EARTH VALOR

EARTH VALOR

EARTHRISE, BOOK VI

DANIEL ARENSON

CHAPTER ONE

Sitting at the helm, Kemi gripped the joystick as the *Marilyn* plunged through the black hole.

"Hold onto your butts!" she shouted.

The ship rattled, threatening to tear apart. Darkness surrounded them, crushed them, yanked at them with such force that Kemi struggled to remain conscious. Around her, the others clung to their seats. Captain Ben-Ari clenched her jaw, face pale, her ponytail whipping from side to side as the ship jerked around. Lailani was shouting out curses, barely audible over the roaring engines and the trembling hull. Marco was silent, turning green, and seemed to be mumbling prayers.

Clutching her joystick with all her strength, Kemi stared ahead into the abyss.

And the abyss stared back.

A funnel of darkness stretched ahead, spinning, roiling, crushing the starship. It seemed almost like a living thing, a great serpent of the cosmos, swallowing them.

"It's tearing us apart!" Lailani cried. "Turn back!"

"We can't!" Kemi said. "Not even with a working azoth engine. It's got a hold on us!"

Lailani grimaced, crossed herself, and began to whisper fervent prayers. Captain Ben-Ari's lips were moving too, and she clutched her Star of David pendant.

But Kemi was too busy to pray. She was struggling to keep the ship together, to adjust their flight to the forces tugging at them. The joystick was struggling to break free like a living creature. She held on. She kept flying. Down through the tunnel. Straight ahead. Deeper into the black hole.

Humans had sent probes into black holes before. None had ever returned any data. In an old experiment, a ship had launched probes on long tethers, only for the steel cables to snap or pull in anything holding them.

The face, Kemi reminded herself. *Marco's face on the asteroid. It had to be a sign. Had to . . .*

The ship gave a loud *crack*. The lights shut off.

They flew in complete darkness.

Kemi couldn't see her crewmates, couldn't see the controls, couldn't see through the viewports. She flew blindly. She wondered if she had passed out, perhaps had died, but she still heard the others call out, heard the ship tearing apart.

"Goodbye," she whispered. "Goodbye, my friends. Goodbye, Marco. I love—"

She gasped.

She narrowed her eyes.

Light.

Light ahead!

She accidentally yawed to the left, and the ship creaked, roared in protest, and the hull dented. She corrected her flight path. She saw it. A point of light like a star in the distance. She flew toward it.

Was this the bottom of the black hole? Kemi had heard that black holes were created when stars imploded. Was this the star it had swallowed?

She kept flying.

If we die, let us die in fire rather than darkness.

The light brightened. She guided the ship onward. Soon the light filled the bridge, blue and gold.

Sounds faded. The rattling eased. The ship plunged forward at incredible speed.

"It's death," Lailani whispered. "We're flying to the afterlife."

Kemi shook her head. "Not today. Not on my watch."

She winced. The black hole's funnel tightened around them. The edges scraped their wings, their belly, their roof. Kemi shot forward, increasing speed, flying toward that light at the end of the tunnel. An old saying from Winston Churchill returned to her: *If you're going through hell, keep going.*

Kemi kept going.

The light blazed against them, blinding her.

Everything was light.

The black hole vanished.

Fire roared around them, then faded into smoke, and blue washed over the world.

"What the hell?" Marco said, speaking for the first time since they had plunged into the black hole. "Where are we?"

"Sky," Kemi whispered, and her eyes dampened. "We're flying in sky."

The blue spread around her. A star shone above—a yellow sun. Scattered fluffy clouds glided.

The ship jolted.

G-forces yanked on them, and they cringed.

"We're *crashing* in sky!" Lailani said.

Kemi flipped switches and hit buttons. Main power was out. Backup power was fading. One wing was damaged, pieces of it fluttering like feathers. The hull was dented, cracked, shrieking as it lost air. Klaxons blared across the ship, and another battery failed.

"Lieutenant, can you still land us?" Ben-Ari said.

"I don't know, Captain." She grimaced, trying to control the descent. The bad wing groaned in protest. Kemi could barely hold the nose up. "It's bad."

Ben-Ari gritted her teeth. "This is just typical of my father. He bought the ship that has a jukebox and ice cream parlor, instead of a proper military vessel that has parachutes."

Marco gaped. "We don't have parachutes?"

"Or ejection seats," said Kemi. "Or an escape pod. Or airbags."

"But we do have all the milkshakes we could eat!" Lailani said, then cringed as the nose dipped. They all nearly fell from their seats. "Holy shit."

Wind shrieked around them and through the *Marilyn.* Kemi yanked back mightily, but the joystick wouldn't move.

"We're going down!" Marco shouted.

"Save us, Captain Obvious!" Lailani shouted back.

They plunged through the sky. Below, Kemi saw the surface of a planet. Grass. Forests.

Earth, she thought. *It's Earth! But how—*

She cringed. They were crashing straight toward a town.

"Lieutenant!" Ben-Ari said.

"I see it, I see it!"

Kemi yanked the joystick, trying to divert their flight. They were going down fast. The town grew closer, closer.

"It's impossible . . ." Kemi whispered.

It was a town out of a storybook. Houses of wood and clay, their roofs thatched with straw, rose along cobbled streets. Smoke plumed from chimneys. A church was the only stone building, and bells were ringing in the belfry. Around the town spread farmlands, but Kemi saw no tractors, only people—at least a hundred—toiling in the fields. Beyond a forest, a castle rose on a mountain.

It's like something out of medieval Europe, Kemi thought. *Where the hell are we?*

But she had no time to contemplate it further. They were coming down fast. They were going to crash.

"Lieutenant, get us away from that city!" Ben-Ari shouted. "We're about to go down right onto those houses!"

Kemi struggled with the joystick. "I might be able to divert us to the fields. But there are too many farmers there. We'll crush them!"

"Better to kill a few farmers than to kill hundreds in the city!" Ben-Ari shouted. The ship was rattling again, the wind shrieking. They all had to shout to be heard.

"The bells in the church are ringing!" Kemi said. "Look, Captain! It's Sunday. The city people will be heading to church! If I can bring us down on the houses, they'll be empty. They—"

"That would destroy the ship!" said Ben-Ari. "And we don't know those houses are empty."

Kemi grimaced. She stared below. She couldn't fly higher. In a minute, maybe two, they were touching down. She stared in horror. The city streets were empty. That had to mean the houses were empty too, everyone at church. Didn't it? She looked at the farms. The farmers were pointing at the sky. If she landed there, she would crush them. She knew it! But maybe she could still save herself, save the crew of the *Marilyn*, save her friends.

"Kemi, you better make a decision!" Lailani said.

What to do? Kemi gave a wordless cry. What to do? Landing in the fields, she would kill dozens. Landing atop the city, she would crush the houses—maybe they were empty, and maybe she would kill hundreds.

They were close now.

They were almost on the roofs.

The crew shouted.

Kemi winced and yanked the joystick sideways with both hands.

"Hold on!" she screamed.

They swerved. They nicked the chimney of an old tavern. They scraped the town's defensive wall. They skimmed the fields, then slammed down, crushing stalks of wheat, and plowing over fleeing farmers.

The peasants tried to escape, but the starship was too fast. The *Marilyn* tore through dirt, wheat, and human flesh. Corpses hit the windshields, ripping apart, and Kemi screamed, shoving the brakes, trying to slow them down. The crew jolted in their seats like rag dolls, heads whipping back and forth, only their seat belts holding them in place. Kemi banged her face against the joystick and blood filled her mouth. The starship drove through a barn, crushing horses, and the windshield cracked, and dirt and hay and blood filled the bridge.

They slowed down.

They came to rest in the field.

For a moment, they were all still, limp in their seats.

Kemi lowered her head, and sobs racked her body. Blood poured from her nose.

I killed them. I killed the farmers. I saved us but I killed them . . .

"Is everyone all right?" Ben-Ari finally asked, bleeding from a gash on her forehead, and she cradled her hand against her chest.

Lailani moaned and unbuckled her seatbelt. "I feel like I just fell through a black hole."

Marco grimaced. "I bruised my elbow, but I'm fine. Kemi? Kemi, are you all right?"

She looked at him. A tear flowed down her cheek, and blood dripped from her split lip. "I killed them, Marco." A sob shook her body. "I killed the farmers."

He embraced her. "It's not your fault. You saved hundreds in the town."

"Maybe," she whispered. "I want to believe that. I do. But what if those houses were empty, if everyone was at church, if we could have saved the lives in the field . . ."

Captain Ben-Ari looked out the cracked windshield, then back at the crew. "The real question is: What are farmers doing inside a black hole?"

Shouts sounded from outside.

Lailani hopped toward the windshield, cringed, then turned toward the others.

"Um, guys? There are a bunch of very angry dudes running toward us. And they have arrows."

A whistle sounded.

An arrow—an actual arrow tipped with metal—slammed into the windshield. A second arrow shot through a crack, whizzed only centimeters away from Kemi's face, and hit her seat's backrest.

Kemi plucked out the arrow in disbelief. Ahead, she saw them—a dozen men or more, wearing chain mail, bows in hand. They were all running toward the ship.

"Where the hell are we?" she whispered.

CHAPTER TWO

Addy drummed on the steering wheel, singing along to the Allman Brothers' "Ramblin' Man," driving the truck through the snowy mountains of Northern Ontario.

"Never pegged you for a country music girl," Jethro said, riding shotgun. The bearded survivalist wore his homemade peg leg, replacing the limb a marauder had munched on. He was busy polishing a rifle that was propped up between his legs, one real and one wooden.

"First of all, it's southern rock, not country," Addy said. "Second, be careful with that rifle, or you're likely to blow your balls off." She bobbed her head and drummed on. "I was born a Ramblin' Man . . ."

Jethro raised an eyebrow. "You were born a man?"

She groaned. "That's what everyone will ask *you* if you keep playing with that rifle. Put it aside! Jesus H. Christ, there will be time for guns later. Sing with me now." The song ended, and Creedence came on the speakers. "My own mix tape."

"I'm not big on classical music," said Jethro.

"Classical music is the shit." Addy's head bobbed along. "No computer sounds. No robots. Just humans pulling strings and beating drums." She kept drumming on the steering wheel.

"You should do less drumming and more steering." Jethro stuck his rag into the crevices of his rifle. "Roads are slippery. Dangerous."

She rolled her eyes. "Says the man who's cleaning a loaded gun."

"She's not loaded, just got a magazine stuck in her." Jethro pulled the magazine out and stuffed it into his pocket. "Better?"

She nodded. "Slightly less suicidal, yes."

Jethro was right, though. The road was damn slippery, and as Addy made a sharp turn, she had to grip the wheel with both hands, press down on the brakes, and curse a couple dozen times. Plow service was in short supply in the post-apocalyptic wasteland, and ice and snow covered the mountain road. The wilderness spread around them: snowy slopes, forests draped with ice, and frozen waterfalls. This wasn't the Rockies, perhaps, but the land was rugged enough, the way treacherous. A perfect place to hide a few thousand people from the marauders.

Those thousands of people traveled behind her, a line of vehicles across the highway. Trucks. Two buses. Beat-up sedans. Motorcycles. A handful of armored vehicles found on battlefields. They were rebels, farmers, and mostly survivors of the liberated slaughterhouse. And they needed a place to lie low, to lick their wounds, and to keep up the fight.

Until Marco comes back here with the Ghost Fleet, she thought. *You better hurry up, little dude.*

"There." Addy pointed. "That hill. Mark it on the map. We'll build a lookout there. We'll raise an antenna too and try to find more rebels."

Jethro nodded and drew an X on a folding map. "And that valley below could make a good camp for a hundred people."

Addy shook her head. "No. Too visible. We need caves. If we can't find caves, we'll use the tanks and blast our own caves."

"We have diggers," Jethro said. "The same big-ass drills I used to build the Ark." His eyes darkened. "I still say we should have stayed in the Ark."

Addy groaned. "We've had that conversation a thousand times. Are you still going to sulk like a homesick baby? The Ark was dangerous! The marauders would have found it sooner or later. Fuck, even I found it just by following the train tracks. It was a death trap."

Jethro scowled. "It was ten thousand square feet of radiation-proof, bomb-proof security, complete with enough food and power to keep hundreds alive for two years."

Addy nodded. "Yes, and the marauders would have torn through it in two hours. Jethro, if you're going to whine the whole trip, I'm going to pull the car over. Don't make me pull over, Jethro!"

He grumbled. "I know, I know. It's just that . . . I spent my life building that place. Decades, Addy. I've known you since you were . . . what, two or three?"

She raised an eyebrow. "I was fourteen, Jethro. Fucking fourteen when I started coming up to your farms to shoot cans off fences and hunt. You thought you were teaching a toddler to shoot?"

He tugged his graying beard. "Whatever, two, fourteen . . . Point is, you were a little pissant girl, and even then I was building the Ark. Waiting for the day we'd need it."

She laughed. "You talk as if I'm some old lady now. I'm only twenty . . ." She frowned and counted on her fingers. "Twenty-six, I think? Fuck me. I don't even know what year it is anymore."

"It's the year one," Jethro said.

Addy raised both eyebrows this time. "We've traveled back in time? When do we get to meet baby Jesus? We can bring him gifts of gun oil and tank diesel."

"It's a new world, Addy." Jethro stared out at the wilderness ahead. "Civilization is gone. Our cities fell. Our fleets collapsed. The old ways are dead. It's the year one—the start of a new era. It's what I've been waiting for all my life."

"Since you were two?" Addy said. "Or did you only start digging bunkers at three when you learned to shoot guns?"

"Since a scum killed my wife and three little boys," Jethro said.

Addy's jaw dropped. She closed it. She took a slow breath. "Jesus, Jethro." She looked at him. "I'm sorry. That's horrible. I never knew. You never said anything." She touched his arm. "Seriously, man. I don't know what to say."

Jethro nodded, staring out the windshield at the frozen hills. "I don't talk about 'em much. I think about 'em a lot. My wife—beautiful, courageous woman. Hair like fire and a personality to match. A warrior. My boys were too. Little but fierce. Would have been about your age now, I reckon, the oldest a bit older maybe. God, they loved fishing!" He laughed. "Those little rascals could spend all day at the lake, come home with a big batch of sunfish and bass, and we'd fire up the grill. Those were good years."

Addy still didn't know what to say, how to comfort him, how to say anything without sounding like a complete idiot. "Sounds like it," was all she could manage. God. She couldn't even imagine such loss. She had lost her parents, lost many friends, but somehow losing your kids seemed a special kind of cruelty. Unthinkable. Unfair. Impossible for her to comprehend.

"The war against the scum was still going on," Jethro said. "But we carved out a good little life up north of the cities. The aliens didn't bother us and we didn't bother them. Until one day, one of those centipede bastards made it onto our farm." He clenched his fists. They shook. "It sneaked into our home at night. Went into the boys' room. It devoured them. It fucking devoured them like a python. My wife fought it. Shot the creature three times before it killed her too. I finally blew its brains out across my oldest boy's room." He lowered his head. "I couldn't live in that old house anymore. Not after what happened. But I knew that my life had new meaning." He looked back up, his eyes now damp and red. "That I could save other families. Other kids. So I devoted the following twenty years of my life to building the Ark.

To preparing for another alien invasion. To saving whoever I could."

Townes Van Zandt's "Big Country Blues" came on the playlist. Addy touched Jethro's shoulder.

"You saved me, Jethro." She smiled. "You saved my life that day I escaped the slaughterhouse. You saved Steve. You saved thousands of people when you stormed the slaughterhouse with me and fought those bastards."

"Only cost me a leg." Jethro patted his peg.

"I'm worth it," Addy said. "What's a leg compared to my brilliant smile?" She gave him a toothy grin.

"Just watch the road!" He cringed.

Addy yelped and yanked on the steering wheel, just barely making the turn. They skidded on the frozen road before she steadied the truck. She blew out a shaky breath.

"See? You just saved my ass again." She frowned. "Does that mean I get another leg?"

"My leg up your ass, if you do that again," Jethro growled, but then his voice softened. He mussed her hair. "You saved me too, Ads. In ways you don't even know, maybe never will. I had some dark years. You brightened them. You're like a daughter to me."

"Aww, shucks." Addy grinned. "Well, you were always like a dad to me. And I'm not just saying that! I had three dads growing up. My real dad when he was alive. Marco's dad who took me in. And you—a grumpy, crazy old loon who taught me how to shoot and hunt and survive. And let me tell you, that came in handy."

Louis Armstrong's "What a Wonderful World" started to play, and Addy cranked up the volume. As Satchmo's trumpet filled the cabin, they kept driving without speaking, watching the beauty around them. The white hills and valleys rolled into the distance, pristine as in ancient days. No war had touched them.

The year one, Addy thought. *A new world.*

But not yet. Jethro was wrong. This was not the year one; it was the year zero. It was the year that they fought. That they bled. That they killed. There were still many battles ahead, and the enemy still filled the world.

But we'll keep fighting, Addy thought. *We'll drive them out. We'll reach our Year One. We'll find peace. New homes. New families. And you better be there with me, Poet, or I'll fly across the galaxy just to kick your ass.*

Jimi Hendrix replaced the Great Satchmo, and Addy began playing air guitar until Jethro forced her to pull over, and he replaced her at the wheel. The convoy rolled on, seeking a new home in the wild.

CHAPTER THREE

"We're on Earth," Marco said, rubbing his eyes. "We're on Earth during the Middle Ages. How is that possible?"

"Guys!" Hopping up and down, Lailani pointed out the bridge's windshield. "Men with arrows! Big sharp arrows! Big sharp arrows flying at us! Questions later, not dying now!"

Ben-Ari nodded. "To the armory. Guns. Now!"

The captain ran off the bridge, heading deeper into the ship. Marco followed, and Kemi and Lailani ran close behind. His wounded elbow was swelling up, and he couldn't move his arm. Kemi and Ben-Ari were both bleeding from head wounds. But fear drove them onward. They ran into the lounge, where the jukebox had fallen over, and the bar had shattered. They leaped over the wreckage, down a corridor, past the crew quarters, and into the armory. All the while, the shouts rose from outside.

"Slay the demons!" boomed a distant voice.

"Slay the metal beast!" roared another man.

Through a porthole, Marco saw the soldiers running toward the ship, their chain mail clanking. They fired more arrows, hitting the hull. Marco blinked and rubbed his eyes. How could this be?

The black hole must be a time warp, he thought. *We're in the past. But how did we end up back on Earth, thousands of light-years away?*

"Guns, helmets, tactical vests," Ben-Ari barked. "I want everyone geared for battle. Hurry!"

They were already wearing their olive drab uniforms and helmets. They quickly grabbed tactical vests, slipped magazines into the pouches, and grabbed T57 assault rifles, grenades, and plasma pistols. Marco thought the weapons excessive—they were dealing with arrows after all, not marauder claws. But, perhaps, better over-armed than under.

"We're gearing up to battle medieval peasants inside a black hole," Marco said. "This can't be happening. It's impossible."

An arrow slammed into a porthole, cracking the glass.

"That arrow begs to differ," Lailani said.

"Into the airlock," said Ben-Ari. She was pale, and her temple bled, but her shoulders were squared and her chin was raised. Only the briefest twitch of her lips revealed her confusion, and her eyes remained hard. "We'll scare them off."

The four stepped into the ship's airlock, and Ben-Ari keyed the code into the control panel. The door opened.

Fresh air filled the airlock—the air of Earth. Marco would recognize it anywhere. He had spent nearly three years straight now in space, first in Haven and then trundling through a variety of spaceships, and had smelled only stale, recycled air. But here—here was *real* air, scented of soil, of growing green things, of life. Yet he could also smell smoke, blood, and the bodies he saw in the crushed fields. The devastation of the crash spread like a trail—crushed stalks of wheat, a deep groove in the field, a shattered barn, and dead livestock and peasants. In the distance, a few kilometers away, rose the medieval town, the spires of its cathedral rising to the blue sky.

Earth, he thought. *Earth long ago. How the hell did we end up here?*

And across the field, the armored soldiers surrounded them, bows and arrows in hand. They wore clanking chain mail, and swords hung from their belts.

"Demons!" shouted one, a paunchy man with a yellow mustache. "Slay them!"

The soldiers tugged back their bowstrings.

"So what do we do?" Lailani muttered, holding her gun. "Kill bloody cavemen firing arrows?"

Ben-Ari stepped forward. She fired a bullet into the sky.

The *boom* was probably the loudest sound the medieval soldiers had ever heard. In their fright, they lost control of their bows, and the arrows whizzed over the crashed starship.

"We mean you no harm!" Ben-Ari cried. "Lower your weapons."

The men hesitated. They glanced at one another. The big brute with the mustache turned red.

"Kill them!" he shouted, loading another arrow.

"Captain—" Marco began.

More arrows flew.

The crew leaped deeper into the airlock. Arrows flew in. One scraped across Lailani's arm, ripping her sleeve, and she yelped. More arrows hit the wall behind them.

"I'm going to kill those assholes!" Lailani shouted and loaded her gun.

No, Marco thought. *Enough have died here.*

He stepped back toward the doorway. The city guards stepped closer, scowling. They drew their swords. Within moments, the crew would be forced to kill them.

We killed enough people today, Marco thought.

He winced, guilt already filling him, and fired his gun.

He hit the mustached guard in the leg.

The man collapsed, screaming, blood gushing.

Marco took a step outside and raised his gun again.

"Run!" he shouted. "Run or we will slay you all!"

"And steal your souls!" Lailani added, firing another bullet, hitting the dirt by a man's foot.

The medieval soldiers turned to flee, carrying their wounded comrade. Across the field, the surviving peasants were running too, and the church bells kept ringing in the distance.

"Infirmary," Ben-Ari said. "Everyone. Now."

They locked the airlock and entered the ship's small medical bay. Everyone was wounded from the crash, but the injuries were superficial. A gash bled on Ben-Ari's head, but she showed no signs of a concussion. Kemi had split open her lip and bled from her nose, but she hadn't broken anything. An arrow had scraped Lailani's arm, and Marco's elbow was swollen. They tended to their wounds. Worse than the injuries was their hunger; they had been living off crackers and jam for several days now.

"All right," Ben-Ari said when they were all patched up. A bandage covered the gash on her head. "Ideas. Where are we?" She turned toward Lailani. "Sergeant de la Rosa, do your sensors pick up anything? Radio towers? Starships above? Satellites?"

Lailani checked her tablet. "Nothing, ma'am. But our ship is banged up like a cat that just ran through the doghouse. Our sensors could be dead."

"Or there's nothing up there," Marco said. "No satellites. No radio towers. No modern technology at all." He blew out his breath slowly. "Arrows. They were using arrows. And you saw that town. We're in the Middle Ages. Somewhere in Western Europe, judging by that cathedral."

Lailani gulped. "Oh dear. They've never seen anyone Asian before. Do you suppose they'll try to trap me, put me in a circus?" She gasped. "And they'll try to enslave Kemi! She's even darker than I am. And Ben-Ari! Oh God, Ben-Ari, hide your Star of David pendant! They'll burn you at the stake, and—"

"Sergeant, calm yourself!" Ben-Ari said. "Nobody is putting anyone in the circus, or enslaving anyone, or burning anyone at the stake. All right? We're not in Medieval Europe. That's impossible."

"So are starwhales," Lailani muttered. "But I remember us flying on the back of one."

Marco spoke slowly, considering each word. "Black holes have immense gravity fields. They're formed when stars implode.

Their gravity is so strong they swallow everything that comes by them—ordinary matter, light, even spacetime itself. If the black hole we entered was sucking up time, that might explain how we ended up in the past."

"But not how we ended up on Earth," said Ben-Ari. "We were thousands of light-years away."

"Well, some believe that black holes can act like wormholes. Portals through space as well as time." Marco scratched his chin. "But the odds of this black hole being a portal to Earth—out of all the billions of planets in the solar system—seems like an incredible coincidence."

"Maybe it's not Earth," Kemi said. "Maybe it's another planet that looks like Earth. Maybe the native lifeforms here just look human."

Marco shook his head. "No. Impossible. While it's true that some alien species are humanoid—they have legs, arms, heads—we've found none that look exactly like humans. The Nandakis are the most humanlike species we've found, and even they're pretty damn alien. There are certainly no aliens who have the same armor, weapons, and architecture as Medieval Europe. Hell, humans aren't even alike between continents; aliens won't be this similar across planets. This is Earth all right. Good old Terra."

"Or a hallucination," Kemi said, staring out the viewport. "A shared dream."

"You know what I'm not hallucinating?" Lailani said. "My stomach. It's clinging to my back. We're on Earth? Great! That means food. Let's go hunting. We might be too early to find a Taco Shack, but a nice juicy deer would sure hit the spot."

Marco wanted to urge caution, to recommend staying aboard the ship for now, but his stomach gave a plaintive growl.

"All right," Ben-Ari said. "Sergeant Emery, Lieutenant Abasi, you two go into that forest." She pointed out the porthole at the trees. "And stay away from that town. See if you can find anything to eat. Hunt and gather. Do not approach any of the locals." She turned toward Lailani. "Sergeant de la Rosa, you and I will stay here to guard—and try to repair—the ship."

"This ship ain't flying anytime soon, Captain," Lailani said.

"She'll fly again if we have to kidnap the local blacksmith to weld her together," Ben-Ari said. "And we'll keep working on those sensors. I want to know exactly where—and *when*—we are." She turned toward Marco and Kemi. "Why are you two still here? Go! Hunt! Gather!"

Marco nodded. He and Kemi left the ship.

As they walked through the field, they saw peasants weeping and collecting their dead. The devastation still spread across the field: a ditch, almost a kilometer long, strewn with corpses. More peasants were approaching, tearing their clothes, and wailing in despair.

"How many people do you think I killed?" Kemi whispered.

"Kemi." Marco took her hand. "Look at me." He touched her cheek. "Look at me, Kemi."

She looked at him. Her eyes were full of tears.

"I'm a murderer," she whispered.

"Kemi, you *saved* lives. You saved hundreds of lives in the town."

"You don't know that," she said. "You can't. I didn't see anyone on the city streets. What if they were all here in the fields or in the church? I could have landed on their empty houses, and—"

"Kemi, listen to me." Marco squeezed her hand. "Listen! You made the right choice. You had only a few seconds, and you made the right choice. We all did. We made that choice together."

"Yet I was the pilot, I had the controls, and . . . Oh God, Marco. They're dead."

He embraced her. "It was an accident. You saved us. You saved *me*. We all would have made the same call. What happened is horrible. People died. But you couldn't stop that. Ben-Ari knows this. Ben-Ari led my infantry platoon in battle. She led many of us to die. She knows that sometimes leaders must sacrifice the few to save the many. All right?" Marco caressed her cheek. "You're right to grieve. But you should not feel guilty. You took some lives to save many lives. It's a horrible choice we all had to face in these wars."

Kemi sighed, tears on her cheeks. "Also, I broke my mechanical hand." She raised the prosthetic and flexed the fingers. "In the crash. There's a connection loose in the middle."

"We'll fix it," Marco said.

"You don't understand." Kemi winced. "The mechanical hand comes with a powerful battery. Enough to send out ten thousand blasts of energy strong enough to knock out a mule. And a connection is loose, Marco. If somebody shakes my hand too tightly, it could kill both of us." She looked close to shedding more tears. "There isn't an engineer within light-years to fix it, and it's connected to my *nerves*, Marco. I can't even remove it, not without ripping out my nerve endings. If the battery jiggles out of place, releasing all its energy, the blast can kill anyone near me. I'm some kind of walking time bomb now, and what if my hand ends up killing somebody else, and—"

"Kemi!" He touched her cheek. "Just . . . don't shake anyone's hand for a while, all right? We'll fix your mechanical hand. I promise you. It'll be fine."

She nodded, wiping away her tears. She turned away from the destruction and faced the forest. "Let's find food."

They crossed the farmlands and entered the forest. Birch, elm, and oak trees rose from crumbly soil, rustling in the breeze. A stream flowed between them, gurgling over mossy stones. Bluebells carpeted the forest floor, and the sweet scents filled the air. Birds and crickets sang. Despite the hunger, the horror, and the confusion, the place soothed Marco. They walked in silence down a dirt road, seeking something to eat.

This is a nice change, he thought. Until now, whenever he reached another planet, it had involved underground mines full of terrors, searing deserts full of massive centipedes, or worlds with endless storms. He had seen such terrors in space. Hybrids creatures in the mines of Corpus, half human, half centipede, twisted and screaming. A ball of skin, twitching, growing his own face, then screaming as Addy tossed it into a vat of molten metal. Aliens tortured in the depths. His friends dying in the sand of Abaddon. Those memories never left Marco. Every night, they returned to him. But here, finally, was a world of beauty. Of trees and flowers and fresh air. A place with no monsters.

"Do you remember how we used to walk like this in Toronto?" Marco said.

Kemi smiled thinly. "In the cemetery. The only green place still left in the city. Bluebells would grow there too." She lowered her head. "Maybe even that cemetery is gone now. Maybe the whole city is gone." She sighed. "I'm sorry. I'm not exactly a ray of sunshine today."

"Look around you." He gestured at the forest. "I don't know where we are. I don't know how we got here. But it's beautiful. I just wish Addy were with us."

"And my parents," Kemi said. "I miss them. I'm so worried about them. About everyone on Earth."

"I haven't seen Earth in nearly three years," Marco said. "Unless this is Earth. Unless we're home now. Just in a different time."

"Or a very, very convincing Renaissance fair," Kemi said, finally showing some teeth in her smile. "I think we should buy some outfits here—a suit of armor for you and a gown for me. And swords! We'll take them to a real Ren Fair when we get home. I'll drag you there. Drag you!"

"Only if you go with me to the *Star Trek* convention."

She laughed. "Hey! I love *Star Trek* even more than you." She gave him a Vulcan salute. "May the Force be with you!" She winked.

"That's *Doctor Who*," Marco said, and he laughed too.

"I thought it was *Space Galaxy*?" Kemi said.

She leaned against him as they walked, and her hand slipped into his.

Yes, this is like being home, Marco thought. *This is like the old walks we used to take. This is the Kemi I loved. The Kemi I still love.*

They kept walking, stomachs growling. They kept searching for food—mushrooms, nuts, berries, anything. They found nothing in this forest. The only animals were sparrows, finches, and robins, birds too small and quick to shoot. Even if they *could* hunt them, they would provide barely any meat.

"I don't suppose we'll run into any coffee bars out here," Kemi said.

"Maybe if we wait a thousand years, a Tim Hortons will open up." Marco patted his rumbling stomach. "I'm looking, buddy."

An hour passed. Then two. Then three. Still they found no food alongside the trail, and they dared not step off it. It would be too easy to get lost in these woods.

"We might have to go into the city," Kemi finally said. "We can buy food at a market."

"How?" Marco said. "We don't have any money. And we're dressed like aliens. We're likely to get put into a gibbet—or just shot with more of those arrows."

"*You'll* be fine," Kemi said. "You look like one of them. You're European. Lailani, Ben-Ari, and I would be burned at the stake. Burn the witches!" She sighed. "We better find some food here in the forest then."

They kept walking, hunger growing. Days of crackers and jam left them weary, and they hadn't even had any of that in hours. If they couldn't find food soon, their quest would end—not by arrows or marauders but simple hunger. Marco found himself thinking of boot camp. He remembered being hungry there too. He had fought Pinky once for a Spam sandwich. A memory tickled him—that day in Greece, when they had sneaked into the old lady's yard to pee, and she had fed them bell peppers stuffed with rice, tomatoes, and beef.

The best day of my life, Lailani had called it.

Marco lowered his head. That had been seven years ago now, almost eight, but he had never forgotten that romance with Lailani. How he had fallen madly in love with the tomboyish, fierce little soldier, with her tattoos, scars, buzz cut, and broken kindness. How he had asked her to marry him. How he had wanted to be with her forever.

But you broke my heart, Lailani. You chose Sofia.

He let out a bitter laugh. What had he expected? He had seen the rainbow tattoo on Lailani's arm, had known she didn't date boys.

But I thought I was different, that you'd wait for me, that you could love me like I love you. That we'd be happy and in love forever.

Kemi was watching him, as if she could read his mind. Marco looked at her. She gave him a small, sad smile. He smiled back and held her hand.

After another hour of walking, and still no sign of fruit or game, Kemi pointed.

"Look!"

Marco looked. A mountain rose ahead, still several kilometers away. On its crest loomed a dark castle—the one they had seen from the sky. Marco couldn't help but shudder. The castle perched like a vulture, seeming to tilt toward them, to watch them.

"There's a bad air coming from that castle," Kemi said. "It looks like a vampire's home."

"Maybe it's Count Chocula," Marco said. "And he'll give us some cereal. I'd kill for some cereal now."

"Marco." Kemi frowned, staring up at the castle. "Back in medieval times, the lord always lived in the castle, right? Whoever lives there might be able to explain all this. Where we are. How we got here. I'm still not convinced this is Earth."

Marco inhaled sharply and clutched her hand. "Me neither. Look!"

Kemi spun around. They both stared.

It stood on a hill between birches, caught in a beam of sunlight. It regarded them, regal, silent, the light dappling its ivory fur and whorled horn.

"Is that . . .?" Kemi whispered.

Marco nodded. "A unicorn."

The animal stood still, eyes golden. One hoof was raised, shining like polished amber, as if caught in mid-walk. It was a female, Marco thought, graceful and whispering of ancient magic, a fay risen into the world. No larger than a deer, inquisitive yet timid. Standing before the unicorn, covered in dirt and wearing a tattered uniform, Marco felt coarse and slow like a goblin risen from a burrow.

"How can this be?" Kemi said.

Marco took a deep breath. "I don't know. I don't know how we ended up here. I don't know if this is Earth. I don't know why a creature of mythology stands before us. I don't know if this is real or just some illusion, some trick, some virtual reality devised by an intelligence we cannot see. But one thing I know." He raised his rifle. "My crew is hungry. Maybe starving. And my crew comes first."

The unicorn burst into a run.

Marco fired.

The unicorn screamed.

"No!" Kemi shouted, pulling his gun down, but it was too late.

They both ran onto the hill. A trail of blood stretched across the forest floor. They followed it, and they found the unicorn curled up beneath an oak, still alive but bleeding profusely. The animal looked up at Marco, met his eyes, and wept. Around her gathered her cubs, mewling and burrowing for milk.

"What did you do?" Kemi whispered, turning toward Marco. "Why?"

Marco trembled. "I'm sorry. I . . . I didn't know she was a mother, I . . ."

Kemi knelt by the unicorn, pulled out her medical kit, and tried to heal the unicorn. But the animal was growing weaker, fading away. One of her legs had broken during the flight, the bone protruding, and the bullet was deep in her belly.

"Kemi, come." Marco gently pulled her back. "I have to do this."

"No!" She wept. "Don't. Please."

But she buried her face in her palms, and Marco did the deed. A bullet into the unicorn's head. He stared at the carcass with searing, dry eyes, and his chest shook, and he loathed himself.

"It's the same as a deer," he said, voice shaking. "Same as a rabbit. It's just an animal, Kemi, and we're hungry. We have to eat or we'll die."

But she wouldn't reply, wouldn't meet his eyes.

"I had to do it," Marco whispered. "I had to."

Several other unicorns approached, staring from the hilltop, and the animals shed tears. The cubs ran to them.

We must sacrifice the few to save the many, Marco reminded himself. But those words he had spoken to Kemi felt hollow.

He slung the dead unicorn across his shoulders. He and Kemi walked back in silence.

CHAPTER FOUR

Brigadier-General James Petty, bedecked with service ribbons and pins, sat alone in his quarters, head lowered, and took another sip of scotch. As the stars streamed outside the porthole, he caressed the framed photo of his daughter.

"I want to make you proud today, Coleen," he rasped. His throat was too dry. He took another sip. "It's all I ever wanted."

The photo showed Coleen as a young woman graduating from Julius Military Academy. She beamed as she tossed her white cap into the air. It had been a glorious day, Petty remembered. The sun had shone, and Admiral Evan Bryan himself, the legendary war hero, had returned their salutes. Sixteen years ago. By God, it felt like yesterday.

Coleen Petty had not been the easiest officer to serve under. He, as her father, knew how headstrong she could be. Many of her soldiers had feared her; some had loathed her. Ben-Ari herself had suffered some of Coleen's legendary wrath. James Petty knew that. He had seen it in Ben-Ari's eyes when the lieutenant had told him of Coleen's death.

But nobody realized how difficult it had been for Coleen. The year she had spent in the hospital as a child. Losing her mother soon after her discharge. Flunking out of flight school—

the first Petty in four generations not to earn her wings. So much fury had filled Coleen when she had joined the infantry—but pride too. Determination to excel. And she had excelled. She had made it into the Erebus Brigade, the most prestigious brigade in the infantry, had risen to command an entire company. That was thanks to her last name, some soldiers whispered, and perhaps there was some truth to that. But he, her father, had also seen her courage, her dedication, her love of the military and Earth.

"Like me, you lived for Earth," he said hoarsely to that old photograph. He took another sip of booze. "You loved Earth more than any living person on it. More than me, perhaps. You lived to defend our homeworld. And you died defending it." His voice dropped. "And maybe in this war I will join you."

No.

He gritted his teeth.

Do not fall again into that hole.

He pushed his glass aside.

He had fallen into that pit twice before. After his wife had died. Again after he had lost Coleen. He would not surrender again to the booze, the despair, the blackness that ever clawed at him. He was a general now. He was the commander of humanity's last fleet, even if that fleet comprised of only several warships and Firebird squadrons. He would remain strong for his warriors, for his species, and for the memory of all those who had fallen.

He took his glass into the bathroom and poured the amber liquid down the sink. He raised his eyes and stared at his reflection. He was old. He was in his sixties, and after his heart attack two years ago, he finally looked it. Sacks hung under his eyes, and his wrinkles had deepened. His face was haggard, but it was still strong. The jaw wide. The eyebrows heavy and black. The eyes like steel. It was the face of a warrior who had seen too many battles—but who was ready to swing his axe until the bastards cut him down.

On his lapel, his communicator beeped.

"Sir," came the voice of Osiris, the *Minotaur*'s android, a piece of hardware the price of ten Firebirds. "We're approaching the graveyard. ETA ten minutes."

Petty spoke into the device. "I'm heading to the bridge, Osiris. Commence shutdown of our azoth engines and have the fleet form a defensive one-two-one formation. I want a hundred Firebirds flying around us constantly."

"Yes, sir. But first, sir, would you like to hear a joke? I—"

"No." He hung up.

Petty stared back into the mirror, at that craggy face.

"Into death, to find life," he said.

He left his quarters.

He walked through his ship. The *Minotaur* was not the largest carrier ever built, but she was a big girl, all cavernous halls and winding corridors. She wasn't slick, elegant, or as pretty as the later generation ships, vessels like the *Sagan* or *Terra*. No. The *Minotaur* was a ship of a different breed. She wasn't built for beauty, not to impress shareholders and ministers and the viewers at home. The *Minotaur*, the first carrier to emerge from the inferno of the Cataclysm, had been built for one purpose: War.

Every last centimeter of her served her purpose. Her bulkheads were thick metal, made to resist alien cannons. Her corridors were narrow and her rooms wide, built to house as many marines as possible; a full five thousand now served here, the entire Erebus Brigade, ready to deploy wherever Petty would command. Her starfighter bays relied not on gadgetry but the steely judgment and quick instincts of the crew. Her fighter pilots too were of a different breed. Petty saw them racing to their stations, pausing only to stand at attention and salute as he walked by. The men had begun to wear thick, coiling mustaches, mimicking the old human pilots of the Golden Age of Aerial Battles. As Petty walked the halls of the *Minotaur*, he returned their salutes. Many of these pilots, he knew, would not survive.

He reached the bridge as the fleet emerged from warp. They quickly arranged themselves in defensive position: the *Minotaur* in front, the *Chimera* and *Cyclops* behind her, and the *Medusa* guarding the cargo ships in the rear. A hundred Firebirds circled the formation in constant patrol.

The ravagers will be on us soon, Petty thought. *We don't have much time.*

He stared through the front viewport. He saw it ahead: The Starship Graveyard.

A thousand human starships, once the pride of the fleet, hovered here in the darkness beyond Jupiter's orbit. Cut open. Dead. Fallen in the first great marauder assault.

Dozens of warships. Three starfighter carriers. Hundreds of smaller vessels. Among them, the husks of thousands of dead ravagers. All had fallen that horrible day. That day Ben-Ari had tried to warn humanity about, ending up in a prison cell for her words.

"The day the marauders arrived," Petty said softly. "A day that will live forever in infamy. Here are its echoes. Here, a thousand dead starships face us in accusation. They fell that day. But they might still save humanity." He turned toward his officers. "Are the salvage teams ready?"

Osiris nodded, her platinum bob cut swaying. "Yes, sir. We've outfitted a hundred shuttles for the job, and they're all staffed by our best technicians. Firebirds will provide cover."

Petty nodded. "Good. We need to move fast. We might only have a few hours before the enemy figures out we're here. Keep all communicator broadcasts at a minimum. I don't want to broadcast our presence. This might get violent—but we will succeed. We must." He turned back toward the viewport, gazing at the dead starships. "There are many warp-capable starships floating here, their crew members dead. They have azoth crystals inside them. We will retrieve them."

"Yes, sir!" said Osiris. "Commencing salvage operation."

From the bridge, they watched as a hundred shuttles emerged from the hangars of the *Minotaur* and her three companions, the *Chimera*, *Cyclops*, and *Medusa.* In the fleet, only those four ships—along with the three largest cargo vessels—carried azoth engines, capable of warp flight. The smaller ships, such as the shuttles and the Firebirds, had to fly within the larger ships' hangars.

If Petty stood a chance of defeating the ravagers, of liberating Mars, he needed more azoth crystals.

Here in these dead starships lay his hope. His secret plan. A plan his scientists and engineers thought was crazy, but which Petty knew would work.

"The Ben-Ari Maneuver," he said softly.

The young captain, it was said, had used the trick when escaping from prison. Petty himself had used the maneuver during his last battle—the only reason he still stood here today. Missiles, bullets, shells—the ravagers could take a lot of their punishment. But warped spacetime tore the alien vessels apart. If Petty could fit azoth engines onto Firebirds, could let the small vessels move close to the ravagers, then bend spacetime . . .

He stood on the bridge, watching as the salvage shuttles flew toward the ruined warships, and hope began to rise in him.

We can tear those bastards apart. He clenched his fist. *We can still beat them. We can still win this war. We can—*

And from the shadows ahead, they emerged.

Hundreds of dark, small ships, jagged and winged and spurting out sparks.

Klaxons blared.

"Ravagers!" shouted Major Hennessy, the bridge's security officer, a tall man with thinning blond hair.

Petty ground his teeth.

"No," he muttered, his chest aching. "Space scavengers. Harpies."

Hennessy shuddered. "I thought we drove those bastards out of the galaxy years ago."

"They're back," Petty said, then spoke into his comm. "Firebirds, engage them! Scatter those harpy ships."

Harpies. Petty stared at them in disgust. Their vessels were shaped like vultures, forged from scrap metal and stolen tech. The harpies, a species of low intelligence but extreme cunning, were the scavengers of the galaxy. They had no homeworld that anyone knew of. Like with the marauders, their origin was a mystery. In the old days, the harpies would hover around space battles, waiting for the violence to end, then swoop in. Like vultures over carrion, they pecked at dead starships, stealing anything they could carry: bulkheads, computers, engines, fuel, even corpses to consume. If old battles on Earth attracted crows, battles in space attracted the harpies.

The *Minotaur*'s shuttles kept flying closer to the wreckage, tasked with retrieving the azoth crystals. As they drew closer, the harpies attacked.

The scrap-metal ships opened their beaks, revealing an assortment of stolen weapons: cannons, railguns, plasma blasters, photon guns, laser guns, and more.

All those weapons fired.

Shells, plasma, lasers, bullets—they slammed into the human shuttles.

The small craft—built for technical operations, not battle—tore apart.

"Firebirds, damn it, engage them!" Petty said into his comm. "Squadrons seven though forty, join the assault!"

Across space, the Firebirds stormed forth. The starfighters fired their arsenals. Heat-seeking missiles flew and slammed into harpy ships. Beaks, wings, and jagged hulls shattered and flew across space. But more and more of the scavengers kept emerging from the dead warships like flies from a rotting corpse. There were thousands, and the humans had disturbed their meal.

Damn it! They didn't have time or resources for this. Any moment now, the ravagers might arrive. They needed those crystals—now. They needed to get to Mars and liberate the colonists before the marauders figured out their plan.

"Photon gun turrets!" Petty said. "Aim at those harpies and fire at will!"

Across the *Minotaur*, the guns fired. Blasts of photons flew and slammed into enemy vessels. Harpy ships collapsed. The battle raged, hundreds of Firebirds spinning, rising, swooping, firing their guns, thousands of harpy ships coiling between them. Flames and explosions and light filled space. Ships spun out of control, slamming into dead warships, knocking vessels into one another. The husks of warships careened into the depths. One by one, the salvage shuttles vanished like fading stars.

Petty stared from the bridge. He inhaled sharply. His fingers tingled.

They're destroying our shuttles. His eyes burned. *When we should be fighting marauders, it's goddamn harpies tearing us apart.*

"Damn it, keep those cannons firing!" he shouted.

"The battle is too crowded, sir!" said Osiris. "We can't risk hitting our own Firebirds."

Petty pointed. "Full speed ahead. Carve a path through the harpies. We need to let those salvage shuttles reach the dead ships."

The android turned toward him, her lavender eyes widening. "Sir, to fly through the battle would—"

"Do it," Petty said. "That's an order."

"Aye aye, sir." Osiris returned to her control board. "Taking the *Minotaur* straight ahead, sir."

The massive carrier, its hangars emptied of Firebirds, charged directly into the battle.

Normally, carriers—warships the size of skyscrapers—blasted their cannons from afar, never engaging the enemy directly. Their Firebirds, tiny vessels in comparison, were those that fought in close quarters. Now the *Minotaur* plowed through the battle like a bull charging through a swarm of bees.

Firebirds and harpy ships fled from their advance. A few were too slow. Harpy ships shattered against the *Minotaur*'s prow like insects against a car's windshield. The carrier shook with every impact, its hull denting, but they kept moving forward—clearing a path toward those dead warships.

"Side cannons, fire!" Petty ordered. "All Firebirds, clear our starboard and port!"

Around the ship, Firebirds rose and fell. From the *Minotaur*'s sides, cannons extended. Shells blasted out, ripping into the harpy ships.

This is what the younger commanders never learn, Petty thought. *You can fly a carrier into battle if you've got the balls for it. And none can match it in pure brutality.*

Yet like that buffalo charging through bees, they got stung.

The scavenger ships, winged and beaked like vultures, attacked from all sides. Their metallic landing gear, extending like talons, slammed into the *Minotaur*'s hull. Steel beaks bit them, bending, twisting, sawing through the carrier. Alarms blared and the ship rattled madly as they charged forth.

"We're losing air pressure on deck 4A!" an officer shouted.

"Seal it off!" Petty said. "Keep moving forward." He narrowed his eyes, staring ahead. "We're almost there."

The starship graveyard sprawled ahead. Petty could see the massive vessels—some larger even than the *Minotaur*—floating in the darkness. A handful of salvage shuttles, protected by the *Minotaur*'s cannons and the fighting Firebirds, managed to reach one dead warship. They attached to it like barnacles, and technicians emerged in spacesuits, clung to the dead hull, and—

A harpy ship stormed forth and slammed into the human technicians, crushing them against the larger, listing vessel.

Petty clenched his fists. Only a handful of salvage shuttles still remained. If they couldn't get to those azoth crystals . . .

"All Firebirds, move to fly around the dead warships," Petty commanded. "Keep those harpies off our technicians! We must—"

The bridge jolted so madly Petty swayed and nearly fell. Smoke billowed.

Alarms shrieked.

"Sir, deck 15A is breached!" an officer cried. "We're being boarded!"

"Seal it off!" Petty barked.

"Sealed, sir, but it's too late. I'm getting reports of enemy combatants already in decks 15B, 15C, 15D . . ."

Petty grunted. Deck 15D was directly below the bridge.

He could hear them. Through the floor. Monstrous screams. Humans shouting. Guns blazing.

Petty turned toward his android. "Osiris, you have the bridge. Security, with me."

As he marched off the bridge, Petty drew his pistol. Soldiers were racing down the corridor. The sounds grew louder. Gunfire rang and creatures shrieked. Petty walked down a staircase, aiming his gun ahead. His security officers walked behind him.

He stepped onto deck 15D to find human corpses—what remained of them, at least—smeared across the floor and walls.

The harpies were here, and they were feasting.

They were ugly bastards. Petty hadn't seen them in years, not since the Scum War. They hadn't grown any prettier. The harpies weren't much larger than humans, but their legs ended with talons large enough to engulf a bulldog. Their brown wings dripped oil, and scales coated their torsos. Worst of all were their faces: bloated, veined, and oozing from open sores. Their jaws were powerful, built to rip open corpses and feast on the rotting innards. Their bulging white eyes blazed with fury. The creatures were intelligent enough to cobble together starships using stolen tech, but they had never developed a language. They screeched wordlessly at Petty, infuriated that he should disturb their meal.

"God, the stench of them," muttered one of Petty's soldiers.

Petty had smelled them years ago and had never forgotten it. Harpies made corpses smell like rose gardens.

The harpies were scavengers, not hunters, and they tended to shy away from battles, preferring to arrive only after the violence had ended. But disturb their meal and they would fight with a fury few in the galaxy could rival.

The creatures lunged themselves at Petty and his men, stretching out those massive talons, their wings beating and scattering droplets of oil.

Petty and his men opened fire.

You couldn't open fire on most modern starfighter carriers, not without piercing the hull. But the *Minotaur* had been built with hostile boarders in mind. Her bulkheads were designed not only to withstand bullets but to capture them, preventing shards from ricocheting and killing your comrades. Petty and his soldiers let rip. Their bullets plowed into the harpies, tearing through scaly bodies, feathered wings, and bloated faces.

Several harpies fell dead, leaking black blood. Others flew over their fallen comrades, withstanding the hailstorm of bullets, and slammed into the humans.

Talons ripped one man's face in half. Another harpy disemboweled a soldier, cackling as the organs spilled. One of the aliens crashed into Petty, wings flapping madly. The beak snapped in a fury. Petty gripped the creature's neck, crushing its windpipe, struggling to shove it away. He tried to fire with his other hand, but his pistol was out of bullets. Even in his sixties, Petty was still strong. But this beast outweighed him, and its beak kept snapping, moving closer and closer with every heartbeat.

And his heart was pounding now. Aching. A heart weakened by the attack two years ago. Sweat drenched Petty. The harpy managed to move its beak closer, slicing through Petty's uniform, through the skin on his shoulder.

Pain pounding through him, Petty swung his gun. He pistol-whipped the harpy, and the creature squealed. Petty kicked it back, grabbed another magazine, and slammed it into his gun.

The harpy leaped back toward him.

Petty's bullet found the back of its throat.

The alien crashed into him, dead, and Petty shoved the creature off with a grunt.

Around him, his fellow soldiers fired more bullets, killing the last of the invaders. Blood, guts, and corpses filled the deck.

Petty took a step, grunted, and gripped his chest.

A grimace twisted his face.

A young soldier raced toward him. "Sir, are you—"

"I'm fine." Petty waved the man off. "Return to your station."

Bleeding from his shoulder, his heart beating against his ribs, Petty made his way back to the bridge. His officers gasped to see their commander coated in both red and black blood.

"Sir, do you need a med—" Osiris began.

"Status!" Petty barked.

"The harpies are falling back, sir," said the android. "Our Firebirds are figuring out their flight patterns and giving them a pounding. The scavengers are scattering, sir. Should we give chase?"

Petty shook his head. "No. Let the bastards run. How many salvage crews remain?"

"Fifteen salvage shuttles with full crews aboard, sir."

Petty grunted and stared out the viewport. His heart sank. The enemy was retreating, but the human fleet had suffered horrible losses. Dozens of dead Firebirds had joined the starship graveyard. Dammit! Petty needed them. His fleet had already been reduced to a mere handful, and now—

He took a deep breath, forcing himself to calm down.

"We still have Firebirds who need azoth crystals," he said. "Get the salvage crews working around the clock. Get me those crystals! Install them in every Firebird that can still fly. We have no more than twenty-four hours here, then we leave. I want full patrols as we work, with our current warp engines primed and ready to engage within an instant. Understood?"

"Yes, sir!" Osiris said.

Petty all but crashed into the commander's seat. His legs ached, his heart still pounded, and his shoulder kept bleeding. He still hadn't caught his breath.

I'm too old for this, he thought.

As it turned out, they had only nine hours.

After nine hours, with a hundred and three azoth crystals salvaged, the alarms blared again.

"Ravagers coming in fast!" shouted his communication officer. "ETA six minutes!"

Petty leaped to his feet. "All salvage crews, back into your shuttles! Gather around the warships! No time to dock. All Firebirds, warp formation—now!"

The smaller vessels raced through space, not even bothering to land in the hangars, just getting close enough to get sucked into a warp bubble.

With seven seconds to spare, the human fleet engaged their warp engines.

They flew through curved spacetime, traveling millions of kilometers per second.

A hundred and three azoth crystals. Crystals to let Firebirds curve spacetime, to destroy ravagers. Petty took a raspy breath. *It better be enough for Mars.*

As a medic stitched up his shoulder, Petty gazed out the porthole. They emerged from warped space beyond the heliosphere, hiding in the darkness from the enemy fleet. Here they could lick their wounds, install the crystals, and prepare to fight again.

Fifty thousand souls on Mars, Petty thought. *Fifty thousand we can still save.*

He knew he was running out of time. If he survived Mars, President Katson would insist they flee across the galaxy, start the human species from scratch on some distant world beyond the marauders' grip. But Petty still hoped, dreamed, prayed.

"Bring back that Ghost Fleet, friends." He placed his hand on the porthole. "Bring me back ten thousand alien starships, and we'll fight together." He pulled his hand back and formed a fist. "And we will win."

CHAPTER FIVE

The forest was cold and shadowy and full of whispers.

Addy walked silently, crossbow in hand, following the hart's trail. She had been tracking the deer for hours now, moving farther and farther from her camp, crossing forested hills and icy streams. Her prey was growing weary, slowing down, his trail easy to track in the snow, leading Addy through the wild. For so long, she had been hunted. Now she was the huntress, hungry, relentless, a predator of the forest.

It was a vast wilderness, lush with life even in winter. Here was the last, the largest true wilderness on the continent. Even before the scum invasion almost sixty years ago, few humans had ever ventured this far north. Even back then, Canada's population had just huddled along the border, only a few adventurers daring to explore the vastness of their northern hinterlands.

Now, with towns and cities in ruins across the globe, it was here in the north, here in this tangled wilderness, that Addy and her fellow rebels had found freedom.

"Ten thousand warriors," she whispered. "Armed. Tough. Survivors. Ten thousand scattered across hundreds of camps. The last free humans."

She had left the Ark last month, feeling too trapped in its darkness, a prisoner between the rusty walls. Here, up north, there was space for her to breathe. There was room for hundreds of bases, some housing only ten rebels, some over a hundred. Some with mothers and children and elders. Others mostly soldiers. Caves. Tents. Bunkers. They had no single point of failure, no single headquarters the marauders could destroy. They were dispersed across the wilderness. While the rest of their race cried out in agony, trapped in the slaughterhouses, here the last free humans hunted, fished, survived . . . and planned their vengeance.

There!

Addy saw movement ahead.

It was hard to be sure. In this thick forest, even with the leaves fallen, an antler looked like a branch, a hoof like a root, a patch of fur like a pile of dry leaves. Addy stood behind an oak, then peered around the trunk, eyes narrowed, toward a cluster of icy maples.

She waited, still.

The tracks stretched through the snow. The animal did not move again. The buck was tired from the hunt, from his hunger. He was slowing down, making mistakes.

Addy turned around the oak slowly, crossbow held before her.

She took a step.

The buck bolted out from the maples. He raced across a ridge, moving between birch saplings toward the safety of a copse of pines, their leaves still thick and green.

Addy loosed a quarrel.

She missed.

With a curse, she ran onto the ridge. She saw the animal making to the pines. Within seconds, he would disappear among them.

She loaded another arrow.

The buck vanished between the branches.

Addy fired again.

From behind the trees, she heard a cry—the animal hit. She heard a *thump*—the deer falling.

Addy licked her lips. "Dinner."

She took no delight in killing animals. She had gone hunting with Jethro sometimes in her youth, and he had taught her to respect her prey, to hunt for food, never for pleasure. Tonight this deer would feed her, Jethro, Steve, and the others who shared their cave.

A crackling sounded among the pines ahead. The branches creaked. The deer was probably still alive, bleeding out. He would not get far. Addy advanced toward the pines, prepared to deliver the killing shot, when—

She gasped.

The severed head of the deer, its skull sliced open and the brain removed, flew toward her.

An instant later, a marauder burst out from the trees, shattering branches.

Addy stumbled backward, heart thrashing. The massive alien leaped toward her, claws lashing, jaws snapping, the deer crushed between its teeth. Addy shouted, scrambled to load another quarrel, but was too slow.

She fell into the snow and rolled. The claws slammed down, slicing her hair, nearly cracking her skull. She tumbled downhill, hit an oak, and groaned.

The marauder vaulted toward her, jaws open wide, shrieking.

Addy grabbed the pistol from her boot, aimed, and fired.

Her bullet slammed into the open mouth, barely fazing the creature. She stumbled aside, and the marauder slammed into the oak, cracking the bole. Addy spun back toward it, firing. Bullets hit the creature's head, bouncing off harmlessly. A claw lashed, hit her gun, and knocked it from her hand.

Fuck!

That left her assault rifle, but it was slung across her back and unloaded. She would only need three seconds to load and fire. She didn't even have one. The jaws snapped at her, and she shoved her crossbow into the marauder's mouth, trying to distract the alien, then yanked her hand back. The jaws snapped shut, shattering her weapon.

Addy ran. It was faster than her. She stumbled downhill, and she saw it below: a frozen stream. She raced with all her speed, the marauder roaring behind her, its claws lashing, missing her by centimeters.

She hurled herself toward the riverbed. Addy had spent her life on the ice. Even without skates, she ran across the frozen surface.

The marauder leaped onto the ice behind her . . . and began to slip.

It was a creature adapted to life in a warm, misty forest. It could climb trees with the best of them, cross great distances on the ground, and explore space in the bellies of its females. On the ice, its six legs floundered, shooting out in all directions, an almost comical sight.

Addy raised her assault rifle, slammed a magazine into it, yanked back on the cocking handle, and aimed.

"Don't fuck with Canada," she said.

Bullets rang out.

They slammed into the marauder, hitting its eyes.

Addy gasped. She hadn't even pulled the trigger yet. Not her bullets!

A man was standing in the cover of the pines, firing at the marauder.

"He's mine!" Addy shouted. "Damn it!"

She stepped closer to the screeching beast. Three of its eyes were already gone. Addy fired a bullet into its last eye. The marauder fell dead onto the ice.

Addy spun toward the pines. "See? Mine! You don't claim that kill. Step out here! Steve, is that you?"

The man stepped out from the trees. No, he was much shorter than Steve—shorter than her too. A thin man with spiky black hair, a gaunt face, and crooked teeth. He carried a string of rabbits across his shoulders, and he moved on two prosthetic legs.

"Hi, Maple," he said.

She gaped at him. She remembered.

"Pinky," she said.

* * * * *

He gave her a thin smile, his crooked teeth pressing against his lips.

"Nobody's called me Pinky in years."

Addy aimed her rifle at him. "Give me one good reason not to shoot you in the balls." She glanced down at his prosthetic legs. "If you even have any balls left."

Pinky nodded. His voice was as raspy as ever. "I deserve that after the shit I pulled. Will you believe I'm sorry now? That I'm no longer that fucking asshole I was at boot camp?"

Addy took a step closer to the small soldier. He still wore his military jacket. Three chevrons, the insignia of a sergeant, were stitched onto the sleeves. Damn, they had made him a sergeant? Who had he blackmailed?

Addy spat. "I don't buy that shit. Once an asshole, always an asshole. I should put a bullet through your ugly face. You made our lives miserable at basic."

He lit a cigarette. "I know. I remember." He barked a laugh. "Yeah, I was a bastard all right, full of piss and fire. God, the shit I pulled!" He grew solemn. "Everything changed at the end, though. When the scum attacked our base. When they ripped off my legs and ate them as I screamed. When you and Poet saved my life."

"Poet saved your life," Addy said. "Not my idea. I just drove the fucking sand tiger. If I knew it was you, I'd have let the scum eat the rest."

"And yet you helped save me," Pinky said. "Well, most of me, at least. Would have been nice to have you show up a few minutes earlier and save the legs too. But hey, I do still have my balls, and they're the most important part of me." He grinned, revealing those crooked teeth. "Hey, kill me now if you like. But you'll be undoing a good deed you and Poet did."

Addy grumbled and lowered her rifle. "What the fuck are you doing here?"

"Came to join the Resistance," Pinky said. "What else?"

She turned away from him. She looked at the bloody hill she had raced down. "Fuck. That damn marauder tore the deer apart. Bits of it everywhere. Spent hours hunting it. Now there's barely enough left to make a cocktail sausage."

"I shot a deer myself," Pinky said. "Mine's still in one piece. Got it right behind those trees. I'll share the meat."

She glared at him. "I don't need your charity." But her stomach growled.

"Not charity," he said. "Just making myself useful. We'll all share the meat. I'm staying in your camp. Already introduced myself to your buddies there."

Addy groaned. "This day is getting better all the time." She began trudging through the snow. "Try to keep up on those rusty robot legs of yours."

As they walked back toward the camp, Pinky told her his story. After the battle of Fort Djemila, he had spent a couple months in the hospital, learning to walk on his prosthetic legs. When the invasion of Abaddon began, he had insisted on shipping out.

"I marched right into my commander's office," Pinky said. "I refused to leave. I said I would fight on these prosthetic legs, or they could toss me into the brig for the rest of the war." He barked a laugh. "Good thing for me, they needed a few million troops. So they shipped me out too, metal legs and all. I never did anything heroic like you and Poet and Tiny. Oh, I heard the stories. We all did. How you killed that fucking scum emperor. But I was there on Abaddon's surface, fighting with the grunts. Killed me a few of the buggers." He pulled up his sleeve, revealing star tattoos, denoting his kills. "I went home proud. And that's where they fucked me over good. It's after the war that you're screwed."

Addy said nothing. She remembered her own experience after being discharged. How she had fled Earth with Marco. How they had suffered in exile, how Marco had nearly gone mad.

"Yeah," she finally said.

Pinky snorted. "What would you know about that, though? I went home and found my mom where I left her. Drunk and drugged out of her mind, lying on the couch in a puddle of her own piss. My brothers were gone—one was in prison, the other shot in a gang war. That's where I come from, Maple. It's what the rest of you never understood."

Addy reeled toward him, teeth bared. "Don't tell what I do or don't understand. I grew up in hell. My father spent his life in and out of prison. My mom was a pathetic drunk, just like yours. And after the army, Poet and I . . ." She breathed heavily. "I saw how the war fucked him up. How he changed. How I tried to save him, but . . ." She looked away. "Fuck it. It's none of your business anyway."

Pinky blew out his breath slowly. "Even Poet? Fuck. War will mess anyone up." He lowered his head. "After the army, I fought another war. I fought on the streets. Gang battles in the alleys. Drugs and cockfights. And I realized something there, Maple. That it wasn't me. Not anymore. That I was no longer that street punk." He looked up, and his eyes were red. "I realized that in the army, I became a better man. That in the army, I was somebody. In the army, I saw what real men were. Guys like Corporal Diaz, like our Sergeant Singh, and . . . yeah, like Poet. Men I wanted to be like. Better men than I was. So when these new fuckers, those marauder pieces of shit, when they came, well . . . I put on my old army jacket. And I decided to fight again. To be a soldier. Because the army was the only time I wasn't a complete fucking failure." He nodded, eyes damp, voice hoarse. "And if I ever meet Poet again, I'll tell him that. That when he saved my life—saved *me*, the asshole who rode his ass throughout boot camp—he saved me from more than the scum. He saved me from myself."

"Touching story." Addy picked her teeth, spat, and scratched her backside. "Fucking beautiful. But I need you to shut up now. We're near the camp and those marauders like to skulk around here. Keep your hands off your balls and your eyes off my tits."

"I wasn't—"

"Shh!"

They walked in silence. The only sound was the snow crinkling beneath her boots and his metal prosthetics. She gazed up, gun raised, seeking marauder webs. The bastards had learned to travel between the branches instead of leaving trails in the snow, and for big aliens, they were amazingly sneaky.

Nothing.

Addy breathed in relief.

She approached the cave, Pinky close behind her. Angela stood guard outside, wearing camouflage, a helmet hiding her fiery red hair.

"I see you met our new friend," Angela said. The girl was only eighteen, had missed being drafted when the marauders destroyed the world.

"An old friend," Addy muttered. She pulled back the leafy branches that hid the cave and stepped inside.

They had set up a little command center here. Radio receivers, phones, tablets, and cables filled the place. Steve and a handful of others were here, working the equipment. Steve, bless his heart, had once asked Addy why Beethoven's parents had named him after a dog, and he still thought *bilingual* meant you were born with two tongues. But the big blockhead was something of an idiot savant; he was a genius at digital and analog communications and encryption. He had rigged this system together, allowing their cave to communicate with a hundred other camps across the forest—and to seek out rebels around the globe.

"Hey, bitches!" Addy said. "We got grub! I'm going to gut this deer outside, so if anyone wants the entrails, let me know now before I feed them to the dogs!"

Nobody answered.

They were all staring at a radio.

A voice was emerging from the speaker, staticky. Addy leaned closer, listening with them. She frowned.

"What language is that?" she said.

"We don't know," said Steve, face somber. "It's been repeating for hours. Priority One message. It's coming to us from Europe."

Her eyes widened. "There are survivors in Europe?"

Steve nodded. "And they're desperate to speak to us. But we can't understand them." He lifted a small device. "This app should be able to detect any language. German, Spanish, Italian, French, Russian, even fucking Klingon. You name it, this device should be able to recognize and translate it. It doesn't even know what language this is, let alone how to translate it. We don't know what the Europeans are saying. But they *really* want us to hear."

Addy frowned at the radio. She narrowed her eyes. "It's a code. Of course it is. Some kind of fancy Pig Latin. If we have one of those translating devices, the marauders might have one too."

Steve lifted a device in his second hand. "That's where this puppy comes in. It detects patterns in codes. It doesn't crack the code for you—you still need a key for that—but it tells you what type of code you're dealing with. Well, I ran it through. Nada. This ain't a code. It's a language."

Addy closed her eyes, listening. The language . . . she had heard it before. Tagalog? She had heard Lailani mumble to herself in that language before. Hebrew? She had heard Ben-Ari use some of that language before. Punjabi, perhaps? Sergeant Singh used to pray in that tongue. As Addy kept listening, more and more memories fired. Older memories. Memories from her earliest childhood. She closed her eyes.

The smell of baking cookies, corn on the cob, and fresh bread. The chinking of beads. Flute music in a parlor, and a little girl running through a garden, picking flowers, and a kindly old man, so ancient he could barely walk . . .

Addy's eyes snapped open.

"My great-grandfather." She hopped onto her feet. "Yes!"

Steve looked at her. "What? What about him?"

Addy trembled with excitement. "I know I look like a Viking princess. That's all my European blood. But my great-grandfather was First Nations. I remember him speaking this language. It's—"

"Cree," Pinky said. He nodded. "Used to buy baseball cards from a Cree guy."

Addy shot him a withering glare. "You just had to steal my thunder, didn't you?"

Pinky shrugged. "Hey, sweetheart, don't hate the player, hate the game. Makes sense, don't it? The Europeans want to talk to us Canadians. They use our native tongue. They probably know it's not in the standard translating apps, in case the marauders got ahold of a translator."

Addy nodded, the deer forgotten. "All right, we've got ten thousand people hiding in these woods. *Somebody* here is bound to speak Cree." She pointed at a few of her people. "Bran, Russ, Jasmine, head out to the nearest camps and ask around. Pinky, you go with them. I want this done offline. I don't want to fuck up our codes and reveal to the marauders that they need a Cree speaker, because they'll find one too. We go to every cave, tent, and bunker in this forest, and if we don't find anyone here, we move north until we reach native villages. If we have to cross the continent, we'll find a Cree speaker, and we'll translate this message."

Steve nodded. He spoke into the radio in English. "Boat stuck in the water. Adjusting our sails and should reach the shore in a couple days." He looked up at Addy. "Old radio trick. Means we're working on the code and should have it cracked within two days." He blew out his breath, fluttering his lips. "Man, back when I learned this stuff, I waded into the lake *three times* before I figured it out."

As it were, it didn't take two days. By that night, they had found Wawetseka—an old woman, well into her seventies but still tough as old leather, a rifle slung across her shoulder and two cigarettes in her mouth.

"Grew up Cree here in Algonquin," Wawetseka said. "Still remember when we had our villages before the scum. Whatever the white man left, they took. But I still honor the old ways. I still speak the tongue. I still fight for my home."

They sat the old woman down in their cave, and they gave her the best slice of deer, and they lit her a third cigarette. And they had her listen.

The old woman clucked her tongue. "Their dialect is different from mine. Cree is all dialects, every village with its own. Each village can understand the next one over, but the more villages you move, the more different the dialects are." She frowned, listening to the message on the radio. "Oh, this young one speaks poorly. But yes. I understand. I will translate. Bring me pen and paper."

Addy frowned as the language was translated onto the page. She raised an eyebrow.

"It's gibberish! It's just nonsense. 'The elephant lost his tusks, so the game of Chinese checkers was lost. Keep an eye on the children from the sea, the tides come in early this winter, but the ball is still on.' What the fuck does that mean?"

Steve lifted one of the sheets of paper. "This," he said, "is our code. Now we have something to decipher."

They were up all night—Wawetseka translating Cree into gibberish English, and Steve and his boys translating the code into proper sentences. The Europeans had been clever. The nouns in the gibberish English represented letters; using only the nouns, they could spell out new words, phonetically, letter by letter. The translation of noun-to-letter came over encrypted too, protected by several layers of passwords. Each password was the name of a Hollywood actor, with only the movie title given; humans would know the actors, marauders would not. Finally, they were able to unscramble the gibberish English, translated from the Cree, into proper sentences. Just before dawn, the code was cracked, the message translated.

Bleary-eyed, Addy stared at the translated message.

"My God," she whispered.

Steve clasped her hand. Silently, they all read the words over and over.

To the North American Resistance,

Do not despair! The Human Defense Force stills stands. Our siblings in air and space have fallen, but on land and at sea, we fight on! Along the Pacific Rim, in the rainforests of the African equator, in the hinterlands of Siberia, in the deserts of Arabia, and everywhere on this small world where the enemy attacks, we will be there to resist him. Many battles were lost. Many brave humans fell. Many still cry out in agony from the inferno of the slaughterhouses. But many still fight!

The tyrant Malphas, leader of the marauders, lurks in his hive in the city once called Toronto. And there we will strike him!

On the first day of spring, the Human Defense Force will invade the fallen continent of North America. We will land in the ruins of New York City. From there, we will make our way north to our final destination.

The Human Defense Force has fallen in North America, but not the human spirit! The Resistance still fights! We call for all Resistance warriors to assist our landing. On the first day of spring, meet us in New York City. Fight with us there. We will invade with all our might, and we will liberate North America—and then the world.

The Earth is an island in the cosmic sea. To quote a great leader: We shall defend our island, whatever the cost may be. WE SHALL NEVER SURRENDER!

Pinky rose to his feet. He saluted. "We shall never surrender."

Steve rose next. "We shall never surrender."

Addy rose with them. She repeated the words. Soon everyone in the cave, all these ragged rebels, stood and chanted these words like a hymn. "We shall never surrender!"

Footsteps thudded.

Angela burst into the cave. The young woman was panting, her red hair in disarray, her rifle in her hands.

"Marauders!" she cried. "Marauders outside!"

Addy grabbed her rifle and ran. Steve and the others followed close behind. They raced outside into the dark forest.

The aliens were everywhere.

From every tree, the eyes stared, black, glittering, beads of darkness. Their claws reached out. Their jaws opened, and they howled—cries that shook the forest, that cracked the icicles, that sent snow cascading and branches falling. Hundreds of them under the stars, creatures from the depths. Hunters. Marauders.

"Never surrender!" Addy shouted and fired her gun.

The marauders leaped toward her, and blazing gunfire and splashing blood filled the forest.

CHAPTER SIX

"Another ship ruined," Ben-Ari said, looking at the damage. "I sure seem good at destroying expensive starships."

"Some women break hearts," Lailani said. "Others break their husband's bank accounts. You break starships. Nobody's perfect."

Ben-Ari smiled wryly. "Oh, hearts and husbands are safe from me. Not so much the *Marilyn*." She lowered her visor and hefted her soldering iron. "Let's get to work."

They stood in the field outside the medieval town, facing their smashed starship. Marco and Kemi were still in the forest, looking for food. Ben-Ari and Lailani had stayed behind to try to repair the *Marilyn*. Thankfully, no more soldiers had arrived to fire arrows, and the peasants in the field gave them a wide berth.

They got to work. Ben-Ari worked on the cracked hull while Lailani tackled the broken wing. Both were badly damaged. Both required tearing metal panels out from the ship's interior. As they worked, the sun beat down, and sweat soaked Ben-Ari. She tried to ignore the hunger in her belly, the weakness in her arms, the pain in her temples, the trembling of her fingers.

She let Bach's *St Matthew's Passion* play in her earbuds as she worked. It was one of her favorite pieces of music. She often played it when troubled. Bach's *Passion*. Mozart's *Requiem*. Beethoven's *Missa Solemnis*. She recognized the irony of it. She, a Jewish woman of the twenty-second century, listening to Christian liturgies from a time when the church had persecuted her people. Yet the music had always soothed her, despite its history, despite the foreign language. She found it beautiful. Soothing. Out of context, a piece of human beauty, of the soul, here in the distant sky.

Einav Ben-Ari had always carried mementos with her to battle. The medals of her ancestors who had fought the Nazis. A book of poems by Abba Kovner. A copy of *Night* by Elie Wiesel. Reminders of the suffering of her people, of the cruelty of tyrants, of why she fought for the downtrodden, why she resisted the bullies of the galaxy. But music . . . music had always been different to her. She had always taken Earth's music into space. Not to remind her of her duty, of the yoke of history. But to remind her of humanity's soul. Of the beauty humans could create. In a cosmos full of cruelty, music was a reminder that humans could be noble.

The music of Bach and Beethoven and Mozart. The paintings of Frida Kahlo and Toulouse-Lautrec and Cezanne—and her own little attempts at watercolors and gouache. Books by Isabelle Allende and Gabriel Garcia Marquez and J.R.R. Tolkien. These were treasures that she could always take out from their box, admire their beauty, seek comfort in them. Perhaps more than the sacrifices of soldiers, more than the ingenuity of scientists, the work of artists inspired her. Art was proof that humanity was worth fighting for.

That is something the scum, the marauders, the bullies will never understand, she thought. *That we humans are not only strong. Not only wise. But that, when we are not cruel, we can be beautiful.*

She supposed it was why Marco wrote stories. Why Kemi danced. Why Lailani had dedicated her life to teaching children to read. To bring beauty into the world. That was nobility.

Ben-Ari had dabbled with her own art. She had scribbled some poems, painted some watercolors. Perhaps in another life, she might have been an artist, lived in a studio by the beach, lived to create. But that had not been her lot.

It's my lot to raise a sword so others can raise paintbrushes and pens. It's for them, the artists, that I fight.

She let out a little laugh as she welded the crack in the hull. The music was making her sentimental. Perhaps when Kemi came back, they would all listen to Buddy Holly and Elvis, would dance instead of contemplate humanity. Perhaps Ben-Ari had always been more of a dreamer than a dancer. Her mother had loved music, had loved to dance . . .

Damn it. And now tears were obscuring her vision. And damn it! Now she had messed up her welding.

She turned off her soldering iron. She had caused more damage than helped, she suspected. She was too hungry. Too tired. Not just the weariness of the body. A deeper, older weariness, one she could not shake.

Lailani had paused from her work. She was looking at her.

"I need another sheet of graphene," Ben-Ari said.

She stepped into the ship hurriedly, wanting to hide her tears. She was still Lailani's captain. Still commander of this ship, of her crew. She needed to be strong for them, to comfort them. They were afraid, she knew. They needed to know she was in control, calm, confident, that she could save them.

She rummaged through the ship, seeking scrap metal she could use, but she found nothing. Damn it! She would have to remove a bulkhead, maybe one between the bridge and the crew quarters. She stepped into the bunk, but the wall was solid. She would need to create a tool, some sort of saw out of engine parts. That could take hours if not days.

We'll starve by then, she thought. *And Earth needs us. And we're stuck here. And . . .*

She could stand the music no longer. She tore out her earbuds. She stood for long moments, shaking, struggling to take deep breaths.

"Be strong, Einav," she whispered. "Be strong. Be calm. Be in control. For your crew. For Earth."

She wanted to continue to work. To fight. She had to always keep fighting. Her crew needed her. Her planet needed her. Her . . .

She sat on her bed, and she covered her eyes, and she breathed deeply. And tears filled her eyes.

I always must be the strong one, Ben-Ari thought. *When do I get to be weak? What if I need help?*

"Ma'am?" Lailani stood at the doorway.

Ben-Ari turned away, her cheeks flushing. She forced herself to speak with a clear, confident voice. "I'll be right out, Sergeant."

But Lailani stepped closer, sat beside her on the bed.

"Ma'am, it's all right to cry," Lailani said softly. "You told me that once, remember? I cry almost every night. Kemi cries. I even saw Marco crying in his bunk the other night, but that might be because I stepped on his sausage when climbing toward the upper shelf."

Ben-Ari laughed weakly. "I could go for a nice big sausage now. I mean—to eat a sausage. I mean—you know what I mean." She frowned. "Stop having such dirty ears."

Lailani grinned—a huge grin that showed sparkling white teeth. "Even officers need to get laid."

Ben-Ari groaned. "Soldiers generally do not tell their officers they need to get laid."

Yet perhaps there was some truth to Lailani's words. Art. Music. Books. Yes, she had taken all those things from Earth. Yet what of the other needs all humans had, even officers? Oh, in her younger days, she had been as wild as anyone, she supposed. Ben-Ari had never forgotten her first sexual experience, a tender, giggly, awkward night with a female friend at age fourteen, another military brat at some forgotten base at the end of the world. There had been a few others after that, all of them older boys, secret romances when her father had been away in space.

Then she had joined the army. She had become an officer. And she had placed all thoughts of romance and love aside. Oh, there was the odd romance novel perhaps, the odd fantasy, but sex?

"My God," Ben-Ari found herself whispering. "I've turned into a spinster."

Lailani laughed. "You're too young and pretty to be a spinster, ma'am."

"I'm twenty-eight!" Ben-Ari said. "That's almost thirty." She sighed. "And while I thank you for the compliment, I'm hardly a heartbreaker. You've said so yourself."

Lailani looked at her lap, and her cheeks flushed. She bit her lip, then looked back up at Ben-Ari.

"I had a massive crush on you at boot camp," Lailani said. "When I first saw you, I thought you were so beautiful. So strong and wise, while I was so weak and stupid. I had a fantasy that on Sunday, you'd call me into your trailer, that you'd order me onto your bed, and then you'd—" She gasped and covered her mouth. "Oh my God. Oh my fucking God. I didn't just say that, did I?"

Ben-Ari stared at her, jaw hanging open. "But—what? Sergeant!"

"I'm sorry!" Lailani covered her face. "I'm so embarrassed." She peeked between her fingers. "It's just . . . I never had anyone strong in my life. My mother died when I was very young. I have no older sisters. And I guess . . . I was attracted to that. To a stronger, older woman. A sort of guardian figure." She laughed awkwardly. "But then Marco put on the moves." She lowered her gaze again and twisted her fingers in her lap. She trembled. "I still think you're pretty. And I still have a crush on you. But I'm silly. I get silly crushes on everyone. Even on Marco. You don't hate me now, do you?"

Ben-Ari sighed. "No, de la Rosa. I don't hate you."

Lailani still wouldn't raise her eyes. "I'm embarrassed. I'm so stupid."

Ben-Ari placed a finger under Lailani's chin and raised the little sergeant's head. She looked into her eyes. "You're not stupid. You're sweet. And intelligent. And capable. And kind. You're my soldier, and I'm proud of you. Always."

Lailani smiled, eyes damp. She reached out, caressed Ben-Ari's hair, then quickly pulled her hand back. She looked away. She spoke softly, hands clasped in her lap. "I want to make love to you now. While Marco and Kemi are away." She took a deep breath, looked back into Ben-Ari's eyes, and took her hand. "You're a good officer. A good warrior. A good leader. But I'm good at this. I'm a good lover. And I want to make you feel good. I want to make you feel less alone. Just say yes, ma'am. You don't need to say anything else to me. You don't have to ever talk to me about it again, even remember it after today, or ever do it again. But today, say yes."

Ben-Ari regarded the young sergeant. Lailani's fingers were trembling, but her eyes were earnest. Hesitantly, she reached out to caress Lailani's cheek, trailing her fingers down to her lips. Her skin was soft, olive toned, her features delicate, her cheek damp from a trailing tear. Ben-Ari thought back to that time in her youth, a time of giddy, nervous lovemaking. She thought of her years of loneliness—an officer, a prisoner, a leader tasked with saving the world. So many years alone. So many years without the warmth, the comfort of a lover. All the cosmos might end tomorrow. All their lives might be lost. Was this place, this world, just a fantasy? Was this just a dream?

Then let it be a good dream, Ben-Ari thought, and tears filled her eyes. *For once, let things be good.*

She took Lailani into her arms.

"Yes," she whispered. "Yes."

Yes, perhaps just a dream. Perhaps just a fever dream in an impossible world. But it felt real. And it felt good. And afterward, when Ben-Ari held her little soldier in her arms, she never wanted this moment to end.

Yet her communicator buzzed. Marco and Kemi were on the way back—with food. Time continued. There were more battles to fight, more struggles to face. And the dream ended.

As Ben-Ari worked outside the ship again, she was calmer, her head clearer, and when she glanced at Lailani, the little sergeant quickly looked away, smiling a small smile. Ben-Ari knew the dream would never return. She knew they would never speak of it again. But perhaps, like her music, her poems, and her artwork, this too could be a warmth to Ben-Ari in the cold. A little memory she could take out when necessary, admire its beauty, then tuck it away for another cold night. It wasn't much. It wasn't the comfort of a spouse, the security of a home. But it was a little light for the darkness that she knew still lay ahead.

CHAPTER SEVEN

The rebels ran through the forest, firing their guns, falling one by one.

The marauders were everywhere.

The dawn revealed more and more of them. Their webs coated the snowy trees. They leaped above. They ran in the snow. They slashed their claws. Their jaws closed around humans, ripping bodies apart, and they laughed as they fed.

"Fight them!" Addy shouted, running through the bloody snow. "Rebels, rally here! Fight them! Aim for their eyes!"

She ran toward the piny hill, toward the tents hidden there in the brush. A handful of rebels ran with her. Steve panted, his leg still sore. Pinky raced on his prosthetics. Angela leaped through the snow, her hair a fiery banner. Even Jethro ran with them, his peg leg thumping. Across the forest, dozens of other rebels were firing their guns. Were dying.

"To the hill!" Addy shouted.

A marauder leaped down before them and bellowed. They fired, peppering it with bullets, shattering its eyes. They kept running. A web shot down from a treetop, grabbed Angela, and yanked her into the air. Addy fired, severing the strand a second before the marauder in the tree could devour Angela. The girl fell into the snow and fired upward, screaming, killing the marauder above.

The rebels reached the hill, pulled back the snowy tarp, and revealed them there: the snowmobiles.

Addy leaped onto one and kick-started the engine. She roared downhill, the snowmobile roaring and thrumming beneath her. The Resistance had mounted machine guns onto the snowmobiles, welding them between the handlebars. Addy fired hers, spraying bullets. Marauders shrieked, falling back from the onslaught.

"Snowmobiles, follow me!" Addy shouted. "Head to the lake!"

She remembered the marauder from the other day. The one who had chased her onto the river, who had slipped on the ice. If she could reach the frozen lake . . .

The other snowmobiles roared behind her. Marauders leaped from all sides, and their bullets sang. Riding beside her, Steve hurled a grenade, and it exploded between the trees, knocking down an oak. A marauder crashed into the snow, and bullets slammed into the beast. Addy lobbed a grenade too, tearing down another tree, knocking down the marauder in the canopy. She kept firing her machine gun, plowing a path through the enemies.

A marauder raced toward her, screeching, claws reaching out. She fired her machine gun, tearing through its eyes. The alien collapsed a second before it could reach her. Her snowmobile hit the corpse, flew into the air, and she fired more bullets at a marauder swinging on a web. She slammed back down into the snow and kept driving.

The trees blurred at her sides. More rebels ran among them, firing guns. Dozens, then hundreds. The marauders were flushing them out from every cave and tent, and corpses filled the forest.

They heard us, Addy thought. *Damn! They heard our communications. They triangulated our location. Fuck fuck fuck.*

"Fight them!" she shouted, firing her guns, roaring forth on her snowmobile. "Never surrender!"

A marauder howled in a tree and shot down a web. A strand caught Addy's snowmobile and lifted one corner. She drew her sword—the sword with the blade made from Orcus's tooth. She slashed through the strand, and her snowmobile fell back onto the snow and kept racing. She lobbed a grenade at the leaping marauder, then ducked her head. She grimaced as the shockwave hit her snowmobile.

Ahead she saw it: the frozen lake.

Hundreds of marauders surrounded it.

Winter was ending. The ice would be thin. But Addy had no time to hesitate. She roared down the hillside, all guns blazing. The enemy leaped from all sides. With a hailstorm of bullets and the burst of grenades, Addy plowed her way through. She shouted, drove her snowmobile over a snowdrift, and flew through the air. She fired bullets at the marauders leaping her way, severing their webs.

She slammed down onto the frozen lake.

A crack raced across the ice.

Addy winced, sure the ice would shatter, but she kept driving across the lake. She spun around to see the other snowmobiles leap over the snowdrift, then slam onto the ice with her. Other rebels raced afoot, vaulting between the marauders, guns blazing. Some fell. Others landed on the ice and scurried away from the bank.

More cracks spread.

This is going to get ugly fast, Addy thought.

The marauders surrounded the lake.

From the beaches, they stared.

"Come on!" Addy shouted, gun raised. "Come and get us, assholes!" The aliens did not move. "Come on!"

The marauders sneered. They drooled. Their eyes blazed. More and more kept emerging from among the trees. Addy and her comrades—twenty rebels on snowmobiles, a couple dozen afoot—stood in the center of the lake.

Come on, onto the ice, Addy thought. *We can fight you on the ice* . . .

The marauders did not move.

Addy fired her gun.

A bullet hit a marauder on the lakefront. It howled. The other rebels fired too. They stood back to back, bullets blazing, hitting trees around the lake, hitting marauders, killing a few. But the aliens were too many, too distant to accurately hit in the eyes.

The marauders grabbed oaks and maples around the lake. These trees had grown here for hundreds of years, and their roots ran deep into the frozen soil. Yet the marauders uprooted these mighty trees as if they were spring saplings. Staring at Addy, licking their lips, the marauders slammed the trees onto the ice.

More cracks spread.

Addy stared.

The marauders smiled at her—horrible, twisting grins full of bloody teeth.

They slammed the trees down again like hammers.

The cracks raced toward the rebels, and the ice shattered.

The water engulfed Addy.

She couldn't breathe. Her heart could barely beat. The cold was terrifying, indistinguishable from heat. She was burning in an inferno. She had fallen into the sun. Agony—pure agony, screeching, biting, searing her—spread across her skin and invaded her innards.

The snowmobile was pulling her under. She kicked, desperate to free herself. Her foot tangled in a strap. She could barely move. Her muscles were stiffening. Around her, she saw others sinking, some already dead.

She gave a wild kick, freed herself, and the snowmobile sank below her. She kicked again, pain exploding with every movement.

Her head burst above the surface.

"Swim!" she shouted. Barely any voice emerged. "To the river!"

Around the river, she saw the marauders. Laughing. Watching her slowly die. Rebels floundered in the lake, trying to grab slabs of ice, falling back under.

"To the river!" she cried. "Swim!"

She swam.

She swam through hellfire.

She swam through the deadly ice.

She kicked off her boots, her jacket, her pants, remaining in her underclothes. Ice was crawling across her skin

But she kept swimming.

The marauders cast their strands into the water. They fished out some rebels, yanked them to land, and tore them apart. Addy swam in zigzags, dodging webs. Steve, Jethro, Angela, and a handful of others swam with her. Pinky was struggling, his metal legs built for running on land, not swimming—let alone in a frozen lake. Addy grabbed the snaggletoothed soldier and yanked him along with her.

"Leave me, Maple!" Pinky sputtered. "I'll slow you down."

Fuck you, Pinky, she thought, not bothering to respond. She kept dragging him. *I'll save your ass, but I'm not wasting breath on you.*

The marauders raced along the trunks of floating trees. They thrust out webs, grabbed rebels, and pulled them into their jaws. Dragging Pinky through the water, Addy dodged one web. Steve slashed his knife, severing a strand that flew his way.

A web caught Jethro.

The one-legged survivalist shouted.

"Jethro!" Addy cried, reaching toward him.

"Addy, swim on!" he shouted as the web pulled him toward the marauders.

"Jethro, no!" Addy began swimming toward him, dragging Pinky with her. "Jethro!"

The marauders grabbed the bearded man. They wrapped him with webs. His blood spurted. Addy screamed.

"Addy, come on!" His face ghostly white, Steve grabbed her. Chunks of ice floated around them. "We have to keep going!"

Damn it. Damn it! She had to save Jethro. He was like a father to her. But more marauders were casting their webs. And she was still holding Pinky. And Steve was tugging her away.

"He's already gone, Addy!" Steve shouted, lips purple as he swam in the water. "We have to go!"

"I'm sorry, Jethro," she whispered. "I'm sorry."

She swam, leaving Jethro behind in the enemy claws.

As marauders screeched, a handful of surviving rebels reached the river. It was a mix of ice, slush, and water, and Addy managed to climb onto a patch of ice and hobble forward. The other rebels emerged onto floating ice around her. They were all shivering, freezing, dying of the cold.

We need fire, she thought. *Or within moments, we're dead.*

The marauders howled and raced along the riverbanks. More webs blasted out.

Addy tried to fire her assault rifle. The damn thing jammed, filled with ice crystals. She tossed her last grenade, and it burst on the riverbank, shattering marauders.

"Run!" she shouted, running off the frozen river. She leaped between the alien corpses and raced through the forest. She had only minutes to live, she knew, unless she found fire. She had removed her frozen clothes in the lake, remaining in her underwear. Her skin was corpse-white, her fingers blue. She kept running. The others ran behind her.

Some brazen marauders raced onto the icy river, only to slip and fall into the water, where they quickly sank. Others still lurked in the trees.

Finally Addy saw it ahead: the lookout on the hilltop. The place where they had raised their antenna.

There would be tents there. Supplies. Big guns. And a campfire.

Wearing only her underclothes, coated with ice, she made her way up the hill. She was nearly dead once she reached the top. Several rebels were here, already dead, marauders feasting upon their corpses. Steve and Pinky fired their rifles—theirs were still working—destroying the beasts.

They leaped behind the sandbags that surrounded the outpost. Three heavy cannons rose here along with several machine guns.

The marauders were racing up the hills around them.

"I'll build a fire," Addy said, barely shoving the words through frozen lips. Her teeth chattered. Every breath, she knew, might be her last. "Steve, help me. The rest of you—fire those guns!"

A handful of rebels manned the weapons, and the air shook as shells blasted down. Explosions rocked the valleys, tearing up trees, sinking craters into the land. Marauders tore apart. Shell after shell flew, raising clouds of snow, frozen soil, trees, and dead aliens, leaving holes that could swallow tanks.

Addy let the others fight. She had a more important task—building that fire. Cold would kill them just as quickly as marauders. The outpost had firewood, and her fingers kept shaking, and she couldn't light the logs. Finally she found gasoline, doused the wood, and a fire roared to life.

Finally, heat warmed her, staving off cold death.

Another minute without heat, and the marauders would have enjoyed a lovely meal of meat Popsicles, she thought.

For hours, they fought, the fire roaring behind them. Marauders kept climbing the slopes, only for the shells and bullets to knock them down. Trees kept shattering. The land shook.

It was afternoon by the time the western chapter of the rebellion arrived, bringing with them the tanks and helicopters. It was dawn again by the time the marauders all lay dead.

Among them, strewn across the forest for many kilometers, lay hundreds of human corpses.

For two days they toiled, salvaging ammo and weapons, re-establishing lines of communication, treating the wounded, and burning the dead. As winter lashed them with its final fury, they mustered in a valley beneath a forested escarpment. They abandoned their caves, their lookouts, their shacks. They all came here, rallying around Addy. The Northern Resistance in all its might: a few thousand ragged souls. A few hundred vehicles. A handful of aircraft. Soldiers. Rebels. Survivors. Humans in a fallen world.

From atop the escarpment, Addy gazed at the thousands in the valley below. She sat astride a horse, one of a hundred the Resistance owned. She raised her banner high, and it caught the wind, unfurled, and displayed its symbol: a blue circle on a black field. Symbol of Earth.

"I am Addy Linden!" she cried, loud enough for them all to hear. "I fought the scum on Corpus and Abaddon! I fight the marauders now! Will you fight with me?"

Across the valley, they roared. They stood in the snow. They stood atop tanks, snowmobiles, and armored vehicles. They rode horses, both live and mechanical ones.

"We will fight!" they chanted.

A great army was sailing from Europe and Africa. Thousands of human warriors were making their way to the ruins of New York City. There, the forces would converge. From there, they would reclaim this continent. Addy did not speak of this to her people. Not when marauders might be lurking in the forest, listening to her words.

But she didn't have to. She knew they would follow her anywhere.

"The time for hiding is over!" she said. "We go south. We go to battle! We go to victory! For Earth!"

"For Earth!" they cried. "For Earth!"

The Resistance began moving south.

The tanks moved at the vanguard. The armored Jeeps brought up the rear. Between them marched thousands of rebels and their families, and trucks carried their helicopters, cannons, and munitions. It was a long road from the Canadian hinterlands to the ruins of New York. As Addy rode her horse between the tanks, she knew that many marauders would wait along this path.

"But we will raise more fighters along the way," she said to Steve. "We will sound the call across the East Coast, and humanity will rise in defiance."

Steve rode at her side on his own horse, his rifle slung across his back. "I always wanted to see New York. Never thought it would be like this."

She smiled thinly. "Me too. New York hot dogs, right?" And suddenly she was remembering roasting hot dogs with Marco, and she missed him and her friends, and she had to wipe tears from her eyes.

Victory, honor, triumph, she thought. *All big words to inspire my people. But all I want is you back, Poet. You and Lailani and Ben-Ari and Kemi. I just want us to be together again, to buy that house on a beach. Somewhere warm where it never snows. Somewhere where we can forget. I miss you and love you.*

The Resistance rolled onward, heading south through the frozen wilderness toward the fire.

CHAPTER EIGHT

They sat around the campfire, slicing pieces of roast unicorn.

"Mmm, unicorn." Lailani bit into a slice. Gravy dripped down her chin. "I can taste the rainbow!"

Kemi shot her a glare. "How could you be enjoying that?"

"Hey, princess, I used to scrounge through landfills for trash to eat." Lailani chomped down, tearing off more meat from the bone. "This is heavenly. Hey, anyone got a piece with extra sparkles?"

They sat near the fallen starship. The *Marilyn* was still badly damaged; she wasn't flying again anytime soon. Ben-Ari had rigged a security system around the wreckage, creating a square of laser beams. If anyone tripped them, an alarm would blare. So far, the city guards had not returned, and the peasants gave them a wide berth. But Marco was worried. When the sun rose again, would knights in armor arrive to slay the demons who had fallen from the sky?

Marco bit into his meal. The meat was gamy and soft. He still felt guilty over slaying such a magnificent creature, but with every delicious bite, the guilt was fading. Even Kemi eventually relented and joined the feast.

"You did good, Marky Marc." Lailani patted his shoulder. "Don't let Princess Kemi make you feel bad. It's no different than eating cow or chicken. Just because unicorns are beautiful doesn't mean they have more rights than a steak."

"First of all, never call me that again," Marco said. "Second, unicorns aren't even real."

Lailani patted her swelling belly. "My tummy happily disagrees."

"You all make me sick," Kemi said. She closed her eyes, took another bite, gulped, and shuddered. "And I hate that this tastes good."

Marco turned toward his captain. Ben-Ari was standing apart from the group, staring up at the night sky. Marco stood up and approached her.

"Ma'am, have you had enough to eat?" he said.

Ben-Ari kept looking up. She spoke softly. "Do the stars look right to you, Sergeant Emery?"

He gazed up with her. The stars shone brilliantly, as bright as he'd ever seen them.

"They're beautiful, ma'am. The stars of Earth. We're home, all right. There's the Big Dipper. There's Orion. And I can see Venus—the bright light there—and Mars above it."

Ben-Ari pointed. "That constellation there. You recognize it?"

Marco stared. He thought for a moment. "Gemini, I think."

She nodded. "Gemini. In the north. In summer."

"Yes, ma'am, so it would seem."

Finally she turned to look at him. "Gemini should be in the east."

Marco frowned. "Are you sure, ma'am? We seem to be in Europe. Maybe from here—"

"I'm sure, Sergeant. And look at Orion. It's summer. We shouldn't even see Orion in the night sky. It's a winter constellation."

Marco's jaw unhinged. "Then we must be in the Southern Hemisphere."

She gave him a wry smile. "With European villages and castles? And unicorns?"

He exhaled slowly. "So where are we?"

"That's what I'd like to know." Ben-Ari turned to look at the dark forest. "And I have a feeling we'll find answers in that castle on the mountain. We'll head there at dawn and—"

A wolf howl tore through the night.

Ben-Ari lifted and loaded her gun. Marco followed suit a second later.

A second howl rose, closer. Another howl from behind.

"Back to the campfire," Ben-Ari said.

She and Marco stepped closer toward the flames. Kemi and Lailani stood there, holding their own guns. The wolf howls surrounded them now, moving closer and closer. These were no ordinary wolves. The howls were too deep, too guttural, demonic.

One of the laser pointers, part of the alarm system around the camp, flew through the shadows and thumped against the dead starship.

"There!" Marco pointed.

Shadows lurched. Figures moved in the night. Marco grabbed his flashlight and pointed a beam.

A creature hissed, eyes searing white, burly and covered in black fur, its fangs bared. It loped back into the shadows.

"Big as a goddamn horse," Lailani muttered.

"What is it?" Kemi said, clutching her rifle.

"Wolves," said Marco. "Giant wolves."

"Wolves smart enough to disable our alarm system?" Kemi said.

The howls rose again.

Ben-Ari knelt, rummaged through her pack, and produced a flare gun. She fired skyward, and the flare rose and blasted out light. A miniature sun now shone above the camp.

"Fuck," Marco said.

The wolves were everywhere. Dozens of them. Massive, bipedal beasts with claws like daggers, with fangs that shone, with red eyes. The creatures tossed back their heads, roared, then charged toward the camp.

"Fire!" Ben-Ari shouted.

Their guns blasted. Bullets slammed into the beasts, ripping through fur and flesh. Wolves fell. As they collapsed, the beasts shrank, changing into human forms. Marco had no time to ponder this. A wolf leaped at him, claws lashing. The beast was easily seven feet tall. Marco swung his barrel, diverting the blow, then released a bullet into its face. The wolf roared, choking on blood, half its jaw gone. It took several more bullets to knock it down. When it hit the ground, it turned into a naked boy.

"They're kids!" Marco said. "They're only kids!"

"Keep firing!" Ben-Ari said, switching to automatic now. She sprayed bullets at the advancing wolves. As they fell, they too became human children, just boys and girls.

"What the fuck is going on?" Lailani shouted, spraying bullets. "Why are they kids?"

"Don't let them reach us!" Ben-Ari said.

The monsters kept advancing, bellowing, lashing their fangs. One wolf managed to reach them, to slash Kemi's shoulder. She cried out, blood pouring, and fired in automatic into the creature. It collapsed at her feet, shrinking into a pigtailed girl.

"We're killing kids!" Kemi said.

"No choice!" Ben-Ari shouted. "Fire at them!"

The bullets kept flying. Another wolf made it through, and its jaws closed around Lailani's leg. She yowled and fell. Marco drew his knife and plunged it down, but he couldn't cut through the animal's thick fur and skin. Lailani struggled, crying out in pain. Finally Marco managed to drive his blade into the creature's eye. All the while, Kemi and Ben-Ari kept spraying bullets every which way. Hot casings flew.

"Back into the *Marilyn*!" Ben-Ari said during a lull in the attack. "Hurry!"

Lailani limped, leaning on Marco, and they made it back into the ship. Marco fired bullets, holding the creatures back, until they slammed the airlock shut. The wolves kept pounding at the walls, shaking the vessel.

Ben-Ari limped toward the bridge, dripping blood.

"Emery, help me!" she said. "We might just have enough juice to scare them off. Front machine guns—fire them!"

Marco saw the wolves leaping through the darkness, slamming against the cockpit. The cracked windshield shattered. A wolf leaped toward the bridge, nearly entering the vessel. Marco fired his rifle, knocking it back, then switched on the ship's control panels.

For an agonizing moment, nothing happened.

Finally the system—badly damaged, running on backup batteries—came online.

Marco fired the ship's front guns. Bullets—far larger than those his assault rifle fired—plowed through the wolf pack. The corpses of children dropped.

As more wolves lunged, Ben-Ari switched on the back engines.

Fire blasted from the ship's exhaust.

The starship screeched forward in the field, too damaged to take flight, still operational enough to skid toward the forest. The inferno blazed out across the wolves that chased them.

Ben-Ari turned off the engines, and they kept sliding forward for several hundred meters, finally crashing into the forest.

The last wolves howled, then fled.

Ben-Ari shut off the engines. The ship lay still and dark in the forest.

Again, the crew gathered in the infirmary.

Again, they had to stitch up and bandage wounds.

From outside came the cries of peasants racing toward the burning farms, trying to put out the fire. They shouted about the demons who burned their farms, who slew their children. But they dared not approach the ship in the forest.

"What were those things?" Kemi whispered, shivering. "Kids. Just kids. And we killed them."

Ben-Ari's face was pale, her mouth a thin line. "They were monsters."

But even the captain seemed shaken. Her fingers trembled. Lailani shivered, covered her face, and tears leaked between her fingers.

Marco felt sick. This wasn't like killing the unicorn, not even the peasants. These had been children . . . at least in death. He wasn't used to this. He had trained to kill bugs, just giant evil bugs from space. Not unicorns. Not peasants. Not children.

"Guys, where the hell are we?" he whispered.

"I don't know," Ben-Ari said, her arm bandaged. "But come dawn, I'm going to find out." Anger filled her eyes. "And we're going to find a way to get home."

CHAPTER NINE

He lurked.

He fed.

He tugged on many strands, saw with many eyes, for he was Master, and his gaze was far, and his legs were long, and his wrath was as vast as the darkness between the stars.

He was Malphas.

He reigned.

He lived in a dark place now. A web among the ruins. He, who had ruled the mighty forests, who had stretched his legs across the void, who had gazed into the Abyss and faced the demons beyond. He, Malphas, Lord of Marauders, he who should reign from palaces of wood and mist and starlight—he hissed, waited, tugged his strands from this small dark place. This burrow. This hive among the ruins of the apes.

This had once been a city.

This had once been a library, for the apes stored their knowledge on desecrated wood.

This had once been the home of two apes. Of Addy Linden. Of Marco Emery. Of names Malphas knew well. Names he had etched into his flesh. Names he dreamed of, tasted with every ape consumed.

From here, this dark place among the crumbling towers, had risen the humans who had defeated the centipedes, had toppled that mighty empire. From here, this very hallowed ground, had sprung the great heroes of humanity.

And so from here Malphas ruled upon their world. From here, he would stretch out his legs and his gaze, and from here he would watch their world fall.

His spheres hung around him on his web. A hundred glass eyes. Through them, he could gaze across this world. He saw the rebels flee deeper into the wilderness; he would find them there. He saw the humans overseas battling in the deserts and forests; he would cut them down. He saw a last fleet, a few ragged starships, hiding in the shadows; he would flush them out.

But only one vision eluded him.

Marco. Ben-Ari. Kemi. Lailani.

Malphas sneered. Somehow, they had fled from his vision. Even his many eyes could not see them. His warriors claimed they were dead. But Malphas knew. He could smell their stench from afar. They were alive. Hiding. Scheming. The ones who had defeated the centipedes. The ones he sought.

And one among them, most special of all humans. One Malphas craved more than any other. The most important ape in the cosmos.

I will find you all, he vowed. *I will make you scream. I will saw your skulls open and cut your brains slowly, over many days, piece by piece, as you beg for death.* His fury flamed through him like the plasma inside a ravager. *You will feel pain like no being in the cosmos ever has.*

"Bring me another!" he rumbled.

One of his warriors approached, crawling across a web. He was a mighty beast, a marauder who had slain countless enemies, and a hundred skulls of a hundred species clattered on his back, but he was but a worm compared to Malphas.

"Another to breed with, my lord?" the marauder hissed. "Would you like the pale one you captured this morning, my lord?"

The harem spread across the burrow. Malphas had collected them, concubines, young human females, delectable, trapped in his web. Their fear seeped through their naked flesh, the scent intoxicating, and his nostrils flared. They were screaming into their gags. Malphas had a harem of ten thousand ravagers, the finest in the fleet, and he had spilled his seed within them all, but he sought pleasures more exotic. On every conquered world, he had them. His beauties.

He would partake of them later, perhaps. Now he craved flesh of a different sort.

"No, my precious," Malphas hissed. "That taste can wait. Bring me flavor of a different sort. Another morsel to feed upon. Young this time. A child. A babe. They are soft. They whet the appetite. They heat the blood."

"Yes, my lord." His warrior-servant nodded. "A nice, soft delectable."

The creature scurried along the web, and the prisoners shook on the trembling strands. The women wept. The marauder grabbed one of the apes at the bottom, a mere babe, younger than one orbit of this pathetic planet around its star. The marauder handed the child to Malphas.

He took the babe in his claws. A sweet little morsel. So soft. So sweet. Malphas lowered his head and sniffed, nostrils flaring, inhaling the scent of the wriggling, screaming creature.

"You are born so weak," he hissed, marveling at it, turning the youngling in his claws. "So useless. So dependent on your mothers. Our kind hatch with claws and fangs. As soon as they emerge from their eggs, they devour their mother, eating her from the inside out. And when their hunger rises again, they hunt. Yet you humans . . ." He caressed the baby's cheek with a claw. "Born so frail. Naked and afraid. Alone in the dark. How have creatures so weak risen so high?" He inhaled again, shuddering with pleasure, and gripped the baby's head. "Ah, yes. There it is. The brain. The delicious, juicy, sentient brain. Nearly as large as the brain of a marauder. A brain capable of such fear, such cunning, such juices that flow down the throat. A true delicacy!"

Of course, the brain of this babe would not sate his hunger. It took larger brains for that. But Malphas wanted to remain hungry. He needed his hunger, needed his cravings unfilled. It kept him alert, kept him on the hunt. He would feed only on these morsels, these snacks, until he caught his prize. Until he fed on Addy. On Marco. On the mighty human heroes who would bow before him.

He opened his jaws and raised the baby toward them.

"My lord!" A voice from the burrow's entrance. "My lord Malphas, we caught a rebel!"

Malphas grunted. He placed the baby aside, sticking it onto his web, and crept down the strands.

"Why do you bring a male ape here?" he rumbled. "How dare you disturb me?"

Three marauders had entered his domain. They bowed on the ground, not daring to touch his webs. They trembled before him. Between them, they gripped a man. A pathetic old ape. His beard was long and gray, and he was missing one leg.

"What is this wretched specimen?" Malphas said.

The marauders bowed lower, holding the prisoner.

"He knows her, my lord!" one said. "He fought with her. He knows the one called Linden."

Malphas inhaled sharply. His eyes widened. He climbed down his web, moved across the ground, and grabbed the human. He yanked the man's head toward him, placed his nostrils against the skull, and breathed in the smell.

Yes. He exhaled, shivering with delight. *Yes . . .*

"Leave us," Malphas said. "All of you! Out."

The marauders—those who bowed before him and those who lurked on his webs—retreated from the hive, returning to the ruins of the city.

Malphas gazed at the old man in his grip.

"Yes . . . you know her." He ran a claw down the ape's face, cutting the skin. "You know Addy Linden. You are . . ." He inhaled again, smelling the brain. "You are Jethro. Yes. You are like a father to her. And you will tell me where she hides. You will tell me everything, and perhaps I will grant you a quick death."

The old man raised his chin. "I have two words for you, buddy. Fuck and you."

Malphas opened his jaws wide, hissing. "Ah . . . the delightful disobedience to mask the terror. I will enjoy this." A grin revealed all his teeth. "Very much."

He tightened his grip on Jethro.

He got to work.

Jethro screamed.

For long hours, Malphas practiced his art. He removed the top of the skull. He poked. He prodded. He cut out bits of the brain. All the while—questioning, sniffing, tasting.

"Think of Addy." Malphas hissed, drooling above the open brain. "No, Jethro. Not about your children." He dug his claws. "About Addy. That's right. Let me have a little taste . . ." He nibbled. He closed his eyes. "Ah yes . . . They are heading to the pile of rubble you call New York. Good. Good. My children will await them there."

Gripped in his claws, tears on his cheeks, Jethro managed to scream, "You son of a bitch! They're going to kill you. They're going to fucking kill you, you space bug, Addy will—"

With a single, fluid flick of his tongue, Malphas slurped out the brain—what remained of it, at least. He swallowed the meal.

Ah . . . delicious.

He had wanted to wait, to save his hunger for Addy, but that was all right. His hunger would grow again. And soon—very soon now—the humans who had slain the scum would be his.

CHAPTER TEN

They slept inside the *Marilyn*, taking shifts guarding. Throughout the night, the wolves kept howling, and the townsfolk kept shouting, but none dared approach the broken starship, still fearing its machine guns, roaring engines, and strange occupants with the booming sticks.

They ate leftover unicorn meat—Marco still couldn't believe it—for breakfast. They decided to split up again. Today, once more, Lailani would stay and continue repairing the ship, and Kemi—still shaken over her experience in the forest—volunteered to stay and help.

"It's you and me, Sergeant Emery," Captain Ben-Ari said. "We head to that castle."

"And try to catch something different than unicorn!" Kemi said.

Lailani raised her eyes from a pile of machinery she was working on. "Have fun storming the castle! Kemi and I will stay and swap juicy stories about Poet. We have *lots* to talk about."

Marco squirmed. "Uhm, maybe *I* should stay and Lailani should—"

"Emery, we're moving out," Ben-Ari said. "Come now."

Lailani and Kemi waved at him, disturbingly quiet, and Marco gulped.

"Emery—" Ben-Ari began.

"Yes, ma'am." Marco rushed to follow her, leaving Kemi and Lailani behind.

They walked along the forest trail, the bluebells and oaks swaying around them. By midmorning, they saw the castle on the mountain. Again, Marco shuddered to see it. The black fortress seemed almost like a living creature, perched high above, watching him approach. No more birds sang here, and the trees were twisted and thin, sending out branches like snagging claws.

"This is where we saw the unicorn." Marco pointed at the hill. "Strange. There's no more blood."

"Very strange," Ben-Ari said, staring at the castle above. Her eyes narrowed.

"What are you thinking, ma'am?" Marco said.

"I'm not sure," said Ben-Ari. "I can think of several possibilities. That we traveled through a time warp back to medieval Earth, and that I'm simply wrong about the stars. That we're in a parallel dimension. That we're on a planet that's simply very, very similar to Earth. That we're all hallucinating, or at least I am. That we're stuck in a virtual reality world—or maybe a physical world that's just set up like a giant medieval theme park. I'm hoping that castle holds answers."

They reached the foothills. The dirt path, which ran from through the forest, zigzagged up the mountainside. Alongside the path, wooden train tracks stretched in a straight line up toward the castle.

"Train tracks?" Ben-Ari said, frowning at them. "In the Middle Ages?"

"Trolley tracks," Marco said. "Look."

A trolley—a little wooden cart, no larger than a bathtub—was working its way up the tracks. Inside were fruit, vegetables, smoked hams, and sausages. A donkey, riderless, was pulling the cart. The animal had an easy job; the trolley moved smoothly along the tracks, its wheels spinning in oiled grooves.

"We'll pay for these later," Ben-Ari said, grabbing some food from the trolley.

Marco's eyes widened. "Stealing, ma'am?"

She nodded, stuffing a cabbage into her backpack. "Stealing. We need to eat, not just meat but fruit and vegetables. Take some. Just enough for a few meals. We'll bring some back to Kemi and Lailani later today."

The donkey brayed, dismayed at the theft, but kept climbing. The animal moved a lot faster than Ben-Ari and Marco, soon vanishing—along with the trolley of food—among the trees farther up the mountainside.

They kept climbing the dirt path, chewing on apples. The trail kept zigzagging. Sometimes, as the path swerved to one direction, the tracks vanished behind trees. But the path always swerved back, and they saw the trolley tracks again, sometimes with more donkeys pulling up trolleys of food—never with riders. At times, the track came within a meter of the path, letting Marco and Ben-Ari pilfer more food. At other times, the track hid behind boulders or brush, impossible to reach.

By noon, they had climbed halfway up the mountain, and they were drenched with sweat. Mostly they were silent, or they spoke of inconsequential things.

Finally Marco spoke the words that had been brewing in his mind.

"Ma'am, there's another option." He looked at her. "That we're dead."

Ben-Ari raised an eyebrow. "I feel very much alive, Emery. The dead get to rest, and my legs are already aching."

"Unless we're in Hell," he said softly.

Now her second eyebrow rose. "I didn't peg you as religious."

"I'm not." Marco shook his head. "But . . . I can't help but think. We flew into a black hole, ma'am. A black hole that should have crushed us. No, I'm not religious. But I also saw monsters—giant centipedes and spiders that eat brains—rise from the shadows. I saw a ghost on Haven, and she gave me a magical conch. I saw luminous whales that swam through space. There are wonders and horrors in this cosmos. Is the concept of an afterlife truly such a leap of faith?"

Ben-Ari sighed. "I've never believed in an afterlife. As an officer at war, an officer who saw her soldiers die, it always seemed like such a cruel concept. That we should suffer so much in one world, should die in agony, screaming, tearing apart, spilling our blood, because there is some benevolent god who wants us in heaven. Or that some devil will punish us in hell because we ate shellfish or said the wrong prayer. No."

"You weren't raised religious?" he asked. "You wear a Star of David. And I've heard you pray."

She smiled thinly. She touched her amulet. "My lucky star. A symbol of my lost country. Of my people. A comfort in shadows. But true faith? It has always eluded me. Besides, Judaism never spoke of an afterlife. That's a Christian concept." She laughed. "To be honest, I think I wear this in defiance of my father. He's a staunch atheist, calls organized religion mere superstition. He always used to say: 'I've seen enough wonders among the stars that I have no time for stories in old books.'" Now some bitterness touched her voice. "Of course, he never took me to see those wonders."

And now Marco spoke other words that had been simmering inside him, words he had not dared speak until now. "Ma'am, I'm sorry. About your father. About how he hurt you."

Ben-Ari nodded. "Noted. But you need not concern yourself with your commanding officer's family affairs. I shared too much, perhaps." She stared ahead and breathed deeply. "It can be hard to let go."

Marco nodded. He finished eating an apple from the trolley and tossed the core aside. They climbed in silence for a while longer.

Finally Marco spoke again. "You're not only my commanding officer, ma'am. You're also my friend."

"Thank you, Sergeant Emery." She pushed aside a branch and kept climbing.

"To grow up on military bases," he continued, "with a father who was never there, to have him run away, fake his death. . . I can't even imagine. My own father died three years ago. It hurt so much. I can't imagine a father intentionally causing such pain, and—"

"Emery, stop," Ben-Ari said. "I appreciate your concern. But right now, you're my sergeant, and I'm your captain, and we're still at war. Do you understand?"

He nodded. "Yes, ma'am. Professional distance. But . . ." He took a deep breath. "It's hard to be alone. I learned that on Haven. You're not alone, Einav. Not now, not ever. And after we win, wherever Kemi and Lailani and I live—you're welcome there with us. Not as our officer. As our friend."

She smiled, and now the smile touched her eyes. "Thank you, Marco. It would be nice to retire someday. To have a . . . normal life."

Marco smiled wryly. "A normal life? I've almost forgotten what that's like."

Ben-Ari laughed. "I think it usually involves a spouse, a house, sometimes kids. I've heard about something called a *job.*" She winced. "To be honest, it sounds dreadful."

Marco laughed. "It can be. I don't think we'll ever find normal lives, though. That ship has sailed."

"I can't imagine myself ever being a wife or mother." Ben-Ari sighed and looked around her. "This is all I've ever known.

Fighting. Approaching danger. Evil breathing down my neck. I'm not sure how I'd make the leap from this to baking cupcakes and driving kids to soccer practice."

"We might never find normal lives," Marco said. "We might never want them. But we can still find peace. A quiet place. Trees and water. No more war. No more officers and sergeants and mountains to climb. Just friends, campfires on the beach, the stars above. And Addy with us."

Ben-Ari smiled and touched his shoulder. "That sounds nice. Something worth fighting for. It's something I sometimes forget—what I fight for." She wiped her eyes. "It's funny. But you, Kemi, Lailani—you're the closest people to me. You're my only family."

"We're glad to have you as our mom," Marco said.

"Hey!" She punched his shoulder. "I'm only a couple years older than you all!"

He gasped. "Does that mean no cupcakes and drives to soccer practice?"

"I make some mean mac and cheese," Ben-Ari said. "I'm an expert at opening that little box."

"Perfect, because I'm an expert at eating it," Marco said.

"You like eating the box?"

He groaned. "Great, so you're not a mom, but now you're telling dad jokes."

"Be thankful Osiris isn't here," she said.

The mountainside grew steeper, and they had to pause from talking and concentrate on the climb. The castle was near now. The dark fortress peered between the trees above, its gargoyles gazing down at them. Even when Marco looked away, he could feel those stony eyes staring.

They reached a ledge of stone, a little place to rest, and saw that the trolley tracks split here into two paths. One path led down south the way they had come. Another set of tracks led down the eastern slope. A lever rose at the intersection. As Marco paused to catch his breath, he tested the lever, toying with moving the rails from one path to another.

"Man, I could go for another apple trolley," he said. "Do you think that—"

Suddenly he heard it. A trolley on the tracks, rolling down from the castle above. He saw the cart far above, full of stones, charging downward at great speed. No donkey pulled it; only gravity was doing its work here.

"Emery!" Ben-Ari grabbed his arm. "Look!"

She pulled him around an oak and pointed south. He stared and lost his breath.

"My God," he whispered.

A hundred meters below, a little girl was tied to the tracks. Gagged. Struggling.

And the trolley was charging down toward her.

Marco ran back toward the lever. He yanked it, changing the rails. They now pointed toward the eastern tracks. Once the trolley reached the intersection, it would miss the girl on the southern tracks. It would instead roll down eastward, and—

—and then Marco saw it.

Down the eastern tracks—partly hidden by the trees. Five peasants were tied to the rails.

"What the hell is going on?" he said.

The trolley from the castle kept charging downward, gaining speed. It would reach the intersection within seconds, then veer onto the eastern track, hitting the five peasants. It looked heavy enough to kill them all.

"What do we do?" Marco said. "We have no time to reach them!"

Ben-Ari was pale. "We choose," she whispered. "Somebody up in that castle is making us choose. One girl. Or five adults."

"Then we don't play!" Marco said.

"You already changed the lever to the east!" Ben-Ari said. "To the five people! We're already playing!"

She grabbed the lever.

The trolley was three or four seconds away.

"Wait!" Marco said and grabbed the lever too. "Together."

She looked at him.

He grimaced.

They pulled the lever together.

At the last second, the rails changed. The trolley raced down the southern track.

It slammed into the girl, crushing her.

The child screamed into her gag, then fell silent.

The trolley overturned, spilling stones, burying the girl.

Marco and Ben-Ari stood, trembling. For long moments they could not speak, could not move.

Then they rushed down the tracks toward the girl.

They cleared away the stones, but there was nothing they could do. The girl was dead.

Silent, breathing heavily, they rushed back toward the intersection, then down the eastern tracks. They drew their knives and freed the five peasants.

"Who tied you here?" Marco said, panting. His pulse pounded in his ears.

The peasants stared at him in fright. "Demons. Demons." They turned and fled into the forest.

"Wait!" Marco shouted. "Come back!"

But the peasants kept running. One of them grabbed the dead girl. They all vanished down the forested mountainside.

Ben-Ari's face was red, her lips tight. She spun back toward the castle above.

"This ends now," she said, jaw tight. "That was deliberate. That was for us. I won't be a rat in a maze." She loaded a magazine into her gun, and cold fury twisted her voice. "Come, Sergeant."

Marco inserted his own magazine. They climbed hurriedly, guns raised.

Finally, in the afternoon, they reached the castle. A plateau spread here, a flat mountaintop. The castle rose from the plateau, dark and topped with towers, but no guards stood on its walls, and no sound emerged from within. The trolley track led through an archway into the castle.

A jowly man stood at the edge of the plateau, gazing down the mountainside.

"Look at them," the man whispered. "Poor sods."

Marco glanced at Ben-Ari, then back at the man. He wore a ragged cloak, and his hair and beard were unkempt. He was obese, belly swelling against his tunic, and had to lean on a cane to support his weight.

"Look at them," the man said again, grief dripping from his voice. He stared down the mountainside. "They will soon die. I wish I could join them. I should jump. I should jump now."

Marco approached slowly until he too stood on the plateau's edge. A cliff plunged downward here, perhaps twice a man's height. The track ran beneath the cliff, heading down the mountain. Farther down, perhaps a hundred meters away, five more peasants were tied to the tracks.

"More fuckery," Marco muttered when Ben-Ari approached.

She stared down at the five peasants on the tracks, then at the fat man on the cliff. Her face paled, and she clenched her fists.

"Come with me, Emery," Ben-Ari said. "We'll free them. We—"

But with a clatter, a trolley came barreling down the tracks. Within seconds, it would hit the five peasants on the tracks below.

"Another test," Marco said.

Ben-Ari crossed her arms. "And I'm not playing."

The fat man stared glumly down at the tracks. The trolley came charging down, emerging around the corner.

Marco grimaced.

Fine. I'll play.

He shoved the fat man.

The man screamed, plunged down the cliff, and hit the tracks.

A second later, the trolley slammed into him.

Bones cracked.

The fat man's skull shattered.

The trolley veered off the tracks and vanished into the forest.

The five peasants managed to free themselves and fled.

Marco turned toward his officer.

"I killed him," he whispered. "I murdered a man. I took a life."

Ben-Ari nodded. "To save five." She stared up at the castle, and she raised her voice to a shout. "Is that what you wanted? To test us? Come out and face me!" She raised her gun. "Come out now! Answer me!"

No answer came.

Marco and Ben-Ari approached the castle's gateway. Two oak doors stood within a stone archway, banded with iron. A bullet made short work of the lock. They shoved the doors, and they creaked open.

A grand hall spread before them. Columns rose toward a vaulted ceiling, and suits of armor stood between them. High above, mezzanines thrust out from the upper floors, lined with balustrades.

Instead of a floor, there was a massive pit.

Marco stepped forward, saw what was in the pit, and gave out a strangled yell.

"Lailani!" he cried. "Kemi!"

He ran forward. Ben-Ari grabbed him.

"Emery, wait!" she said. "Assess the situation!"

He stood, Ben-Ari clutching his shoulder. His eyes burned, and his hands trembled around his rifle.

Monsters. Monsters filled the pit. Slithering creatures, pale, slimy, eyeless. They reached up clawed hands and snapped their teeth. They were vaguely humanoid, but twisting, oozing, screeching. Their jaws protruded from their wrinkly skin, the teeth long and sharp. Hundreds of them filled the pit, climbing over one another like naked mole rats. And they were hungry.

Above the pit stood a massive, gilded statue of Lady Justice, nude and blindfolded. Her head nearly reached the ceiling several stories above. She held out her arm over the pit, and from her hand dangled balancing scales. The scales had two metal pans, each about the size of a bathtub. The creatures in the pit were leaping up, desperate to reach the scales, but the pans were just out of reach. The scales were now perfectly balanced. Should one pan dip, the creatures would reach it.

In one pan of the scales, the one closer to Marco, lay a stuffed sack. There was a slit in the sack, and sand was flowing out, cascading into the pit. The grains sprinkled the monsters who screeched and leaped up.

In the scale's second pan, this one farther away from Marco, stood Kemi and Lailani.

Both women were bruised, their uniforms torn, and somebody had taken their guns. They were leaping up, trying to reach a mezzanine above, but it was too high. As the sack kept losing more sand, the pan with Kemi and Lailani kept dipping closer toward the monsters. The creatures howled, drooled, and kept jumping toward the two women. The monstrous claws nearly reached them now. One brazen monster managed to graze the bottom of the pan, and Kemi and Lailani screamed.

And still more sand spilled into the pit.

Kemi and Lailani sank another centimeter.

Marco wanted to run forward, but there was no way around the pit. No bridge. No ledge. He could not reach them.

"Lailani, get on Kemi's shoulders!" Marco cried to them. "Try to reach the mezzanine!"

"What the fuck is a mezzanine?" Lailani shouted to him, barely audible over the screeching monsters.

"That balcony above you!" Marco shouted.

"So why not call it a balcony?" she cried back.

"Balconies are outside of buildings," Marco yelled, "mezzanines are inside, and—oh for chrissake, it doesn't matter, just try to reach it! Onto Kemi's shoulders!"

Kemi knelt, and Lailani climbed onto her shoulders. When Kemi straightened, Lailani reached up, trying to catch the mezzanine.

The sand kept spilling out the split sack.

Lailani's fingertips grazed the mezzanine.

The pan she and Kemi were in dipped farther down—closer to the monsters.

"Come on, Lailani, you can do it!" Marco said.

"Stand on her shoulders!" Ben-Ari cried. "Stand up on them! Acrobat style!"

"I'm not a fucking acrobat!" Lailani shouted back, but she obeyed. Gingerly, swaying, she rose to stand on Kemi's shoulders. She reached up toward the mezzanine, and—

A monster leaped from below and hit the bottom of the pan. Kemi swayed. Lailani fell, and Marco's heart skipped a beat. Lailani nearly tumbled into the pit, but Kemi caught her and pulled her back into the pan.

They made another attempt, but the sand kept draining, and the scales kept tipping. Lailani and Kemi sank. Deeper. Deeper. Soon they were so low the monsters kept scratching the pan. One creature grabbed the rim, and Kemi kicked its claws, and it tumbled back down to its brethren.

But within seconds, Marco knew, Kemi and Lailani would tip the scales.

And the monsters would feast.

Marco began to fire his gun. Bullets slammed into the pit. Monsters squealed and died, but the living tugged down the dead and climbed over them. Ben-Ari added her fire to his, but the pit ran deep with creatures. Whenever they killed one, the living pulled its body down and climbed back up.

Soon they were out of bullets.

Marco tossed his rifle into the closer pan, the one with the draining sack, adding three kilos of weight. Ben-Ari tossed her gun too, adding another three kilos. They tossed their backpacks in next, then their helmets, then their boots.

Lailani and Kemi rose a meter higher, momentarily saved from the leaping monsters.

But the sand kept draining.

Soon they would sink back into the pit.

"We need more weight!" Marco said.

Ben-Ari nodded. "We'll get stones from outside."

They ran toward the doorway, but the doors slammed shut and locked. Marco and Ben-Ari banged against them. They wouldn't budge.

"Damn!" Marco shouted and ran back toward the pit.

The sand kept draining.

Kemi and Lailani were low in the pit now. The monsters were scratching and grabbing the rim of their pan.

The two women looked at him.

"Goodbye, Marco," Kemi said. "I love you."

"Goodbye, Marco," Lailani said, tears in her eyes. "Ruv you always."

Marco stared.

So here it was.

His final test.

He inhaled deeply.

He raised his chin.

The scales tilted farther.

Marco ran, leaped toward the scales, and landed in the pan with the torn sack.

At once, his weight shoved his side of the scales downward. Kemi and Lailani shot upward, high enough to grab the mezzanine. They quickly scurried up to safety.

Marco sank into the pit.

As the claws grabbed him, as the teeth tore into him, he gazed above, and he saw Kemi and Lailani on the mezzanine.

Safe.

They were safe.

I saved them. I saved them . . .

Claws ripped his skin, tore out his flesh, and the monsters feasted. He sank into their darkness.

CHAPTER ELEVEN

He saw it ahead, hovering in the darkness.

The Red Planet.

The God of War.

Mars.

General Petty stood on the *Minotaur*'s bridge, hands clasped behind his back, staring.

There it is, he thought. *The hour of our greatest triumph . . . or the hour humanity falls.*

It was eerily silent on the bridge of the HDFS *Minotaur*, flagship of the human fleet—or what remained of that fleet, at least, which wasn't much. Officers stood at their stations, ready for battle, watching the planet grow closer.

Petty placed his hand on a railing as if to caress his ship.

Here, from aboard the *Minotaur*, the fate of humanity would be decided.

The *Minotaur*—badly damaged, her hull breached at several places, two of her engines, three of her launch bays, and six of her cannons destroyed. Even before the ravagers had battered her, the *Minotaur* had been old, rattling, days away from being decommissioned and sold for scrap metal. She limped, she creaked, but she was still ready for battle. And she was still the best damn ship Petty had ever flown.

"You can still fight, old girl," Petty whispered—too softly for anyone to hear. His chest felt too tight; it had felt wrong since the heart attack two years ago. "We're both old and broken, but we both still have a lot of fight left in us."

Through the viewports, Petty saw the other ships in his fleet.

There weren't many.

Only several years ago, humanity had flown with tens of thousands of mighty vessels. With a massive armada, among the largest in the galaxy, they had struck the scum in their homeworld, had emerged victorious. Humanity had become a superpower of the Milky Way, a dominant military force none could challenge. They had forged a galactic empire.

Today that empire was gone.

Today, from that vast armada, only shreds remained. Only three warships flew around the *Minotaur*. The HDFS *Cyclops*, badly scarred, barely flying, her cannons still ready for battle, her thousand marines still eager to fight; the HDFS *Chimera*, the legendary ship that had torn apart scum formations in the old war, that had saved thousands of lives, that today was ready for one more battle; and the HDFS *Medusa*, among the oldest vessels in the fleet, the warship where Petty himself had first served as a young man.

Between these mighty beasts of steel glided their last Firebirds, single-pilot starfighters. At the height of the scum war, a hundred thousand Firebirds had fought for humanity. Today only hundreds still flew.

Petty thought back to himself as a young lieutenant, a cocky pilot in his twenties, during the years following the Cataclysm. He had flown the first generation of Firebird. The legendary Evan Bryan himself had taught him, had commanded his wing. Back then, the fleet had felt so new, so vigorous, the might of humanity growing every year. What did the young pilots feel today? Not hope. Not that feeling of immortality and unbridled power Petty himself had felt as a young man. It was likely they would not return from this war; they all knew it.

We were stronger then, Petty thought. *The cosmos was ours to conquer. But we are wiser now. And we are braver. And we will not turn away from our duty.*

"Sir, we're detecting several thousand ravagers orbiting the planet," Osiris said. The android turned toward him from her control panel. "They're taking battle formations. They've seen us."

Petty nodded, hands clasped behind his back. "Open a fleet-wide channel, Osiris."

The android nodded. "Yes, sir. Channel open, sir."

Petty cleared his throat. For a moment, he could not speak.

For a moment, he needed a drink.

For a moment, he wanted to lower his head, to despair.

For a moment, the pain—of losing most of his fleet, losing thousands of soldiers, losing his family—was too great.

But the moment passed. He shoved that grief and terror aside. He was a Brigadier-General. He was a leader. He was a father to the thousands who still fought for him, many of them war orphans. He led, perhaps, humanity's last chance at survival. And he would keep fighting until victory or death.

He spoke into his communicator, his voice carrying across his fleet.

"This is Brigadier-General James Petty. In a few moments, we will arrive at Mars. Nine months ago, the marauders captured the planet, destroying all its defenses. Based on our best intelligence, fifty thousand colonists are still alive down there, prisoners of war. Thousands of ravagers still orbit the Red Planet, and thousands of marauders are still on the surface. We expect heavy resistance. We expect the enemy to fight hard. We, the last human warriors, are outnumbered and outgunned. We fly to war with only four warships—the *Minotaur*, the *Cyclops*, the *Chimera*, and the *Medusa*. We carry only several hundred Firebirds and only eight thousand marines. We are the underdogs in this fight. But fight we will! With human spirit, determination, and unflinching courage, we will do our duty. We will defend our colony. We will defend our species. Our mission is simple: We must destroy the enemy, every last one, and free the colonists. We will succeed! We must. Humanity depends on us today. We are soldiers of the Human Defense Force! And we will prevail." He raised his chin. "All Firebird squadrons—emerge from your hangars and take attack formations. All marine companies—head to your landing craft and prepare for invasion. Follow your commanders. Take courage from your comrades. And fear no evil. Good luck, warriors of humanity, and may God, the stars, and the cosmos bless you."

The warship hangars opened. The *Cyclops*, *Chimera*, and *Medusa* released fifty Firebirds each. From the larger *Minotaur* emerged two hundred of the starfighters.

Each Firebird carried a shard of azoth inside a small metal heart.

Normal azoth crystals were the size of bullet casings—large enough to bend spacetime itself the way a diamond scattered light. From the starship graveyard, Petty had retrieved nearly a hundred of these priceless artifacts. Painstakingly, the fleet's best engineers and androids had labored day and night, cutting the azoth crystals into smaller shards, each no larger than the stone in an average engagement ring. Such a small crystal would not bend enough spacetime for a massive warship, but it was just enough for a Firebird . . . and maybe enough to crush those damn ravagers.

Petty inhaled deeply, struggling to calm his nerves. The physicists always warned pilots about bending spacetime too close to a planet; the interference could rip a ship apart. According to them, the smaller crystals might work near Mars without crushing the Firebirds. Might.

They were drawing close now. The enemy was charging toward them. It was time to roll the dice.

Hundreds of ravagers came charging toward them, claws opening to reveal their flaming innards. Thousands more orbited

Mars, shielding the planet. On the surface, Petty knew, thousands of marauders were waiting.

The Firebirds took formations above the warships, streaming forth. The best sons and daughters of humanity flew them, prepared to give their lives if necessary. Petty had never been prouder of them—and more afraid to lose them.

They are all my children.

"All warships!" Petty said as the ravagers stormed closer. "Fire a volley."

The warships' cannons blasted out their rage.

Shell after shell flew toward the enemy.

Explosions rocked the ravagers.

"Another volley!" Petty said.

More shells flew. They burst against the ravagers, cracking their formations, washing them with fire.

Yet from the inferno, the enemy fleet emerged with barely any losses. The hundreds of ravagers kept charging forth.

"First wave of Firebirds—fly!" Petty said.

A flight of Firebirds charged toward the enemy, then scattered into several smaller formations. They flew around the enemy like claws stretching around prey. The ravagers blasted out plasma. The flames washed over Firebirds, melting a few of the starfighters.

"Firebirds, engage azoth engines!" Petty shouted.

Ahead, only a few kilometers away, the starfighters' engines glowed blue.

With flashes of light, they warped spacetime and blasted away, leaving only blue streaks.

The ripples of spacetime cascaded out, tossing the ravagers into tailspins.

"Fire!" Petty shouted.

From the warships flew a barrage of cannon fire. The shells slammed into the reeling ravagers. Explosions rocked the ships. Shells drove between their claws, entering their fiery cores, and ravagers burst apart.

"Second wave, fly!" Petty commanded.

The hangars opened. Another flight of Firebirds—the second half of the fleet—charged toward the enemy.

This time the ravagers were better prepared. The enemy broke its formation at once, sending ravagers flying in every direction like the shrapnel of a grenade. The clawed ships tore through the Firebird squadrons. Starfighters shattered, burst into flame, and careened into the darkness. Missiles and plasma flew. Every instant, claws or plasma tore apart another Firebird.

"Engage azoth engines!" Petty shouted.

"Sir, they're not in formation!" cried Osiris. "They'll slam into one another, they—"

"Engage now!" Petty ordered, knowing he had no choice.

In the cloud of battling starships, the surviving Firebirds engaged their azoth engines, bending spacetime through their crystal shards.

The ripples burst out.

Ravagers—but also other Firebirds—shattered.

Some Firebirds, traveling at millions of kilometers per second, slammed into their fellow starfighters. Lines of light criss-crossed, and fire blasted where they intersected, and metal shards cascaded.

"Warships, fire!"

Again the shells flew, slamming into the assaulting ravagers. Many of the enemy ships had fallen, but hundreds still flew toward the warships, closer every instant—too many to repel without the Firebirds.

Come on, where is that first flight . . .

There!

With streams of light, the first flight of Firebirds returned from warped space.

"Charge at them and reengage your warp drives!" Petty ordered.

The Firebirds swooped, firing missiles, drawing near the ravagers. But the enemy kept changing formations, a massive swarm, writhing, expanding and contracting. It was impossible to engulf them all in a neat bubble. Their plasma ripped through the Firebird formations.

One by one, the starfighters were blasting back into warped space, casting out ripples that shattered ravagers. The second flight returned. They rejoined the battle. Firebirds zipped through the enemy lines, flying as close as they could to the ravagers, then bending spacetime again, knocking the enemies back, only to return instants later for another volley.

Slowly, they were destroying the ravagers . . . but not fast enough.

Too many Firebirds were falling.

And from the planet ahead, thousands more of the clawed, living starships charged toward them.

"Shoot them down!" Petty said. "Damn it, shoot—"

The thousands of ravagers tore through their ranks.

The *Minotaur* shook. Fire blazed. Plasma washed across them. Explosions rocked the vessel.

"Ammunition bay three is breached!" a voice cried out.

"Sir, the *Cyclops*! She's—"

Through the viewport, Petty saw it. Hundreds of ravagers were tearing through the *Cyclops*, the mighty warship that had slain many scum and marauders. Only a few kilometers away, she cracked open. Explosions rocked the legendary starship. With blasts of searing light and flying shrapnel, the *Cyclops* shattered into a million pieces.

Petty stared, for a second frozen.

He had known every commanding officer—and many enlisted soldiers—aboard that ship. They had been his friends, as close as family.

Gone.

A thousand lives—wiped out.

And more ravagers kept coming.

Petty clenched his jaw.

"Osiris, take us full speed ahead. We plow through those bastards."

The android spun toward him. "Sir, we can't withstand their—"

"That's an order."

"Yes, sir!"

The *Minotaur* began to lumber forth, plowing into the battle.

Back in the starship graveyard, they had shattered the harpy vessels in their path. But ravagers were larger and tougher; it would be like a man charging into a hailstorm of bullets.

"Osiris, engage our azoth engines," Petty said.

"Sir!" She spun toward him again. "We're too large, too close to Mars. We cannot—"

"Slingshot maneuver," Petty said. "Captain Sinclair used it successfully in the year 2106. Raise our nose. Position our ship to slingshot around Mars's orbit. We'll spin around the planet, aligning our warp curvature with the gravitational forces. We might knock out more of those orbiting ravagers too." He smiled thinly. "The gravitational pull will only increase the effect."

Osiris gasped. "Sir, that story is just a myth! A tale soldiers tell. The math on that would take . . ." She frowned, scrunched up her lips, and tilted her head. "Math completed." She winced. "It might work. But the odds are small."

"That's all I need." Petty nodded. "All Firebirds, give us a wide berth! We're going into warp."

Along the prow and starboard, the cannons were firing in a fury, desperate to knock the ravagers back. Mars grew closer ahead, larger than a full moon from Earth's surface. The Firebirds pulled back to a safe distance, still firing missiles at the ravagers.

"Engage!" Petty said.

The *Minotaur* rattled. Its azoth engines, still warm from their flight here, blazed with blue fire.

They blasted forth.

Moving faster than light, they skimmed the orbit of Mars.

Below them, ravagers shattered in the shock waves.

Smoke filled the bridge. Cracks raced across the walls and viewports.

The planet grabbed the *Minotaur* as they roared past. Gravity yanked them. Petty clung onto the rails as the ship—still at warp speed—spun around the planet like a slingshot, then hurled itself forward back into the battle.

Hundreds of ravagers shattered in their wake.

"Disengage our engines," Petty said. "Bring us back to where we started."

Spacetime smoothed out around them, and they rumbled back toward the planet. Ahead, their two remaining warships—the *Chimera* and *Medusa*—were firing all their guns. The Firebirds were taking out the last ravagers.

The bridge of the *Minotaur* was cracked, full of smoke, tilted to one side. Petty grabbed his communicator.

"All ships, make your way to the planet and enter orbit. Prepare for heavy resistance from the surface. Respond to enemy fire but be careful; there are colonists down there."

The surviving warships flew toward the planet: the mighty *Minotaur*, the *Chimera*, and the *Medusa*, the last three branches of a mighty oak, all three now scarred and cracked and charred. Among them flew the surviving Firebirds and the lumbering cargo vessels. A few ravagers still flew at them, but the heavy shelling knocked them back.

They entered orbit around the Red Planet.

Petty took a moment to catch his breath, to gaze down at the beauty of Mars. He still remembered how, as a child, he had admired Astronaut Szabo, the first man to walk on Mars. How, as a young officer, Petty had met his wife on the Red Planet; she had been a graduate student studying ancient microbial life found under the Martian surface. How, when Coleen had been young, Petty had taken her on a trip to the planet, had shown her the canyons and soaring volcanoes and sweeping red landscapes. This planet was dear to him—and now its people cried out in pain.

He saw the colony below, magnified on the viewports. Ares—a city of fifty thousand settlers. A city of domes and walkways, shielded from the radiation of space and the harsh Martian environment. A city now draped with marauder webs.

"Sir, we're detecting thousands of marauders on the surface," said Osiris. "Many might be inside the colony too. We can't detect them through the domes."

"Thank you, Osiris," Petty said. "We have seven thousand marines in our fleet. We'll liberate this planet if we need to sweep door to door."

"Should we ready the landing craft, sir?" Osiris asked.

Petty shook his head. "Not yet." He narrowed his eyes, staring below. "It's too quiet. It—" He inhaled sharply. "There."

He magnified the viewport. Cannons, coated with red dust to camouflage them, were emerging like serpents from holes. They were all over the surface. The guns swiveled toward the armada above, then fired.

Balls of flaming steel flew toward the orbiting fleet.

"Fire defensive missiles!" Petty said.

A barrage of missiles—thousands of them—flew from the warships. Seconds later, they slammed into the projectiles soaring from below.

A few of the marauder shells made it through. Metal balls, engulfed with fire, slammed into the fleet. Several Firebirds shattered. The *Chimera* took heavy shelling, its hull cracking open. The *Minotaur* shook, the enemy assault crashing against it, breaching a deck.

"Return fire!" Petty shouted. "Use our bunker-busting bombs."

The bombs fell.

Clouds of dust rose over Mars.

"Careful to avoid the colony," Petty said.

"Sir, some of the enemy fire is coming from the colony," Osiris said. "The marauders placed cannons between the domes. Should we—"

"No." Petty shook his head. "Do not bomb the colony. Not even if marauders are firing from there. We can't risk hurting those settlers."

Osiris tilted her head. "Sir, by my calculations, if we take out the cannons in the colony, we will kill between three to five hundred colonists. It might help us save tens of thousands. Ethically, it is a sound judgment, and—"

"I said no." Petty grunted. "We will not bomb our own people. Keep hitting the surface."

They swapped fire for hours.

Vessels kept traveling from the cargo ships to the bombers, transporting new shells. Those shells kept peppering the surface of Mars, taking out the guns and webs of the marauders that sprawled around the colony. With every shell that exploded below, pride grew in Petty.

During the first marauder assault, we crumbled, he thought. *But now humanity is regrouping. Now we're fighting back. Now we're gaining ground.* He bared his teeth. *We can still win this war.*

Normally, he might have bombed from orbit for days, made sure he wiped out all the marauders he could before landing.

But he had no time.

Lord Malphas, he knew, would hear of this assault. No doubt, the marauder king was already mustering his forces, perhaps flying here already. Any moment now, thousands of new ravagers could arrive to destroy what remained of humanity's fleet—and the colony below. Petty had to get the colonists out—and fast—and then fly the hell out of here.

He turned away from the viewport. He spoke into his communicator. "Marines of the HDF, this is James Petty, commander of the human fleet. We prepare now for landing. On the surface, you will meet heavy resistance. The enemy will attack you at every turn. He is strong and determined. Do not underestimate him. His claws are long, his jaws sharp, his cunning ruthless. But you can defeat him! Aim for the marauders' eyes; that is where they are weak. Listen to your commanders. Fight courageously. Fight for your species. I will be fighting with you. We will overcome!"

A hundred landing craft detached from the three warships.

With Firebirds streaming alongside, they made their way down to the Martian surface.

Inside, the warriors of humanity wore their exoframes—heavy metal suits, built for war. Within these wearable robots, the soldiers were faster, deadlier, sturdier than any soldier in history. Thousands crammed into the landing craft, blazing down toward the red desert.

And James Petty rode with them.

Perhaps he was being foolhardy. He was the commander of the fleet, should oversee the battle from above. But let President Katson remain in the sky. Petty had begun his military career fighting in the trenches, and even now, past sixty with a bad heart, he would not back down from a fight.

As the landing craft shot down, the enemy fire rose.

The marauders still hid cannons on the surface. Their flames blasted skyward. Firebirds streamed below, bombing cannon after cannon, but they couldn't stop the assault. A shell skimmed the landing craft where Petty rode, tossing the vessel into a tailspin. Soldiers shouted until the pilot corrected their descent. At their side, enemy fire tore a landing craft apart, and a hundred marines spilled out, crashing down toward the surface, some still alive.

The surviving craft landed outside the colony domes in a sea of marauders.

The creatures were everywhere, racing across the canyons and hills, shrieking, casting their webs.

The landing craft doors opened, and the wrath of humanity emerged.

Tanks rolled forth, firing their cannons. Armored troop carriers blasted their machine guns. Infantrymen ran in their exoframes, firing flamethrowers into the eyes of the enemy.

"Forward!" Petty shouted, leaping in his exoframe. "Fight them! To the colony!"

Encased in a towering metal suit, he felt like a young man again. His metal fists swung into marauders, shattering their teeth, their eyes. His plasma gun fired, tearing out their legs. Around him shouted thousands of human warriors. Petty had been fighting for decades, but he had never been so proud of humanity.

Many of his comrades died.

But many made their way forward, leaving piles of dead marauders.

They fought for hours, pounding the marauders in canyons and on mountaintops, among the dunes and at the colony gates. Tanks burned. Armored vehicles overturned. Soldiers died by the hundreds. But still they fought. Still they pounded the enemy. On the red surface of Mars, they avenged their brothers and sisters on Earth. Here, in exile, their homeworld lost, the sons and daughters of Earth struck the enemy with wrath and vengeance and pride.

And the enemy fell before them.

The marauder corpses twitched in the sand.

The husks of ravagers smoldered around them.

The aliens that had crippled the human fleet, that had devastated the Earth—here on Mars they fell.

Petty panted, gazing at the dead marauders on the red landscape.

For the first time in this war, we won a battle. We proved that it can be done.

Leading a company of soldiers, Petty stepped toward the gates of Ares, the Martian colony. The soldiers stepped inside . . . and found terror.

For a moment, they could only stand still, staring.

"Hell," Petty whispered. "We're in Hell."

Behind him, one soldier vomited into his helmet. Another fainted.

Petty looked over his shoulder. "Medics!" he cried. "We need medics!"

He walked through the colony that brave human settlers had built within the domes. When Petty had visited here with Coleen years ago, he had found an idyllic civilization. Farmers in overalls and straw hats had plowed the Martian soil, singing as they worked. Families had lived in clay homes. Dogs had run between trees genetically engineered for this foreign soil. A small colony, a baby compared to a place like Haven at Alpha Centauri—but a colony of peace, of beauty.

Today Petty saw a vision of Dante's *Inferno.*

The farms were burnt. The houses lay in ruins. Webs rose everywhere, coating the dome, hanging between poles, covering the ground. Corpses piled up, forming hills—naked, bald, brutalized, the skulls carved open and the brains removed. The stench—God, the stench of the place. Petty could smell it even through his helmet.

But most of all, the living broke Petty's wounded heart.

Thousands of settlers were still alive.

The hardy, smiling settlers Petty had met years ago were gone. These people looked like ghosts. They shuffled forward, naked, skeletal. Their skin draped over their bones, and he could count their ribs; Petty could barely believe they were still alive. Their heads were shaved, and bruises and cuts covered their naked bodies. Men, women, children, babies—the marauders had turned them all into wretches. They reached out, weeping, whispering in joy, tears streaming down their gaunt cheeks. Some settlers were missing limbs. The limbs that remained were only skin and bones, the joints bulging. One man still lived with an open skull, the brain exposed. Other people could only crawl.

"What did the marauders do?" a soldier whispered, tears in his eyes. "What the hell did they do here?"

"Those bastards." Another man clenched his fists. "Those fucking bastards."

The soldiers moved through the colony. Petty's nausea grew. He approached a web behind a water tower, and he struggled not to gag.

The marauders had not done this just for food. Just for conquest. They had done this for sick pleasure.

On the web, the aliens had installed living, twitching artwork—humans broken, reformed, stitched together. A man with two heads, one sewn on and rotting. A man and woman carved in half and stitched together, forming a conjoined twin, still alive and whimpering. Some humans hung with bellies sliced open, their organs exposed, pulsing, still alive. A few women were pregnant, their thighs tied together. Children were flayed alive. The remains of the dead—skulls, severed hands, peeled faces—hung on lurid strings around them. It was . . . an art installation? A web of trophies like something a serial killer might collect?

"Medics," Petty whispered, then forced himself to shout. "Medics!"

A clattering rose behind him.

Petty turned around and saw a marauder there.

The beast drooled, shivering, missing four legs. It knelt in the dirt. A child's severed arm was stuck between two of its teeth, and human skulls clattered on its back. Its guttural voice emerged from its jaws.

"I . . . surrender . . ."

Petty's hands shook.

He roared in fury.

He fired his rifle, and his plasma slammed into the creature, slaying it in the dirt.

He fell to his knees, crying out in agony.

"Evil," he whispered, tears in his eyes. "Those sick, goddamn evil bastards."

He trembled. He knew these visions would never leave him. He knew that for the rest of his life—whether he died in this war or thirty years from now—the memories of this place would haunt him. And that the survivors, even should they be nursed back to health, would never recover their joy.

He wanted to remain in the dust, to weep, to tremble. But he was a soldier. And his discipline drove him to his feet.

"Soldiers!" he said. "We might have only moments before the enemy arrives with reinforcements. Help me get the survivors into the shuttle craft. We're taking them into the cargo ships—and off this rock."

They moved as fast as they could. Petty had not slept in days. If not for the metal suit encasing him, he might have collapsed from exhaustion. But he kept working, helping the survivors into the shuttles. Thirty thousand survivors still lived, and it took the shuttles several trips to finally ferry everyone into the cargo ships above. These hulking, heavy vessels had been built to store weapons and supplies, not for comfort, and they offered only metal floors to sleep on, but Petty imagined that it was heaven compared to the hell these people had endured on Mars.

Not moments after the last human was off Mars, and Petty was back on the *Minotaur*'s bridge, the alarms blared again.

"Ravagers!" Osiris said. "Hundreds coming in!"

"Azoth engines, engage!" Petty said. "Get us out of here."

"Where should I—" Osiris began.

"The Oort Cloud," Petty said. "We'll lose them in the dust. Go!"

The surviving vessels—only three warships, a handful of cargo hulls, and their retinue of Firebirds—blasted off.

Within seconds, Mars was too far to see.

And may I never see that planet again, Petty thought, and his eyes burned, and a lump filled his throat. *Please, God, let me forget what I saw there.*

They flew through the Oort Cloud, finally losing pursuit among the radiant gasses and dust. The last fleet of humanity—survivors, fighters, weary and brave souls—floated in the darkness. Lost in shadow. Alive and victorious.

But even in victory, Petty did not forget.

One planet still cried out in agony.

One planet still needed him.

I have not forgotten you, Earth.

CHAPTER TWELVE

Marco bolted up, panting, drenched with sweat.

He lay on a cot.

He stared around, heart pounding, ready to fight the monsters in the pit, to die fighting them, to—

He froze and stared around.

He was alive.

He was back in the HDFS *Marilyn.*

Specifically, in the crew quarters. Three other cots were here, and his fellow Dragons—Ben-Ari, Kemi, and Lailani—slept in them.

Marco rose from bed, and the world swayed. He grabbed his head and took deep breaths, struggling to steady himself.

"Wake up, everyone!" He stumbled toward the nearest cot, the one where Kemi slept. "Wake up!"

Ben-Ari was the first to wake up. She leaped out from bed, but she too clutched her head and nearly fell.

"Slowly," Marco said. "You'll be dizzy." His head still spun. "I think we were drugged."

Kemi and Lailani rose next, leaning on each other.

"What happened?" Lailani said, blinking and looking around. "How did we get back here?"

"I was hoping you'd tell me," Marco said. "Last I remember, I was up to my eyeballs with monsters." He looked down at his body. It was banged up, bruised, scratched, but still in one piece.

"I remember climbing onto the balcony," Lailani said. "Oh, sorry, Marco. *Mezzanine.*" She rolled her eyes.

"That's the last thing I remember too," Kemi said, then winced. "And I remember Marco falling into the pit. The monsters tearing at him." She gave him a soft look. "You sacrificed yourself for us."

Lailani's eyes also softened. She rose to her feet and gave Marco a hug. "Thanks, buddy." She leaned her head against his shoulder.

Ben-Ari checked her gun. Still out of bullets.

"Sergeant de la Rosa, lend me and Sergeant Emery some spare ammo," the captain said. "Everyone—guns loaded. And follow me. We're not in the clear yet."

They left the crew quarters, guns held before them. They saw nothing but darkness through the portholes. The ship's lights were on, eerily pale. The crew walked toward the airlock and paused.

Lailani checked a control panel on the wall. "There's air outside." She hit buttons on the touchscreen. "The ship hasn't moved. Same coordinates where we left it." Her eyes widened. "And all her systems are back online! I can access the *Marilyn*'s navigation system, weapons system, life support, even the entertainment library. The works." She turned toward the others. "Guys, somebody fixed the *Marilyn* while we were asleep."

"And somebody brought us back from that castle," Ben-Ari said. "Somebody I'd very much like to speak to. Follow me outside. Let's take a look."

She opened the airlock, and they leaped outside, pointing their guns.

They all froze and stared.

"Fucking hell," Lailani said. "Would you look at that."

"The sky!" Kemi said. "It's . . . it's . . ."

"It's beautiful," Marco whispered.

The night sky was no longer black. It was deep purple, indigo, and swirling silver. The stars shone, huge and yellow, nearly the size of the moon, haloed with light. The colorful swirls looked like paintbrush strokes.

"Starry Night," Ben-Ari whispered, staring up, the light in her eyes. "Van Gogh's Starry Night. We're in a painting."

"Not everything is paintings and books, Marco!" Lailani said. "Sometimes you—Oh. Ben-Ari said that. Sorry, ma'am. I'm just used to Poet being the one talking like that."

Ben-Ari shook her head wildly as if to clear her thoughts. She grabbed her flare gun, and soon a flare hovered above them, illuminating their surroundings. The light brought another shock. The farmlands, the medieval town, the forest, the distant castle—all were gone. The landscape was barren. They still saw the groove along the ground where they had crashed, and the mountain still rose in the distance, but all other features were gone. No wheat.

No grass. No sign of any life. The world where they had crashed was desolate, a dark desert.

"Look!" Kemi said, pointing. "There, between those stars! It's the black hole!"

They all stared. Yes. Marco saw it. A section of the swirling blue and golden sky was missing. A black hole hung in the sky like a black splotch in the painting.

"So we did survive the flight through the black hole," Marco said. "And this isn't Earth."

"So where are we?" Kemi said.

Marco pointed skyward. "Look. See those? Lights. Moving lights."

They all stared. The lights were tiny, so small they were barely visible. They floated like satellites in the depths of space.

"The Ghost Fleet," Lailani whispered, and tears filled her eyes.

They turned back toward the *Marilyn.* The ship seemed fully repaired. The windshield had been replaced, the hull cracks mended, the wing patched up. The companions raced into the starship, and Kemi sat at the helm.

"All systems are ready to go," the pilot said. "They even repaired our azoth engine! I can't believe it. There's a new crystal installed. Bloody hell, they did good work. I haven't seen engines calibrated this well since flight simulators. They didn't just repair the *Marilyn.* They souped her up."

"Who is *they*?" Lailani said.

"We're about to find out," said Ben-Ari. "Lieutenant Abasi, take us up there. Let's get to the bottom of this."

They reached space within sixty seconds. Or was it space? They had never seen such a place. Space was black and empty. But here the cosmos was all coiling purples and indigos and beams of golden light. Marco indeed felt as if they flew within Van Gogh's Starry Night.

"Look at the black hole." Kemi pointed. "I can see our universe."

They all looked. Through the black hole they could see it: their old universe. The blackness of space punctuated by small, white stars.

"We're in a different universe," Marco said. "A different reality. A place where space is colorful and dreams come to life."

"Dreams?" said Ben-Ari. "Whatever we encountered down there seemed real enough. Our bodies are still wounded."

"And I'm still full from unicorn meat." Lailani hiccupped and covered her mouth. "Excuse me." She checked her instruments. "It's bizarre in here, wherever we are. Half my functions are breaking. The sensors are working, they just don't know what to do with the data. It's as if the constants of the universe are all wrong here."

"Because this isn't our universe," said Marco.

"A parallel dimension?" said Lailani.

"A parallel *universe*," Marco said. "A thousand years ago, humans believed there was only one world: Earth. The idea of multiple planets seemed laughable, even heretical. It challenged the notion that we humans are at the center of creation. But then we discovered Mars, Venus, Saturn, the other planets of our solar system. Fine, people thought. So there are multiple worlds. But at least there's only one sun, and the universe revolves around it. But then we discovered that the stars were distant suns, that they have their own planets, that the galaxy is massive. But surely, we thought, there's only one *galaxy*, and ours is the center of the universe. Well, we know how that ended up. We found other galaxies, found out that our own Milky Way is quite ordinary. Do you see where I'm going with this?"

"That you want to bore us all to death?" Lailani said.

Marco rolled his eyes. "Very funny, Tiny. Look, we went from planet, to sun, to galaxy, then to believing that there's only one universe. Well, here we go. There are more universes than ours, maybe billions, maybe *infinite* universes. And that black hole is a portal between our universe and this new one. At least, that's my theory. If anyone has a better one, I'd love to hear it."

"That doesn't explain all the weird shit we saw down on that planet," Lailani said.

"No," Marco said. "But *they* might be able to explain it."

He pointed.

They all stared.

Ahead they saw it: distant lights, growing closer, taking form.

A fleet.

A massive fleet.

"The Ghost Fleet," Lailani whispered. "They're real. I always knew they were real."

"Help for Earth," Kemi said, tears in her eyes.

"Hold it together, everyone," said Ben-Ari. "We don't know what we're dealing with yet. We don't know if they're friends or foes. Lieutenant Abasi, take us closer. Slowly. Let's get a better look."

The *Marilyn* glided forward. The alien fleet came closer into view. Marco couldn't help but gasp. He had seen many amazing sights during his journey—alien ships of crystal and light, starwhales that swam through space, and worlds of wonder—but he had never seen anything like this.

Ships floated ahead. Tens of thousands, maybe hundreds of thousands. Some were massive, as large as cities. Others were no larger than cars. Small or large, they all had the same design. They were formed of three disks: a bottom disk of dark metal, a central disk of light, and a top disk of metal again.

"They look like giant checker pieces stacked together," Marco said. "A black piece, a glowing piece, then another black piece."

"They look like giant Oreo cookies to me," Lailani said. "Giant space Oreos with glowing creamy centers."

"How can you be so tiny when you're always thinking about food?" Kemi said. "I just *smell* food and gain three pounds."

The ships ahead weren't moving, even as the *Marilyn* flew closer. But their lights were still on. They were obviously still functional to some capacity, despite their antiquity. If this was indeed the Ghost Fleet, legends claimed these ships were a million years old, that they had flown to battle when humanity's ancestors were still swinging from trees.

"They're sending out signals," Lailani said, hunched over her controls. "They match what we detected from the Oort Cloud." She turned to look at the others, eyes shining. "We found them."

Kemi laughed and wiped tears from her eyes. "We finally found them."

But Marco did not share the others' enthusiasm. He remembered all too well the horror on the world below. He remembered feeling like a rat in a maze, tortured with cruel visions. The wolves. The trolleys. The monsters in the pit. Had these aliens tested the crew? If so, were they evil?

Ben-Ari seemed to share his concerns.

"That's close enough, Lieutenant," the captain said. "Stop here. Keep us battle ready. Sergeant Emery, man the cannons and be ready to fire within an instant's notice. Sergeant de la Rosa, send out a signal. Tell them we come in peace. But be ready to fight."

Lailani nodded, her smile fading. "Aye aye, Captain. Sending out our greetings."

They sat in the idling *Marilyn*, facing the Ghost Fleet. Waiting. The signal beeped, heading out into the void.

Will they understand us? Marco wondered. *Are they truly friends, an ancient force for good, as the legends tell? Or are they the beings that tormented us on that planet, and will they torment us still?*

For a long time—silence.

The Ghost Fleet hovered ahead, perfectly still. Marco wondered if anyone was on those vessels at all, whether their occupants had died long ago, and they had simply forgotten to turn off the lights.

"I'm detecting increased activity," Lailani said. "The ships are transmitting. They're talking amongst themselves. I can't interpret their signals, and nothing is broadcasting on our frequency." She chewed her lip. "They're talking about us but won't talk *to* us. Are your ears all burning?"

"Take us a little closer, Lieutenant Abasi," Ben-Ari said. "Another thousand kilometers, then stop. We'll see how they react."

"Yes, ma'am," Kemi said, nudging the ship another thousand kilometers closer, then came to a halt.

Nothing.

Silence.

Stillness.

Then—

"There." Marco pointed. "Look! The large ship in the center."

According to their scanners, the round ship was five kilometers in diameter, dwarfing even the largest warships humanity had ever built. The alien vessel's central disk pulsed with light, illuminating the metal disks that sandwiched it. In the bottom disk, a hatch opened, revealing a shadowy chasm.

The crew looked at one another.

"They opened a door for us," Lailani said.

"It could lead to danger," Marco said.

"Poet, it's a ship the size of Manhattan," Lailani said. "If it wanted to kill us, we'd be red smears on the planet below right now."

They looked back at the alien vessel. Marco had trouble grasping the sheer size of it. A ship the size of a city . . . and behind it hovered hundreds of other behemoths, just as large. Between them flew thousands of smaller vessels. Marco had seen massive fleets before. He had flown with thousands of human warships against the scum. But he had a feeling that the Ghost Fleet could easily destroy any human armada.

And hopefully the marauders, he thought.

"Captain, what do you think?" Marco said, looking at Ben-Ari. "A door has opened. Do we enter?"

She turned toward them. She was pale. Her temple was still bandaged. Blood stained her uniform. But their captain smiled—a warm smile. A smile full of love, hope, and the hint of mischief.

"When have we ever turned away from an open door?"

Kemi smiled too, then bit her lip as if trying to suppress a grin. "I'll guide us in, ma'am."

"Great," Lailani muttered. "Our first contact with a new alien civilization, and we're flying a 1950s diner. I just hope they like Buddy Holly."

The *Marilyn* flew closer toward the mighty alien ship. More details emerged. Marco could see glyphs engraved onto the dark metal of the ship's upper and lower disks. The runes were shaped as suns, stars, pulsars, orbiting planets, and even humanoid figures. Marco saw no portholes, no weapons, but grooves seemed to denote moving parts, perhaps other hatches that could open.

"I'm hungry for Oreos," Lailani whispered.

"Hush!" Marco said.

They flew toward the open hatch. The opening was just large enough for the *Marilyn* to enter. They glided into a massive, empty hangar, and Kemi brought them down.

Behind them, the hatch thudded shut.

The *Marilyn* stood alone in the hangar.

The walls soared toward a distant ceiling. More glyphs were engraved on the walls, displaying stars, planets, and humanoids. They reminded Marco of crop circles. Light filled the hangar, its source hidden.

For a few moments, the crew waited in silence.

Finally Lailani spoke. "Do we wait to be seated or go find a waiter?"

"Not everything is about food!" Marco said.

"We wait," said Ben-Ari. "A little longer."

They waited in silence on the *Marilyn*'s bridge. Still nobody came to greet them.

"Maybe the aliens are dead," Lailani said. "Maybe the hatch is automatic. Like grocery store doors." She glanced at Marco. "When you go buy Oreos."

After several more uneventful moments, Ben-Ari nodded. "All right. We go investigate. No guns, no grenades, no knives. Leave all weapons behind."

"Is that wise, ma'am?" Marco said. "If anyone's still alive here, they might not be friendly. The planet below certainly wasn't."

"If they wanted to kill us, they could have done so long ago," said Ben-Ari. "We don't want to antagonize our hosts. We represent humanity now." She looked at their tattered, bloody battle fatigues and sighed. "I wish we had proper service uniforms, but this will have to do."

"There are the old vintage clothes in your father's closet," Kemi said.

"No." Ben-Ari shook her head. "We won't greet aliens looking like the cast of Scooby-Doo."

They stepped out of the ship and into the hangar. There was no need for spacesuits; the air was breathable, just like down on the planet. Their footfalls echoed in the towering chamber. Standing out here, the runes on the walls seemed even larger, towering circles, beams, and stick figures. Marco felt like an ant who had wandered into a castle. Were these aliens giants?

They walked deeper into the hangar, leaving the *Marilyn* behind, heading toward the far wall.

"Do you see those patterns on the wall?" Ben-Ari pointed ahead. "That looks like a round doorway. Let's knock."

The four soldiers stepped closer, and Marco felt naked without his rifle. Lailani was still mumbling something about cookies; she was scared, Marco knew, using humor to alleviate her fear. He had spent enough time with soldiers to know that humor sprang from horror. Kemi too was nervous, clenching and releasing her good fist, and she kept reaching to her belt as if seeking her pistol. If Ben-Ari was scared, she displayed few signs of it, only pale cheeks and tight lips. She walked at the lead.

They were a hundred meters away when the round doorway dilated.

The aliens emerged.

The crew froze.

Marco couldn't help it. He took a step back.

"Ugly fuckers," Lailani whispered.

The aliens scuttled forward, thin and pale and tentacled. They moved at incredible speed, their digits flailing like ribbons. Their actual bodies—the central abdomens—were no larger than basketballs, covered with bulbs that were perhaps eyes. Most of their mass seemed in those tentacles that whipped about in every direction, propelling the creatures forward. They reminded Marco of giant brain cells or perhaps crazed jellyfish.

"They don't look friendly," Kemi said, voice strained.

Marco gulped, curbing the instinct to flee.

"Hello, friends!" Ben-Ari said, raising her hand. "Greetings from Earth! We come in peace."

The aliens reached them. The tentacles shot out. Marco grimaced and turned his head aside. The tentacles trailed across him, poking, prodding, feeling, squeezing. Suction cups connected to him, then pulled back. Needles poked him.

"Ow!" Marco blurted out. He heard similar sounds of protest from his friends. The creatures were nicking them, drawing drops of blood. They sucked up the liquid as if tasting. Nostrils opened on their tentacles, and they sniffed.

"What are they doing?" Lailani said.

"Studying us," Marco said. "Smelling, tasting, analyzing our blood. They're curious fellows."

The flailing creatures retreated. Tentacles whipping in a frenzy, the aliens scurried back through the doorway, vanishing deeper into the ship.

"Still nicer than the hostess at Denny's," Lailani said.

They all readjusted their clothes and took a few moments to shudder.

"The round door is still open." Ben-Ari pointed. "I take that as an invitation."

They walked through, entering a second chamber, and Marco lost his breath.

"My God," he whispered, looking around with wide eyes.

"A cathedral." Lailani crossed herself. "A cathedral of life."

Ben-Ari had tears on her cheeks. "It's a forest. It's a galaxy."

Trees grew here. Hundreds, maybe thousands of trees, their trunks and branches as black as the floor and walls. Their leaves hung like the leaves of weeping willows, long and woven of pure light, shimmering, sparkling with internal stars. Runes were engraved onto the walls and ceiling, shining, forming constellations. Crickets sang and a breeze rustled the leaves.

"They're mimicking their home planet," Marco said softly. "It's a bit of their world. Here on the ship."

The companions walked deeper into the woods. The hanging leaves brushed against them, veined and full of luminous beads. The air smelled like autumn evenings after rainfall, and fireflies danced. They reached a clearing. A throne rose ahead, taller than a man, formed from coiling roots and branches. A figure seemed to sit here, gazing down upon them, cloaked in shadows.

The companions paused.

Ben-Ari raised her hand.

"Greetings, friend! We are humans of Earth. Peace!"

A voice rose, sonorous, androgynous, vibrating with life.

"We know your world. Whether you are friends shall be seen."

Marco narrowed his eyes. Something about that voice triggered an old memory.

He took a step closer. "Will you reveal yourself?" he called out.

"Marco." Ben-Ari placed a hand on his shoulder.

He looked back at her, and he saw fear in her eyes. He nodded at her, gently, and she removed her hand.

Marco stepped closer to the throne of coiling wood. "Who do we speak to?"

The alien descended from the throne. She moved on digitigrade legs, like those of an animal. Her frame was delicate, but each of her hands sprouted three fingers tipped with powerful claws. She wore a wispy dress, the fabric silvery like gossamer, and a wooden mask. It reminded Marco of a kabuki mask.

He knew her.

He had seen her on Haven.

The ghost who had given him the conch.

"Tomiko," he whispered.

CHAPTER THIRTEEN

Petty sat in his quarters, reading a dog-eared paperback of *The Moon is a Harsh Mistress*, when the knock sounded on the door.

President Katson stepped into the room. "You wanted to see me, General?"

Earth's president looked ruffled. Haggard. Her suit showed a handful of wrinkles. Her hair had not been done in days. When Petty had first met her, he had thought Katson intolerably prim and proper—and that was coming from a general who folded his socks. Yet over the past few days, cracks had shown in Katson's steely exterior, and some light, some warmth, had shone through. She had barely left the colonists since they had rescued them on Mars. For days now, Katson had walked among them, comforted them, helped feed and tend to them.

I almost thought you were an android at one point, Petty thought. *Now I see the woman behind the armor.*

He placed his book aside. He stood up.

"Yes, Madam President, thank you for visiting me here."

She looked at a framed photograph on the wall. "Your daughter, yes? Captain Coleen Petty?"

"Major Coleen Petty," he said softly. "They promoted her posthumously."

Katson looked at him. "I'm sorry for your loss, James. I never met her, but I heard she was a remarkable woman."

Petty couldn't help but snort a laugh. "She was proud, impetuous, stubborn, and rude. She drove me up the wall, and half the time I wanted to strangle her. But I love her. She was my little girl."

Katson nodded. She lowered her head. "I too lost someone dear. I lost . . ." She cleared her throat and looked up. "What did you want, General? I'm needed on the cargo ships among the survivors."

Petty stared out the porthole. Several cargo ships floated nearby, as large as the warships. The survivors of Mars were crammed inside. To make room, they had emptied the vessels, loading the warships with ammunition to the brim. But inside those cargo hulls there was still plenty of food, oxygen, and water. Enough for several months, even with the survivors aboard.

"Yes," Petty said. "That's what I wanted to tell you. That you should be there. Among them. That you should lead them—out of the solar system, out of the marauders' empire. Lead them to a new world, Maria. Somewhere the marauders can't reach." He turned toward her. "But I'm staying. I will not abandon Earth. I will fight on."

President Katson inhaled sharply. A line appeared on her brow. "Liberating Mars was one thing, General. But Earth . . . There are so many ravagers there. Even with a thousand warships you could not defeat them." She gripped his arm. "You promised, General. I need you with me."

"You will have the HDFS *Sphinx*," he said. "She never fought on Mars. I ordered her to remain in the darkness, backup in case we all fell. I'll give you her coordinates, and she knows to wait for you and the cargo ships. I'll send a hundred Firebirds with you too. And the *Chimera* and *Medusa* as well; they will defend you." He smiled thinly and placed his hand on the bulkhead. "But this old girl . . . the *Minotaur* . . . she will remain. She will never abandon her home. She was built for war, and this war she will continue to fight. If Earth goes down, we will go down with her."

Katson exhaled in disbelief, but then her eyes hardened. "And what of your soldiers? You will doom them too to go down with Earth?"

"I will force no man or woman to remain," Petty said. "Every soldier will be given a choice—to fly under your command into the distance, to seek a new home thousands of light-years away, or to remain and fight for Earth, even if it means their death. I have a feeling that I'll have more volunteers than I can fit on this ship."

Katson let out something halfway between laugh and scoff. "You soldiers." She shook her head. "Why are you so eager to die?"

He looked away. He looked at the portrait of his daughter. "No, Maria." He spoke softly. "You misjudge us. Soldiers do not wish for death. We hate killing. We hate dying. We hate war. We hate the roar of guns and the shrieks of jets and the rumble of tanks charging forth. We love green hills, blue waters, clear skies. We love freedom and our families. We love peace. And that is why we fight—because we love these things. Because we wish to protect them. Because we are willing to suffer horrors so that others may live lives of joy. Die? No. We do not wish to die."

She clutched his arms. "James. If you stay here, you will die."

He gazed into her eyes, and he saw something there—true concern. Maybe a hint of admiration.

"Maybe, Maria. But I believe in something. Soldiers always do. We believe in miracles, or the human spirit, or our courage or luck."

"And what do you believe in?" Her eyes softened.

"In heroes," he said softly. "In Captain Einav Ben-Ari. In her soldiers. In a small group of people who, against impossible odds, will find help. Who will return here with an alien fleet ready for battle. And when they return, Maria, I will be here waiting for them. And I will charge with them to battle! To victory! To glory and the days of peace that follow."

Katson caressed his cheek.

"Goodbye, James," she whispered.

He saluted. "Goodbye, Madam President."

She returned his salute, eyes damp.

Petty stood on the *Minotaur*'s bridge, watching the rest of his fleet fly out. The HDFS *Medusa* and HDFS *Chimera.* The cargo ships full of survivors. A hundred Firebirds flew around them, defending the larger ships. With bursts of light, they blasted into warp speed—traveling into the unexplored depths of the galaxy, seeking a new home.

Petty smiled thinly and patted one of his control boards.

"Are you ready, old girl?" he said softly. "Our time together is not yet over."

Osiris turned toward him from her controls. "The rest of the fleet made a successful jump to warp space," the android said. "Where to, sir? Shall I set a course to Earth?"

"Not yet," Petty said, gazing into space, and his voice dropped to a whisper. "But I hope that soon."

Osiris nodded. "Yes, sir. While we wait, we have many repairs to make. We'll be in prime condition for the next battle."

For one last battle, Petty thought.

One last chance to give his life meaning, to fly with the Ghost Fleet, and to win this war.

CHAPTER FOURTEEN

Tomiko, Marco thought, staring at her.

But of course, Tomiko wasn't this alien's name. It was merely the name Marco had given the character in *Le Kill*, inspired by this mysterious figure in the kabuki mask—the figure who used to haunt him in the underground of Haven. Here before him, on an alien vessel across the galaxy, she stood.

"I saw you!" Marco said. "I saw you in Haven!"

The alien stepped closer to him. Through the mask, he saw her eyes for the first time. Blue eyes, shimmering, speckled with white dots like stars. She stood only five feet tall, slender, yet those claws looked powerful, and she had the aura of ancient strength like the roots of an old oak.

"We have never met, child of man, and none of my kind have ever visited your worlds." The alien bowed her head, her long black hair dipping to the floor, then looked at him again. "We are those of the forest. We are the spirits who remember. We are of light in darkness and consciousness in the void. We are the whispers among the living and the memories among the dead. That is only part of our name. You may call our kind *yurei*, for you speak in single words. I am Eldest. That is what you may call me. To my sisters, I am known by names you will not understand. To my sisters, I am many things, and my meaning is deep. To you, I will be Eldest of the yurei."

Marco glanced at the others. Lailani, Kemi, and Ben-Ari stood beside him, a mixture of confusion, fear, and awe on their faces.

"You've met her before?" Ben-Ari whispered to him.

Marco bit his lip, then turned back toward the alien.

"Perhaps I mistook you," he said. "Perhaps it was one of your sisters that I met. I lived in a city called Haven on a planet called New Earth. There, I met one of your kind. A yurei. She . . . helped me. On a dark night."

Marco lowered his head to remember that night, perhaps the worst night of his life. The night he had walked onto the roof of a tall building, had approached the edge, had wanted to jump. That night he had come within seconds of taking his life. The sight of the stars, after so long in the storm, had eased his pain, had pulled him back from the edge. It was then that a yurei had emerged. Had spoken to him. Had given him a gift.

"She gave me this." He reached into his pocket and pulled out the conch. "A gift from the cosmic ocean, she called it."

Eldest's eyes shone bright blue. She reached out and caressed the conch with one of her claws.

"This is a soulcatcher," the yurei whispered. "It is a precious gift, given only to those most deeply grieving. Your soul must have been greatly hurt."

Marco glanced at the others, a little embarrassed by this revelation. Kemi gazed at him softly, Ben-Ari was still staring at the alien with narrow eyes, while Lailani was staring at the floor, lips tight.

Marco turned back to Eldest.

"I've come here to ask for help again," he said. "We are in danger, and—"

"Was it you?" Lailani suddenly shouted. She stepped forward, fists clenched. "You who tortured us on the planet?"

"De la Rosa—" Ben-Ari began, voice strained.

"Tell me, ghost!" Lailani said, ignoring her captain. She thrust out her chest at Eldest, chin raised, fists ready to fly. "Down on that planet below. Somebody was fucking with us. Sending werewolves and monsters and shit our way. Forcing us to play games. To kill people." Her eyes were red. "To play games with lives. Forcing Marco to sacrifice himself to save me." Now her tears flowed. "That was fucked up, lady. Fucked up! Tell me. Was it you? Because I'm ready to shatter your goddamn—"

"Sergeant de la Rosa!" Ben-Ari boomed, grabbed the little soldier, and pulled her back. "Calm yourself! That is an order." But the captain too stared at Eldest with angry eyes. "I apologize for my soldier. She will be disciplined for her outburst. We come here in peace, not to fight you, Eldest. Yet I too pose the same question to you. Were you controlling the environment on the planet? Was it all a show, a simulation?"

Eldest gazed at them, one by one. From the forest behind her, more aliens emerged. They all had the same animal legs, the same wispy dresses, the same clawed fingers. But their kabuki masks were all different, some with round eyes, others with square eyes, some painted with red lines, others pure white, some formed of raw wood, some peaceful, some demonic. They stood among the glowing leaves and twisting black trunks, staring.

"You came into the World Beyond," said Eldest. "Into the Deep Sky. We have retreated into this void to seek peace, to build new worlds of imagination. For many eras, others sought us, seeking our strength in battle, our wisdom, our healing. For many eras, we hid away, for the concerns of the Old Sky are no longer ours. You are the first to have entered the Deep Sky. We sought to determine your worth. To reveal your souls."

Marco understood.

"With tests," he said. "With ethical dilemmas. In a simulation of Earth."

Eldest nodded. "Yes. We can only judge a soul's strength in the forge of hardship. We needed to see. To see if you would crash your starship in a farm or a city. To see if you would slay children of your kind if they took monstrous form. If you would kill the few to save the many." She looked into Marco's eyes. "If you would sacrifice yourself for your friends."

"Why?" Marco said. "Why test us?"

"Because you come seeking aid in war," said Eldest. "We know this. And we are beings who fight only for righteousness. Only to slay the few to save the many. We had to see if you shared our values. Most in the Old Sky do not."

Kemi stepped forward. She spoke for the first time, voice hesitant. "Why Medieval Europe, then? Why not a world more familiar to us?"

Eldest regarded her, head tilted. "Perhaps we made a mistake. When we last observed your world, it was nine hundred years ago. If your world has changed since then, we have not seen those changes."

"But you did see modern humanity," Marco said. "You saw Haven, at least. One of you did. The one who gave me this conch. This soulcatcher."

"No." Eldest shook her head. "Not yet. Time is fluid. That has not yet occurred."

Marco frowned, not sure how to take that.

Ben-Ari stepped forward, placed a hand on his shoulder, and gently guided him back to the group. The captain faced Eldest and her sisters.

"Have we performed to your satisfaction?" she said, just the hint of harshness to her voice. "Did we pass your tests?"

Eldest tilted her head. She turned back toward her sisters. The yurei huddled together, whispering, touching their claws together, a witches' mass in the forest of haunted souls. Finally Eldest turned back toward the group.

"Inconclusive," she said.

"Inconclusive!" Lailani blurted out. "Fucking hell! Marco gave his life for us! And he did whatever he could to save the people on the train tracks. He told me all about that. And—"

"And you slew children," Eldest said, gazing at her.

"Werewolves!" Lailani said.

"Children nonetheless," said Eldest. "Marco sacrificed himself to save you and Kemi, women he loves. Yet his compassion did not extend to children afflicted with a disease that turned them monstrous. You all slew many children to save only the few." The alien looked at Marco. "A curious being. Willing to shove a man onto the train tracks, to take a life, to save many lives. Yet perhaps too eager to kill. Perhaps too quick to shoot the unicorn when only a few moments away, he would have found carts of apples. Curious indeed. Your kind can display great nobility, great sacrifice. Yet so much pettiness. So much impatience. So much aggression."

"I'll show you goddamn aggress—" Lailani began, fists raised, then yelped and stumbled back.

The yurei leaned forward. And they changed. Their kabuki masks split open at the mouths, the jaws dislocating, dropping like the jaws of snakes. The yurei's mouths opened wider, wider, their chins soon reaching their knees, revealing chasms lined with teeth. Each being became a predator, a creature of snapping jaws and fangs and burning red eyes, hair wild, claws extended. Shrieking, ghostly, demonic.

The aliens spoke together, a chorus of high-pitched screeches and rumbling bellows.

"You will not threaten the yurei! We are the ancients. We are the dwellers of the deep. We are the devourers of souls."

Lailani gulped, raised her hands, and gave a nervous laugh. "Nice ghosts, nice ghosts . . . No need to devour my soul." She cringed and shoved Marco ahead of her. "Here, Poet, you talk to them."

Marco faced the yurei. The ghostly aliens hissed, drooling from their massive jaws, eyes blazing, demons of claws and fangs and wild hair. But Marco stared at them, refusing to back down.

I've faced worse demons, he thought. *And my soul already shattered too many times. I will not fear them.*

"Yes," he said. "We are an aggressive species. We are petty. We are hateful. For most of our history, we butchered one another. We shared a single small world, a mere blue dot lost in the emptiness. And we raised empires to slaughter our fellow inhabitants of that speck. We tortured, burned, destroyed, hurt countless innocent lives. We rose, bloodthirsty apes, from the sea of life on our world. Not with wisdom. Not with kindness. But with cruelty. Thus did we conquer our planet, and thus did we raise our first vessels into space."

"So you confess the crimes of humanity!" shrieked Eldest, jaw still extended.

"I confess them!" Marco shouted. "I myself have seen the cruelty of humanity. I saw the cruelty of an admiral who led millions to die, sacrificing their lives to save a single soul. I saw the unbearable isolation of humanity in the storm of Haven, the madness and loneliness that twists our souls, that breaks us down. I myself, mad in a cage, hurt others. I loved a girl. I loved one called Anisha. And I hurt her, and I betrayed her, and now she lies dead on a distant world." His eyes dampened. "And I hurt others like her. I hurt Addy, my best friend. I hurt the people I love."

"Then why should we fly with you, human?" rasped Eldest, her jaw distending all the way to the ground. "You confess your guilt!"

He stared into her eyes. "Because I saw nobility too. In the cruelty of humanity, I saw a light shine. I saw sons and daughters leave their homes, fly to war, and sacrifice their lives to defend their families at home. I saw Sergeant Singh, a mentor, a leader, give his life to save his comrades. I saw Beast, among my dearest friends, sacrifice himself to save me." Now his tears flowed. "I saw Lailani, a woman I love, rise from the most unimaginable darkness, claw her way up from poverty and despair, to become strong, become decent, to dedicate her life to helping others. I saw Kemi, a woman I love just as much, survive horror in the mines of the scum but emerge stronger, kinder than before, and still she fights for her friends. And I saw Einav Ben-Ari—my leader, my lodestar, my captain—devote her life to defending her soldiers, her species, her world. There is kindness and honor and empathy in their hearts. We humans are risen apes, not fallen angels. But we reach toward divinity. We still climb. We still reach to the stars, though they harbor much darkness, with curiosity, unending courage, and our hand outstretched in peace. Take that hand, yurei. Shine your light with ours."

The yurei's mouths closed. Their wooden masks snapped back into place. Once more they were as young girls, hair and dresses flowing, eyes curiously gazing through the holes of their masks.

"You speak nobly," said Eldest. "You speak as the yurei do. Of many things. Of many meanings. You are creatures of darkness and light. Very confusing."

"The marauders are not confusing," Ben-Ari said, stepping up to stand beside Marco. "They are beings of pure cruelty, pure conquest, pure evil. All they do is destroy. We need help fighting them. If the marauders destroy humanity, their cruelty will spread through the galaxy—the old home that you still love." She nodded. "Yes, you still care about your old universe. That's why you remain so close to the portal. Why you still watch. Because you are guardians. And now the galaxy is threatened. We humans do indeed stretch out our hand in peace, but our other hand holds a sword. Now is the time to raise our swords together."

Eldest regarded the captain. "Interesting. You are complex beings who speak of symbols and emotions. Such confused creatures! Some species know only hunger, others only logic. You are beings of pictures, stories, feelings, myths, beings of many facets like crystals that shine. Deep. Yes, deep paintings of many colors and songs of many notes, forests of many growing things."

Marco looked at Eldest. And he thought back to that night on the rooftop.

It is her, he thought. The same mask. Same voice. It had to be her. Not another yurei, but Eldest herself. The one who had inspired Tomiko, the heroine of *Le Kill.* Who had given him the conch.

Marco reached into his pocket and felt it there. Cool, smooth, comforting.

And he thought he understood.

"You never visited Haven," he said. "But you will. In the future, you will go back in time. Time is fluid, you said."

Eldest gazed at him. "For us yurei, time is a forest, every tree an era. For you it is a path you cannot stray from."

Marco nodded. Yes. He understood.

"Eldest, hear me," he said. "You can't judge my soul with games. With simulated tests. The world you created below was magnificent, but it was false. To truly understand me, you need to see my real life. All the ugliness inside me. All those I hurt. But also my strength. My courage. How I stepped back from darkness. You can only judge a soul's strength in the forge of hardship. You need to visit me on Haven." He held out his conch. "And you need to give me this. It will save my life. It will bring me here."

Eldest took the conch from him. And it seemed to Marco that her eyes softened. That there was compassion there.

She nodded.

"I will visit you in shadows," she whispered.

The yurei retreated, moving deeper into the forest, fading between the trunks and leaves. Eldest climbed onto her throne of coiling roots, curled up into the shadows, and closed her eyes.

The human companions huddled together. Kemi smiled softly at Marco and slipped her hand into his. Soon they were all linking hands, standing silently in the forest of lights, for a few moments at peace. The luminous leaves swayed, the crickets chirped, and the whole forest sang.

Finally Eldest stepped off her throne. She approached slowly. The humans turned to face her.

"I watched," said Eldest. "And I saw."

Marco nodded. "I remember."

"I carved your face upon a great stone," Eldest said, voice soft. "A legacy for the ages. An invitation to draw you here. To me. For you are beautiful, and you are good."

Slowly, almost hesitantly, Eldest removed her mask.

Marco stared with shock that soon flowed into pity.

Eldest's face had perhaps once been beautiful. Now it was badly scarred. She looked like a burn victim, her skin raw and pale. Deep grooves, like the marks of claws, ran across her face, adding to its ruin. But her eyes were still beautiful, large and oval and glimmering.

"I saw you," Eldest whispered, and her eyes were damp. "Now see me. See the scars of war."

The other yurei removed their masks too, also revealing scarred faces. Some were missing their noses, their ears, their mouths, even eyes. Some barely had faces left.

"Once we were beautiful," one yurei said.

"They deformed us," said another.

"They took our faces," said a third. "They took our beauty."

"They tortured us," whispered one yurei, trembling. "They broke us."

"Who?" Marco whispered.

"An ancient enemy," said Eldest. "An evil that swept across the galaxy before humans had risen on Earth. They destroyed our world. We fought them. Millions of us died. We banished them into the great emptiness, and we sealed them there, but not before our planet burned. We, the last survivors, fled in shame. Scarred. Forever ugly. Our homeworld gone. We took our fleet of soulships. We fled. We built worlds of memory, and aboard this fleet, we keep our culture alive."

Marco hesitated, then reached out and caressed her scarred face. "You are still beautiful, Eldest. And you are good. Now we humans face evil. Now we might lose our world. Will you help us? Will you fight with us against this new enemy that threatens to destroy the galaxy?"

A tear rolled down Eldest's cheek. "There can be no victory without sacrifice. There can be no peace without war. There can be no joy without pain. I will help you, Marco. But the price will be terrible. If we go to war, one among you—among the four humans who gather here—will die."

Marco's heart seemed to freeze, then shatter.

He looked at his companions, then back at Eldest.

"One of us?" he whispered. "Me? Or Lailani? Or Kemi? Or Ben-Ari?"

Eldest nodded, tears falling. "That is the price the cosmos demands. The yurei will help you. But we will take a life from you. That will be your choice, Marco. Not a simulation. Not a game. A true choice, a true death. If you wish, you may fly with your companions to the world below, and we will create a paradise there for you, a world like your Earth, peaceful, indistinguishable from your true planet. You may have your home by the sea there, grow old with your friends."

"But not with Addy," he said.

Eldest shook her head. "No. She remains in darkness. To save Addy, to save Earth, you will have to sacrifice one of these four."

Marco raised his chin. "Then take my life. I sacrifice myself."

"Who will die is not a choice you can make, Marco," Eldest said. "The future is fluid, always changing, and even we yurei cannot see all its paths. Yet that is the price the cosmos demands. Who among you will die? That we cannot choose. But if you fly to war, one of you must die."

Ben-Ari stepped forward. Her voice was forceful, but her face was pale. "To save Earth, yes, we will sacrifice one of our lives. Can you guarantee victory?"

Eldest turned toward her. She reached out to stroke Ben-Ari's hair. "The proud captain. So wise. So strong. So noble, perhaps noblest among her crew. So ready to pay the horrible price."

"It is a price every soldier is willing to pay for victory," Ben-Ari said. "For peace."

"Yet victory I cannot guarantee," said Eldest. "We are mighty, yet the marauders are many, and strong, and cruel. Even with all our wisdom, we yurei might be unable to defeat them. The hope for victory is small, for the enemy is great. Even if you sacrifice a life, you might lose this war. Would you still choose death—for yourself or one of your soldiers—for but a glimmer of hope? Even if your sacrifice will likely be in vain?"

Ben-Ari inhaled deeply. "This is a choice we will make together."

The four humans faced one another. They held hands, standing in a circle. Marco looked at them. The people he loved so much. Lailani, small and fierce, her brusqueness hiding her kindness, a woman who had risen from privation, who still fought to lift others to nobility. Kemi, wise and gentle, a woman who loved dancing, old music, and silly B movies, yet also studied the stars and fought for humanity. Ben-Ari, a leader who, every day, taught Marco to be a better man. How could he lose one of them? And just for the faintest of hopes, the slightest fighting chance?

But he knew the answer to this ultimate test.

They all did.

"For Earth," Ben-Ari said.

"For humanity," said Lailani.

"For family," said Kemi.

"For Addy," Marco whispered.

They turned toward Eldest. They nodded.

"Yes," they whispered, one by one, and it was the most devastating word they had ever uttered.

Eldest placed the mask back on her face. She raised her hands, and lights flowed across the branches of the trees and filled the runes engraved into the walls. Her voice thrummed through the forest of souls.

"For the first time in many eras, the yurei will fly to war."

Marco had spent months dreaming of this moment, yet now the horror overwhelmed him. The companions embraced one another, and even this forest of lights seemed unable to cast back the darkness.

CHAPTER FIFTEEN

She grabbed him.

"Here," Addy said. "Now. In the back of the truck."

Steve was busy hauling radios and antennae into the armored truck, and sweat glistened on his forehead. He looked around him. "Lots of people moving about, and—"

She yanked him into the truck. "I'm not asking you. I'm telling you."

Steve sighed. "No point putting up a fight when you're in the mood."

Among boxes of munitions and radios large enough to crush a stegosaurus, they made hard, sweaty love. Whenever she could, Addy had sex before a hockey game and before a battle. It sharpened her senses, woke the huntress within her, reminded her what she was fighting for. She lay on her back, eyes shut, legs wrapped around him, and she dug her fingers into his back, and when she climaxed she bit his shoulder so hard she tasted blood.

"Ow." Steve winced. "You're a fucking marauder, not a human."

"Don't talk about them here," she said. "Just hold me. For a moment before the fire."

She cuddled against him. Sex to feel like an animal. Cuddling to feel like a woman. Fierce and loved. Deadly and safe.

Another battle lies ahead, she thought, holding him close, her eyes closed. *I never want to leave his arms. I never want to face the horror again. But I will fight—for him. For Steve. For the man I love. For my friends who are still out there, fighting for us in the darkness. For Earth. For a dream of someday ending this nightmare. For someday finding a home.*

She felt so cold when she left Steve's embrace. With stiff fingers, she got dressed for war. Her old military uniform. Her tactical vest and pouches, all full of bullets. War paint. Her helmet, the words *Hell Patrol* scrawled across it. Guns and grenades. A soldier. Once more, just a woman bred to kill. Her body covered in metal and death. Hollow inside.

"Girls always take so long to get ready," Steve said.

Addy punched him. "Shut up."

The Resistance rolled out. Tanks and trucks. Humvees and sand tigers. Helicopters and drones on massive transporters. Civilian vehicles had joined their forces too: pickup trucks with machine guns thrusting over their tailgates; roaring motorcycles with guns welded onto the handlebars; bulldozers painted with fangs and flaming eyes, marauder skulls glued to their roofs; and armored buses full of troops and mounted with cannons. Ten thousand warriors traveled south along the highways to New York City. Many were HDF soldiers, their units destroyed, their commanders killed; they now followed Addy. But most were civilians, a mixed bag of veterans and survivalists who had joined the fight. The Resistance had only a loose structure and not much discipline; they were more mob than army. But every man and woman here was ready to sacrifice their life for victory.

And along the road south, more joined them.

The ruins of every town held a pocket of rebellion. Partisans lined the roadsides. Hundreds, soon thousands more joined the Resistance. Some fought only with knives, others had rifles, and some carried machine guns and grenade launchers. Some walked afoot or drove beaten sedans; others had armored military vehicles. Some had families with them: elders, children, babies. Most were alone. The Resistance swelled, and as they crossed the wilderness of America, tens of thousands of humans rallied behind Addy's banner.

And on the way, they saw more slaughterhouses.

Many slaughterhouses were behind metal walls—walls the rebels shattered with shells and bulldozers. Others were merely webs in the wilderness, holding captive humans like flies. Hundreds of the slaughterhouses dotted the land. The rebels' destination was New York City. They moved to meet the enemy there, to join with the European and African forces landing among the ruins. But Addy would not abandon the prisoners in these webs. Every few kilometers, they fought a battle. They shattered gates and burned the enemy. They suffered losses but freed naked, tortured, starving prisoners. They left a trail of corpses, both human and alien, but also a trail of victory, of liberation. And with every slaughterhouse liberated, Addy knew that the visions would never leave her, that more demons would howl in her nightmares.

Throughout the winter they fought, and finally, on the first day of spring, they saw them in the distance: the ruins of New York City.

Many of the skyscrapers had fallen. Marauder webs hung from the buildings that still stood. The Freedom Tower rose highest among them—knocked down by the scum nearly sixty years ago, rebuilt, and now crawling with marauders. In the port, Addy could see it: the Statue of Liberty, rising in the dawn, alien webs draped over her torch. Between here and the city sprawled the industrial wasteland of New Jersey, lying in ruins. Dead boats listed in the Hudson, and the carcass of a massive starship—the length of several city blocks—lay on the riverbank.

Addy carried a pair of trinoculars—electronic, next-generation binoculars able to gaze farther than normal lenses, even connect to the Resistance's spy drones and tap into their video feeds. It was among the most expensive toys the Resistance owned. When Addy looked through the trinoculars, she could see a full view of Manhattan and the ocean beyond.

She saw no humans.

The marauders must have moved them all to the slaughterhouses—or killed them. And she saw those marauders everywhere. They crawled over the towers. They scurried along the streets. They bustled across webs that draped over Central Park. They shrieked at the advancing Resistance, and their ravagers hovered over the ruins, claws extended. Their screams of fury rose from the city, goading the Resistance on.

"Come and die!" rose a howl.

"Bring us your flesh!"

"Humans, come to feed us!"

"Come, apes, into your graveyard!"

The aliens cackled. Their ships gathered fire. Thousands of them—eager to kill, to feed.

Addy and Steve stood on a hilltop, gazing at the ruins of New York, once the largest city on the continent. The wind ruffled their hair—the first breezes of spring, scented of death and desolation.

"New York is fallen," Steve said, standing at her side on the hill.

Addy held a banner pole, and her flag unfurled, displaying the blue Earth. "She will rise again."

"Where are the others?" Steve said, gazing through his trinoculars past the ruins at the Atlantic. "The Europeans and Africans. They should be here. It's the first day of spring."

"They will come," Addy said. "We will tenderize this city for them." She raised her flag high. "Artillery! Roll forth!"

The guns of the Resistance rolled onto the hills. Cannons. Tanks. Simple pickup trucks with launchers on their backs. They stood just across the river from Manhattan.

And they began to fire.

The shells pummeled the city. Buildings collapsed. Webs burned. Holes tore open on the streets. The fury of the Resistance pounded the enemy.

And the marauders fired back.

The ravagers soared, blazing plasma. Grenades flew skyward, slamming into some of the alien starships, tearing them down—but far too few. Fire gripped soldiers, and trucks burned. A munitions truck burst, showering metal shards. People ran, screaming, aflame, and marauders raced into the camp, tearing into human flesh.

For hours the Resistance fought, shelling the city, as the ravagers burned them, as the marauders tore through their ranks. Hundreds, soon thousands of rebels fell. And still the enemy stormed forth from the ruins, an ever-gushing river of flame and claw and tooth and hunger.

"We have to fall back!" Steve shouted as the sun fell. "They're too many! We can't resist them."

"We have to fight them!" Addy said, dodging a lashing claw. She fired her gun into the marauder's eyes. "For the eastern army!"

"They're not coming!" Steve said, firing his gun at a marauder that leaped forth. The alien squealed and crashed down. "This city is lost."

Addy looked around her, panting, coated with blood—her own blood, the blood of her enemies, and the blood of dead comrades.

And she knew that Steve was right.

Half the Resistance vessels burned. They had felled a few ravagers with grenade launchers and helicopter attacks, but hundreds still flew. They had slain many marauders, but thousands still lived, still poured forth from the ruins of New York.

And so many rebels lay dead.

Men. Women. Some were mere children, wearing helmets too large for them, clutching rifles in their small cold hands. The price of her rebellion. The people who had followed her here, who had believed in her, who had died under her banner.

And the enemy surged forth in the night, emboldened by the darkness, shrieking with new fury.

We lost, Addy thought, firing her machine gun, screaming as the monsters stormed forth. *We lost this battle, this war, this world. I'm sorry, Marco.*

Marauder webs slammed into her, and Addy fell into the mud, bleeding, out of bullets, the monsters swooping in. An alien pinned her down, roared above her. She struggled to free herself, could not.

I wanted to hold you one last time, Marco. I'm so sorry I couldn't hold out long enough. I love you. I love you so much.

The claws gripped her. Her eyes rolled back.

From the east—horns.

Deep, keening. Foghorns like those of ships in the mist of ancient stories.

Horns—mournful. Beautiful. Horns of hope.

Around her, the marauders screamed. The alien pinning her down rose, shrieked so loudly Addy's ears rang, then fled.

She gasped for breath and struggled to her feet. Corpses lay strewn around her. The marauder had ripped open her bulletproof vest. In another instant, it would have clawed out her organs. She stumbled forward, staring to the east.

The horns sounded again in the darkness.

Lights.

Light on the Atlantic.

Tears streamed down Addy's cheeks.

"They're here. Hope is here."

Steve limped toward her, covered in blood and ash. A marauder eyeball quivered on his bayonet.

"The Eastern Resistance," he whispered. "The Human Defense Force."

Addy could see them now. Ships. Thousands of ships on the ocean. Some were massive warships. Three were aircraft carriers, and fighter jets soared off their decks. Thousands were smaller vessels—a flotilla of barges, landing craft, cargo hulls, even motorboats with soldiers aboard.

Humanity had lost the sky. But the seas were still theirs.

The ravagers swooped toward the fleet, raining down hellfire, and the ships responded in kind, blasting their cannons, and the fighter jets fired their missiles, and hot metal hailed into the Atlantic. Through the storm, the ships reached the city, and soldiers—entire divisions—stormed the beaches and charged, screaming and firing their guns, into the ruins.

"For Earth!" Addy shouted. "Resistance, follow!"

They stormed forth.

Motorbikes, tanks, trucks, bulldozers—they stormed across the bridges. Thousands ran, fighting afoot. As the

European and African forces invaded from the eastern sea, the North American Resistance crossed the river and entered the ruins with them.

They fought through the night.

They fought along rubble-strewn streets.

They fought from rooftops of crumbling buildings and behind fallen skyscrapers.

They ran from the fire of ravagers and fought in the subway tunnels, firing at the marauders underground.

They charged over piles of bricks and metal, tearing into the alien horde.

They burned the webs stretching across Lady Liberty's crown.

They fought through dawn and another day, and when night fell, they fought some more.

They fought through the steel canyons of Manhattan, skyscrapers collapsing around them. Massive marauders, genetically engineered to grow as large as dinosaurs, climbed the Empire State Building, and their stingers sprayed venom onto men below. It took a hundred attack helicopters to finally tear them down. Other marauders raced across the George Washington Bridge, ripping through its steel cables, bringing it down as rebels tried to cross. Marines and aliens fought in the Lincoln Tunnel, and fire filled the darkness, and thousands perished in the inferno. Atop the Statue of Liberty, men and aliens fought with guns and claws, and blood draped Liberty's *tabula ansata.* From the World Trade Center, where once the city had wept, the rebels tore down a massive alien cube-ship, slaying thousands of the beasts within.

New York City trembled, burned, crumbled . . . yet kept fighting.

And through day and night of war, the Eastern Forces kept landing. They lost thousands. But they kept storming the beaches, kept fighting in air and sea, kept filling the city and the ruins beyond.

Within three days, a million troops—Europeans and Africans—landed in North America and raised the flags of Earth in the ruins.

On the fourth dawn, Addy stood on the roof of the Chrysler Building, and she gazed upon a city in ruins. Fallen skyscrapers. Mountains of rubble. Dead warships in the water and ravagers smoking on city blocks. Standing here, hundreds of meters above the city streets, she raised a flag.

It was not a flag of America, this land. It was not a flag of Canada, her homeland. It was not a flag from Europe or Africa from where so many soldiers had come, had died here, had fought to liberate this city.

It was a flag of Earth.

A blue planet on a dark sky. From the distance, just a pale blue dot. A mote of dust in the dark cosmos, yet a world that meant everything. The homeworld of humanity. A world in ruins.

"A world we will reclaim," Addy whispered.

Across the ruins, the soldiers of humanity raised their fists, and they chanted her name. From the rooftop, Addy returned the salute.

"We have won one battle!" she cried into her megaphone. "But the war rages on. In the north, in the ruins of Toronto, he lurks. Lord Malphas, leader of the enemy." The crowd booed, and Addy spoke louder. "Lord Malphas! Hear me now! We are coming for you. We are coming to kill you. We are coming to reclaim our world. This is Earth!"

And from across the city, they roared. "This is Earth!"

"Earth rises!" Addy cried, and they repeated her call.

"Earth rises! Earth rises!"

CHAPTER SIXTEEN

For the first time in a million years, the Ghost Fleet flew to war.

Soulships, the yurei called them. Ships as small as starfighters. Ships as large as cities. Thousands of ships, each formed of two dark disks sandwiching a glowing center. The great fleet of the yurei, their home destroyed, flew to war.

Marco gazed through a viewport at them.

"Hope," he whispered. "From the darkness—light."

Lailani stood at his side. She chewed her lip. "I'm telling you, they're flying Oreos. I always did want to fly inside of a giant cookie."

Marco looked around them. They stood inside one of the yurei soulships, the one where they had met Eldest, the ancient yurei who had given him the conch. Ben-Ari and Kemi were back aboard the *Marilyn*—Marco could see the retro starship outside, so small by the massive soulships, barely a speck.

"The *Marilyn* looks so small from here," he said.

Lailani nodded. "Like an Oreo crumb."

He rolled his eyes. "You think Oreos are everything."

"Oreos *are* everything! They are the light and the way."

Marco had asked Eldest if he could stay a while longer on her ship. It was still a long flight back to Earth, and he wanted to soak up the magic of this forest. Lailani had opted to stay too, saying she had never gone hiking in a forest before, and if all she had was a forest aboard an alien starship, well, she would take it. Ben-Ari had grumbled a bit at first, but she relented after Marco and Lailani had agreed to take double cooking, cleaning, and maintenance shifts on the *Marilyn* the following week. Marco wasn't sure how they'd cook the alien foods the yurei had given them—a variety of breathing fruits and tentacled plants—but figured that anything would taste good after some time in the deep fryer.

He turned away from the porthole, ready to explore that forest right now. The yurei soulship was several kilometers in diameter, providing enough room—several times the size of Central Park—for a rich biosphere. There were no corridors, not even trails, just the trees growing from the dark soil, their bark silvery, their leaves luminous. Alien plants grew between their roots, sprouting feathery appendages, bulbous pods, and gleaming flowers. There were animals too—pets to the yurei, perhaps. Glowing caterpillars crawled on branches, and furry little creatures peered from holes in the trunks, eyes large and luminous.

"They look like tarsiers," Lailani said.

"What are tarsiers?" Marco said.

"A kind of monkey we have in the Philippines," she said. "They're only about the size of a hamster, but they have massive round eyes. Half their head is just eyes! Tourists buy them sometimes. Illegal pet trade. I've never seen them in the wild, though." She hopped toward a tree where the alien critters were burrowing. "Hey there, little buddies!"

Several aliens emerged from a burrow. These ones too were hamster-sized. They had no limbs that Marco could see, however.

"They're balls of fluff with eyes," Marco said.

The creatures hopped along Lailani's arms and nuzzled her. She cooed to them. "Cute little guys. Think the yurei would let me keep one?"

"Not if they've seen 'The Trouble with Tribbles,'" Marco said.

She groaned. "You think twentieth-century references are everything."

He nodded. "They are the light and the way."

Lailani rolled her eyes. They kept walking through the terrarium. They saw only a handful of yurei, and only from the corner of their eyes. The ghostly aliens drifted through the forest, robes fluttering, vanishing whenever Marco or Lailani turned toward them.

"Shy creatures," Lailani said. "Like me."

"You're shy?" he said. "Only last week on the *Marilyn*, I saw you dancing around in your underwear, rapping that you like big butts."

"*I* wasn't rapping that!" Lailani said. "It was a hiphop song I had playing on the speakers. I might have just mouthed the words a bit." She looked over her shoulder and sighed. "Besides, my butt is tiny. The tarsiers have more ass than I do." She looked back at him. "And yes, I'm shy around strangers. I'm only comfortable around people I know. Around you and the others. Remember how shy I was at boot camp?"

"I don't remember you rapping there," Marco confessed.

"See? Shy. I remember how—" She frowned. She took a few steps. "What's that?"

Marco saw it. A tree, but different than the others. Its bark was white, its roots twisting, and crystals hung from its branches instead of leaves. As the soulship moved through space, the crystals jangled. Images flickered within them.

"I saw . . ." Lailani touched one crystal, and her eyes widened. "Poet! Look!"

He looked into the crystal with her. He blinked and rubbed his eyes. "It's us. How could it be us?"

They gazed into the crystal together. It showed an image from RASCOM, their first day in the military, almost eight years ago. Marco was standing in formation with Addy and the others. Elvis was there. And Beast. And Caveman. And Sheriff. His lost friends. Sergeant Singh was there, putting the platoon together. In the crystal, Lailani ran up to them, late to join the group. She was so young, so small. Her hair was buzzed short, and she looked like a little boy in her father's uniform.

There was no sound in the crystal, but Lailani—the current Lailani, twenty-six years old, her hair longer—whispered the words with her younger self.

"I'm here, Sergeant!" Tears flowed down the present Lailani's cheeks. "I'm here and ready to kill fucking scum."

Marco watched as the younger Lailani did her push-ups, punishment for being late, then came to stand by Marco—by the younger Marco, that scrawny teenager with the ill-fitting uniform.

"How can this be?" he whispered.

Lailani pointed. "Look! There's something in that crystal too."

They turned toward a second crystal that hung from a branch. It showed an image of a beautiful town in Greece. The soldiers of their platoon were there. God, they were all so young. Addy and Elvis were joking around; she wore a hockey jersey, and he wore leather pants and a leather jacket. Marco was there too, wearing an undersized pink shirt and green trousers. Lailani looked beautiful in a blue summer dress and a wide hat. In the crystal, they sneaked into a house's yard, seeking a place to relieve themselves. A granny fled into the house, but then emerged moments later, carrying a pot of stuffed cabbages for the platoon.

"I remember that day," Marco whispered. "We had the drill in Greece. We all had to pretend to be casualties of a scum attack, to let the medics practice on us. But God, we goofed around all day. It was a great day." He smiled, his eyes damp. "I loved that dress of yours. I told you that you looked like Audrey Hepburn."

Lailani smiled and slipped her hand into his. "I look nothing like her! Well, maybe the Asian version of her?" She leaned against him. "It was the best day of my life."

The other crystals showed other scenes from their past. Eating in the mess hall. Playing soccer in the desert. Discovering the vending machine and emptying it of candy. Laughing. Lots of laughing.

"It's a memory tree," Marco said. "It's showing our memories." His eyes widened. "Look at that one!"

He held the crystal. Lailani looked with him. In this crystal too, they appeared back at boot camp, their first Sunday there—their first day of freedom. Addy, Elvis, and the others all left the tent to play ball. Left alone with Marco, the young Lailani pulled off her uniform, then lay naked on the bed.

She gasped. "My tiny little butt!" She covered the crystal. "Don't look!"

"I thought you weren't shy with those you know." Gently, he pulled her hand away, watching them make love. When his own backside made an appearance, he shoved the crystal away. "Yeah, this one is boring."

"Hey, I was watching that!" Lailani grabbed it again. She grinned. "Look how *skinny* you were."

"Hey, I'm still skinny!" Marco said.

She shook her head. "No. You've filled out. In a good way. You're not a scrawny teenager anymore." She sighed. "I still have the body of a broomstick, though." She tapped her chest. "Two mosquito bites."

"I like your body," Marco said. "I think you're perfect."

She lowered her eyes. "Now you're making me shy again." She leaned against him. "Tank you."

"Tank you? You want to run me over with a tank?"

She nodded and gave him a little shove. "Boom."

He feigned injury, falling down onto the forest floor, then grabbed her hand and pulled her down too. Lailani squealed and fell onto him.

"Careful!" she said. "I'll squish you."

He lay on his back, and she lay atop him, and they stared into each other's eyes. He caressed her hair—black, silky, just long enough to run his fingers through.

"I like you with longer hair than that old buzz cut," he said. "Less androgynous."

"You mean I looked like a robot once?"

"Androgynous, not an *android*," he said.

She spoke in a robotic voice. "I am Lailani the android! Resistance is futile! Surrender, human!"

"I surrender," he said, then kissed her lips.

She blinked. She looked away.

"I'm shy," she whispered. "I'm scared."

"Of what?" he whispered, holding her against him.

"Of hurting you." She nestled against him. "Of being hurt. Of losing somebody I love." Tears filled her eyes. "The yurei said we'll lose somebody. I'm so afraid."

Marco kissed away her tears. "I'm afraid too. And I love you."

She looked at him through her tears. "You ruv me?"

"I love you," he whispered. "For real. I'm not afraid to say it."

She smiled, tears on her lashes. She had always been shy about kissing, even in their youth, perhaps fearing the intimacy. At most, she had given him quick pecks on the lips. Now, for the first time, she kissed him deeply.

They undressed while kissing, and his hands explored her, caressing the curve of her hip, stroking her thigh, and when he moved his fingers farther down she laughed.

"You're touching my tiny little butt!"

He kissed away her words, and her fingers moved down too, stroking him. Their bodies had changed, grown harder, scarred with war, but it felt like they were eighteen again, just two youths in love, hesitantly exploring. They made love for what felt like hours. She sat on his lap, rocking slowly, then lay him down and rode him wildly, his hands on her hips, and when she rolled onto her back, when he lay atop her, she moaned into his neck, eyes closed.

"I love you," she whispered, and they climaxed together under the tree of memories, creating a new memory, one to warm them in the darkness again.

They lay on their backs under the crystals, naked, sweaty, holding hands.

"That," Marco said, "was amazing."

She stuck her tongue out at him. "You mean it was nicer than an army cot with sergeants barking outside?"

He nodded. "Much nicer."

She cuddled him, and he held her close. Eldest's words, the deal she had struck with them, echoed in his mind.

One life.

One life for the fleet.

Him or Ben-Ari or Kemi or Lailani.

I don't want to lose you, Lailani. I don't want to lose any one of you.

He gazed up at the tree of memories, at the visions in the crystal leaves. So many good times. He could see some of his own memories in those leaves: himself with Lailani, but also his days with Kemi back in Toronto, and good times with Addy, and beautiful, bittersweet memories of him and his father. So many moments of his life, all reflected here in this alien tree. Lailani's memories filled the leaves too. Some Marco recognized; they were shared memories. But the tree also reflected memories that belonged only to her. In one leaf, he saw Lailani as a child, scrawny, dressed in rags, playing with a stray cat. In another leaf, she was only a toddler, held in the arms of a girl no older than thirteen—her mother, he surmised. In some memories, Lailani was an adult, standing in an observatory, perhaps in the Oort Cloud, watching the stars and laughing with friends. In another memory she was strolling through a park with Sofia, her lost lover.

And in one crystal leaf . . .

Marco frowned.

In one crystal, high above, Lailani was back in the *Marilyn*. And she was with Captain Ben-Ari. Kissing her. Making love to her.

He looked at Lailani. She was still cuddling against him, eyes closed.

"You and Ben-Ari?" he whispered.

She opened her eyes and looked up. "Shit."

Marco sat up. "Why didn't you tell me?"

Lailani sat on the forest floor. "I didn't know I had to report to you every detail of my sex life." She sighed. "I'm sorry. That sounded harsh. I just . . . You're not hurt, are you?"

He got dressed quickly. He stood up. "No."

Lailani hopped up too and pulled on her clothes. "Great. You're hurt. You're sulking."

He turned away. "I'm not sulking."

She laughed mirthlessly. "That's sulking!" She stepped around him and held his hands. "Look, Marco, you don't need to be upset. It's not like I cheated on you."

He nodded. He couldn't meet her eyes. "It's not. We're not together or married or anything, after all. I get it. We all like sex. You have it. With me. With Ben-Ari. With whoever."

"Hey." Her eyes narrowed. "I'm not like that. Don't you say that. Don't you insult me."

"Then don't keep secrets from me!" He gave a bitter laugh of his own. "You come here, and you sleep with me, and you tell me that you love me, and you make me feel like . . . like there's a chance. That we could be together again. A couple. An actual, real couple. And then I see that?" He gestured at the tree.

Anger filled her eyes. "As if you weren't making moon eyes at Kemi all this time. I know about you two and your little dance and milkshake dates. And besides, I'm sure you slept with other women in Haven. So what? I never said a word about that! I didn't care. I wanted you to be happy!"

"And I want you to be happy." He looked away again. "If Ben-Ari makes you happy, then I won't get in the way. I'll—"

"Marco!" She groaned. "For fuck's sake. When I said that I love you, I meant it. I didn't know the tree would show you that!"

"You didn't know." He nodded. "That explains it."

She let out a longer, louder groan. "Don't be a baby. God! Marco, I was scared, all right? I thought we'd die on that planet. I still think we might die! Ben-Ari was lonely. She was scared too. The woman hadn't had sex since the Beatles broke up. She needed somebody to hold her, to be with her, if only for a short while. And . . . I needed her too, all right? After I lost Sofia, I . . . I just needed somebody to hold me. Somebody strong, who could make me feel safe. Make me feel loved."

"I could have been that person," he whispered. "I love you. I've always loved you. And you left me, Lailani. You didn't wait for me. When we were stationed at different bases, you didn't wait. And even on the *Marilyn*, when we were together again . . ."

Tears now filled her eyes. She looked away, blinking too much. "Marco, haven't you learned that already about me?"

"Learned what?"

Lailani's tears fell. "That I'm broken. That I can't be the woman you want. I can't be sweet and kind and loyal like Kemi. You want a wife. Somebody holy, somebody who'll cook you dinner every day, who'll be forever yours, who'll go on dates and drink milkshakes and be sweet and wholesome. And I can't be that person. I can never be Kemi. I . . . I'm someone who'll always come and go, Marco." She held his hands, gazing at him through her tears. "I'm someone who can never settle down, never be that perfect wife that you want. That you deserve."

"Lailani! I didn't fall in love with you because I thought you'd cook me dinner or be a sweet, charming housewife. I fell in love with you because you're strong, brave, a warrior."

"Then I'm sorry I hurt you," she whispered, trembling, and wiped her eyes. "But I'm not sorry for who I am. For what I did. And you're wrong to make me feel bad."

And now Marco felt like shit.

And now guilt filled him.

And now he wanted to apologize, but he remained silent, torn between shame and pain.

He nodded. "I understand. It's all right." He attempted a smile, but it came out sour. "Hey, what say we head back to the *Marilyn*? I kind of miss sleeping on a real bed."

She nodded. "Me too."

They walked through the forest in silence. They reached the alien airlock. They signaled the *Marilyn*, and Kemi flew toward the soulship and entered its hangar.

As the *Marilyn* floated back into space, Marco looked through a porthole at the fleet outside. Thousands of circular, luminous soulships flew all around, each with forests inside them. Ships of beauty, of war, and of memory.

We fly to Earth, he thought. *We fly to the greatest battle our species has ever known. And yet I'm like some lovesick boy, jealous, caught in a love triangle. Who has time for such nonsense when the fate of humanity is on the line?*

And yet thoughts of Lailani, of Kemi, of Anisha, of the other women in his life still filled him. That ancient, intrinsic need to find a partner. To belong. To feel safe. Even with humanity crumbling, he could not stop feeling it.

Because if I'm not fighting for love, what the hell am I fighting for?

He entered the crew quarters. Kemi was already there, asleep on her cot. She opened her eyes as he entered, gave him a sleepy smile, waved, then fell back asleep.

Marco climbed into his bed beside her. He looked at her serene face, so beautiful in the shadows, then out the porthole. He watched the stars.

For Lailani, he thought. *For Kemi. For Ben-Ari. Because I love all of them. Because I love Earth. Because I love books. Because I love trees and tarsiers and Oreos and milkshakes. Because even if I'm confused, even if I'm broken, I can heal. And Earth can heal. And I don't want to die in the dark.*

He closed his eyes.

I don't want any one of us to die.

Memories flashed through him. The laboratory back on Corpus. The scum experimenting, creating hybrids, half human, half centipede. Tying Kemi to a table. Preparing to deform her. The ball of skin Marco had found, the one that grew his face, that screamed when Addy killed it. The thousands of scum scurrying through the tunnels. And his slain friends—Elvis, Beast, Diaz, the others—resurrected, half human, half centipede, and him killing them, and—

He took a deep breath.

No. He could not fall down that hole again.

Instead, he brought to mind Addy's face.

Addy. His best friend. Smiling, laughing, shouting, crying, always a torrent of emotion, always brave, always strong. Always dear to him. He remembered their good times together—children having snowball fights, youths laughing in boot camp, adults who had formed a deep bond, one that no hardship or distance could break.

I will find you, Addy. I promise. I fight for Earth. But I also fight for you.

Finally he drifted off to sleep, and he dreamed that Addy was with him again.

CHAPTER SEVENTEEN

Ben-Ari sat in the commander's seat aboard the *Marilyn*, gazing into the darkness. They were halfway home. In a few weeks, she would see Earth in the distance. She had done what she had promised. She had found the Ghost Fleet. She was returning with aid. Yet the thought of coming home terrified Ben-Ari.

When I reach Earth, what will I find?

Would humanity still exist? Had the marauders kept humans alive as food, or had they extinguished the species during her quest?

And even should she save the world, what awaited her? Her soldiers still acknowledged her command, but her superiors had demoted her to private, had sentenced her to death. Would her crimes be forgiven now, or would they return her to her cell to await execution?

And even if I save the world, she thought, *and even if I'm forgiven, what life is there for me? The life of a soldier? I've seen too much death, too much war. A life as a civilian? I don't know what that means. I wouldn't know how to live such a life. What do I have on Earth? Nothing. My career is over. My country was destroyed. What do I have in this cosmos aside from this ship, from its crew? From Marco, Kemi . . . Lailani?*

She looked at her little sergeant. Lailani sat nearby, fiddling with her instruments.

Ben-Ari looked away. Her cheeks burned. Damn her pale cheeks! Whenever she blushed she turned into a tomato.

First of all, Einav, what you did is illegal, she told herself. *You're her commanding officer. You're an authority figure. You cannot just do . . . what you did.* She cringed. *Second, you need to focus on the mission. Nothing else. Not on such matters. You're not Marco, for God's sake. That boy would hump an android if there was no woman within ten meters, but you're a commander of a starship.*

She sighed. She knew all that. Yet she had been unable to resist that day. She had been scared, angry . . . and lonely. She was almost thirty, and she had gone nearly a decade without sex before her encounter with Lailani, not since those flings in her youth, those wild boys on the beach, acts of rebellion against her father. Did she not deserve to fill a basic human need? Was she not human, just because she commanded a starship? Did she not deserve to hold someone, to feel loved?

It happened one time, Ben-Ari thought. *It won't happen again. But . . . I'm grateful, Lailani.* She looked at her sergeant, then quickly looked away, praying the girl didn't see her blushing cheeks. *I'll remember it fondly.*

Ben-Ari checked the monitor readouts for the umpteenth time. Perhaps she should count the ammunition stores again. Or maybe double check the engine repairs, or—

No. Damn it. She was too nervous. The ship was on autopilot, everything was fine, and she needed to relax.

She pulled out a dog-eared paperback copy of *The House of the Spirits* by Isabel Allende, translated from Spanish. It was a novel she reread every couple years. She put on headphones and browsed through her library of music. She considered *La Boheme*, one of her favorite operas, but thought the singing might distract from her reading. She chose instead Brahm's Symphony No. 2; it was hefty enough to ground her during her more turbulent moods. All she was missing was a glass of wine—a strong Cabernet would match the music—but she settled for a juice box from the ship's stash. Grape. A cartoon vampire on the box boasted of seven essential nutrients, most of them probably sugar.

She opened her book, took a sip of juice, and cranked up the volume.

This isn't so bad, she thought. *I'm in my own ship. With friends. With music and literature. With a fleet of thousands around me. I can relax for an hour. I can—*

The alarms blared.

Of course.

Of course they did.

She slammed the book shut and yanked off her headphones.

Another time, Isabel, Johannes, and Count Grapeula.

"Captain!" Kemi burst onto the bridge. "Captain, ravagers approaching!"

Ben-Ari nodded. "I know, Lieutenant. Take the helm. Take us out of autopilot." She switched on the ship's speakers. "Sergeant Emery, report to the gun turret. Hold fire until an order from me." She turned to Lailani. "Sergeant de la Rosa, how many ravagers are you reading?"

Lailani stared at her monitors, cringing. "All of them, I think." She loosened her collar.

Only moments ago, Ben-Ari had cursed the blood that had rushed to her cheeks. Now she felt that blood drain from her face.

"How is this possible?" she said. "We're still light-years away from their territory."

"Well, ma'am, they've never really been ones to respect borders, have they?" Lailani said. "They'll be here in moments."

Ben-Ari reached to the crystal the yurei had given her. She tapped and tilted it, trying to get it to work. Finally Eldest's reflection appeared in one facet. The yurei gazed at Ben-Ari through the holes in her wooden mask.

"Eldest, do you see them?" Ben-Ari said. "Enemy ships! Ravagers! Thousands of them approach."

"We see them, child of Earth," said the yurei, and her voice hardened. "They are wretched. They are destroyers. They are evil. For the first time in many eras, the yurei will fight."

Ben-Ari nodded. "We're going to engage the enemy with you. We'll get out of your way but do our best to assist."

She placed aside the crystal. She stared through the central viewport. She saw them now. Thousands of them. Dark, clawed, living ships, roaring forth. The claws bloomed open. The plasma roiled.

Ben-Ari turned toward Lailani. "Sergeant, open a communication channel."

"Captain?"

"Do it."

Lailani nodded. "Yes, ma'am, communication channel opened, broadcasting on marauder wavelength."

Ben-Ari spoke into her communicator. "Marauder fleet! We are flying in neutral space. Close your claws, hide your fire, and disengage from our flight path. If you continue your aggression, we will—"

Before she could complete her sentence, the enemy blasted forth streams of plasma.

Kemi yelped and tugged on the joystick, dodging jet after jet. The *Marilyn* rocked.

"Emery," Ben-Ari spoke into her communicator, "choose a target and fire."

Marco sat at the elevated gunner's station. He hit buttons, and a missile flew.

A few seconds later, the missile exploded in the open jaws of a ravager, and the ship collapsed.

The thousands of other ravagers charged.

The plasma blasted out.

Kemi whipped the ship from side to side, but one jet streamed against their shields, knocking them into a tailspin. Alarms blared. All around them, plasma slammed into yurei soulships. Explosions rocked the larger vessels. Some of the smaller yurei ships, even smaller than the *Marilyn*, careened and crashed into one another, and explosions rocked the armada.

Ben-Ari stared in horror.

The yurei ships—they were falling apart!

She had imagined them to be nearly invincible, ancient gods of war, powerful beyond measure. Yet the ravager fire was melting their hulls, destroying their fighters.

Terror filled her.

The *Marilyn* still spun madly. Another blast hit their port side. They jolted, careened, too unsteady for Marco to keep firing.

The ravagers stormed closer, instants away from ramming into the *Marilyn* and the Ghost Fleet.

And then the yurei sent forth their wrath.

The light along the soulships' central disks grew brighter, coalescing into points, thrumming, beaming like stars . . . then blasting out searing, furious beams.

The streams of light slammed into ravagers. Where they hit, they melted metal. They bored holes into the living starships. Ravagers tore apart, claws flying.

Kemi managed to steady her flight. She had to dip to dodge one of the yurei beams that blasted overhead, bathing the *Marilyn* with radiation.

"Emery?" Ben-Ari said.

He nodded, perched up at the gunner's station. "Continuing fire, ma'am."

Shell after shell flew from the *Marilyn*, pounding the ravagers ahead.

But thousands of the ravagers still charged toward them, moving closer, closer . . .

"Hold on!" Kemi shouted.

"Full power to shields!" Ben-Ari cried.

With the fury of collapsing worlds, the two fleets slammed together.

Fire and light flowed over the battle like a supernova.

Everywhere around them, the yurei light beamed, slamming into enemy vessels, criss-crossing space. The claws of the enemy tore into soulships, gripping, shattering, cracking open holes and filling them with plasma.

Kemi flew in a frenzy, dodging light, fire, and flying shrapnel. Ahead of them, a ravager tore apart, scattering claws the size of oaks. Three other ravagers slammed into a soulship, and their claws tore it open. Air, trees, and yurei flew out from the breach, and the ravagers filled the ship with plasma. Everywhere, ships large and small were battling. Thousands of yurei starfighters, disks the size of merry-go-rounds, spun madly, blasting out beams of light, tearing ravagers apart. Other ravagers fought back, grabbing the disks, cracking them, burning them. High above, one of the massive yurei soulships—kilometers wide—cracked open. Explosions rocked it, and its disks shattered, showering flame and metal and light, destroying a hundred ships—both yurei starfighters and ravagers—that flew around it.

"Shouldn't this be easier?" Kemi shouted over the din of battle. "I thought the Ghost Fleet is invincible! Like the Army of the Dead that Aragorn raised at Dunharrow."

Ben-Ari raised an eyebrow. "*Lord of the Rings*? Never pegged you as a fan."

Kemi groaned. "I shared a ship for two years with Noodles, remember?"

"Just focus on flying," Ben-Ari said. "De la Rosa, divert more power to our engines, shields, and cannons—give us everything you've got from all power sources, primary and backup. Emery, keep our guns blasting, damn it!"

As the *Marilyn* whizzed through the battle, firing its weapons, Ben-Ari's nervousness grew. Kemi was right. This should have been easier. It seemed that for every ravager they destroyed, a soulship collapsed. Ben-Ari too had imagined an invincible fleet, ghost warriors that no enemy could destroy. The yurei were capable fighters—their beams were deadly, and they were searing many ravagers—but they were far from unstoppable gods of war.

This better be enough, she thought. *Or we summoned a paper tiger.*

A mob of ravagers—a hundred or more—slammed into another massive soulship, tearing at its glowing central disk. Half the ravagers shattered in the beams of light, but the others tore into the ship. The central disk exploded, blasting out white light like a supernova, pulverizing the ravagers around it.

Kemi swooped hard. Chunks of metal slammed into the top of the *Marilyn*. Marco cried out from the gun turret.

"Our cannon is blasted!"

"Fire our photon guns!" Ben-Ari said. "But only when you see an opening into the mouth of a ravager. Don't waste ammo on their metal hulls. De la Rosa, divert more power to Emery. Take it from life-support everywhere but the bridge. And keep our shields up!"

"Full power to shields, guns, *and* engines all at once?" Lailani muttered. "For the next battle, we'll install hamster wheels instead of chairs, so we can generate more power as we fly."

While power was at a premium, there was no shortage of ravagers to fire on. The living ships were everywhere. Three charged toward the *Marilyn*, claws opening to reveal their flaming gullets. Marco fired the photon guns, and one ravager exploded. The two others blasted their plasma. Kemi dodged one jet, but the second stream washed across their starboard.

The lights shut down on the *Marilyn.*

They listed, helpless in the sky.

"De la Rosa, get us backup power!" Ben-Ari shouted.

"I—" Lailani began when a ravager slammed into them.

They all screamed.

Claws slammed against the shields, tearing, ripping.

Air shrieked.

"Our cargo bay is breached!" Lailani shouted.

Ben-Ari cursed and hit a button. Deeper in the ship, a door slammed shut, sealing off the cargo bay. She could see their supplies—food, water, medical kits, fuel cells—hurtling out into space.

Damn.

"Got it!" Lailani said, hitting controls, and power came back on. "I'm routing power from the cargo bay's shields. We don't need them anymore, and—"

The claws slammed into them again.

"Kemi!" Ben-Ari shouted.

"Got it!" The pilot gripped the joystick, snarling, pulling them upward. "Marco, get ready!"

The *Marilyn* swooped toward the ravager below. It opened its claws to blow fire.

Marco filled its mouth with bullets.

Kemi yanked the stick, and they flew through raining debris and roaring fire.

The battle lasted for hours. The *Marilyn* soon exhausted its missiles, then its bullets, leaving it only with photon blasters.

When the dust settled, a victor emerged.

The yurei fleet glided through a cloud of shattered ravagers.

"We won." Kemi slumped back in her seat. "We beat them."

"But at a heavy cost," Ben-Ari said, looking out at the devastation.

She couldn't count how many soulships had fallen. But it was hundreds. Maybe thousands.

Some of the round vessels floated, dead, their hulls cracked open. Others had shattered into countless pieces. Some of the disks had torn off, cracked in half, and were floating away. Among the wreckage floated dead trees and dead yurei.

Ben-Ari gazed at the fallen, eyes damp.

"We roused them after a million years of sleep," Lailani whispered. "Now so many have died."

Ben-Ari forced herself to raise her chin, to square her shoulders. "But thousands of their ships still fly. The Ghost Fleet is still strong."

But Lailani only covered her face, trembling. Kemi lowered her head and said nothing. Ben-Ari knew what they were feeling. She felt it too, overwhelming her.

Guilt.

They died for our war. So many—dead. Because of us.

The surviving soulships floated in place, no longer advancing toward Earth.

Ben-Ari pulled out the crystal Eldest had given her.

"Eldest of the yurei," she said to the crystal. "This is Captain Ben-Ari. My crew and I are here to offer any assistance you need. We can provide medical care and engineering services. Please let me know how we can help."

No reply came.

The crystal reflected her own face back at her.

For a long time, they floated in silence, waiting for some communication from the yurei. As they hovered here in the battlefield, Lailani and Marco both donned spacesuits and began repairing the damaged hull, soldering the cracks. Most of their supplies were gone, but a few—a crate of food, some more ammunition, and some battery packs—they found floating among the wreckage.

Still the soulships floated around them, answering no communications, making no move. Thousands of those ships were still functional—their central disks were glowing—but they might as well have been more floating wreckage.

Ben-Ari was dozing off on the bridge—she was so tired—when Kemi hopped in her seat.

"Captain, look!" The pilot pointed. "The dead yurei!"

Ben-Ari blinked and rubbed her eyes, embarrassed that she had fallen asleep. She stared outside and gasped, her sleepiness instantly vanishing.

Thousands of dead yurei still floated through space, most too small to see without the viewport's magnification. All across the battlefield, wispy light was now rising from the dead. Each fallen yurei seemed like a seed, sending out luminous sprouts. The glowing strands coiled toward the soulships that still flew. They flowed into the central disks, adding to their glow.

Lailani, who was outside in her spacesuit, spoke through the speakers. "Are you seeing this, Captain? Lieutenant?"

"We're seeing it all right," Ben-Ari said. "It's beautiful."

Lailani's voice was awed. "The souls of the dead are rising."

Ben-Ari smiled wryly. "I've been all over the galaxy, Sergeant, and I've never seen any evidence of an afterlife."

"Until now." Lailani hovered outside in her spacesuit, wrench in hand. "They're returning home. To the surviving soulships. To their forests. To their trees of souls."

They all watched in silence as the glowing strands floated from the dead.

Souls? Ben-Ari had never believed in souls. To her, consciousness had always been an illusion, just a byproduct of the physical brain. And perhaps it was for humans. But who was she to understand these mysteries of the cosmos? There were more wonders in the galaxy than poets and artists had ever imagined on Earth.

"There are more things in heaven and earth, Horatio, than are dreamt of in your philosophy," she whispered. A quote Marco had once used. Words that returned to her time after time on her journey.

This is why my father traveled, she realized.

Her crystal came to life.

Eldest spoke from it.

"The council of the Old Ones is convening in our forest. Send forth your elder, Captain Einav Ben-Ari."

If she bristled a bit at being called an elder—she was only twenty-eight!—she swallowed her pride.

She returned into the large soulship, the one that had first swallowed the *Marilyn.* She walked through the forest, following a trail of lights, until she found a henge of stones engraved with runes. By every stone stood a yurei, these ancient beings with tattered gowns and flowing hair, with wooden masks hiding their ravaged faces. In their claws, they held their tools of divination: crystals and feathers and leaves and strings of beads.

"Captain Einav Ben-Ari of Earth," said Eldest. "The council mourns the loss of many of our sisters. All the yurei grieve. For many eras, we lived in peace, remembering our home, living among the light of memories and souls. We have joined you on your quest, but we have suffered too much loss. The council has decided. The yurei will return to the Deep Sky, our home in the cosmos beyond. We have lost our war."

Ben-Ari stared.

Horror pulsed through her.

"You won!" she blurted out. "You beat the enemy! You destroyed the ravagers! You can't go back now. We're only halfway to Earth!" She trembled. "We still need you! The cosmos needs you."

The yurei all turned their masks toward her.

Slowly, they removed those masks, revealing their scarred faces.

"We fought for this cosmos long ago," Eldest said, speaking through the ruin of her mouth. "We suffered. We suffer still. We were wrong to come back. Wrong to think we could fight again." The yurei lowered her head. "Now so many have fallen."

Ben-Ari nodded. She spoke softly. "I lost many too. I lost many of my soldiers. I lost many of my friends. I lost millions of my kind." She raised her chin, tears in her eyes. "I understand. If you go back to hiding, to living in memory, I understand. This cosmos is full of pain and loss. And why should you suffer the slings and arrows when you can build a wall around yourselves, when you can live eternally in the memories of your crystal trees?"

The yurei looked at one another, then back at her.

"You do not approve," Eldest said.

Ben-Ari shrugged. "It's not for me to judge you. If I were in your place, maybe I'd do the same thing. So what if species are going extinct? So what if your old universe—the one you come from, that you fought for, suffered for, lost so many friends for—falls to the enemy? You have a safe space. You can live there forever. Hiding. Remembering the old days. Living in the past. Why not, if the future is so grim?"

Anger filled the yurei's eyes.

"We are not some cowards who would hide in a cave while the forest burns!" said one. "You cannot understand our kind. You cannot understand our wisdom."

"Oh, very true," said Ben-Ari. "Many times on my own planet, we had civilizations like yours. That I could not understand. That were far too wise. That looked away while my people were being slaughtered and burned in ovens. That turned a blind eye to poverty and despair. That built walls and fences while their neighbors cried out in anguish, dying, desperate for aid."

"We did not abandon the cosmos!" said Eldest. "We fought!"

"And now you would retreat!" Ben-Ari said. "Tell me, yurei. Why did you test us with ethical dilemmas? Why did you force Marco to sacrifice his life to save two of his comrades? You told me it's to see if we're worthy of aid. If we're moral. If we're willing to sacrifice the few to save the many, even to sacrifice ourselves. Well, now you face the same test!" She panted, rage now pounding through her. "You stand where Marco stood. Above a pit of monsters, and the only way to save your friends is to jump in. My soldier passed that test. You failed." She turned her back to them. "I'm returning to my ship. To my war. Good day."

She began walking away.

A hand held her shoulder—a hand with three wide fingers, each tipped with a claw.

Eldest's voice was soft. "Einav. Wait, child."

Ben-Ari turned back toward the yurei. She waited. The aliens donned their masks again, and they huddled together in the henge, speaking in their language. The runes engraved in the stones glowed, and the trees rustled around them.

Finally, when Ben-Ari's feet were sore and her bladder was full to bursting, Eldest turned back toward her.

"The council has considered your words, and we cannot agree amongst ourselves," the yurei said. "Therefore, each sister shall take her own path. Some of us will return home. To our cosmos beyond the cosmos. To our memories. The others will continue with you."

Ben-Ari took a shuddering breath. Relief flowed through her.

"How many will come?" she said.

"Three soulships will continue with you," said Eldest. "The largest ships that carry our forests. With them will fly three thousand seedships, the small fighters we fly in battle. The rest return home."

Ben-Ari gasped. "That's it? But . . . there are tens of thousands of ships here! Even after the battle, there are—"

"The rest will return home," Eldest repeated. "They will try to forget."

Dejected, Ben-Ari returned to the *Marilyn.*

The fleet flew on.

From a hundred thousand, they were down to a handful.

Three large soulships, forests inside them.

Three thousand smaller disks, the single-pilot starfighters of the yurei.

And one dented, limping human starship, four souls trapped inside her—four who had agreed to be three. Four grieving. Four scared. Four lost in darkness, hope only a flicker ahead.

The darkness stretched out before them, and they headed to Earth.

CHAPTER EIGHTEEN

The signal came from Earth.

A human signal.

A message from home.

General Petty stood in the *Minotaur*'s war room, a chamber deep inside the ship. If the bridge was the central hub of command, managing all aspects of the ship, the war room was a place for deep thinking, for strategizing, for scrutinizing. The ship was floating in the asteroid belt, hidden from the marauders, waiting in the darkness far from home.

Perhaps, Petty dared to hope, the message was an invitation to come back.

The message repeated over the communicator. Petty and his officers frowned.

"We've unscrambled it," said his communication officer. "That's all we've got."

Petty scratched his chin. "What language is that?"

"We're not sure, sir," said the officer. "It's not in any of our translation services. It sounds like an obscure language, probably chosen in case the marauders grabbed translation software from Earth."

Petty turned toward Osiris. The android stood at his side, the only one not frowning, a smile on her synthetic face.

"Do you recognize this language, Osiris?"

The android's smile widened. "No, sir! I am programmed with over two hundred languages, sir, including rare tongues such as Aramaic and Gaelic, but this one doesn't exist in my memory banks. Would you perhaps like me to recite some Mongolian poetry, sir?"

He groaned. "No. But I want you to interface with our PA system, and to broadcast snippets of this recording—just the first sentence—across the ship. On my cue."

She nodded. "Happy to comply!"

Petty grabbed a communicator and broadcast his voice through every speaker on the *Minotaur*.

"This is Brigadier-General James Petty speaking. We are seeking a translator. If anyone can translate this following message, please report at once to your commanding officer."

He nodded at Osiris, and the android streamed the first sentence of the message into the speakers.

They waited in the war room. There were over five thousand officers and enlisted soldiers aboard, a diverse crew from across Earth. Petty just hoped somebody spoke that language.

He didn't have to wait long.

Within only moments, the door opened, and an officer escorted a young private into the war room. The lad gulped, looked around with wide eyes, and seemed ready to faint at the sight of so many senior officers. The boy—he couldn't have been older than eighteen—managed a trembling salute.

"Uhm, Private Doyle, Computer Programming and Engineering, reporting for duty, sirs," he squeaked. Sweat beaded on his brow, and his legs shook.

Petty struggled to stifle a smile. He remembered himself at that age, a green cadet; he had trembled the first time he reported to a Master Sergeant, and a war room full of generals would have probably made him faint.

"Are you cold, Private?" he asked, trying to hide his amusement.

Doyle nodded. "Yes, sir! I mean, no, sir. I'm very comfortable aboard the *Minotaur*, sir. Very honored to serve here."

"You seem nervous," Osiris said, peeking over Petty's shoulder. "Would you like to hear a joke to ease the tension?"

Petty groaned inwardly. "Not now, Osiris." He turned back toward Doyle. "Did you understand the message we broadcast on the speakers?"

"Yes, sir!" Doyle said. "My grandfather insisted on teaching me, sir. Said it's our duty to keep a dying language alive. I can speak Cree fluently, sir. Well, almost fluently."

"Cree," Petty said. "So that's the language."

Doyle nodded. "Yes, sir! I'm a quarter Cree myself. A quarter Russian, and the rest is English, sir. Well, there's also some Scottish in there too. My family immigrated to America back in the nineteenth century, though, so it's been a while. Well, not the Cree part of the family, obviously, but—"

Petty cleared his throat. "Can you translate this message for us, Private?"

"Yes, sir! Well, I think so, sir." He was trembling again. "There are many Cree dialects. But I can try, sir. If, uhm, I have security clearance, sir?"

"You just got it," Petty said. "Of course, after this meeting, we'll have to wipe your memories clear."

Private Doyle wobbled. He looked ready to pass out. He gulped and managed to squeak, "Of course, sir, but if you could just leave me *some* memories—maybe the good ones, like of my grandfather, and that time Betty Adams and I—"

Petty sighed. "Sit down, Private. And start translating."

The private seemed thankful for the seat. For a long time, he worked, listening, frowning, rewinding and scribbling on a piece of paper. It was a different dialect than his, but slowly the message came together.

"Here, sir." Doyle handed him the paper. "It's the best I could do, sir." He loosened his collar. "Now, sir, if you could just be gentle with that memory wiping machine . . ."

Petty sighed inwardly. "We already used it, Private. Did you forget?"

Doyle's jaw unhinged. He nodded vigorously, saluted, and stumbled out of the room.

Petty read the message again. He read it aloud for the group. With every word, his heart beat faster, and his fingers tingled.

To any human ships who hear!

This is a message from the Human Resistance of Earth. Throughout fall, spring, and winter, we have been fighting the enemy. We fight him in the hills. We fight him on the beaches. We fight him in the ruins of our cities. We have suffered many casualties, but we fight him still.

After a year of war, the time has come to strike the snake's head! On the Ninth of May, known across much of our globe as Victory Day, we will launch our largest offensive yet. We will assault the city of Toronto, once fair, now overrun by the enemy. Within those ruins he lurks, he who calls himself Lord Malphas, commander of the marauders. We will fight until he is captured or slain!

On the Ninth of May, the ending begins. The enemy is strong, determined, and will fight well. But we will not be cowed. We will fight until the end. Until total victory. Until Earth is free again.

If you receive this message, join our fight! Return to Earth. Join us in our assault on the enemy's stronghold in the ruins of Toronto. Together we are strong. Together we will be victorious.

For humanity and for Earth!

With pride,

Addy Linden

The Resistance

In the war room, there was a long silence.

"Addy Linden," Petty repeated.

"A figurehead," said one of his officers. "Probably just a myth."

Petty shook his head. "No." His voice was soft. "It's really her. The same Addy from the Scum War. One of Ben-Ari's soldiers." He looked out the porthole. "And where are *you*, Ben-Ari?"

Another officer cleared his throat. "May Ninth is only a few days away, sir. We can't possibly attack Earth alone, not without Ben-Ari and her Ghost Fleet—if such a fleet even exists. There are thousands of ravagers orbiting our homeworld."

Petty gazed outside into the darkness. For a long moment, he was silent. Then he turned back toward his officers.

"No, we can't wait for Ben-Ari," he said. "Not any longer."

His officers all stared at him. He knew that they would follow him on whatever path he chose.

He reached into his pocket and touched his daughter's dog tags.

"Years ago, Earth faced the scum menace," Petty said. "Earth stood alone. Yet we emerged the victors. Once more, Earth stands alone. Once more, it seems, no help will come to us from elsewhere. It is up to us. And Earth will fight! The *Minotaur* is the last ship in a once-mighty fleet. And she will give a mighty, final roar! May Ninth. On that day, we make our final stand. On that day, we liberate Earth or die in her sky. For Earth."

"For Earth!" they repeated.

Only a few days. A few days to complete repairs on the ship. To prepare the soldiers. To draw up battle plans.

To finally, after so long in exile, go home.

CHAPTER NINETEEN

"All right, boys, ante up." Addy took a puff on her cigar. "Five-card stud and suicide kings are wild."

"Get yer stinkin' feet off the poker table." Pinky shoved her boots. "You're crushing the cigs!"

Addy blew smoke in his face. "You're just jealous cuz I have feet, Bladerunner."

Pinky scowled. "I'm the one who has to smell your stinkin' kickers." He placed a cigarette on the table. "Ante up. I'm in. And no cheating this time, Bigfoot."

Sitting across from them, Steve stared morosely at his stash—he had lost most of his cigarettes, candy bars, and other valuables in the previous rounds.

"Come on, lover boy," Addy said to him. "I ain't sleeping with no chicken. Show us you got a pair and ante up!"

Steve groaned. "I hate playing poker with you." He added a candy bar to the pile. "Fine! I'm in."

Addy slapped down a bar of soap—her own ante—and shuffled the cards. They sat in a tent fifty kilometers south of Toronto, close enough to smell the stink of the city when the wind was right. Tomorrow was May Ninth. Tomorrow the assault on the city—her home—began.

Tonight she wanted to forget.

She took a swig of beer and dealt the cards.

"All right, boys." She puffed on her cigar. "No cheating, and if you bluff, I'll kick you in the balls."

Pinky glared at the pot. "You put down a bar of soap. A bar of soap ain't a proper ante."

"It is when you stink like you do, pipsqueak." Addy blew more smoke at him.

She was winning the game. A pile of cigarettes, candies, soap, razorblades, toilet paper rolls, buttons, and other valuables piled up at her end of the table. She had even won the cigar she was smoking. She took a swig of beer.

Let me drink and smoke and fuck and live and laugh tonight, she thought. *Tomorrow we all might die. Like Jethro died. Like Caveman. Like Elvis. Like—*

"Come on, your bet!" she growled at Pinky. She wanted to get this game going. She didn't want to think. To remember. To fear tomorrow.

Pinky nodded. "All right, I'm down for another cigarette." He added it to the pile.

Steve stared at his cards, his face glum. "God damn," he muttered.

"Stevie-boy, you in or out?" Addy said.

Steve winced. "I guess . . . in." He pulled off his wristwatch and added it to the pile. "Cheap knockoff."

Addy's eyes widened. "Dude, that's a Rolex. That's gold."

Steve harrumphed. "I wish! My dad bought it in Thailand for a couple bucks. Doesn't even work. Well, it works twice a day."

Addy stared at her cards. She had a pair of queens and a suicide king. A good three of a kind. Even if Steve was bluffing, it should be enough to beat his ass.

"Fuck it, I'm putting down these Cubans." She added an entire box of cigars to the table.

Pinky slammed his cards face-down. "Too rich for my blood."

Addy clucked like a chicken, ignoring Pinky's withering glare.

They swapped no more cards and made no more bets. Addy blew smoke at Steve.

"All right, lover boy, what have you got?"

He sat with slumped shoulders and heaved a sigh. "Nothing much." He placed down his cards. "Just a straight flush." He leaped up, suddenly grinning, and did a little dance. "Read 'em and weep!"

Addy leaped up too. She roared and lunged forward, knocking over the table, and slammed into Steve.

"You son of a bitch!" She punched him. "I said no bluffing!"

"You said no *cheating*." Steve laughed, trying to hold back her kicks. "Ow, ow! Stop biting me!"

"My Cubans!" she said. "My precious Cubans! You stole them! I only got to smoke one . . ." She sighed and lifted the cigar, which had fallen into the mud. "You really are a stinker, Steve. Way worse than Pinky."

Pinky pulled the table back up. "All right, all right, come on! Another round. My deal. We're playing Texas Hold 'Em. That's real poker."

They sat down for another round. It was late, but nobody wanted to sleep. Nobody wanted to face the nightmares.

"I'm winning back my Cubans," Addy said.

Steve snorted. "You wish! I'll be smoking them in your face all month."

"If we live that long!" Addy said. "Tomorrow we'll probably all be dead." She bit her lip. "Sorry. I shouldn't have said that. That was fucked."

They were all silent for a long moment, staring at the table.

"You're right," Pinky finally said, voice low. "Tomorrow might be the end. Tomorrow we're hitting the marauders' greatest base on Earth. We won't all make it out."

"We might," Steve said, but he didn't sound optimistic.

They were all silent again.

Addy lowered her head. She didn't think she could bear losing Steve. Losing anyone else. She had already lost almost everyone—her parents, nearly all her friends. She reached under the table and clasped his hand.

I can't lose you too, Steve.

"If you could be anywhere in the world tonight," Pinky said, "where would you be? For your last night on Earth."

Addy raised her eyebrow. "You mean, playing poker with you isn't the best night in the world? I'm shocked."

"Very funny, Canada," he said.

Addy chewed her lip. "I suppose I'd be at a Leafs game. Of course. And I'd have a nice cold beer, not this warm stuff. And three hot dogs topped with jalapenos and cheese and spicy mustard. And the Leafs would win the Stanley Cup. And Marco would be there." Suddenly her eyes were damp. "And Kemi too. And Lailani. And Ben-Ari, though she'd probably hate it. And I'd even let this big dumb galoot Steve come with us." She wiped her eyes. "Fuck, that would be a good last night." She turned to Steve. "What would be your best last night? And you better give the same answer!"

Steve leaned back in his seat. "Well, I'd be in Hawaii, hanging out on the beach outside the bar I own. And a bunch of bikini babes would be feeding me grapes, while—"

Addy punched him. "I'm going to feed you my fist!"

"Ow, ow!" He cringed. "Fine! Just one bikini babe. You."

"Better." She nodded. "But you better be wearing a Speedo. A tiny one."

"Babe, a tiny one won't fit," Steve said.

Addy scoffed. She turned to Pinky. "What about you, pipsqueak? What would your perfect last night look like?"

"You mean smelling your stinky feet isn't the best night in the world?" Pinky said, then ducked as she threw an empty beer can at him. "Well, I'd spend my last night with my wife and kids."

Addy's jaw unhinged. She stared at Pinky and rubbed her eyes.

"You're kidding me." She frowned. "*You* have a wife and kids? *You*? Human ones or some pillows you drew faces on?"

He rolled his eyes. "Very funny, Canada." He pulled out his wallet, flipped it open, and showed them a photograph.

Addy couldn't believe it. In the photo, Pinky—the same damn Pinky who had made their lives hell at boot camp—had his arms wrapped around a woman and two children, a little boy and girl.

"Fucking hell," she said. "You look . . . normal. You're smiling, for God's sake. It's a smile that could break mirrors, but it looks honest."

He put his wallet back into his pocket. "Yeah, they make me smile. Tamed me a bit." He barked a laugh. "An army of shrinks and doctors and juvy counselors couldn't do that. Took the love of a good woman and a couple of little kiddos." He sighed. "Wish I were with them now. I miss them. I love them. That's why I'm here, you know. Fighting. For them, to bring the world back for them."

And suddenly, Pinky—the Pinky who had raised hell at Fort Djemila, who had been their worst nightmare for weeks in the desert—was crying.

"Pinky, man!" Addy moved her seat closer to him. "Dude, here." She handed him a tissue.

Pinky looked away. "Fuck. I didn't want you to see me like this." He growled at her. "Not a word to the poet."

"Not a word." Addy patted his shoulder. "It's all right, little dude. I cry almost every night. Steve does too."

"Only because you keep kicking me in the shin in your sleep!" Steve said.

She kicked him again. "I'll show you kicks! Admit it. You cry because you're scared too. Because you're hurt. We're all terrified. We're all homesick. We're all fucked up and miserable here." And now her own eyes were damp. "This war. This place. This whole fucking situation. It was never meant to be like this. We were supposed to beat the scum and live happily ever after. But . . . maybe life's like that. You leap from the frying pan to the fire. But you gotta keep jumping, all right? You got to keep fighting. You got to keep *living*."

"I intend to keep living for as long as I can," Steve said. "I plan to grow old with you, babe."

Pinky nodded. "I plan to grow old with my family. Fuck those marauders. I ain't dying tomorrow. I'm going to live to see my kids grow up. To walk my daughter down the aisle when she gets married. To play with my grandkids." He wiped his eyes. "We're all going to make it tomorrow."

Addy grabbed the box of Cubans from Steve. "Cigars for everyone, boys!" She passed them around.

"Hey, those are mine!" Steve said, then winced when she kicked him.

They lit their cigars, filling the tent with smoke. Pinky dealt the cards. They played on through the night, waiting for a red dawn.

CHAPTER TWENTY

Captain Julian Bryan stared into the mirror, terrified of the man he saw.

"I'm not him," he whispered. "I will be better than him."

Across the world, they knew his grandfather's face. Evan Bryan—the great hero of humanity. The pilot who, fifty-eight years ago, had nuked the scum's homeworld, killing millions of centipedes and ending the Cataclysm. For decades, that roguish face had adorned cereal boxes, winked from posters, growled while blasting aliens in video games, and inspired generations of soldiers.

Then, only eight years ago, it all changed.

Then that face became hated.

Then that face became shameful.

Now, as Julian stared at his reflection, he saw the same face. His grandfather's face.

He tightened his fists. That young face, perhaps handsome by any other name, twisted into a snarl.

"I am not him. I am not a warmonger. I am not a murderer."

He turned away from the mirror, jaw clenched. That damn, square jaw, a jaw that another man would be proud of, that only reminded Julian of his grandfather.

His grandfather who had ignored the scum's overtures of peace.

Who antagonized the enemy for decades.

Who extended the war for fifty years longer than it should have lasted.

Who caused the death of millions.

Who Marco Emery and his friends had finally killed.

"I am not him," Julian said again. "I will fight my war differently."

One of his three bunkmates moaned and stirred on his cot. "Just fight it quietly." He tossed a pillow. "We're trying to sleep here."

Julian left his bunk, leaving his fellow pilots to sleep. There wasn't much room here aboard the *Minotaur*. Even Firebird pilots shared bunks. At least Julian only shared his quarters with three others; the poor marines, and there were thousands aboard this ship, had to share rooms with their entire platoons.

The corridors were crowded, even this late at night. There was never true night aboard the *Minotaur*. At any given hour, a hundred pilots were on high alert, hundreds of marines wore battle armor and were ready to deploy, and an army of specialists were bustling across the starfighter carrier, keeping the massive starship flying and battle-ready. The size of a skyscraper, the *Minotaur* was home to six thousand officers and enlisted soldiers who served aboard her, not to mention a host of androids and robots big and small.

The last starship, Julian thought as he wormed his way through the crowd, moving down the cluttered corridors. *The last hope of humankind.*

It was hard to believe that Earth had once commanded a hundred thousand vessels. Now this was all that remained.

Julian smiled grimly.

Then again, Grandpa defeated the scum with a single Firebird.

He finally reached the officer's lounge, a small chamber above the engine room, functioning as a bar, rec room, boardroom, and library. The floor vibrated as the engines hummed below, and pipes and cables ran along the walls. Several faux-leather couches filled the room, arranged around low tables. As Julian entered the room, two heads rose from behind a couch: a young man and woman, privates by the looks of them, gunners by their tattoos, both very naked. The couple grabbed their clothes and made a beeline to the door.

"Sorry, sir, sorry, sir," they mumbled as they hurried by.

Julian stifled a smile. He didn't mind the enlisted using the officer's lounge; it was the only semi-private place on the ship. And they were all scared for tomorrow.

Tomorrow was May Ninth.

Tomorrow they flew to their final stand.

Tomorrow, it was likely that they would all die.

Julian went to the bar to grab a drink, reached for a bottle, and his hand froze.

Somebody had pinned a photograph of Evan Bryan to the bar. That same old famous photo, smiling at the camera. The most famous photograph in the world, showing twenty-one year old Lieutenant Evan Bryan returning from nuking Abaddon.

On the photo, somebody had scribbled with a marker: *Clear his name! Bryan was a hero! Earth Power!*

Beneath the words, they had drawn a swastika.

Julian's fists trembled. He grabbed the photograph and ripped it apart.

"If I find who did this, I will kill them," he swore. "I will kill them myself. I will strangle them dead. I—"

A voice spoke behind him, deep and raspy.

"I hope you're talking about the marauders, Captain."

Julian turned around.

His heart burst into a gallop.

James Petty himself, commander of the *Minotaur*, entered the lounge.

Muted with shock, Julian stood at attention and saluted. Even after a year aboard the *Minotaur*, he had rarely seen the general. Petty mostly kept to his quarters and the bridge, rarely mingling with his soldiers.

"Sir!" Julian finally managed to say, chin raised, heels pressed together. "Looking forward to killing marauders, sir!"

Petty returned the salute, the hint of a smile on his lips, and approached the bar.

"Care for a drink, Captain?" he said, reaching for a bottle. "What's your poison?"

Julian blinked. To share a drink—with a general?

"Uhm . . . rye, sir," he managed.

Petty nodded. "Excellent. How about Gold Creek?"

"Yes, sir!"

Petty turned toward him. He gave the slightest roll of his eyes. "I'm asking what drink you'd like, Captain. You don't have to agree with my first offer."

Julian allowed himself a small, relieved smile. "I've always been more of a Moose Jaw man, sir."

"Very good. Strong, solid rye." He poured two glasses—one of Gold Creek for himself, another of Moose Jaw for Julian. "Cheers."

They clinked their glasses. They drank. The rye was strong and rich with hints of oak.

For a moment, they sat in silence. A monitor showed a rerun of a soccer game. A rerun from last year. From before the world had fallen. They watched the game in silence. Santos scored a goal.

Finally Julian managed to find his voice again. "Sir, I'm sorry for my outburst earlier. It was unbecoming of a pilot. I found . . . a disturbing message. About my grandfather." Maybe it was the drink that was bringing those words to his lips. "A moment of weakness. I would never harm another soldier, only the enemy."

Petty took another sip of his drink. He made a small noise of satisfaction and placed his cup down. "Captain, did you know my daughter?"

"I know *of* her, sir," he said. "Captain Coleen Petty was a company commander in the Erebus Brigade. Very brave. A soldier who fought honorably at Corpus, who gave her life for the Human Defense Force."

Petty nodded. "Yes. And she was a huge pain in the ass."

Julian couldn't help but gasp. "Sir?"

"Oh, I loved her. I loved my Coleen with all my heart. I still do. I would give my own life ten thousand times to bring her back. I miss her every day. But she was headstrong. Rude. Arrogant. And yes, a huge pain in the ass." He gave a small laugh. "She had a good heart, but Lord above, she was prickly on the outside." He looked at Julian. "We don't have to be like our family, Captain. We're our own men."

Julian took another sip. "Some men cast long shadows, sir."

"So we shine a light," said Petty. "We cast the shadow back."

Julian stared into his cup. He looked at his commander. "Sir, do you really think we can do it? Defeat the enemy? Win this war? Or should we have gone with the other ships into exile?" He winced. "I'm sorry, sir. It doesn't behoove me to question orders. Forgive me, sir."

Petty placed a hand on his shoulder. The general's hair was graying, his face lined, and dark sacks hung under his eyes, but those eyes were iron.

"There is hope, son. There is always hope for us. For our war, our lives, and our legacy."

Julian nodded. "Thank you, sir. I vow to you: I will fly well tomorrow."

"You always do, Captain. Now go get some sleep. Dawn comes early on the *Minotaur*. And with it comes war."

"Yes, sir!"

He saluted and left the lounge. As he passed by the trash bin, Julian stopped, was about to toss in the crumpled photo of his grandfather. Instead, he carefully ripped off the bottom half, where the words were scrawled. He folded the upper half, showing his grandfather's eyes, and placed it into his pocket. He would not forget where he had come from, the shadow that loomed over him. He would shine his own light.

* * * * *

Petty remained in the lounge, sitting at the bar, staring at his drink.

"Hope," he muttered. "Yes, I gave the boy hope, maybe."

He took a sip.

But did I lie to him?

Tomorrow, they would reach Earth.

Tomorrow, the final battle for their homeworld would begin.

How many of my young pilots am I sending to death? Petty thought. *Did I make the wrong choice? Should I have taken Julian and five thousand other young soldiers into exile, to begin a new life on a new world? Am I leading them into fire for a planet that is already lost?*

He thought again of the message from Addy. The hope of the Resistance. Yet how could they hope to defeat the marauders, this enemy that had torn through their fleet, that had conquered star after star?

Hope. Yes, Petty still had hope. In the courage of his warriors. In Ben-Ari returning to him. In humanity. Yet what was hope but a fool's drink, offering courage where prudence failed?

He shoved his drink aside.

He rose to his feet.

He stood, watching the monitor. The old football game. Families in their seats, waving flags, cheering, laughing. The sun shining. A mascot dancing. Earth. Life. Joy.

All those things lost.

All those things he fought to reclaim.

"I can still turn away," he said softly. "I can still join the other ships in exile. I can save their lives. Save Julian and the others."

He turned toward another monitor, a small screen showing the view outside. He could just see it in the distance—the pale blue dot. Earth. A world wrapped in darkness. A world where Addy and her Resistance were still fighting, still dying.

Petty thought of the great heroes of his family, those who had fought the scum, fought even older monsters on Earth. He thought of brave men and women who had marched into the fires of war.

He spoke softly to the empty room. "True heroes are given a choice. They have a path to safety yet choose the path of thorns. We must keep going." He closed his fist around his daughter's dog tags. "We must fight. We must win. We will not abandon Earth. Even if we die. Even if I watch them all die and their blood is on my hands. They are all my children too, Coleen. Julian and all the others. And I will lose some of them too, maybe all of them." His voice shook. "But I will keep going."

The *Minotaur* glided on in the darkness, approaching home.

CHAPTER TWENTY-ONE

They pushed north through the rain, their cannons heralding their coming.

They marched along the Appalachian Trail and the coast. They flowed across the northwestern plains. Their ships traveled down the Saint Lawrence River. From across the continent, the divisions of the Resistance moved toward Toronto. Toward Lord Malphas. Toward defeat or victory.

The generals of the Resistance—officers from what remained of the Human Defense Force—wanted Addy to travel in armored vehicles, hidden among the troops, protected. She was the face of the Resistance, after all, too precious to lose. She was the heroine who had saved Earth from the scum, who had escaped from marauder captivity, who had raised North America in rebellion. Addy wondered if her looks—she was still young, tall, and not the ugliest soldier in the army—added to her appeal.

But she had refused the generals. She couldn't stand traveling hidden in an armored truck, even with the constant marauder attacks. She rode at the head of the army on her motorcycle, the wind ruffling her short blond hair, her rifle slung across her back. Patches of body armor covered her, and she bore her ivory sword at her side. She rode onward, a Joan of Arc of grease and diesel and gunpowder. Thus she would return home. Not in hiding but riding at the vanguard, proud and free, the wind in her hair.

Here was not a technological assault like the attack on Abaddon in the Scum War. Here was a slow, bloody migration, slugging it out for every step along the trail.

And every step, they left people behind.

Along forest trails, their warriors fell to marauder claws.

Along mountain roads, their vehicles burned in ravager fire.

Through ghost towns they rode, the marauders attacking from every roof and alley, tearing into them, spilling their blood across the pavement.

Along the plains, as a hundred thousand soldiers marched below, ravagers and jets battled above, and plasma rained as grenade launchers fired up.

It was an invasion of courage and a trail of tears. They marched toward victory and they left a wake of their dead behind them.

Addy fought in every battle, from massive assaults where thousands of marauders attacked to skirmishes with rogue aliens on the roadsides. She fired her rifle. She hurled her grenades. She rode her motorcycle through the lines of marauders, cutting into their eyes with her bayonet, and she rode atop armored sand tigers, firing machine guns as the vehicles charged into the enemy. Twice she shot down a ravager from the ground, firing her shells into their flaming maws.

Every battle left another scar. Scrapes and burns on her body. Wounds on her soul. She felt dead inside, barely able to feel the horror anymore, and if at night she wept into Steve's embrace, at dawn she fought again.

She worried what Marco would find when he returned, if he would recognize the woman she had become. Where was the Addy he had loved, the girl who laughed, played, wrestled him for sport, always with a grin on her face? That girl had died somewhere between Haven and the ruins of this world. With every new scar, with every new terror she faced, Addy's realization grew: Not only graves hold the soldiers who died at war. Even those breathing, talking soldiers who return home died upon the battlefield, their souls burned in the fire.

"Rest today," Steve whispered to her in the mornings, holding her in his wide arms. "Ride at the back. In an armored truck. Sleep. Laugh."

But every morning, Addy shook her head. "I started this. I must lead them."

Every morning, they woke up in another bed—on a roadside, in a forest, in an abandoned house. Every morning, she made love to him. No, not made love; that was too tender a thing. She fucked him urgently while her wounds ached, while her soul screamed, clutching him until she drew blood, desperate to forget—if only for a few moments, to forget the pain. And they fought on.

The tanks roared.

The helicopters and jets rumbled overhead.

The thousands of soldiers fired their guns.

The marauders fought for every centimeter of land. For every step, they took a life.

And with every step, Addy's fear grew that Marco would never return. That he had fallen on his quest to find the Ghost Fleet. Perhaps he had fallen in Haven itself, only moments after the marauders had kidnapped Addy. Perhaps there was no help for Earth. Their quest for the Ghost Fleet had surely failed. Earth alone fought this war. Earth alone would have to win it.

And with every step, another fear grew. A fear that she would lose her war. That her hosts would break against the ruins of Toronto, the stronghold of marauder might on the planet. That Malphas was letting her claim these early victories, drawing her nearer like a spider drawing a fly. That his web awaited her.

"I'm scared," she whispered to Steve one night, lying with him under the stars. "What if I can't do this? If I'm leading us all to slaughter?"

Steve kissed her forehead. "You defeated the scum. You can defeat the marauders."

"I didn't defeat the scum," she said. "I was just following orders then. I had Ben-Ari and Bryan and other brave, smart officers to lead me. I'm not an officer. I'm not brave. I'm terrified all the time. Steve, am I leading us all into a web?"

"Probably." He nodded. "But we'll burn that web down."

Or end up like flies, she thought. *A meal for the spiders.*

Dawn rose.

She straddled her motorcycle.

She rode on.

They were near now. Behind Addy, the divisions of the Resistance converged. Hosts of armor, battalion after battalion of tanks that roared across the land, raising clouds of dust. Formation after formation of artillery, the massive cannons rolling forth. Countless trucks full of engineers and builders. Tens of thousands of infantrymen, some riding in armored transport carriers, most marching afoot, several divisions of them, banners raised. Cargo trucks crammed full of munitions, food, water, blankets, medical supplies, and all the other necessities of war. Above flew their air force, jets and helicopters and bombers, unable to reach space but deadly in the sky. Most of these warriors came from the Human Defense Force and still wore its uniforms, but many were rebels gathered along the long roads, rising up against the enemy. A hundred rebel groups fought together, joining under one banner. Here it was, in all its strength—the Resistance.

As Addy rode at their lead, she saw it ahead, rising from the haze.

Toronto.

Its spires rose like chipped teeth in the rotting jaw of a giant. Smoke plumed from the ruins, forming a charcoal shroud above. A cloud of specks swarmed around what remained of the skyscrapers like bees over a carcass—ravagers. Addy didn't know if any humans still lived in her old city. If they did, they were in hell. Here was a nightmare, a vision of the underworld.

The Resistance stopped outside the city.

Rain began to fall, mixed with ash.

Silence covered the land.

Addy rode along the front lines on her horse, banner raised, like a knight from an old tale. She let the troops see her, salute her, know that she, this figurehead, this heroine, was fighting with them. Inside she was trembling. Inside she was still that little girl, facing the ruins of her home, so afraid. But as she rode by them, tall, chin raised, shoulders squared, the wind in her golden hair, she was a symbol to them. She was like a living statue—strong, eternal, the warrior who had defeated the scum, who would deliver them now from evil.

And all I want to do is hide, she thought. *Every part of me shakes. I comfort them. I am strong for them. But who can I turn to for comfort?*

She turned back toward the city.

She sat on her horse atop a hill, staring.

Toronto.

The city where she had been born to a junkie mother and a prison dad.

The city where she had fought on the street, poor, ragged.

The city where they had stuck her into the remedial class, locked her up with the freaks.

The city where she had wept, had fought so many battles against boys twice her size, where she had wanted to die, where she had watched her parents slain.

The city where she had felt trapped, an animal in a cage, crying out, enraged, tortured by countless whips.

The city where she had met Marco.

Where she had watched the stars with him.

Where she had moved into his library, learned about old stories and music and art.

Where she had met Steve.

Where she had played hockey and laughed so much.

Where she had become a woman, learning the ways of love.

Where she had collected her coins from precious memories, from hockey games and movie nights and street fairs.

Where she had loved people.

Where she was at home.

Where she was not this figurehead, not this heroine, just a girl.

Where she would return to today.

I wish you were with me, Marco, she thought. *I miss you so much.*

One of her soldiers, a speechwriter by trade, had composed Addy's message to General Petty and his fleet. A marauder had torn out that writer's guts two days south from here. But Addy would still speak to her soldiers today, try to inspire them. Her horse nickered and sidestepped. She patted the animal, and she spoke into her communicator, broadcasting her voice across the camp—and, she hoped, to the marauders in the city ruins.

"To the warriors of the Resistance!" she said. "This is Addy Linden. Some of you call me the Golden Knight. Others the Steel Witch. Some of you, I've heard, call me 'that crazy bitch with the tattoos.'" She cleared her throat, mustering herself for an attempt at eloquence, knowing these words would echo through the ages. "Anyway, listen up. The final battle is ahead. In the city ruins, the tyrant Lord Malphas waits. The king of the marauders. And many of his warriors guard his lair. It'll be a tough battle. But I believe in you! You are strong, you are brave, you are human. That means a lot. That means you don't take shit from nobody!" She winced. Again, she had failed to sound exactly Churchillian. "What I mean to say is: There comes a time in our lives when we must stand tall. When we must raise our heads. When we must march toward danger, through fire and rain, through darkness, to seek the light. Today we will rise! Today we will be noble! Today, like the great heroes of old, we will . . . we will . . ." She twisted her lips, words failing her. "Ah, fuck it. I'm no poet. Let's just go kill that Malphas asshole and go home. Kick ass, everyone!"

She nodded. Good enough.

The artillery began to fire.

The attack on Toronto began.

CHAPTER TWENTY-TWO

It flew toward Earth.

A single, massive, clanking warship, an old bull with one last fight in its gnarled heart.

The *Minotaur*. The last starship of humanity.

Petty stood on the bridge, staring ahead at the pale blue dot.

"The poet's eye, in fine frenzy rolling, doth glance from heaven to Earth," he whispered.

Earth—there, growing larger, in all her fragile beauty. A marble in the depths. The spring of humanity, art, music, all things dear to Petty. A world afire. A world fallen. A world in chains.

Around the planet they flew. The ships of the marauders. The deadly ravagers. A hundred thousand or more of those living ships orbited his world.

Petty and his ship—they flew toward the enemy. Alone. Two aging warriors facing their last fight.

"It is likely that we fly to our deaths," he said to his officers. "It is likely that today, we lose our war, that our last flare of independence goes dark. But we will fly forth nonetheless. And we will fight well. Here at the end."

They flew past the moon. They flew onward. Earth grew from a marble to a great sphere against the stars, limned with a band of blue sky. It was May ninth. Below on the surface, the assault on Toronto would be commencing.

And as General Petty and his warriors flew toward their world, the ravagers flew out to meet them.

Thousands of them.

Petty gave a thin, tight smile.

Good, he thought. *We'll draw a few away from Addy.*

"Full power to forward shields," he said.

"Aye aye, Captain," Osiris said. "I should warn you, sir. With our shields at full power, our cannons will only fire with half their usual deadliness."

"I am aware, Osiris." He nodded. "Remember, the enemy has more ships than we have ammunition. But we can distract those ravagers. We can hurt them. We can give Addy some breathing room."

The ravagers were flying nearer, charging at incredible speed.

Osiris looked over her shoulder at Petty.

"So we're cannon fodder, sir?"

"No," he said. "We're the galaxy's biggest damn bull in its biggest damn china shop. Now damn those ravagers, and full speed ahead!"

Osiris smiled. "Full speed ahead, sir."

The *Minotaur* charged.

The thousands of ravagers stormed toward it.

Space exploded with fire and metal and light.

Plasma roared across the *Minotaur*'s shields, showering out, forming a great cone of flame. The ravagers flew through the inferno, slammed against the *Minotaur*'s thick metal hulls, scratching, digging, clawing.

The engines roared.

The hull creaked and screeched and grumbled.

They kept charging.

All along the port and starboard, the side cannons blasted. Shells tore through the enemy, and fire pulsed.

The ship's front cannons fired, blasting out shell after shell, ripping through the ravagers.

But mostly, it was the pure girth of the *Minotaur* that did the damage.

The ravagers were large starfighters; they were far larger than Firebirds. But the *Minotaur* dwarfed them. They were like insects crushed against a charging, enraged bull. Their constant assault pattered against the *Minotaur*, a hailstorm.

The hull dented.

A deck cracked open.

Alarms blared.

"Keep streaming power to our shields!" Petty said. "Everything you've got!"

"No more power available, sir!" Osiris said.

"Divert some from the engines! Burn up more fuel! We need to keep those shields up."

"If I tap into the fuel for power, sir, we won't have enough to fly away."

Petty gripped his controls. "We're not flying away, Osiris. This is our last stand. Keep those shields up!"

They kept charging through the ravagers, knocking them aside. Their guns kept firing. Another deck cracked open. Marines spilled out into space, soon burned in the enemy plasma. Petty could barely see Earth; the fire was everywhere, washing across them. Life support died in the lower decks. One engine burst and the ship rocked. A viewport cracked.

"They're tearing us apart!" an officer cried.

"Keep charging!" Petty shouted. "Onward! To Earth!"

Through fire and metal, they flew.

Another deck cracked.

Fire raged through the ship.

Ravagers clung to them, digging, ripping open holes.

Sirens screamed.

"We're being boarded!" shouted an officer. "Deck 17B breached!"

"Deck 23A breached!"

"Storeroom 7 breached!"

From across the ship, gunfire raged. Monitors showed marauders racing through the corridors of the *Minotaur*.

"All marines, fight for your ship!" Petty said, speaking into his communicator. "Hold them back! Fight for your lives!"

Marauder after marauder crawled into the warship. Gunfire blazed. Smoke filled the ship and blood splattered. A marauder burst onto the bridge, and security guards fired their guns, tearing it down.

A hundred more ravagers formed a wall before them.

"Sir!" Osiris screamed, and Petty could have sworn there was fear in the android's artificial eyes.

"Onward," he said.

They stormed onward.

They slammed into the wall of ravagers.

Their central viewport shattered.

Fire filled the bridge.

Metal screamed and the hull creaked.

They broke through.

The curtains of fire parted, and ahead he saw it: Earth.

They were close now, so close that Earth filled those viewports that were still working. Many ravagers still orbited the planet, turning toward the damaged, limping *Minotaur.* On the surface, Petty knew, hundreds of thousands, maybe millions of marauders were waiting. Osiris turned the ship toward North America.

"Magnify a view of Toronto," he said.

On one of the viewports, he saw the ruins of the city.

The battle had already begun. Petty couldn't see the details, but he could see hundreds of trails of smoke arching through the sky—the trails of artillery shells, flying toward the city ruins.

The Resistance was bombing Toronto.

The invasion of the city was about to begin.

And we will join it, Petty vowed.

More ravagers kept flying from behind them, and their engines roared out fire, and their back cannons blasted. Within the *Minotaur*'s twisting halls, the battle still raged, but the marines were getting the upper hand, slaying the last marauders.

"Bring us directly above Toronto, Osiris," he said. "We're going to bomb a path through the ravagers, then send down our marines."

"Yes, sir!" the android said. "Heading toward Toronto, sir!" They slammed into more ravagers, knocking them aside. "Sir, do you know why Canadians don't wear short sleeves? Because they're not allowed to bear arms. It's funny because it's cold there, so they all wear jackets. And did you hear about the Canadian who took a test? He got an eh. It's funny because—"

"Osiris, focus on flying," Petty said. "Bring us within five hundred kilometers of the surface. Our shuttles can make the jump from there. We—"

He stared.

For an instant, he couldn't speak.

My God.

Three marauder warships were flying toward them from around the planet.

Not ravagers. They were far larger—larger even than the *Minotaur*. They were shaped as cubes, patched together with metal sheets, and spikes thrust out from them, each like an obelisk. Here were no living starships; Petty could see the bolts and rivets. Here were ships the marauders had built. Massive warships. And they were charging toward the *Minotaur*.

Petty clutched his communicator, his grip so tight he nearly shattered it.

"All Firebirds, fly!" he shouted. "Get down into the atmosphere and help the Resistance! The *Minotaur* will handle these behemoths."

The massive alien ships were closer. Seconds away.

Petty cursed. He was still too far. He needed to bring the *Minotaur* directly above Toronto to launch his marines.

He stared in horror as the cubical warships drew nearer.

"Fire everything!" he shouted, and the *Minotaur*'s cannons blasted out, and shells burst against the massive cube ships.

Instants later, one of the cubes—twice their size—slammed into the *Minotaur*.

They careened through space, spilling out Firebirds like a mother spider ejecting her spawn.

Across the bridge, officers flew from their seats. Petty fell and banged his hip. He struggled to rise.

"Osiris, steady us! Take them on!"

The android leaped back into her chair and grabbed the controls. "Yes, sir, I—"

Another cube ship plowed into them.

Klaxons wailed as another deck was breached.

The *Minotaur* spun through the sky, plowing through ravagers and Firebirds alike.

"Osiris, charge at them!" Petty cried. "All cannons firing! We'll slam them into one another, and—"

Shrieks tore through his words.

Three marauders leaped from a corridor onto the bridge, webs flying, claws lashing.

Petty cursed, drew his pistol, and opened fire.

The cube ships slammed into them again. The lights died. Only the glow of the monitors—at least, those monitors that were still working—lit the ship. The marauders moved in the darkness, ripping into officers. One of the creatures grabbed Osiris, yanked her out of her seat, and tore the android in half. She screamed and fell, limbs twitching, electronics spilling out.

The *Minotaur* spun toward Earth. Bridge officers lay dead at their posts, torn open.

Nobody was flying the ship.

They stormed toward the atmosphere.

A cube hit them again.

The *Minotaur* jolted.

Petty realized what the enemy was doing.

They're going to slam us down onto the planet. We'll hit with enough power to wipe out cities.

The marauders kept rampaging across the bridge. Marines burst in, firing at them, taking one down. Petty lurched forward, fell. He rose to one knee. His chest ached. He thought he was having another heart attack. He ignored it.

He fired his gun, hitting a marauder, knocking it back.

He pulled himself toward the helm, shoved a dead officer out of his seat, and yanked on the controls.

The engines roared.

They turned away from the planet, charging back to space. Their engines sputtered, and Petty tugged a lever, and they roared with new fury.

One of the cube ships loomed ahead, and Petty fired all their cannons.

Explosions rocked the cube ship ahead, and Petty yanked the control wheel. As large as several city blocks, lumbering, leaking out air, the *Minotaur* flew alongside the cube, skimming its surface, cracking its hull.

He fired the starboard cannons.

The guns blazed, scraping across the cube, ripping through it, tearing it apart. Shards of metal fell toward Earth, flamed in the atmosphere, and slammed into the ocean.

Petty fired more shells.

The cube tore apart, exploding into a million pieces, peppering the *Minotaur* and cutting through its shields.

Petty kept flying, moving them farther from the atmosphere. Smoke and shards of metal trailed from them.

If we had fallen onto Earth, we would have been like the asteroid wiping out the dinosaurs, he thought.

But his relief was short-lived. Two of the massive cube ships were still flying, and they were now charging toward the *Minotaur*. Many Firebirds still flew, but they faced thousands of ravagers, and they were falling fast.

They were hovering over the Pacific now. Petty somehow had to make it around the globe, to bring his ship above Toronto, and to let down his marines.

It would be easier to dig through a boulder with a spoon.

Their ammo was running low. Many decks were losing air. Two decks were burning. And more ravagers were rising from the planet.

Petty gritted his teeth, forced down the fear, and kept flying.

CHAPTER TWENTY-THREE

I was in darkness.

Marco stood in the shadows, head lowered.

I thought I was alone.

He closed his eyes.

She was with me.

"Addy," he whispered. "I'm coming."

Light streamed outside as the *Marilyn* flew through the heliosphere, leaving the vast empty space between the stars, entering at last the solar system. Home. Heading toward that distant star, still small and pale, soon to grow into the sun.

For many days now, here aboard the ship, Marco had been thinking not of Earth, not their destination, but of New Earth, that stormy planet orbiting Alpha Centauri. Of the colony of Haven. He thought about the two years he had spent there—two missing years of his life. Two years of trauma. Addiction—to alcohol, to sex, to grief, to self-destruction. Two years of living with Addy in a box, floating through a storm. Two years of pushing her away. Of hurting her. Of losing her friendship.

I nearly lost my life in Haven, he thought. *I nearly jumped off that ledge, fleeing the ghosts of war that still chased me. But almost losing you, Addy, was worse. Because you're better than I am. You've always been better.*

You've always been the best part of me, the best reason for me to live. He took a shuddering breath. *And I'm going to find you now, Addy. I'm going to save you. And I'm never letting you go again.*

He stepped between the four empty cots in the *Marilyn*'s dark bunk. He placed his hand on the porthole, gazing outside into space.

The Ghost Fleet flew there.

Most had not made it this far. Most had died in battles along the way or fled back home. But three motherships, large as towns, had flown with the *Marilyn* all the way here. Three thousand smaller seedships, the starfighters of the yurei, flew here too. Large and small, they all looked the same: two metal disks encircling a central disk of light.

A small fleet, Marco thought. *But it will be enough. It must be enough. Or we have no chance.*

He refocused his eyes, gazing at his reflection in the porthole.

Would Addy even recognize me?

He had changed. He looked haggard, he thought—despite what Lailani had told him. He had been too skinny on Haven, but after six months in space, eating little, he had lost even more weight. His eyes looked too large in his gaunt face. Leaping into the pit of monsters in the simulation, an act as devastating as nearly leaping off the edge at Haven, had etched his face with weariness. For the first time in his life, he had gray hairs. Just a few of them. But they were there at age twenty-six.

For Addy, if she was still alive on Earth, twice as long would have passed since Haven. Time flowed differently in the cosmos, depending on gravity and speed. Six months had passed for Marco since Haven. A year or longer for Addy.

"Have you survived this long, Addy?" he whispered. "Hang on a little longer." His eyes dampened. "You helped me when I needed you most. I'm coming for you, Addy. When I was in darkness, you were there, and I'm coming for you. Just survive a little longer."

A voice answered from the doorway. "She will, Marco. She's strong. She's alive. I can feel it."

He looked up to see Kemi entering the bunk. He felt his cheeks flush.

"Sorry, I think out loud sometimes when I'm alone," Marco said.

Kemi hugged him. They gazed out into space together.

"They're beautiful," she whispered. "The soulships."

"Not as beautiful as you," he said, then suddenly laughed. "I can't believe I said that. Such a horrible line!"

She pouted. "You don't think I'm beautiful?"

He looked at her. Her high cheekbones. Her curly dark hair. Her full lips.

"You are beautiful," he said. "I've always thought so."

Kemi smiled and lowered her eyes. "You silly boy." Her smile faded. She leaned her head against his shoulder. "I'm scared, Marco."

He held her, stroking her hair. "Me too."

"Do you think the yurei spoke the truth? That one of us will die? Me or you? Or Lailani? Or Ben-Ari?"

"I don't know."

Kemi's tears wet his shoulder. "I can't imagine losing any one of you. I'm so scared one among us will die, or more than one. I'm so scared that my parents are dead. We're almost home, Marco. Almost back on Earth. Back in Toronto. Our home. What will we find there?"

"Ruins," he said. "Death. War. But also, maybe, victory. Also, maybe Addy and your parents." He held Kemi's hands. "Also, maybe a chance for a new life. To rebuild. To be happy."

"How can we be happy again?" she whispered, tears on her cheeks. "How can we forget everything?"

"Forget?" Marco said. "No. We won't forget. I tried to forget in Haven, but the memories chased me. We'll remember, Kemi. We'll remember how we fought. We'll remember those we lost. Every day, when we wake up in peace, we'll remember, and we'll mourn, and we'll be grateful for what we have."

"For our house on the beach?" She bit her lip, eyes hopeful.

He nodded, smiling. "For our house on the beach. That big house we'll all share. The water on one side and trees on the other. Campfires at night on the sand. Roasting marshmallows."

She grinned. "*Star Trek* marathons on the big TV!"

He laughed. "And long walks along the beach, collecting seashells. And you can wear a hula girl outfit."

Kemi gasped. "You wear one, hula boy!" Her grin grew, revealing sparkling teeth. "You'll be my little hula boy." She touched his cheek. "I love you, little hula boy."

He placed his hands on the small of her back. "I love you, Kemi."

She kissed him.

They kissed for a long time. Kemi smiled nervously, biting her lip, as she pulled him onto a cot. They kept kissing, but then Kemi pulled back. She grew serious. She placed a hand on his cheek and gazed into his eyes.

"Marco, eight years ago, we made love for the first time. Our only time." Her eyes welled with tears. "And I broke your heart then. I chose a military career over you. And I regretted that ever since. I'm sorry, Marco. I want to make love to you again. Because I really love you. You're the love of my life." A smile shone through her tears. "Well, you and Captain Kirk."

"I can't compete with Kirk," Marco said. "You'll have to settle."

He kissed her again, more deeply this time.

"Just . . . be careful with my hand," she said. "You know, the loose battery. I know that I'm shockingly sexy, but I don't want to shock you for real."

"I'll find other parts to interest me," he whispered, reaching toward one of particular interest.

She gasped. "Naughty hula boy! Even Kirk was more of a gentleman."

They kissed again. And they made love again. And they lay in each other's arms, laughing, remembering home. Remembering their long walks among the trees in Mount Pleasant Cemetery, the last green space in the city. Their lunches at the Indian restaurant, their favorite haunt. Their evenings watching movies and having popcorn wars. Their Sunday mornings, reading Shakespeare plays aloud, acting out the parts in the living room. Being kids. Being happy.

As Marco lay beside Kemi, he thought of Lailani. He thought of falling in love with her. Of making love to her just weeks ago in the forest aboard the soulship. He had loved other women on Haven. He had loved Anisha, had slept with many others in his daze and darkness. But here, aboard the *Marilyn*, aboard this small ship, were the two great loves of his life. Kemi, of sweetness and pain. Lailani, of fire and ice. Two women he had given his heart to. Two women who had broken his heart. Two women he still felt torn between.

Maybe someday, he thought, *we will choose loyalty. Maybe someday, we will be healed, and we will live normal lives. Maybe someday, I will marry a woman, settle down, grow old with her. But right now, I must think of a third. Of my best friend. Of Addy.*

"Hey, hula boy," Kemi said. "We still have an hour before our shift at the bridge. Wanna watch a *Star Trek* episode?"

He rolled his eyes. "We live on a spaceship, and you want to watch old science fiction shows from before the moon landing."

"Hey, our spaceship doesn't have a Gorn!" She pulled out her tablet. "You're watching an episode with me if I have to tie you down."

She curled up against him. He wrapped his arms around her, and she laid her cheek on his chest. They watched Kirk battling the Gorn as the *Marilyn* flew onward, as the Ghost Fleet followed, as they headed closer and closer to Earth.

CHAPTER TWENTY-FOUR

"Armor—charge!" Addy shouted from her sand tiger. "For Earth!"

The artillery fired their last shells.

Across the countryside, the armored divisions stormed forth.

Thousands of tanks charged, firing their cannons, raising storms of dust. Thousands of sand tigers charged with them, machine guns rattling. Thousands of troop carriers, great boxes of metal, carried infantry brigades to battle. They had painted the vehicles with fangs and flaming eyes, had mounted them with marauder corpses, and their banners fluttered in the wind. They raced toward the city, all guns blazing. Above them flew the choppers, the fighter jets, the drones. The great Resistance—they charged with all their might.

After hours of shelling the city, it was time to come home.

And from the ruins of Toronto, the enemy emerged to meet them.

Ravagers flew above, raining down plasma. Thousands of marauders scurried across the land, howling for war. And thousands of new horrors rolled forth too, great balls formed of twisting metal and spikes and crackling electricity, marauders rolling inside them, the aliens' version of tanks.

The two forces stormed toward each other.

Addy drove her sand tiger, a lumbering beast of steel she had dubbed Matilda. She gripped the controls with both hands, guiding the heavily armored vehicle. She had fought her first battle as a sand tiger driver, all the way back at Fort Djemila eight years ago. She would fight her last battle from one too. Her old brother-in-arms, that little bastard Pinky, stood in the gun turret, firing the machine gun. An infantry squad gathered below him, waiting in Matilda's hold, prepared to leap out once they entered the ruins. Hundreds of other sand tigers roared around them. Addy drove at the vanguard, leading the charge.

The marauders grew closer.

Addy lit a cigar and grinned.

"Let's kill some bugs," she said.

With a sound that shook the Earth, the two forces slammed together.

The sand tiger plowed into several marauders and spun madly. All around her, thousands of vehicles crashed into the enemy. Claws tore at them. Jaws ripped into iron hulls. The marauders' spherical vehicles rolled everywhere, lashing their scythes, crashing through the human assault. Above, the jets and ravagers slammed together, burning, crashing down. Addy screamed, gripping the steering wheel, spinning madly, trying to steady the sand tiger.

"Addy, damn it!" Pinky shouted from the gun turret. "Are you drunk?"

"I'm trying!" she shouted. "Fuck!"

Back at Fort Djemila, her sand tiger had plowed over the scum like a car over cockroaches. But the marauders were larger and tougher. Every one she hit knocked her back. Matilda weighed over sixty metric tons, but the vehicle could barely slog through these aliens. The creatures clawed at the armored hull, rammed into the front, and bit at the caterpillar tracks.

Addy was just glad that sand tigers had been upgraded since the scum war. Back then, Marco and Lailani had stood in an open gun turret, exposed to the enemy; he had fired the machine gun, while Lailani had spun the winch to aim it. The new model had a closed turret, protecting Pinky, and a gun he could move and fire at once.

"Pinky, the marauder attacking our tracks!" Addy shouted. "Shoot it down or we're dead!"

His machine gun blazed. Through a monitor, she saw the bullets slam into the marauder biting at their caterpillar tracks. The creature squealed and fell back, eyes popping. Addy pressed down on the gas, and they charged forward.

"Pinky, ahead of us!"

"I got 'em!" he cried, and his machine gun fired at the marauders ahead.

Some of the creatures fell. Addy drove Matilda another few meters forward.

More marauders leaped onto them. Matilda was encased in thick plates of metal that could take a grenade like a prize fighter taking a mosquito bite. The marauders dented that armor like knives into rotting wood. They tore one armored plate free. Claws ripped into Matilda's hull, and the crew inside—a squad of infantrymen—shouted and stabbed at the beast.

"Pinky!"

"I see him." Pinky wheeled his machine gun downward and fired. His bullets shattered the skulls along the marauder's back, but he missed the creature's eyes. The marauder yanked the crack wider, and its jaws entered Matilda. Inside the sand tiger, a soldier screamed, blood spurting. His comrades fired their guns. Bullets slammed into the invading marauder, and the creature finally slipped off the hull, leaving a gaping hole.

"Fuck," Addy said as she drove onward. Sand tigers were falling all around her. Nearby, the tanks were slogging it out, battling for every meter. Their cannons kept firing, knocking back marauders, only for more aliens to replace them. All the while, the ravagers flew above, swooping to rain down plasma like dragons burning charging knights. The ravagers outnumbered the Resistance's helicopters and jets a hundred to one, overwhelming the human air force, tossing the flying machines down.

They were still several kilometers from the city.

It felt like a galaxy away.

Addy pressed the gas pedal to the floor, charging forward.

"Steve, you with me?" she said into her communicator.

He answered from his own sand tiger. "Right behind ya, babe. I'm the one with the dead marauder dangling off his nose."

Addy looked through the reverse viewport. She saw his sand tiger rolling behind Matilda. A dead marauder hung from his front, claws stuck in the metal shielding.

"Nasty booger you got there, lover boy," she said. "Want me to shoot it off for ya?"

"You guys keep shooting at the marauders ahead," Steve said. "Let's plow through those buggers. Last one to Toronto is a rotten marauder egg."

Addy kept driving, but the marauders were everywhere. She slammed into another one. Pinky shot it back, but three more marauders replaced it, lashing at the hull. A claw tore through the front shielding, emerging by Addy's head. She winced, pulled out a pistol, and when the claw pulled back, she fired through the hole. She hit the marauder's eye, then slammed into the shrieking alien. Matilda rolled over the creature, crunching its legs.

"Fucking hell, our armor was built to withstand cannon fire," she muttered. "And those claws are ripping through us like we're tinfoil."

Already, across the field, sand tigers and tanks lay overturned, burning, torn apart. Marauders were ripping off the armor and feasting on the soldiers within. Gunfire blazed. Infantry warriors, their vehicles destroyed, were fighting afoot; they weren't meant to fight yet, not until they entered the city. The ravagers kept streaming above, spewing fire. One of the living ships flew ahead of Addy, scooping up infantrymen with its claws, then scattering them across the field. A second ravager swooped directly above her, and its plasma rained.

"Incoming!" Addy shouted, pushing down on the gas.

Matilda rumbled a few meters forward, slammed into several marauders, and ground to a halt.

An instant later, the plasma showered them.

Addy screamed.

She covered her face.

Flames leaped through the crack beside her, licking her arm, melting the body armor. She cried out and ripped off the searing pieces. She heard soldiers screaming in the hold, and she glanced over her shoulder to see that the flames had entered the sand tiger. Soldiers burned.

Fuck.

Addy leaped out of the driver's seat. She stepped into the hold, cringed at the flames, and grabbed a fire extinguisher. She sprayed foam as the soldiers screamed.

When the flames died, she saw that the soldiers had opened the back hatch, that several had escaped the inferno. Two had remained inside the sand tiger. They lay, charred and bloody, not moving. Addy couldn't tell if they were dead or alive.

The hatch was still open.

A marauder stood outside, staring at her.

The beast leaped into Matilda.

Addy, without an instant to think, sprayed foam from her fire extinguisher, blinding the alien.

The creature slammed into her, jaws snapping. Teeth tore through her bulletproof vest. One of her grenades tore loose and rolled. She screamed, fell back, and the marauder pinned her down. She raised her pistol, but claws swiped it aside. Her rifle was pinned under her back. The creature drooled above her, cackling. The foam dripped off its eyes.

"I know you," the marauder said. Its tongue reached down to lick her face. "Addy . . ."

She screamed and struggled to free herself but could not. It was crushing her. She couldn't breathe. She reached blindly, seeking a weapon, found none. The jaws opened wide above her, and she stared into the gullet of the beast.

With a battle cry, Pinky dropped from the gun turret onto the creature's back.

"Hey, you son of a bitch!" Pinky grabbed the marauder's horns. "Get the fuck out of our ride!"

The marauder shrieked, voice echoing in the hold, so loud Addy's ears rang. Riding the creature like a mechanical bull, Pinky drew a knife and slammed it down—right into an eye.

The marauder screamed and leaped upward with incredible force.

Pinky slammed against the ceiling, crying out.

Addy winced to hear a bone snap.

The marauder landed on the floor. Pinky still clung to its back, his arm at an odd angle. But still the little bastard fought, stabbing his knife down again, taking a second eye.

The marauder yowled and jumped up again, slamming once more against the metal ceiling.

Pinky howled.

The broken bone pushed through skin.

Addy managed to rise to her feet, to grab her rifle. She aimed just as Pinky took out a third eye. She fired but she missed the fourth and last eye. Her ears pounded.

The marauder leaped again, slamming Pinky onto the ceiling—again, again, crushing the little soldier, and Pinky kept screaming.

Addy fired a bullet. She missed again. Again. Again.

The marauder finally managed to rip Pinky off and toss him aside. When the creature leaped at Addy, she fired her last bullet, hitting the creature's final eye.

The marauder slammed down dead, burying Pinky beneath it.

Gunfire blazed outside. A marauder fell, riddled with bullets. Steve leaped into the sand tiger, his rifle smoking.

"Addy!" he said.

"Help me!" She grabbed the marauder pinning Pinky down, grimacing. "Steve, help me lift this fucker."

It was like lifting a dead horse. They both groaned, straining, shoving against it. Finally they managed to toss the dead alien outside. Steve pulled the hatch shut, though the hull was still cracked. The battle raged on across the field.

Covered in blood, lying on the floor, Pinky groaned.

"Steve, you got another driver for your ride?" Addy said. "Can you man the gun above?"

Steve nodded. "I'm on it, babe."

He scurried up the ladder into the gun turret, and while Matilda was immobile, at least Steve was now firing the machine gun.

Addy needed to get back to the driver's seat. Any instant now, a ravager might burn them. She had to keep storming forward with the others.

But instead, she knelt above Pinky. She touched his cheek.

"Pinky! Pinky, stay with me, you bastard."

He looked up at her, blinking. His arm was a mess. Half his face was bloodied, crushed.

"Addy . . ." he managed to whisper, hoarse, voice slurred.

Fingers shaking, she rummaged through her medical kit. She slammed a needle into him, giving him a shot of morphine.

"I'm here, Pinky," she said. "You're all right. Just a bit uglier than normal, but that's not much of a difference."

He coughed. His teeth were loose. His back was crooked, she saw. He had soiled himself.

His spine is broken, she thought.

"My name is . . . Peter . . ." he managed to whisper.

She clasped his hand. "All right, Peter. You hang in there. We'll get you a medic soon and he'll stitch you up. You might just need a metal spine to go with your metal legs. Kinda like Corporal Diaz, remember?"

His hand shook in hers. His hand was so small. Like a child's hand.

"Tell Poet," Pinky rasped. "Tell him . . . I'm sorry. Tell him I'm sorry. That . . . I'm his friend."

"I will," Addy whispered, tears in her eyes.

Pinky managed to give her a crooked, bloody smile. "Win this war, Addy. For the Dragons Platoon."

She nodded, her tears splashing him. "I will."

His breath died.

He stared up at the bloody ceiling, the smile locked on his face.

Addy returned to the driver's seat. The cracked sand tiger, with Steve now in the gun turret, kept driving.

But the battlefield was ugly.

Everywhere Addy looked, she saw the ruin of the Resistance. A helicopter lay smashed nearby, burnt pilots inside its wreckage. The husks of tanks smoked everywhere. Thousands of dead soldiers lay across the field, and marauders were cracking their skulls open to feast on the brains. Much of the Resistance was still fighting, but they were struggling for every meter of ground, and Toronto was still several kilometers away.

And the damn ravagers still covered the sky.

We're not going to make it, Addy realized.

She stared at the ruins ahead. Malphas was there. She was so close to killing him.

But we'll die outside his door. We can't break through.

The ravagers streamed above, and more plasma fell. Addy cursed, swerved her sand tiger, and dodged a jet of fire. She kept plowing forward, slamming into marauders, desperate to reach the city, knowing already that she could not.

CHAPTER TWENTY-FIVE

The Firebirds streamed through space, all guns blazing.

All around them, the battle for Earth flared with light and fire and searing metal.

Above them, the *Minotaur* was ramming into the two massive cube-ships. Below them, Earth was burning, the bombs exploding. And here around them, everywhere, thousands of them, flew the ravagers.

Captain Julian Bryan clutched his joystick, leading his squad of Firebirds.

"All right, boys and girls, stay in formation and let's blast those sons of bitches," he said. "Remember, don't get drawn into a brawl in orbit. Our destination is Toronto. Let's rock this joint."

They stormed down toward the planet—his fifteen starfighters and around them hundreds more.

The ravagers charged at them from all sides, plasma flaring.

Julian fired.

His heat-seeking missile flew, curved, and slammed between the claws of a ravager, hitting its fiery innards. The ship exploded.

"Remember, guys, aim for the fire," Julian said. "Don't waste ammo on their hulls; they're too heavily armored. Get 'em to open their claws and hit 'em where it hurts."

Enemy fire blasted toward him. He swooped, releasing another heat-seeking missile. It rose and hit the ravager, and the alien ship exploded, scattering severed claws. Julian thrust his Firebird forward, barrel-rolling, dodging the shrapnel. One cloven ravager claw, the size of a tree, slammed into a Firebird behind him, knocking the starfighter into a tailspin. Plasma took out another bird. The rest of his squad were firing their own missiles, cutting a path through the ravagers ahead.

"Forward, to Earth!" Julian said. "With me—spear formation!"

All around him, the other Firebird squads were charging at the ravagers. The living ships grabbed starfighters in their claws and ripped them apart. Walls of fire rose. Ships chased one another in dog fights, plasma and missiles and bullets flying. More Firebirds fell. Julian pulled his ship up, dodging a charging ravager, then spun and sprayed it with bullets. When the ship turned toward him, fire blasting, he shot another missile. The alien ship exploded.

Another one of his Firebirds shattered. Its pilot ejected, only for a blast of plasma to roast him.

Julian pulled his starfighter back toward Earth. The atmosphere was close now, only a few hundred kilometers away.

Between him and the blue sky were still thousands of enemy ships.

No fear.

He stormed forth.

No pain.

He flew through the fire.

For Earth.

He fired his missiles.

The ravagers slammed into his squadron, tearing Firebirds apart. He heard his comrades screaming. He saw them dying. A burnt corpse slammed into his cockpit and flew off, smearing blood. Plasma flew toward Julian, and he flew left and right, up and down, unleashing his arsenal.

He fired his Gatling guns, trying to hit the ravagers' flaming mouths. He hit them with bullets. He blinded them with photon blasts. One ravager clipped his wing, and he spun madly, spraying bullets, finally steadying himself.

Around Julian, scores of Firebirds burned and fell down toward the planet.

Squads shattered and reformed.

More pilots fell.

Behind him, the *Minotaur* was still roaring, a wounded bull, battling the behemoths.

I'm going to die here, Julian thought. *We're all going to die.*

He bared his teeth.

No.

"Hey, boys and girls," Julian said, broadcasting his words to the entire wing. "You remember the Garrote Move from flight school?"

One of the squad leaders answered. "Yeah, you mean, the move we were told to never, ever use?"

"That's the one!" Julian said. "I say it's time to give her a try. What say you?"

The other Firebirds kept firing missiles and bullets, unable to break through.

"Let's roll the dice!" came the reply.

With a few quick commands back and forth, the Firebirds changed formation.

They charged toward the enemy.

Instead of scattering and looping, they kept flying straight forward, and each Firebird blasted out cables from its sides.

The cables were normally used for docking on unusual surfaces—an asteroid, say, or even the back of a larger starcraft. The Garrote Move had never been tried in actual battle.

But it works in theory, Julian told himself, wincing.

His cables attached to the Firebirds at his sides.

Their cables snapped onto his starfighter.

A hundred Firebirds charged, forming a great net of metal cables between them.

The plasma roared toward them.

Julian cringed as the flames washed around his ship.

The cables slammed into the ravagers.

"Release them!" Julian cried, hitting a button.

The cables detached from the Firebirds, tangling around the ravagers.

The ravagers spun madly, unable to navigate, trapped in the net. They crashed into one another. They burst on impact. Ravager after ravager careened. Several slammed into the cube-ships, punching holes into the hulls.

The surviving Firebirds—by God, so few remained—flew onward.

They reached the atmosphere.

They plunged into the sky, the fires of atmospheric entry burning around them.

They roared over the Atlantic, flying at thousands of kilometers per hour.

They flew close to the water, blazing forth toward the coast. They stormed over forest and field and the ruins of cities—two hundred Firebirds, the last among tens of thousands.

They flew until they saw the ruins of Toronto ahead and the battle that raged there.

Julian lost his breath.

He had fought in many battles. As a young lieutenant, barely out of flight school, he had battled the scum at Abaddon. As an experienced captain, he had fought marauders at Pluto, at the Starship Graveyard, at Mars. But Julian had never seen a battle like this, never seen such destruction.

The city lay in ruins. Barely any buildings still stood, only the husks of some skyscrapers. Across the countryside, leading to the ruins, smoked the wreckage of thousands of tanks, troop carriers, trucks, and fallen helicopters. Thousands of corpses littered the fields.

But still the Resistance fought.

Still their surviving armored vehicles were trying to reach the city. Still their artillery fired. Still their infantry marched.

And more kept falling.

The marauders were everywhere, leaping onto humans, ripping them apart. Great mechanized spheres, bristly with blades, were rolling between the human troops, marauders operating them from within. The ravagers swooped everywhere, plucking up soldiers in their jaws, breathing fire, tormenting the Resistance.

Here was the great human uprising—and they were losing.

Julian tightened his grip on his joystick.

These ravagers might have destroyed tanks, helicopters, and even fighter jets. But they hadn't faced Firebirds yet.

"All right, pilots," Julian said. "Spearhead battle formations. Full assault mode. Let's tear these bastards apart."

The Firebirds swooped toward the city.

The ravagers shrieked and turned up toward them, spurting up fire.

The Firebirds blazed forth their wrath.

Missiles, bullets, and photon blasts tore into the enemy. Ravagers exploded, careened, and slammed down onto the city.

"Phoenix Squadron, get the bastards on the ground!" Julian said. "With me."

The Firebirds dived and fired their machine guns, tearing through formations of marauders in the field. The creatures screamed and died. The Firebirds rose toward the sun, spun, swooped, and fired again, ripping apart the lines of marauders. Their spherical vessels burst. Their severed claws flew.

Emboldened, the Resistance soldiers cheered and stormed forth, charging toward the city.

And below, Julian saw her.

It had to be her.

She stood atop a tank, waving a flag with a blue sphere on a black field. A cigar thrust out from her mouth. An ivory sword hung from her side, and her golden hair shone in the sun.

"Addy," Julian whispered.

Marauders leaped toward her, and Julian fired his machine guns, tearing them down. Addy and her armored vehicles kept moving, crossing the last kilometer to the city ruins.

Julian and his Firebirds kept flying.

Firebird after Firebird fell.

They were the last pilots. They were the survivors, the best at their trade. They were the pride of humanity. They tore down ravagers. They plowed through marauders.

Yet the enemy ships outnumbered them by hundreds to one. More kept flying toward the Firebirds, rising from the city like flies from a corpse.

The fire was everywhere.

Julian dodged one spray of plasma. Another blast hit him, and he spun, barely steadied himself. At his side, a Firebird burned. Another crashed, hitting a crumbling skyscraper, shattering what remained of the building.

Julian gripped the controls.

If I go down, I go down fighting. For Earth. With courage. With honor.

A blast hit him.

His engine caught fire.

Julian screamed, and even as his Firebird dived down, aflame, he kept firing bullets. He kept killing the enemy.

He hit the ground, slamming into a host of marauders, ripping into them.

His cockpit cracked.

His starfighter kept driving forth, scraping across asphalt, plowing through the enemy.

The marauders screamed everywhere.

The fallen starfighter screeched to a halt along the city streets.

Julian moaned, head bleeding. His leg was twisted. The bone was broken.

With shrieks, the marauders leaped onto the Firebird. Their claws shattered the cockpit. Julian reached for his pistol. He fired. Again. Again. The bullets glanced off them. The aliens grabbed his hand and tore it off, and Julian screamed.

The aliens paused for an instant. A hundred or more circled the crashed starfighter.

Julian knew he could not fight them all off.

He smiled thinly, delirious with pain.

This is heroism, Grandpa.

Several bombs still hung from his Firebird's weapons racks.

The marauders leaped into the cockpit and tore into him. As they ripped his belly open, Julian pressed the button.

The bombs detached, hit the ground, and fire raged, and—

CHAPTER TWENTY-SIX

Sitting at the helm of the *Minotaur*, General Petty fired the cannons and drove his ship forward, ramming into one of the hulking marauder cubes.

The great alien ship, large as a mountain, slammed into its brother.

Petty fired again.

Again.

He hit the cannons one last time—firing the *Minotaur*'s nuclear weapons.

Massive explosions tore through space.

Blinding light flared over the *Minotaur*'s bridge.

Petty yanked on the controls, and the hulking *Minotaur* rumbled into the distance.

The two enemy cubes shattered into millions of pieces that rained down into the Atlantic below.

For a moment—only a moment—Petty allowed himself to breathe.

Below him, a path of clear space and empty sky led to Earth.

Behind him, thousands of enemy ships still flew.

And here it is, Petty knew. *My choice. Two paths. Death upon my world or death above it.*

He gazed down at Toronto. He magnified the image on his viewport.

His heart sank.

The Resistance was struggling to advance.

The *Minotaur*'s fleet of Firebirds was doing some damage, but barely any remained.

Soon the war would end. And the marauders would reign supreme upon the world.

And Petty knew his path.

"Osiris, are you with me?" he said.

The android lay on the floor, torn in two. Her legs twitched in the corner. Her upper half lay slumped nearby, spilling out cables and electronics. Around her, several bridge officers lay dead.

"I . . . am here . . ." The android blinked at him, voice staticky. "I . . . malfunction."

Petty guided his ship down, closer to Earth, cannons firing at the ravagers around him. "Osiris, I need you to interface with the *Minotaur*. I need your help. We're going to attempt a Samson Maneuver."

Osiris blinked at him. "Sir! There's no recovering from a Samson Maneuver! The *Minotaur* can enter the atmosphere, but she'll never rise into space again."

Petty nodded, flying closer to Earth. "Yes, Osiris. This is our last stand. Last flight of the *Minotaur*." He smiled softly. "She had a good run."

A Samson Maneuver. In theory, it should work. In practice, it had never been attempted.

We won't go down as scrap metal, he thought. *We go down in a blaze of glory.*

"Yes, sir. Interfacing with the ship now, sir." Osiris nodded from the floor, unable to move but able to reach the controls wirelessly. "Should I guide her down, sir?"

He shook his head. "I'll fly her, Osiris. You keep controlling the shields, the engines, the cannons. When I give the order, I want you to launch our landing craft and send our marines to the surface." He gripped the controls. "No offense, but it takes a human touch for this."

He increased speed.

"All marines!" he boomed into his communicator. "Into your exoframes and into your landing craft. Prepare for launch!"

He kept diving.

The *Minotaur*—her hull cracked and dented, her shields nearly gone, her wounds leaking smoke—plunged toward Earth.

Ravagers rose to meet them. The ship barreled through them. The cannons kept firing. They dived into the atmosphere like a whale into the ocean.

Air shrieked around them. Fire roared. The ship creaked. Shields tore off the hull and flew. The ship rocked madly and control panels rattled.

"She's falling apart, sir!" Osiris cried.

"Do what you can to keep her together! Seal the leaking decks! All power to the shields!"

It was only a minute. It couldn't have been longer. But that minute of entering the atmosphere, flying a ship the size of a skyscraper, was the longest minute of Petty's life.

The ship rattled.

More shielding tore free.

Fire blazed across the ship.

An entire deck collapsed.

Flames engulfed them.

They plunged down, crashing through the clouds of ravagers, cannons carving a path before them. From below, they must have appeared as a massive asteroid, falling with the vengeance of the gods, heralding extinction.

He could see Toronto below. He guided the ship toward the ruins.

Twenty kilometers above the surface, he cried out, "All marines! Deploy, deploy!"

Hatches opened on the *Minotaur*'s belly. The landing craft emerged, one by one, firing their guns. Each held a platoon of space marines, the deadliest warriors in the Human Defense Force, each fighter encased in an exoframe. Their vessels swooped, mighty warships in their own right, blasting their cannons.

From the ruins of the city, the ravagers rose to meet them.

Hundreds of these living starships flew upward.

Then thousands.

The landing craft blasted their cannons, trying to carve a way through. Ravagers slammed into one vessel, tearing it apart. Plasma washed over a second landing craft. Their marines ejected, plunging toward the surface in their exoframes.

But most of the ravagers were attacking the *Minotaur*, biting at it like piranhas at a charging whale.

Petty gritted his teeth and kept flying, the yoke wheel threatening to rip from his hands.

He leveled off a kilometer above the city, raising their nose. The swarm intensified. Ravagers shattered their hull. They slammed into the bridge, shattering another viewport. Claws tore through the metal only meters away from Petty. Air shrieked through the holes.

"Sir!" Osiris screamed.

"Keep us firing." He bared his teeth. "Empty our arsenal down to one percent."

Their cannons blasted.

Their last missiles, bullets, photons bolts, and lasers—all fired in a storm.

Ravagers fell below them.

"More power to the engines!" Petty said.

They increased speed. They skimmed the skyscrapers of the city—a massive ship as large as the crumbling buildings below. They drove through the swarm of ravagers, knocking hundreds back, snapping their claws. Explosions filled the sky. Metal hailed onto the ruins.

The *Minotaur* roared.

The last flight of an ancient ship. The last cry of a legend.

Below, the Resistance was struggling to cross the last few hundred meters to the city. A swarm of marauders still covered the ground, forming a living wall of claws and fangs around the ruins. The human tanks and infantry could not advance.

"Osiris," said Petty, gliding the ship downward, "would you like to tell one last joke?"

"Why did the android cry, sir?" she said, tears in her eyes. Her engineers had actually given her tears. "Because it was an honor to serve her commander. Goodbye, sir. I am proud."

He flew lower, his cannons blasting the marauders on the ground, slaying hundreds.

The creatures tried to flee.

Petty emptied the ship's last reserves of ammunition, tearing through their lines.

He took a deep breath.

He slammed down onto the army of marauders.

Hundreds shattered below him.

The *Minotaur* kept plowing forward, digging ruts through the earth outside the city, tearing up marauders, scattering aliens like a plow driving through a field of insects.

Fire filled the bridge.

The walls shattered.

The engines tore off, rolled, and exploded.

Cannons detached and tumbled into the crowds of aliens, crushing them.

The hull cracked open.

Hundreds, maybe thousands of marauders tore apart.

They kept driving forward, too fast to stop, and slammed into buildings, knocking them down, digging up streets, scattering houses. And with every meter, they crushed more marauders.

A steel beam slammed onto Petty. Shards of metal leaped up from the floor. The ceiling collapsed above him. His instruments exploded, showering him with glass and metal and silicon. Fire raged.

Finally, in the heart of downtown Toronto, countless marauders around them, the *Minotaur* came to a halt.

Petty lay on the floor.

Debris covered him.

He groaned, reached out, struggling to rise. Osiris reached out to him, trapped under a metal beam. Their hands clasped.

From outside, he heard the screeches of a thousand marauders racing toward them, ready to feed.

But I killed many, Petty thought. *I did my part. I went down with pride. A warrior.* He pulled his daughter's tags from his pocket and clutched them as the marauders advanced. *I'll be with you soon, daughter.*

With his other hand, he pulled out his pistol.

The marauders leaped in.

Petty fired his gun.

CHAPTER TWENTY-SEVEN

Addy stood atop the tank, banner raised.

"Forward!" she cried hoarsely. "Into the city!"

Her tank roared forth beneath her. Thousands of other vehicles—tanks, Humvees, bulldozers, sand tigers, motorcycles, even mechanical horses—followed. Thousands of infantry soldiers ran.

The massive warship had plunged from the sky, had plowed a road through the ruins. The Resistance now charged down this path of hot metal and uprooted asphalt. Lines of tanks, several deep, formed the flanks, holding back the marauders that still lived. The infantry ran between them. Addy rode at the vanguard, rifle in one hand, banner in the other.

After so long at war, so many battles, so many scars, she entered her city.

Toronto was not an old city. It had never survived ancient wars like Jerusalem, falling and rising again, time after time. It had never been the center of the world like Rome or Athens or New York City. It had never kick-started revolutions like Paris, never seen empires conquer and crumble. It was a city in the far northern corner of the world, a city not used to great deeds or monumental events. A city that had never been of much importance. Yet to Addy, it was the most important city in the world. It was her home.

Not, she supposed, that much was left of it.

As the tanks rumbled into the city, she saw only ruins. Half of the buildings had fallen. The others were punched full of holes, burnt, crumbling. The marauder webs were everywhere, draping over buildings, burning on the streets, and some still held corpses. It was eerily quiet. Only sporadic gunfire sounded, and they saw only a handful of marauders that quickly fled before them.

Addy stood atop her tank, speaking to its driver through her communicator, leading the army through the city. Lord Malphas, they said, had taken residence atop the ruined library. He had chosen her house to build his hive. Addy took the old roads home.

The city lay in ruins, but here was still her home, and tears filled her eyes as she rode. She passed by a Firebird burning in a smoldering yard, a place where she had once played soccer. An old factory where she had worked one summer, assembling shells for the war, lay in a pile of rubble, and corpses—both human and marauder—lay atop it. The street where she had been born was gone, just a pile of ash strewn with corpses.

As she traveled down the streets, the army behind her, Addy saw two cities superimposed. She saw the ruins, the devastation, the death. But like ghosts, translucent patches of color, she saw her memories overlaying the city. Children playing.

Trees rustling. Families laughing. Her and Marco. Her life. Her youth.

"We will rebuild," she whispered, tasting her tears. "This city will rise again. It will be good again. I will be happy again. And you'll be back here, Marco. You have to come back."

Thousands of tanks and soldiers were in the city now, traveling down the highway, heading toward the library. Still they saw barely any marauders, only a handful that scurried away from their advance.

The tank's hatch opened behind her, and Steve climbed onto the roof with her. He stared around him in amazement.

"Fuck me," he said. "The city is empty. The buggers all spilled out of Toronto to face us on the field. We won this war."

Addy bit her lip. Her fingers tightened around her gun. A marauder stared at her from a rooftop, hissed, then fled. But she had seen no fear in its eyes.

"No," she said. "This is too easy. They're planning something."

The tanks rumbled onward down the street. Addy raised her assault rifle, staring from side to side. They traveled deeper. She lifted her communicator and hailed the back of the line.

"How are we doing back there?"

One of her officers answered from several kilometers behind. "There are still several thousand marauders in the field, but they seem beat. They're barely putting up a fight. We're bringing the last few troops into the city now."

Addy breathed heavily. The marauders in the field—barely fighting anymore. The marauders in the city—fleeing before them. There were a few ravagers that still flew above, but they seemed disjointed, not even blowing fire.

Her heart pounded, and cold sweat washed her.

"It's a trap," she whispered, then spoke into her communicator. "Keep a brigade of tanks and infantry outside the city! Don't let anyone else in! We—"

Shrieks and screams flowed over the communicator.

"What's going on?" Addy shouted.

The officer on the other end cursed. "They're raising walls! The marauders! They're raising walls of metal and stone! They're blocking the roads!"

"They're trapping us in the city," Addy whispered, then shouted, "Turn back! Blast open those barricades! We have to get out, we—"

From the roofs and alleyways around her, countless marauders shrieked and pounced.

From the sky above, thousands of ravagers swooped, spewing fire.

The trap is sprung.

For an instant, Addy could only stare in horror.

They herded us into our graveyard.

Then she screamed and fired her gun.

Then I die fighting.

The marauders were everywhere. The swarm rose from the sewers, emerged from windows, and coated the city. The ravagers hid the sky. Steve tried to leap back into the tank, to pull Addy in with him, when three marauders slammed into the tank, grabbed the caterpillar tracks, and lifted the vehicle. They overturned the tank as if it were a mere sedan. Addy and Steve leaped, landed on their backs on the pavement, and fired their guns as the enemy drove in from all sides.

All across the road, soldiers screamed.

Addy crawled, huddled by the overturned tank, fired her gun, and stared.

A few meters away, a tank burned. Burning soldiers emerged from inside. Another tank rolled, hit a building, and marauders tore it apart. Everywhere, the infantry soldiers were running, fighting, falling, dying. A horse ran through the battlefield, burning, wailing. The ravagers kept roaring along the highway, only several meters overhead, raining down their inferno. Addy pushed herself against the overturned tank, cringing, the fire licking her boots.

All down the road, they burned. Soldiers. Men. Women. Boys and girls. Some barely even teenagers. Living torches, they ran, screaming. A few meters away, a marauder was tugging out a soldier's entrails, cackling as the boy wept, as he called for his mother. Beside them, a marauder carved open the skull of a screaming woman, picked out her brain, and tossed the corpse aside. A war dog wandered the battlefield, his jaw ripped off.

"Break out," Addy whispered into her communicator. Her hand shook. "You have to break out of the city."

She heard only screams.

Then static.

She rose to her feet. She took a step, dazed. The highway curved upward to the north, back toward the countryside. She gazed along a road of death.

A hundred thousand soldiers or more covered that highway.

And they were falling. They were dying.

The ravagers swooped in wave after wave, blasting their plasma. The soldiers tried to flee onto side roads, only for marauders to cut them down. They were trapped along this artery. Some tried to retreat out of the city, only to hit the barricades the marauders had raised. And still more of the creatures were emerging from every hole in the city, screeching, laughing, feasting.

"We should never have come here," Addy whispered as soldiers died around her. "After all this, to fail, to die, so close to home . . ." She lowered her head. "I'm sorry, Marco. I'm sorry, Earth. I failed."

She fired her last bullet.

The marauders were moving in from all sides.

Addy reached out and clasped Steve's hand. He pulled her against him, wincing. The ravagers descended from above, fire gathering.

"I love you, Addy," Steve whispered.

"I love you, Steve." She held him tightly, waiting for the fire.

Light.

Light flared above her.

Addy cringed, expecting the agony of fire.

But it was a soft light. A white light. Not the furious red light of plasma.

She blinked and stared up.

A beam, pure and white as moonlight, slammed into a ravager and knocked the ship back.

More beams flared, hitting other ravagers, destroying the ships.

Light flowed across the street, blast after blast, searing through marauders like sunlight through a magnifying glass burning ants.

Addy stared upward, squinting, and she saw them there.

Starships.

Thousands of starships.

They were circular, shaped like three disks, the outer disks metallic, the central ones glowing with light. The beams were blasting out from those central disks, tearing into the ravagers, burning marauders, filling the sky with light.

Addy gazed up at the ships, and tears flowed down her cheeks.

"The Ghost Fleet," she whispered. "You did it, Marco. You did it."

CHAPTER TWENTY-EIGHT

Finally, he was home.

Finally, he was flying over Toronto.

Finally, the great last battle was here.

The Ghost Fleet had come to fight.

Marco sat in the gun turret of the *Marilyn*, flying over the ruins of his city, firing the cannons. All around him flew thousands of soulships, small fighter vessels, no larger than his own ship. As he fired the cannons, the yurei ships blasted out beams of light, tearing into the thousands of ravagers that flew over Toronto, burning the countless marauders that still scuttled below.

"We got here too late," Marco said as he fought, shelling the enemy. "The city has fallen."

From the bridge behind him, Ben-Ari answered. "No. We're not too late. Humanity still fights."

The *Marilyn* swerved and flew lower, gliding over a highway. Marco stared down and lost his breath.

"The Resistance," he whispered.

They had received signals from the Resistance on the outskirts of the solar system, had thought them already lost. But some still fought. Some soldiers still lived. They were trapped on a highway, ravagers above, marauders at their sides. Many lay dead across the road, and tanks burned.

But some still lived.

Marco's eyes watered.

"Addy, are you here?" he whispered.

A ravager flew toward them. Marco fired, and photon blasts hit the living ship, ripping it apart. A dozen other ravagers charged in formation. Soulships spun toward them, beaming out their rays, burning the enemy. The ravagers crashed into buildings below.

"Can anyone see her?" Marco said, struggling to keep his voice calm. "Can anyone see Addy?"

"I can't see her!" rose Kemi's voice from the helm.

"I can try to zoom in on soldiers below," said Lailani, sitting at the engineering station, "but—"

Ben-Ari interrupted them, voice harsh. "Abasi, you keep flying. Emery, keep those guns firing!"

Marco tightened his lips, trying to shove aside the fear. Thousands of corpses burned below. He couldn't bear the thought of Addy among them. He took a deep breath, aimed the *Marilyn*'s cannons at another ravager, waited for the ship to open its claws, and fired into its fiery mouth. The ravager tore apart, spilling eggs—the ship was pregnant—onto the city. With every breath, another ship crashed down, ravagers and soulships alike.

"Captain!" Lailani cried. She laughed. "I—"

Fire roared.

A ravager flew toward them.

Somebody screamed.

Claws grabbed the *Marilyn*, ripping into the hull.

"Emery, damn it!" Ben-Ari cried.

Cursing, he spun the gun turret, aiming the cannon. The ravager was crushing their ship in its massive metal claws. A claw tore into the hull. Marco fired. Again. Again. Pulse after pulse of energy flew out, pounding the ravager. Finally the living ship released them, and they began to rise again, sputtering, only for another ravager to grab them.

The gun turret shattered open.

A claw ripped out the cannon.

Marco found himself staring into the jaws of a ravager.

Fire gathered, bathing him with heat, swirling like a cauldron of molten metal, ready to fill the gun turret.

Marco wanted to leap deeper into the ship. Instead, he raised his assault rifle, switched it to automatic, and emptied a magazine into the ravager's maw of flame.

He leaped out of the gunner's station as the ravager exploded.

The *Marilyn* rocked, dipped, rose again, and tilted. Smoke rose. Flames gripped the ship.

"The cannon's toast!" Marco cried.

"We're going down!" Kemi shouted, gripping the controls.

"I saw her!" Lailani said. "Marco, I—"

They slammed into the jagged top of a broken skyscraper.

They skidded higher, then plunged down.

They all screamed.

"Kemi!" Ben-Ari cried.

"I'm trying!" she said, gripping the joystick. "We've got only one engine left and a wing is broken, and—" She grimaced. "I'm bringing us down! Hold onto something!"

The battle raged around them as they shot downward. Ravagers and soulships were flying everywhere. Fire and light pounded the city below, killing both humans and marauders.

Kemi aimed the ship toward a highway.

Screaming, she tugged the stick back with both hands, desperate to raise the ship's nose.

Spilling fire and smoke, the *Marilyn* slammed onto the highway.

Marco thudded against a wall and reached out blindly. Strapped into her seat, Ben-Ari grabbed his hand. He clung to her.

The *Marilyn* screeched along the road, tearing into the asphalt, slamming into marauders on the way. Finally they veered off the road, hit a building, and lay still.

For a moment, they all sat in silence, breathing heavily.

"Kemi," Lailani finally said, "you suck at landing."

"It's not my fault I always have to land after being crushed by ravagers or a black hole," the pilot said.

Marco rose to his feet, legs shaking. "Kemi, whatever ship you fly on needs to come supplied with extra underwear."

She rolled her eyes. "Usually my passengers are potty trained."

The door to the bridge tore open.

A marauder sneered.

They all opened fire, killing the beast.

"All right, soldiers," Ben-Ari said. "We have a war to fight. And it's out there on the streets. If you're well enough to joke around, you're well enough to fight. Follow me."

They were four. Ben-Ari, their leader. Kemi, their pilot. Marco and Lailani, gunner and navigator. Friends. A family. Together, guns raised, they stepped out of the crashed *Marilyn* and onto the highway.

Soulships were landing around them. Hatches opened, and the yurei emerged. Normally, they were meek creatures, hiding in shadows, as dainty as mist. But in war, the yurei were terrifying. Their jaws extended halfway down their chests, lined with fangs. Their claws lashed. They carried crystal amulets that blasted out rays of light, and the beams seared through marauders. The yurei swept through the city like ghosts, casting their light, tearing into the enemy. From each soulship, these astral warriors emerged.

"God damn," Lailani muttered. "These ghosts are badasses."

The marauders were screeching, dying, but fighting back. One marauder grabbed a yurei and tore her open, scattering glowing white blood. Another leaped through a beam of light, losing three legs to the ray, but the marauder still landed on a yurei and bit deep. While soulships and ravagers battled above, the war raged on the streets, marauders and yurei fighting for every city block.

And humans were fighting too.

Marines ran in exoframes, firing their guns.

Tanks rolled down the roads, cannons blasting.

Infantry battled along the highways.

And there, standing atop a tank, she stood.

A tall woman, the wind blowing her short blond hair. A woman with a rifle in one hand, a banner in the other.

Marco stared at her, his breath catching.

Across the distance, she stared back.

Their eyes met.

Her eyes widened and she leaped off the tank. She stood on the road, staring.

Marco took a step closer to her.

She tilted her head, eyes narrowing.

Marco took another step.

She ran a few steps, froze, stared at him again, hesitating.

"Marco?" she whispered.

No. Marco didn't recognize her. It couldn't be her. She was different. Rawboned. Covered with blood and burns. Her hair was too short, her cheeks too gaunt. Her eyes were different. Haunted eyes. Hurt eyes. Eyes that had seen too much.

"Poet," she whispered, tears drawing white lines down her cheeks.

It was her.

Tears filled his own eyes.

Marco ran.

She ran toward him down the highway.

As the battle flared around them, she leaped into his arms, and he wrapped her in an embrace, squeezing her, and they wept together.

"Addy," he whispered, chest shaking with sobs. "Addy. Addy."

She touched his cheek. "I knew you'd come. You silly poet. You're late." She squeezed him in a crushing hug, not even letting him breathe. "I'm never letting you go again."

The others reached them. Kemi wrapped her arms around them. Ben-Ari followed, smiling through her tears. Lailani hopped onto them, clinging like a monkey, laughing and crying. Above and around them, the lights flared, the war continued, but here, for this moment, they were together again. Here for a moment the world was good.

"Now come on!" Addy finally said, pulling herself free. She took a shuddering breath. "Lord Malphas took over our library, Poet. Let's end this. Let's go home."

* * * * *

The city lay in ruins.

Kemi couldn't curb her tears.

My house is gone. Are my parents dead?

Her mechanical hand crackled. Electricity shocked her, making her jump. Kemi looked at her prosthetic.

It gave another crackle, and electricity raced across it. Kemi winced.

After Malphas had bitten off her hand—God, it had been nearly three years now—Kemi had replaced it with a weaponized prosthetic. Its battery had enough power to fire ten thousand bolts of pure energy, each strong enough to knock out a dinosaur.

And now the hand was thrumming, ready to burst.

Kemi had damaged it during her first crash, plunging through the black hole. Since then, its parts had jiggled, making her nervous. She couldn't even remove the damn thing, not with it connected to her nerves, to her skin, to her bones. It was a part of her.

A part that could kill her.

And now, in this second crash, she had damaged it further.

Now the disk on her palm, which could once blast out her energy bolts, hung loose. Now the parts inside jangled with every movement, including the battery.

One wrong move, Kemi thought, *and it'll blast enough energy to light up my bones like a neon skeleton.*

She reached into her pocket and pulled out the bandage she kept there. They had taught her in the army to always keep a bandage in her pocket. Gingerly, she wrapped it around her mechanical hand.

"We just got to win this war, then find a mechanic to fix you, hand," she said. "Don't blow me up before that, okay? Please don't blow up."

Around her, her friends were firing their assault rifles. The marauders still swarmed across the streets, battling humans and yurei.

Lailani raced up and grabbed Kemi—thankfully, by the good hand.

"Come on, Kemi!" she said. "We're heading to the library."

Kemi nodded. The library. The place where she had spent so much of her youth. She nodded and ran with the others, her broken hand chinking with every step.

Hold on, my hand, she thought. *And if you're alive, hold on, my parents. Soon this will be over. Soon I'll be with you again.*

CHAPTER TWENTY-NINE

For the first time in years, Marco went home.

He walked down Yonge Street, the road he had traveled countless times in his childhood and youth. He walked with his friends at his side. With Addy. With Kemi. With Lailani. With Ben-Ari. He walked toward his old library. He walked toward the beginning and the end.

Here my story began, he thought. *Here let my war end.*

The road lay in ruins, the old cafes and shops destroyed. The library was gone now too; he had seen it demolished before the marauders had even attacked. A new structure rose above the library's ruins. Marco shuddered to see it.

"A marauder hive," he said, pausing on the road.

Standing at his side, Addy hefted her assault rifle. "Ugly, ain't it?"

They stared at it together. Jagged metal shards, blocks of stone, and tarry black material—foul paste the marauders spewed—spiraled upward, forming a dark tower. Sticky webs, the strands as thick as ropes, draped across the structure, holding it together. It looked almost like a pile of rubble, not an actual dwelling.

Kemi stepped up beside him. Cradling her damaged prosthetic hand, she stared at the jagged tower. "That's what the overrun prison looked like, the one Captain Ben-Ari and I found. The marauders coated it with rocks and strands and that sticky black tar. This is a marauder dwelling all right." She cringed. "It looks just like the hive where Ben-Ari and I first saw Lord Malphas. Where he bit off my hand."

"He's not biting off any more of us," Marco said.

"Fuck no." Addy slammed a fresh magazine into her assault rifle, yanked back on the cocking handle, and spat. "It's time to squash some spiders." She placed a hand on Marco's shoulder. "Poet, old boy, let's go take our home back."

Ben-Ari and Lailani joined them, both loading their own rifles.

"Together again." Lailani spat into her palm, then held it out. "Like in the good old times. Siblings-in-arms."

"The Dragons Platoon," Ben-Ari said, taking Lailani's hand, and her voice softened. "Like in the good old days. We beat the scum emperor. We can beat Malphas too."

They all clasped their hands together. They looked at one another, silent, determined. Weapons held before them, they advanced toward the dark tower.

Behind them, the marauders and yurei were still fighting. Above, the ravagers and soulships still battled. But ahead, the street was empty. Only two marauders leaped toward the Dragons, quickly slain with bullets to the eyes. Without further resistance, they reached the hive.

Addy held out her arm. "Wait," she said. "What if it's a trap? Shouldn't we bomb the place from the air?"

"And then we'd never know if Malphas was killed," Ben-Ari said. "Even if we find a corpse under the wreckage, it would be too mangled to recognize." Her eyes flared with uncharacteristic rage. "I want to see the bastard. To recognize the monster who bit off Kemi's hand. Who landed me in prison. Who ruined the world. I want to stare into his eyes before I riddle them with bullets. Malphas told me once that we would meet again." She bared her teeth. "He was right."

Marco stared at his captain. It was rare to see her get angry. He wondered if the anger impaired her judgment, if perhaps Addy was right. He too, however, could see the wisdom of meeting their enemy face to face.

"A clean corpse of Malphas could be displayed to his forces," Marco said. "It would perhaps dissuade the marauders from further aggression. Maybe we can even capture Malphas alive, put him on trial, and—"

"No," Ben-Ari said. "We kill the bastard."

Marco nodded. "All right. We kill him."

He took another step toward the hive, but Ben-Ari reached out and stopped him.

"Emery," the captain said, "I've met Malphas before. You haven't. He's not like other marauders. He's larger, for one, twice the size of a normal marauder. But he's also smarter. I saw the intelligence in his eyes. I never forgot it. Cruel, vicious intelligence. Be careful in there. Whatever he might say to you, ignore it. The instant we see him, we shoot him." She looked at the others. "Is that clear?"

They all nodded.

A tall crack gaped open before them, allowing passage into the hive. Ben-Ari made to enter first, but Marco placed a hand on her shoulder.

"Ma'am," he said, "allow me. This is my home. If this is a trap . . . I should be the one to spring it."

She nodded. "I'll be right behind you." She smiled wryly. "Maybe not *right* behind you. In case of that trap." She gave him the smallest, yet the warmest of smiles Marco had ever seen.

At that brief moment, he loved his captain as much as he had ever loved anyone.

The words of Eldest returned to him.

One to die.

He tightened his lips, swallowing the terror.

Then let it be me.

He stepped into the hive.

A tunnel stretched ahead, its walls formed of marauder webs, tar, and stone. Marco took a few steps forward. He lit his flashlight. It felt like walking into the womb of a giant beast. Human corpses hung on the walls, some little more than skeletons, their skulls sawed open. They stank so badly Marco struggled not to gag.

He looked over his shoulder, reporting what he saw to the others. They entered the tunnel with him, lighting their own flashlights.

They walked deeper down the tunnel, passing by more corpses that hung on the walls. Some were the corpses of children. Some of babies. Some of the bodies were fresh and showed signs of torture. Some had been flayed.

Marco's revulsion grew. Many believed—himself included—that the war against the scum had been unnecessary, that Admiral Bryan's aggression had extended that war for too long. But there could be no doubt here. The marauders weren't merely mindless predators like the scum. The marauders were evil, and they delighted in it.

Marco took another few steps down the tunnel, then paused.

He sucked in air.

Weeping came from ahead. Human weeping.

A scream rose.

"Please, master!" rose a voice ahead. "No more! Please."

Marco narrowed his eyes.

His legs trembled.

He couldn't breathe.

He knew that voice. Impossible. Impossible!

The scream rose again, and Marco ran down the tunnel.

He burst into a large, hollow enclave where the library had once stood. The old bookshelves were gone. Marauder webs filled the place now, clinging to metal and stone towers. Shadows swirled like mist, and a hot stench assailed Marco's nostrils. Deep, inhuman laughter echoed.

He took another step forward, moving his flashlight back and forth.

Somebody sobbed.

Something creaked.

Shadows stirred.

Drops splashed onto Marco's hand. Blood.

Marco flicked his flashlight up, and his heart seemed to stop in this chest.

He inhaled sharply and pointed his gun.

Ben-Ari, Kemi, Addy, and Lailani—they ran up toward him, pointed their flashlights upwards too, and they gasped and cursed.

Addy aimed her gun.

"Wait!" Marco said. "He'll kill them. Oh God, he'll kill them."

Lord Malphas, the largest marauder Marco had ever seen, hung above like a rancid chandelier of black limbs, claws, and fangs, so large that if he dropped down, he would cover the five soldiers below.

Each of his six legs pinned down another prisoner, claws pointed at their hearts.

The prisoners were all human, all bound in webs, and all bleeding. Their skin was torn, their faces bruised, their bodies bleeding.

"Marco!" a prisoner cried out, and yes. He knew that voice. And his tears fell.

Impossible. It couldn't be her. She had died on Haven! He had seen her house burnt to ashes!

But it *was* her.

"Anisha," he whispered.

Another prisoner called his name. Then another. He had not recognized them at first, not in these shadows, not with blood and dirt covering them. But he recognized them now. Women he had known in Haven. Women he had loved, had hurt. Women he had thought were gone.

All but the last prisoner. The sixth prisoner.

The sixth prisoner was a man. Gray-haired. Middle-aged.

And Marco wept.

"Father," he said.

Addy's face turned red. Her hands trembled around her rifle.

"You fucking liar!" she shouted up. "Malphas, you fucking piece of shit liar! Carl Emery is dead! He's dead, you idiot!" She laughed hysterically, tears on her cheeks. "Heart attack. What is that, a fucking puppet?"

The massive horned marauder laughed—a grumbling voice like rolling thunder.

"Hello, Addy." The creature's voice was boulders rolling, bones cracking, blood dripping. "Hello, Lailani." Malphas opened his jaws in a lurid grin. "Hello again, Einav and Kemi." Finally his eyes turned toward Marco. "Hello, Marco. I have been waiting for you all. For a very long time."

The alien etched his claws along Father's chest.

Blood dripped.

"Father!" Marco shouted, trembling, unable to breathe. "It's impossible. Impossible!" Ben-Ari tried to calm him, but he ignored her, shouting. "You lie, Malphas! My father died three years ago!"

Father looked down at him from the web above. He was so thin, so ashen. "Son . . ."

"Yes, Marco," said Malphas, and his dripping tongue emerged to lick his teeth. "It is your father. He lives. A heart attack?" He cackled. "That is the story my slaves told your kind. I collected him, Marco. Long ago. The way I collected the others that you love. Like I collected Anisha, who screams so beautifully when I hurt her. Like I collected the rest of your harem, these females who cared for you, whom you betrayed, whom you doomed to torture and death."

Marco trembled so wildly he could barely hold onto his gun.

"Take me instead!" he shouted upward. "Take me, Malphas, and let them go! Take my life for theirs!"

The marauder's laughter grew. "Oh, dearest Marco . . . I already have you."

His stinger rose, and webs sprayed out. They hit the tunnel, blocking their escape. When Ben-Ari raced toward the blocked exit, another web shot out, grabbed her feet, and knocked her down. More webs wrapped around the captain, and she shouted, unable to free herself.

"Fuck this shit!" Addy shouted and opened fire on Malphas.

"Addy, no!" Marco shouted. "He'll kill them!"

He tried to grab her, but Addy kept shooting. Lailani shouted wordlessly and opened fire too.

But Malphas kept cackling. The bullets glanced off him harmlessly. One ricocheted and hit Ria, a sweet girl Marco had dated for a month on Haven. Another scraped across Anisha's side. Some bullets seemed to hit Malphas's eyes, but they caused him no harm. Marco caught the glimmer of protective shielding—like some alien contact lenses—coating them.

The massive marauder cast out more webs.

Strands caught Addy and Lailani's rifles and yanked them free. More strands wrapped around the two women, bundling them up, knocking them down. Ben-Ari screamed, struggling to free herself, before more webs wrapped around her mouth. Kemi too fell, strands trapping her, gluing her to the floor.

Marco grabbed a grenade. He was about to toss it, to break his way out, when webs wrapped around him too.

The strands pinned his arms to his sides. His grenade thumped against the floor, pin still inserted. Another strand lassoed his torso. He stood directly below Malphas, unable to move, only to gaze up into the beast's maw. Malphas's saliva dripped onto him, sizzling-hot and rancid.

"As I was saying, Marco," the alien said, "I already have you. Do you know why I took those that you love? Why I took your harem? Why I took your father? Not as bait, Marco. Not as hostages, not as a human shield." The alien's grin grew. "I took them for pleasure, Marco. For the pleasure of killing them as you watch. For the pleasure of seeing their deaths reflected in your eyes. For the pleasure of breaking your heart—like you broke their hearts. Yes, Marco. You hurt these people. You love them and you hurt them. Now it's time for me to hurt you. Now it's time to pay for your sins."

A strand yanked Marco's head back, forcing him to stare upward, forcing him to look.

Malphas grinned.

"Marco," Anisha whispered, hanging above, tears in her eyes. "I love you. I forgive you."

Malphas thrust his claws, piercing Anisha's chest.

"No!" Marco screamed.

Her blood fell around him. Anisha gazed down at him, smiling softly, and the life left her eyes.

"You fucking bastard!" Marco shouted.

Malphas laughed. "Good. Good! Such exquisite pain."

He thrust another leg, piercing another woman's chest.

Marco shouted, struggled against the strands, but could not free himself. His fellow soldiers were shouting too, trapped in the webs.

A third woman died.

A fourth.

A fifth.

All those women Marco had loved in Haven. All those women he had hurt. Now his heart broke for them.

"Such pain!" Malphas said. "Such beautiful tears! Such lovely screams! This is delightful, Marco. Your pain is so wonderful." He licked his lips. "It floods your brain. I can smell it. I will delight in feeding upon that brain soon. But not yet, Marco. Not yet. First you must watch me kill my last prisoner. Your father."

Marco trembled.

He gazed up at his father.

"Dad," he whispered. "I'm sorry."

Carl Emery gazed down at him. "I love you, son. Look away."

Marco nodded, sobbing, and closed his eyes.

But he could still hear his father gasp. Still hear the scream. Still hear the blood drip. And when he opened his eyes, Father was gone.

For a second time, I lost him.

Marco hung his head low.

"Why?" he whispered. "Why, Malphas?" He looked up through his tears, the strands still wrapped around him. "Why?" His voice rose louder. "Why do you torment me? What have I ever done to you?" He was shouting now, fists clenched. "We never hurt you! Why do you torture us? Why, you sick bastard, why?"

Malphas stared down at him. The mirth left the alien's face.

"Still you don't understand," the marauder said.

"So tell me!" Marco shouted.

Malphas snarled, rage filling his eyes. "I killed your father, Marco, because you killed mine. Because you killed thousands of my brothers and sisters."

"Bullshit!" Marco shouted. "I never met any of your kind before they invaded our worlds."

"Oh, but you did, Marco," said the alien. "You did long ago. On a distant, dry world. Deep in a dark hive. You killed the one you called the scum emperor. The one I called . . . Father."

Marco stared up at the alien. At the marauder.

"It can't be," Marco whispered. "You're not a scum. You're not a centipede! You're a different species!"

The marauder stared down at him. A massive creature, larger by far than a scum, a creature with six legs instead of thirty-six. A creature with massive jaws, with a bloated abdomen. A creature with sentience beyond anything the scum had possessed. But as Marco stared, he saw the same hard shell. The same claws tipping the legs. The same hunger. The same cruelty.

Lord Malphas spoke, voice deep and raspy. "Deep in the mines of a world you call Corpus, we were born. They created us there. You never did learn what the centipedes were creating in that mine, did you? You never did question the purpose of their experiments. Of the creatures they were breeding, half scum, half human. Hybrids with the physical strength of a centipede, with the sentience of a human. We were created there, Marco. We, the marauders. And I, Lord Malphas, was spawned from the cells of the scum emperor himself. He was my father. You killed him,

Marco. You and your friends. For years, I sought you. And now, Marco, now I will have my revenge."

Marco stared up in horror.

"You . . . are half human?" he whispered.

The creature nodded. "Yes, Marco. Half of my DNA came from the scum emperor. The other half came . . . from you."

"No," Marco whispered, trembling. "No. You're lying."

Malphas shook his massive horned head. "I'm not lying, Marco. Do you remember that time in Corpus? Touching a ball of flesh? Do you remember how it grew your face? My creators took your DNA then. In the burrows of Corpus, long after you departed, I grew quickly. I bathed in the nuclear waste of your bombs. I mutated. I gained my sentience. I spawned thousands of children. My host of marauders. My sweet ravagers. We grew from a mix of scum and human, brewing in the radioactive ooze. From you, Marco. We are the cruelty inside you. We are the broken, haunting demon that tormented you on Haven. The demon that has always been inside you. The savagery of man, so integral to your rise, to who we are. I am your son, Marco, just as surely as I'm the son of the centipedes. See me and see yourself."

Marco could only hang his head, only tremble, the terror too great, the truth too horrible, too impossible.

He didn't know if this creature spoke truth or not.

But he knew that this war was over.

He knew that he would die here in his old home.

And he knew that this death would come as a relief.

The strands tightened around him. They yanked him upward. Malphas began reeling him up like a fish on a line.

"Now, Marco, I rid myself of my weakness," Malphas said. "Now I consume my shame. Now we truly become one."

The alien kept pulling Marco upward toward his waiting jaws.

"Marco!" Kemi shouted. "I love you!"

Malphas paused from reeling him up. Marco dangled on the strands.

"Your turn will come, Kemi!" Lord Malphas said, cackling again.

Kemi ignored the alien hybrid. Trapped in the web below, she looked at Marco. "I love you, Marco. I love you so much. And I know that you love me. I know that you love me more than Anisha, more than any of the others. Even though you hurt me. Even though you broke my heart."

He stared at her. "Kemi . . ." he whispered.

She smiled at him, tears on her lashes. "I love you, Marco Emery. And I know that I'm your greatest love."

He understood.

"Don't," he whispered.

Above them, Malphas hissed. He tossed Marco back onto the floor, shot down a web, and yanked Kemi up toward him.

"Ah yes." The alien gripped Kemi in his claws. "Kemi Abasi. Your high school sweetheart, Marco. You love her too. Of course you do." He licked his jaws. "Now watch me eat her alive, Marco. Watch me break her. Watch as I tear her apart. Your own death will wait a little longer." He stared into Marco's eyes. "Watch, Father."

The jaws opened wide, ready to engulf Kemi.

She looked at Marco.

"I love you," Kemi whispered, eyes damp, then slammed her fist into her mechanical palm.

Electricity crackled around the prosthetic.

Malphas leaned in to feed.

Kemi slammed her thrumming, buzzing hand against him.

Energy surged out, blue, searing, hot as lightning, slamming into Malphas. The entire creature lit up, blue, smoking, shrieking. The power surged back into Kemi, blazing across her. Shock waves pulsed out like ripples on a pond. The energy intensified, pounded through Kemi, and still she held her hand against Malphas.

The alien screamed.

He thrashed on his web.

His teeth shattered.

His eyes burned.

His webs tore.

Marco fell.

An instant later, Malphas fell from the ceiling too. The creature hit the floor by Marco, twisting. Fire raced across him.

Kemi lay beside the alien, her hand still pressed against him, pulsing out every last drop of energy into the creature.

With a *crack* like shattering boulders, Malphas's head hit the floor and burst.

His legs gave a few twitches, then fell still.

His eyeballs oozed out from empty sockets.

Malphas, lord of the marauders, was dead.

Marco yanked off the torn, smoldering webs that still bound him. He ran across the floor and knelt by Kemi. He grabbed her.

"Kemi!"

She lay in his arms, broken, burnt. But she was still alive. Her breath was shallow, her eyes glazed, but she was still alive.

"Hi, Marco," she whispered.

He looked over his shoulder. "Ben-Ari! Lailani! Get a medic!"

Lailani was untangling herself from the web. Ben-Ari had already freed herself; she was busy carving a way out of the chamber.

Marco returned his gaze to Kemi.

"Hang in there, Kemi," he whispered. "They're getting help."

Kemi laughed weakly. With her good hand, she reached up and caressed his cheek. "I told you about my hand. How it's dangerous."

He nodded, tears falling. "You warned me."

She smiled through her tears. Her breath was so soft now. "I was always worried, Marco. That it would be you. Or Ben-Ari. Or Lailani. Turns out it's me. The one to die."

"You're not dying today, Kemi." He squeezed her hand. "Do you hear me? Not for many years."

She blinked up at him, smiling. "You gave your life for me. In the simulation. In the black hole. Do you remember? You jumped into a pit of monsters to save me." She gave a weak laugh. "Seemed only fair that I should return the favor." She shivered. "It's getting cold, Marco. It's getting so cold. But it'll be over soon. Hold me."

He held her in his arms. He rocked her gently and kissed her forehead. "I have you, Kemi. You're safe. You're safe."

"I love you, Marco," Kemi whispered, voice fading. "I've always loved you. Be good, Marco. Be happy. Whatever you do, be happy."

Her eyes closed.

Her head fell back.

Marco lowered his head, holding her close, crying softly.

CHAPTER THIRTY

He carried her out from the hive into the ruins of the city.

Kemi lay in his arms, peaceful in death, and Marco stared ahead, eyes dry, feeling empty, feeling shattered.

His companions walked behind him. Ben-Ari, pale and bloody. Lailani, chin raised, eyes red. Addy, somber, almost unrecognizable without her broad smile and long hair. They walked together, silent, grieving, guarding their fallen friend.

Around them, the battle was dying down. Humans and yurei fought together, slaying the last marauders. Marco spotted a familiar face: Steve, Addy's on-again, off-again boyfriend. The towering hockey player was covered in ash and blood, standing over a dead marauder.

Addy and Ben-Ari pulled on strands of web, dragging the dead Malphas from the hive. Seeing the corpse of their lord, the last marauders cried out in fear. The aliens fled into the meat grinders of the human machine guns. The city barricades, built to trap in humans, now trapped the last few marauders, and they perished under the human onslaught.

"The war is over," Marco said softly. "We won. But there is no joy today. There is no victory. There is only grief. Only loss. Kemi, you are gone."

Around them, some soldiers were cheering. Cries of "Victory, victory!" filled the streets. Marco walked silently, Kemi in his arms.

A wispy shadow stirred, and Eldest came walking toward him. Her tattered dress and black hair fluttered in the dusty wind, and ash stained her wooden mask. She stood before Marco, and she raised a hand. She placed her three long, clawed fingers on Kemi, and she looked up into Marco's eyes.

"I am sorry, Marco," Eldest said.

Sudden anger flared inside of Marco, mingling with his grief. "You knew, Eldest. You knew she would die. You told us one would fall. Why didn't you stop this? Why—"

"I can only observe the paths of the future," Eldest said. "They are ever flowing, a river breaking into a thousand rivulets. I could not stop this tragedy, not without losing this war. Victory is always bought with grief. Peace is always bought with blood. Many have fallen, both of your kind and mine. Many hearts have stopped beating, and many now mourn. We kill and we die and we break ourselves so that others may live in peace. We wet the soil with our blood so that trees may shade our children. Thus it has always been."

"Your words don't comfort me," Marco said. "You're speaking loftily about the nature of war and humanity." His voice caught in his throat. "I lost a friend."

Eldest's eyes seemed to soften. "Place her down, Marco. Here in this yard."

She led him to a little house, its roof gone. The yard had burned, but there was a patch of clear, soft soil between a tank and a fallen Firebird. Here he laid Kemi down. A wind chime, a vestige of the life that had once filled this city, sang an unearthly song. Ash fell from the sky like snowflakes. Kemi had always loved the snow. And then Marco recognized this place. The Indian restaurant where they used to eat. They had eaten their last meal here before his draft.

"Marco, do you remember what I told you in Haven?" Eldest said. "On the roof of a tall building on a dark night in a storm?"

Marco nodded. "You gave me a gift. A conch. A soulshell, you called it."

The yurei placed her hand on his arm. "Do you have the soulshell, Marco? Do you remember what I told you to do with it?"

"To use it in my darkest hour," he said. "That it would light my path. And I used it, Eldest. In the darkness at the edge of space. When our engine was dead, when we floated, lost, hungry, facing starvation and death in the emptiness. I used the conch and I summoned the starwhales."

"That was not your darkest hour, Marco." Eldest seemed to smile through her mask—a sad smile, her eyes teary. "The conch did not summon the whales, and that is not its purpose. Use the shell now, Marco. Use the gift that I gave you."

He pulled the conch out from his pack. He ran his fingers across its smooth, bluish surface. His friends gathered around him, and his tears fell.

"She loved the sea," Marco whispered. "We planned to live together by the sea. To collect seashells on the beach. To be happy." His voice cracked. "To finally be happy after so much pain. She deserved it. More than anyone. I can't believe you're gone, Kemi."

Kemi lay on the ground, and Marco knelt beside her. He held her hand. It was already growing cold. His tears fell, and when they hit her skin, they rose like steam. Glowing. Golden.

Standing above them, Addy gasped. "Marco! Your seashell!"

Through his tears, Marco gazed at it. Golden wisps rose from Kemi, coiled through the air like ink in water, and flowed into the conch.

Awe filled Lailani's eyes. "It's her," she whispered. "It's Kemi's soul."

Marco held the conch with both hands, watching in amazement as the wisps of light rose from Kemi, as they entered the seashell. When the last wisp had entered the conch, the light still glowed from within. The soulshell was warm in his hands. Comforting. And when Marco looked at Kemi again, he didn't see her. Her body was still there, but it was no longer *her*, just an empty shell. The shell in his hands was full.

"How can this be?" he said. "Eldest, what does this mean?"

"We do not know," Eldest said. "But our people have their myths, their traditions. We believe that the soul is eternal. That after we die, the soul can glow within our ships, light our forests, and dance among the stars. We believe that our bodies are but vessels. And we believe that with our soulshells, we can give a new vessel—if only temporary—to the light within." She smiled sadly. "Yes, Marco. I can see many paths along the coiling tree of time. And long ago, when I met you on a rooftop in a distant city, I judged you to be kind. To be good. To be walking toward this dark hour, the loss of your friend, the price of your world's victory, of your own peace. And so I gave you this gift. For you. And for her."

Addy looked with huge eyes between Eldest, Marco, and the conch.

"So . . ." Addy rubbed her eyes. "Kemi turned into a seashell?"

Lailani groaned. "Addy! Her soul rose from her body. It entered this mystical vessel. The soul is a force of light, of energy, of consciousness, and we witnessed a miracle here. We witnessed her soul rising. And . . ." Seeing Addy's perplexed expression, Lailani sighed. "Fine. Yes, Addy. She turned into a seashell."

Addy gave an impressed whistle. "Damn. That's some Buddhist magic right there."

Marco looked up at Eldest, holding the conch with both hands.

"What do I do with it?" he whispered.

"We'll take her with us!" Addy said, answering for the yurei. "We'll carry seashell-Kemi everywhere! We'll buy her a seat at hockey games, give her a place at the poker table, and at night, she can sleep in a fishbowl."

"Addy!" Lailani groaned.

"Fine, fine," Addy said. "We'll buy her an aquarium. A small, affordable one. Maybe a couple goldfish for company."

Lailani pulled Addy back. "Come, Addy, let's give Marco some space. Let's go find some tall buildings to raise our flags on."

Blessedly, Addy liked the idea, and she wandered off with Lailani.

Same old Addy after all, Marco thought.

He gazed at the seashell in his hand. He looked back up at Eldest.

"Can Kemi hear me?" he said. "Is she still conscious? Do we do as Addy said, and just . . . keep her in here? You said that the shell is temporary."

Eldest placed a hand upon the shell. She gazed into Marco's eyes.

"I do not know the mysteries of the afterlife," Eldest said, "only legends, only songs and tales from ancient days. But I know, Marco, that the soul will not live forever in a shell. Every turn of the moon, more of her light will escape, until one day the shell is cold and barren and the soul is nothing but a memory."

"Then why did you give me this shell?" Marco said. "That seems cruel."

Eldest removed her mask, revealing her scarred face, a face destroyed by a war long ago. She smiled at him sadly. "So that you could say goodbye. So that I can take her with me, if you wish it. We keep some yurei souls in our ships, where they fill our forests, where they power our engines, where they shine their light upon our enemies. We release others among the stars. Some we release onto the surfaces of worlds, where they live in memory forever, or so our tales tell. If you wish it, I will take the soulshell with me. And I will release Kemi in the Deep Sky, and there perhaps she will find eternal peace and joy among the fallen yurei, living in a world of dreams and memories."

Marco thought back to the illusionary world inside the black hole. The place that had tested him. Perhaps the yurei could create such a world for Kemi. A place of fairytales. Of unicorns and knights and castles. Yet it seemed to Marco unbearably lonely. To spend a second life, perhaps an eternal one, on a distant world, a mere illusion, to be among the souls of alien life who could never understand her experience?

"No," he said softly. "I will find a place for her here. On Earth. The way some among us spread the ashes of the dead in beautiful places, I will release her soul in a place of peace. Here upon her world that she fought for, that she died to save. How long do I have, Eldest? Before she fades away?"

"Perhaps a year," said Eldest. "Perhaps two or three. I don't know how it will be with human souls, and this future I cannot see. It depends on how strong her soul is."

"It's strong," he said.

Eldest smiled again, and this time her smile was warm, a smile full of goodness, of joy. She placed her hands atop his.

"Heed her advice, Marco. Be happy. Should the darkness creep again, should the weight of memories seem too heavy to bear, look at the stars. We will be there, Marco. We will be with you always, even in your darkest hours." Eldest placed a small wooden box in his hands. "When you're ready, when the grief is too great, open this box. This is my parting gift to you. Goodbye, Marco."

Eldest placed her kabuki mask back on. She hovered away like a ghost, fading into the gliding ash. All across the city, the yurei flowed away, as if they too were wisps of souls. Their ships rose higher in the sky, vanishing into the light.

* * * * *

Addy climbed the stairwell, banner in hand. Lailani climbed behind her, still holding her gun, seeking marauders. They found no more aliens. Not in this building. Not anywhere on their way here. The enemy had fallen. The city was theirs.

Earth is ours, Addy thought.

"Fuckin' marauders." Lailani panted behind her on the staircase. "Worst thing they ever did was break the damn elevator."

"Come on!" Addy said. "It's only thirty stories."

Lailani gave a sound halfway between groan and squeal. "Easy for you! Your legs are longer than my entire body."

Addy rolled her eyes. "Yeah, well, you also weigh about as much as one of my legs, Tiny, so you should have an easy climb."

They kept climbing. Finally they emerged onto the roof of the building, one of the few that still stood in Toronto. From up here, they could see for kilometers in every direction.

Addy stared upon her home.

"Damn," she said.

Nearly all the city was gone. Buildings lay flattened. Street after street lay in ruins. Piles of rubble rose everywhere. Piles of corpses too. Addy had been a soldier for years, but she had never seen such destruction.

"It looks like the ruins of Stalingrad from the old photos," she said.

Lailani emerged onto the roof behind her. She fell to her knees, panting. "At least most of the tall buildings are gone. Bloody hell."

Addy didn't answer. For a moment she couldn't speak, only gaze at her home. She could see her old street from here, the place where she had grown up. A few streets away, she saw the block where the library had stood. Her childhood, her youth—gone. All these places—existing now only in memory.

She could see Steve below. That hulking, stupid, lovable brute had joined Marco, and the two were clearing away rubble, seeking survivors. Addy knew there would be few. Almost everyone she had known growing up here was gone.

"I fought the marauders for a year," she whispered. "And every day, I thought that I would die." Her voice choked. "I lost many friends. I thought our battle was doomed, that dying in battle was preferable to dying in the slaughterhouse, fattened up and butchered like an animal. I wanted to die in battle, Lailani. But we won." She turned toward her friend, tears on her cheeks. "We won."

Lailani embraced her. "We won."

"So why does it feel so bad?" Addy whispered.

Lailani wiped her eyes. "There are no true winners in war. There is no victory without sacrifice. There is no peace without spilling blood to earn it. We won, but we lost so much. We found new life, but we saw so much death. And it hurts. And it will always hurt. And we'll always miss those we lost."

Addy thought of them, all those who had fallen. Her parents. Most of her friends from basic training. Most of her fellow rebels. Kemi, one of her dearest, oldest friends. And she thought of Haven, how even after defeating the scum, they had fought the memories for years. How they had never left the abyss of Corpus.

"Can we ever be happy again?" Addy said. "Or will this be like after the scum? We go back to a haunted, scarred life, wretched beggars in the ruins of a world we saved?"

"We will be scarred," Lailani said. "Our bodies. Our souls. We will be haunted. Peace? Not for us. There is never peace for veterans. We fought for another generation. We fought so that the children born after this war can grow up in peace, in joy. Those children will never understand us. When they grow up. When they rebuild this world. They won't understand the pain we lived through. And that's good." She laughed through her tears. "Let them worry about other things."

Addy looked over the ruins and sighed. "So, off to a life of nightmares and poverty."

Lailani smiled thinly. "No. Not poverty, maybe." She reached into her pocket, then held out her palm. "Before they left, the yurei gave me this. They told me I have to share, but . . ." She shrugged and winked. "We'll see."

Addy's eyes widened. "Fucking hell! Are those azoth crystals?"

"I think so," Lailani said. "Unless they're fake. The yurei know they're valuable to us humans, that we use them for interstellar travel. They're worth a lot, you know. More than diamonds. People will still need to build azoth engines, to power the great starships of the future." She hefted the azoth crystals in her hand. They chinked. "I don't think we'll be poor."

Addy rubbed her eyes. "Are you telling me we're rich?"

Lailani nodded. "We're rich."

"We're rich," Addy repeated.

"Yes, as I said."

Addy laughed. "We're rich! We're wealthy! We can buy all the hot dogs we could eat! We can buy mansions and thrones and—" She bit her lip. She looked at Lailani. "We should probably use the money to rebuild, right? To help the survivors."

Lailani nodded. "That would be the noble thing to do."

"But we can keep a little bit," Addy said. "Just enough to build that house on the beach. Marco would insist. Can't let the boy down."

"That Marco!" Lailani shook her head. "He'd probably insist we buy a few pet Dobermans too. Cute ones. With floppy ears."

"He's so selfish!" Addy said. "He'll insist we buy new hockey gear too. And a new motorcycle." She shook her head sadly. "Some people just won't think of others. Now come on. Let's raise this flag so we can go shopping."

They unfurled the flag, and they hung it from the edge of the building. It billowed in the wind, a blue circle in a black sky. The flag of Earth. Below, across the city, survivors saw the flag waving, and they stood and saluted.

Earth, Addy thought. *Our planet. May you never more weep. May blood and tears and ash never more stain your soil. Earth. You are our world. You are precious. You will forever be our home.*

* * * * *

James Petty groaned, shoved aside the metal beam, and saw sunlight.

He gasped like a fish out of water.

Cold air flowed into his lungs.

The air of Earth.

He grunted, pain pounding across him, and shoved aside another beam. He gripped a crack in the hull, and he pulled himself toward the light.

Coughing, Petty managed to crawl out onto the battered, burnt roof of the HDFS *Minotaur*.

He knelt, struggling for breath, looking around him. The massive warship lay in the ruins of Toronto, stretching across several city blocks. He knew it would never fly again. The bridge had shattered. The engines had detached from the hull. The hangars had caved in. The old bird, the oldest and toughest in the fleet, was dead.

But you went down with honor, girl. You went down with a roar.

The battle, it seemed, was over. Human troops were marching through the city, chanting of their victory. Marauders lay dead on the roadsides. The ravagers lay smashed across the city.

"We won, sir." The voice came from beside him. "The Ghost Fleet was here! You missed it, sir. They were beautiful. They were so beautiful."

Petty turned to see Osiris lying nearby on the *Minotaur*'s roof. The android was still missing her lower half, and cables dangled from her torso. Petty groaned and sat down beside her. Below, rescue crews and medics were rushing in and out of the ship; they had carved openings in the hull. Petty knew that he should join them, should help them seek survivors. But right now, he couldn't stand up.

He rested beside Osiris, gazing at the ruins with her.

"I'm sorry I missed the Ghost Fleet," he said.

Osiris smiled. "They flew all over the world, sir! Many are still flying. I'm picking up reports from major cities around the globe. Tokyo. Beijing. Jerusalem. Paris. Hundreds of other cities. The marauders are fleeing Earth, sir. Those that still live, at least, and there aren't many of those. They're leaving our planet." She clasped his hand. "We won, sir. We won this war."

"And you served admirably, Osiris," he said. "When they first assigned you to my ship, I disliked you. I mistrusted androids. But you are a fine officer. I'm proud to have fought with you."

Osiris placed a hand on his knee and smiled. "Why did the android lose her legs, sir?"

"Why?"

"Because the marauders shook her starship while she was shaving them. It's funny because androids don't shave their legs, sir. We're naturally hairless."

Petty couldn't help it. He burst out laughing.

"We'll get you new legs," he said. "Hairy ones this time."

She gasped. "Sir!" She thought for a moment. "Yes. Yes, I'd like that."

He was laughing again when he saw the soldier below on the street.

His laughter died.

She was a young woman, grime staining her long blond hair, ash and blood covering her face. She wore a tattered olive green uniform, and a rifle hung across her back. She paused below the *Minotaur*, and she gazed up at him.

Petty rose to his feet. Carefully, he climbed down toward the road. His body was bruised and scratched, and every movement shot pain through him, but he forced himself to keep moving. He limped toward her.

She smiled, eyes damp, and saluted. "Sir."

Petty felt a lump in his throat. He returned the salute. "Captain Ben-Ari."

She gave a small sound halfway between laugh and sob. "I've been demoted to private, remember, sir?"

He could no longer speak. He pulled her into his arms. "You did it, Einav."

She wrapped her arms around him and laid her cheek against his chest. "We both did, sir." Suddenly Ben-Ari was crying against him. "And we lost many."

Petty nodded and stroked her hair.

Yes, we lost many.

Thousands of soldiers he had commanded—gone. His family—gone.

He reached into his pocket, and he felt Coleen's tags there.

I lost one daughter, he thought, holding Ben-Ari. *But I gained another.*

The medics rushed toward them, and Petty let them tend to him. His wounds would heal quickly, he knew. Earth's wounds would take longer to heal. It would take years, maybe decades to recover, to rebuild. Even centuries later, perhaps, Earth would reel from these two devastating wars. There was still much work to do.

I can no longer save this world for you, Coleen. But I can make this a good world for millions who still live. For millions of young men and women who will seek a new life, who will defend this world from future enemies. They are all my children. I will build a good life for them.

*****

They buried Kemi in the northern woods. For a year, the forces of the Rebellion had hidden among these trees, had fought here through the winter and searing summer, and the forest still bore the memories of their war. Bullets and casings, marauder claws, burnt army vehicles, and skeletons littered the forest.

But Marco and his friends found a hill lush with maples and oaks, and from its crest they could see a meadow and lake. Dragonflies flitted over rushes, and crickets and blackbirds sang. In a desolate landscape, here was an oasis of beauty. Marco realized that he knew this place, that he had hiked here once with Kemi, that they had paused upon the hill, gazed at the lake, and rested in the shade of the maples. He knew that she should rest here.

They buried her on the hill under a maple. They buried her with a view of the water. But Marco knew they were burying only an empty vessel, and when they lowered her into the grave, he felt the soulshell's warmth in his pocket.

He stood above the grave, and he looked at his companions. At Ben-Ari. At Lailani. At Addy.

"I don't know what to say." Marco lowered his head. "I'm a writer. I'm trying to be a writer, at least. I've always loved words, have prided myself on my ability to weave them. But right now, I don't know what to say. I want to speak about how much I loved Kemi. How much her smile warmed my heart. How, even through so much pain and struggle, she remained so sweet, so happy. How whenever I felt lonely or sad or scared, just seeing her smile, just being in her presence, instantly made me so happy. How she was so brave, strong, intelligent, but much more importantly—how kind she was. And how she made everyone around her instantly smile with her."

Ben-Ari touched his shoulder. "I think you know exactly what to say, and you just said it." The captain turned toward the grave. She spoke softly. "You were not only my soldier, Kemi. You were not only the best pilot I've known. You were also my friend. You were my best friend. I loved you like a sister. Goodbye, Captain Kemi Abasi."

She had given her pilot a posthumous promotion. Captain Abasi, heroine of Earth.

Lailani knelt and placed lilacs on the grave. "Goodbye, Kemi," she whispered, able to say no more, then stepped back and leaned against Ben-Ari.

Addy hesitated, then placed a single coin on the grave. "I saved it," she said. "It's from when you and I went to a movie together. Remember? Marco was supposed to join us, but he stayed home to study, because he's a huge nerd." She shot Marco a glare, then looked back at the grave, and her eyes softened. "But we had lots of fun, Kemi. We became really good friends that day. I'll miss you. Even though you turned into a seashell, and you're probably eavesdropping from Marco's pocket." She sniffed. "I promise that whenever I eat oysters, I'll think of you."

Marco placed a hand on her shoulder. "I think we get the point, Addy, thank you. That was beautiful."

Addy blew her nose. "I didn't get to the part about how mermaids wear seashell bras because B-shells are too small and D-shells are too big."

"Jesus, she's turned into Osiris," Marco said.

Lailani took hold of Addy's arm. "Come, Addy, it's walking time again."

After the two women stepped downhill, Marco remained by the grave, staring down at it.

"Are you all right, Marco?" Ben-Ari said softly. She put a hand on his shoulder.

He nodded, wiped his eyes, and smiled. "Yes, ma'am. For the first time in a very long time, I think that I'm all right."

Surprising him, his commander kissed his cheek. "I'll go join the others. Take as much time here as you need."

Marco remained on the hill, alone with Kemi, for a long time. He listened to the maples rustle and the insects chirp. He watched ducks in the lake below and the butterflies that flitted between the wildflowers. He inhaled the deep, rich scent of the forest.

"It's Earth, Kemi," he said. "We saved it. We did it. I'll miss you. I'll miss you so much, and I love you. Goodbye, princess of the sky. Goodbye."

He walked downhill between the flowers and trees, and he joined his friends.

CHAPTER THIRTY-ONE

Under the searing summer sun, they toiled. Sweat soaked them. Calluses grew on their hands.

"This is harder than the goddamn war!" Lailani wiped her brow, then continued digging.

Even Steve, who could make gorillas look scrawny, moaned about his exhaustion.

For long hours and days, they labored.

They buried the dead.

They pulled survivors from the rubble.

They hunted down the last marauders, clearing Toronto of lingering enemies, as across the globe soldiers drove out the aliens from their final strongholds.

They fought the seeds of fascist, communist, and theocratic uprisings that sprang across the city, groups that sought to seize control of Earth in the chaos. They exiled their leaders into the wilderness.

They prayed, those with faith. They meditated. They reflected.

Mostly, they built. They built shelters and field hospitals. They treated the thousands of wounded. They hunted in the fields. They hauled buckets of water from the lake into the camps.

Every day, sifting through the rubble of Toronto, Marco was sore, blisters on his feet, his skin peeling in the sun.

"I miss war," Addy said miserably at one point, hauling buckets of water.

She was joking, of course. Marco knew that. He saw the pain that flickered across her eyes, the old memories.

Someday, maybe, I'll ask Addy about what happened to her in this war, Marco thought. *But not yet. Maybe not for a long time. Not until she's ready.*

So he only smiled, patted her shoulder, joked with her. Sometimes, during their days of toil, he saw that Addy would just stand. Just stand and stare at the distance, face blank, and she seemed to be gazing ten thousand kilometers away. Ghosts seemed to dance in her eyes. When that happened, Marco would wait beside her, and when she returned to this world, he would plant a kiss on her cheek, muss her hair, tell a joke. Sometimes he just embraced her. Just held her as she trembled. Just stood with her, comforting her, until she could work again.

Someday maybe you'll tell me, he thought during one of those times, holding her. *When you're ready, Addy. I'll be with you always.*

That night Addy slept in his arms, and whenever the nightmares seized her, Marco stroked her hair until she calmed.

"I love you, Addy," he whispered in the darkness. "Always. We'll never be apart again."

She mumbled in her sleep, nestled closer to him, and slept until dawn.

They toiled through the days.

They remembered during the nights.

Brick by brick, grave by grave, they scoured the city. They reclaimed their home.

But as the days went by, with every new street cleared, Marco's realization grew.

This was no longer his home.

He had been born in Toronto. He had lived here until age eighteen. But he was twenty-six now. His adult life had been spent in searing deserts, in a storm on an alien world, in the darkness of space. The city he had known—it was gone.

And he knew that he would not live here again.

This will always be the place where I fell in love with Kemi, he thought. *Where I met Addy. Where I lived with my parents. Let it stay that place in my memory.* He wiped sweat from his brow and paused from his labor. *I've emerged from the fire, and I'm still alive, though so many are gone. Let me find a new place. A new life.*

"Marco, would you come north with me today?" Lailani said to him one morning. "I want to explore the forests for mushrooms and game."

They took an old army Jeep which coughed and trundled along the highway. They headed into the forests north of the city, parked, and hiked along old trails. They spoke of good memories. They laughed about the time Caveman had emerged for morning inspection in firetruck pajamas, how Sergeant Singh's eyes had bulged out. They remembered how one Christmas, back at the library, Addy had lost her watch while stuffing a turkey. They smiled to remember those days in Greece long ago, pretending to be wounded, the closest thing to a vacation they had ever had. They spoke in hushed voices about the tree of memories in the soulship, about the good times they had seen. They spoke of Kemi.

They reached a clearing where they found mushrooms, and they knelt to collect them. When they both reached for the same mushroom, their fingers touched. They stared at each other, and on a whim, Marco leaned forward and kissed Lailani's cheek.

She looked away.

"Marco," she said softly, "I wanted to tell you something. That's why I asked you to come here."

"I know," he whispered.

Lailani looked up at him, eyes damp. "I'm going home, Marco."

His own eyes dampened. He took her hands. "Lailani, I—"

"Marco, don't."

But he plowed on. "Lailani, I love you. I've loved you since the first time I saw you, since that day eight years ago when you joined my platoon. Our war is over now. We can be together. We . . . we can get married. I forgive you for Sofia. For Ben-Ari. We can start a new life now. I love you."

Lailani stared into the distance, tears in her eyes.

"I come and I go." Her voice was soft, barely a whisper. "It's how I've always been. I come to you, and I love you, and I leave, and I return, and I go again. Because I've always been broken. I've always been a wanderer. I wandered the slums of

Manila as a child, orphaned, hungry, afraid. I wandered fields of war. And I wandered between the beds of lovers. I broke hearts and I had my heart broken. I saw terrors and I saw beauty too. I fell in love. I fell in love with many." She looked back at Marco and touched his cheek. "I always knew that I would hurt you. I told you that when we first met. But I come and I go. And that is who I am, and who I must always be. You're an oak, Marco, and your roots have always sought purchase. But I'm like dandelion seeds, visiting tree by tree, and I can't give you what you want. I can't give you roots."

Marco looked at her. She was beautiful. She was so beautiful.

"Where will you go?" he whispered.

"To where I began." Lailani smiled and wiped her tears. "To where I was born. To where Sofia died. To continue my work. We have money now, Marco. I sold the crystals. I'll use my portion to open a school. A real school. Not just a wagon of books, but a school with brick walls, with desks, with a library. Then another school after that, and another, and as many as I can build. I once thought that I was meant to be a soldier. That I was meant to die in battle. But I was meant to live, Marco. I was meant to do this. I'm going home."

He wanted to ask Lailani if he could come with her. But he had asked her that before, long ago. And he knew the answer.

You come and you go, he thought. *You are like dandelion seeds.*

"It's a good plan," he said instead, forcing himself to smile, and he found that his smile felt very real, that it filled him with joy. Joy for her. For the purpose she had found.

Lailani smiled too, and her smile grew into a grin, and light filled her eyes. "You should go to Greece, Marco. Remember our time there? When the granny fed us stuffed cabbages? You should go back. Build your house there on the beach. Fill it with books. Fill it with friends. Fill it with laughter and light. I'll visit. A lot. And you'll visit me. Remember, it's a small world that we saved."

After all, it was.

The trip to Greece only took a few hours. After traveling to the Cat's Eye Nebula and back, it seemed barely a hop and skip. During the flight, Marco tried to read a book, but Addy kept singing, dancing in her seat, and poking Marco's ribs whenever she leaned over him to look out the window. Marco had to admit: he was somewhat mortified that she had invited Steve to join them. When Addy pulled her hulking boyfriend into the airplane bathroom with her, she was embarrassingly loud.

Ben-Ari sat behind them, headphones plugged in, enjoying her own book, even getting some sleep. When Marco tried to nap, Addy elbowed him again and insisted that he let her hold Kemi's seashell—just one more time.

Marco groaned and gave her the shell. But one treasure he kept hidden. He still had not opened the wooden box Eldest had given him.

When you're ready, when the grief is too great, open this box, she had said. Marco kept it closed.

The plane landed.

They traveled through a bustling Greek city.

"God, Addy, why am I carrying your backpack too?" Steve grumbled, buckling under the weight of two packs.

"Because you're a big, strong, manly man!" She puffed on a cigar, examining a folding map of the islands. "And I'm holding the map."

He groaned, shifting her backpack across his shoulders. "What did you pack in this thing, rocks?"

"Just a few bricks from home," Addy said. "I wanted to use bricks from the library as cornerstones for our new house."

Steve groaned louder. "I knew it. Rocks! She packed rocks!"

They made their way down to the beach. Ben-Ari. Marco. Addy and Steve. They found a place an hour outside the city. A place with water on one side, with trees on the other. A place of sunshine at day and clear stars at night. The place they had dreamed of for so long.

They put down their packs.

They put down their bricks.

And may we put down roots, Marco thought.

That night, their house still only blueprints, they built a campfire on the beach, and Addy roasted hot dogs, and they slept under the stars.

* * * * *

These were strange days for Einav Ben-Ari.

At first, she had insisted on building the house herself. She had made lists of suppliers in the nearby islands, bought wood and bricks, refined blueprints, collected tools. She had fought two wars. She had escaped from prison. She had flown across the galaxy and back with an ancient fleet. She could surely build a *house*. It took Marco to touch her shoulder one day, to comfort her after her electrical wiring had nearly burned down their island, and convince her to hire builders—and then get out of their way.

"You've earned a vacation, ma'am," he told her. "Spend the next few months relaxing on the beach. Catch up on reading. Keep working on your memoirs."

For the millionth time, she told him, "You can just call me Einav now. I'm your friend now, no longer your commanding officer."

He tried it. They all did for a few days. But they kept naturally slipping back to "ma'am" or "Captain" and once Addy even saluted her by mistake. Old habits, like memories, died hard.

She found idleness intolerable. For a few days, Ben-Ari lay on the beach and read, completing the memoirs of Winston Churchill. But soon she found herself antsy, unable to enjoy the peace. Marco could spend hours just gazing at the waves, contemplating, meditating, but Ben-Ari needed to do *something*. She tried to keep working on her own memoirs, which she had begun in prison, and in a mad three-week dash, working from dawn to midnight each day, she chronicled her part in the marauder war. And yet she found it difficult to write the end. The end? She was only twenty-nine. Was this truly the end? Now, not even thirty, she retired and would grow old on a beach?

"You earned it," Marco told her, but that did not solve her restlessness.

She began to explore the ruins on the island, to walk between the columns of ancient Greek temples, and once she even found a few coins dating back thousands of years. She wondered if the modern cities of the world—Toronto, Tokyo, Paris, Tel Aviv, New York, and others destroyed in the great alien wars—would someday become treasure troves for a future amateur archaeologist.

Often at night, the nightmares emerged. Ben-Ari rose in a cold sweat on the beach, struggling to breathe, haunted with memories of her prison cell, of the scum, of the marauders, of creatures in the darkness. Under the starlight, as the others slept, she would undress and walk naked into the water. She would let the salty waves of the Mediterranean soothe her, wash away her sweat, her memories. She would look up at the stars and try to see them as things of beauty, not the dens of monsters.

Often on these dark nights, when she felt so alone, she thought about Lailani. She remembered that forbidden day, making love to her in the *Marilyn*, and her cheeks flushed. She would push the memory aside, embarrassed by it . . . but not without savoring the sweetness of it.

Perhaps that's what I need, Ben-Ari thought. *A lover. A man who can cook and tell jokes, who's tall and strong and can fight, but who's also smart enough to discuss literature and science and history.* Yet the thought seemed laughable to her. She had always been married to her duty. To her career.

Now she had no duty. Now she had no career.

After two months, when their house was taking shape, Ben-Ari had to admit: *I'm shell-shocked. I'm lonely. But mostly, I think that I'm bored.*

The day before their house was finally ready, while they were already planning a moving-in ceremony, a Military Police jet landed on the beach.

Ben-Ari froze.

Her heart leaped.

Marco and Addy ran toward her. They had no guns, but Addy drew a knife.

"Fuckers!" Addy spat. "What do they want?"

Ben-Ari fought the urge to run. There was no use running from the MP. If they wanted to find her, they would find her. She stared at the vessel on the beach, heart pounding against her ribs.

"I'm still technically an escaped prisoner," she said softly. "And they found me."

"We're not letting you go back to prison," Marco said and clasped her hand.

"No way in hell," Addy said, grabbing her other hand. "We'll fight them as hard as we fought the aliens."

A hatch opened on the jet. Two soldiers emerged, wearing the red armbands of the Military Police, and stood at attention.

A third soldier stepped out of the jet, walking between the guards. He was a tall man in his sixties, his hair graying, his eyes dark and hard. He wore many service ribbons on his uniform, and a golden phoenix shone on each of his shoulders, denoting him a general.

Ben-Ari's eyes widened. She gasped.

"General Petty," she whispered.

She snapped to attention and saluted. Marco and Addy glanced at each other, then followed suit. They weren't sure if they were civilians or soldiers now, outlaws or heroes, but in the presence of a general—the hero who had piloted the *Minotaur* during the great last battle—they all felt awe.

Petty approached and stood before them on the sand. He returned their salute. He nodded at them, one by one. "Sergeant Linden. Sergeant Emery. Captain Ben-Ari."

For a moment, Ben-Ari wanted to hug him. She had hugged him back in Toronto. But that had been in the heady aftermath of a great battle, with both suffering from blood loss, both celebrating a victory. Here and now, with the dust settled, would he do his duty? Would he drag her back to prison?

"Sir!" Ben-Ari said. "It's an honor."

Petty inhaled deeply, a thin smile on his lips, and looked at the water. "A beautiful place to hide, isn't it?"

Ben-Ari cringed. "I'm sorry, sir. I'm not hiding. I know I broke the law. I know I escaped prison. I—"

"Einav," he said softly. "You saved the world." He looked at Marco and Addy. "You all did. I'm not here to arrest you. You are heroes." He raised his chin and saluted again. "I am here to honor you."

Addy's eyes widened. "Are you going to give us medals?"

Petty laughed. "Eventually, yes, you'll get your medals. Once you're wearing proper uniforms and I can pin them to your chests."

Addy and Marco looked down at their clothes. Addy was wearing a bikini bottom, Crocs, and a shirt with a cartoon sausage and the caption: *Sorry for being a brat, I'm the wurst.* Marco's shirt featured Johnny Cash flipping the bird. Their cheeks both turned red.

"What?" Addy said. "Medals would look great on these outfits!"

Petty sighed. "You'll be an officer now, Linden. You and Emery both. Along with your medals, I'm giving you battlefield commissions. You're both becoming lieutenants. You need to look the part."

Their eyes widened.

"Poet and me, officers?" Addy said. "Damn. Poet, we'll have to start wearing pants and everything."

"I always wear pants!" Marco said.

Addy scoffed. "Not if there's a girl within five kilometers."

Petty sighed. He turned toward Ben-Ari. "Einav, walk with me."

She nodded. "Yes, sir."

Leaving the others behind, they walked along the beach. For a long time, the general was silent, seeming to simply enjoy the sea air. The jet, guards, and house were soon distant, and they walked between ancient Greek columns and shattered pottery.

Finally Ben-Ari could bear the silence no longer.

"Am I in trouble, sir?" she said. "I know that I'm a criminal."

Petty knelt to lift a piece of pottery. He hefted it in his palm. "Funny. It probably lay here for thousands of years, through the endless wars of men and two devastating wars between worlds. And the world spins on." He placed the shard back down, then looked at Ben-Ari. "I'm giving you a full pardon, and I'm promoting you to major. As of right now, you are Major Einav Ben-Ari."

She gasped. "Thank you, sir. It's an honor!" She meant it. Few achieved the rank of major before their thirtieth birthday. Hope sprang inside her. She was forgiven! She was promoted! She could return to do good, honest work, to help rebuild this world, to lead, to—

"And," Petty said, "right now, I'm giving you an honorable discharge from the Human Defense Force."

She blinked at him. "I . . . I'm not sure what to say."

She stared at the sea in stunned silence.

"I guess it's the best possible result," she finally said. "I can't return to the military, not after the secrets I leaked, not after all my crimes." She sighed. "But yes, thank you. An honorable discharge—with a higher rank for bragging rights—is a lot nicer than being led back to prison in chains." She looked around her. "Beach retirement it is for me. Maybe I can spend the next fifty years seeing how long I can grow my toenails."

Petty smiled thinly. "Einav, we've been working in secret for a long time now. We began a program a few years ago, back during the Scum War. We had to mothball things for a while when the marauders attacked, but now the program is charging forward again."

She looked at him. "Sir?"

"We call it the Human Outreach Program for Exploration. HOPE. It's a government institution dedicated to exploring space, to finding friendly alien civilizations, and forming alliances with them. Your father has been involved in HOPE, actually, as a consultant. NASA never recovered from the Cataclysm. But HOPE will replace it. In all our travels, even including the journey you took to the Cat's Eye Nebula, we humans have explored only one percent of the Milky Way galaxy. The rest is still out there, waiting to be discovered. HOPE will reach to the stars not with weapons, not with soldiers, but with curiosity and friendship."

Ben-Ari stared at the sky. The sun was setting, and the first stars were emerging. "There's a lot out there that's not very friendly, sir."

Petty nodded. "I know. Which is why I insisted on enlisting ex-military officers to command the HOPE fleet. We'll be launching the flagship next year, a state-of-the-art vessel with a crew of five hundred scientists and explorers. We call the ship the

Lodestar, and her mission is simple: not to fight but to explore. Einav, I want you to command that ship."

She looked at the sea.

She turned to look back at the house on the beach, at the soft lights that glowed there, where her friends waited.

She looked up at the stars.

After everything, after so much pain, do I dare go back up there? Do I dare lead men and women again, maybe into danger, maybe to death?

Marco had told her to relax. To read. To enjoy her retirement. And this island was beautiful. And she loved her friends. And she was miserable here.

She gazed at the stars again. She had sailed among them before. She had found danger, had found monsters. But she had seen beauty too. The noble Nandakis. The graceful starwhales. The beauty of the heavens.

Tears filled Ben-Ari's eyes, because she would miss her friends. She would miss them so much.

She nodded.

"Yes," she whispered.

They walked back to the house as the sun vanished behind the sea.

CHAPTER THIRTY-TWO

During his long days at war, Marco had imagined a full house on the beach, bustling with life. In his dreams, Lailani would be running around, chasing all the stray dogs she adopted. Ben-Ari would spend much of her time reading, writing, and painting in her studio in the attic, but come down in the evenings to light candles, to sing, to feast with them. Addy would organize poker games and field hockey matches, and Kemi would put on music and dance and force everyone to dance with her. Marco would complain about them, of course, call them all too loud and crazy and a nuisance, but he would be happy. He would be with his family.

As it turned out, he ended up moving into the beach house with Addy and Steve.

With *just* Addy and Steve.

He felt like in that old apartment in Toronto. It was only missing Stooge on the couch.

The days went by, and they made it a home.

There were many empty rooms, but the house was never silent, not with Addy around. Marco put together a studio for himself on the second floor. His window afforded a view of the sea, and on his shelf, he placed model ships and seashells, one among them a precious conch. He found a used bookshop in a nearby town, and he began to purchase the old books and fill his house with them. A hardcover set of *The Lord of the Rings*, another of *The Chronicles of Narnia*. Copies of *Tigana* and *The Chronicles of Amber* and several books by Heinlein. Several rare, leather-bound Dickens novels. Every book Carl Sagan had written. A few works by local, contemporary authors when he could find English translations. A copy of Ben-Ari's memoirs of the war, which he still dared not read, fearing the memories inside.

And he wrote his own words.

Every morning, he made a pot of coffee, then sat by the window to write.

He wrote a new story, a fantasy about knights in armor, noble elves from mystical forests, dwarves who mined for gems in the depths, and dragons that soared. His story grew into a novel, then into a trilogy of novels. And as he kept telling his tale, Marco realized that here was not just an adventure story, not just escapism, though he had originally intended the story to be escapist. With every chapter, Marco realized that he was writing about himself.

The dwarves dug too deeply for their gems, and they awoke an ancient evil—like Marco and his friends had found evil in the mines of Corpus. The heroes, humble farmers from a peaceful village, traveled through dangers untold to seek the aid of the noble elves—like Marco had sought help from the yurei. The dragons soared and battled the demons from beyond, much like the human fleet had fought the scum pods and the ravagers in space.

A year after he began writing, Marco completed his trilogy, and he named it *The Dragons of Yesteryear*. To his surprise, a local publisher printed a thousand copies, and they sold across the islands. Then a larger publisher bought the trilogy, and they printed half a million copies, and they sold across the ocean. They sold out.

For the first time in his life, Marco was sharing his writing with more than his friends. He kept a drawer in his desk for fan letters, and when he received one from Lailani—who had found a copy of his book all the way in the Philippines, where she had opened her school—it made his year.

Loggerhead and *Le Kill* remained, unpublished, in the second drawer.

In the days that followed, Marco began to take long walks.

He walked along the beach for kilometers. He hiked among the hills. One time, he spent three days hiking around the entire island, sleeping on the beach, before circling back home. His royalties arrived in his bank account every month, leaving him free to spend his days hiking, lost in thought. He kept Kemi's soulshell in his pocket, a constant warming presence. He remembered what Eldest had told him, that he had to release her soul before it withered, yet he could not bring himself to do it. Not yet. It still hurt too much. And so he took Kemi with him on his walks, and he spoke to her, though she could not answer.

On his walks, Marco got to know the people who shared the island with him, most just by face if not name. He waved at the old fishermen. He exchanged pleasantries with the young man who sold gyros in the town. He became good friends with the old married couple who owned the local bookshop, the only bookshop on the island. Most people here spoke only a smattering of English, but Marco spent some evenings with them, dining on fried calamari and crunchy fish with chips and lemon, washing it down with strong *arak*.

But mostly he walked alone.

Mostly he preferred walking alone, reflecting, daydreaming.

During his walks, one familiar face caught his attention more than most. She was a young woman who seemed to live on the beach. Often Marco saw her fishing on a pier. Sometimes he saw her sleeping by the water, and sometimes he caught her hiking among the hills. A couple times, he nodded and smiled at her, but she looked away shyly.

One night, Marco woke up before dawn, cold sweat covering him, the blankets tangled around him. Once more, a nightmare had roused him. Oddly, it wasn't about the war, not about scum or marauders in the darkness. In his dream, he had been back on Haven, back in the call center, trapped among the desks, desperate to please his superiors, wasting away. Trembling, he walked to the sea, and he swam until dawn, then walked along the beach, wearing nothing but his shorts. Often at home, he felt shy about walking with his shirt off, even in the heat, for he still carried scars from the war. Today the beach was deserted. He walked in the sunrise.

It was on this dawn, of all days, that the shy girl approached him.

She met his eyes briefly, then looked at her feet, cheeks flushing, and twisted her fingers.

"I wanted ask you, sir," she mumbled. "Are you being Mister Marco Emery, sir?"

He couldn't place her accent. She wasn't Greek; her accent sounded vaguely Asian, though with a touch of the west. Her hair was black and smooth, her eyes dark and slanted, and she seemed very young to him, barely older than a youth.

He nodded. "I am."

She kept staring at her toes, swishing them through the wet sand.

"I am being a fan, Mr. Emery. Of *The Dragons of Yesteryear*." She dared glance up and meet his eyes. "Your books help me so much. Take me to new places. Adventures. Maybe you sign my books?" She pulled three books from her pack, along with a pen. Her hands were shaking.

He smiled. He had never signed a fan's books before.

"Of course," he said. "Who should I make them out to?" When she blinked at him, confused, he said, "What's your name?"

"Ah." She smiled and pointed at herself. "This is Tomiko. I say right? I mean: I is being Tomiko."

Marco blinked at her.

He frowned.

"Tomiko?" he whispered.

She bit her lip. "I say bad? I no speak English well. Or Greek." She pointed at herself again. "Name is being Tomiko."

Marco couldn't help but laugh.

Tomiko.

Nobody had ever read *Le Kill* aside from Addy. Nobody else knew that Tomiko was the heroine in his unpublished manuscript. And standing there on the beach, signing the books for her, Marco realized that there were as many mysteries, as much magic and wonder, here on Earth as in the vastness of space.

He hesitated for a moment, the words on his lips.

Come on, you've faced scum and marauders in battle, he thought. *You can ask a girl out for dinner.*

So he did.

And Tomiko grinned—a huge, happy grin that made her eyes light up—and accepted his invitation.

They ate at his favorite place, the little taverna on the boardwalk in town, and he ordered the calamari and fried fish and two bottles—real glass—of Coca-Cola. Over dinner, Tomiko told him her story. She had grown up in Osaka, had managed to flee the burning city during the marauder assault. She had turned eighteen during the war, and during the chaos, she had never received her draft to join the military; Japan's HDF command had collapsed in the marauder assault. So she had begun to make her way west, to Paris, hoping to find her French father, a seaman who had romanced her Japanese mother but had returned to

France soon after Tomiko's birth. Tomiko had reached Greece when she learned that Paris, like so many other world cities, was gone.

"So I decide I stay here in Greece," she said over her plate of calamari. "I like the beach. Weather is being good. I catch fish and sing for money."

Marco walked her home, to her tent on the beach, and for the next few days, he couldn't stop thinking about her.

He walked by her beach again, and she smiled to see him, and he invited her for another dinner, this time at his house. Again she accepted. That evening, Tomiko seemed shy, almost frightened, around the loud and brash Addy and Steve. She seemed relieved when Marco walked her home along the beach.

"Addy can be loud, huh?" he said.

Tomiko laughed nervously. "She very nice. I is just being shy. I am shy around new people." She slipped her hand into his. "Not with you, though, Mr. Emery."

He laughed. "You can call me Marco."

When they reached her tent, Tomiko stood on her tiptoes and kissed his cheek.

"Goodbye, Marco," she whispered. Then she blushed furiously and fled into her tent.

Soon, Tomiko was coming over for dinner almost every evening. Soon, she and Marco kissed goodbye every night—at first just pecks on the cheek, soon on the lips, and then longer kisses while lying on the beach.

In the spring, Addy sat Marco down on the couch in their living room, placed her hands on her hips, and told him, "Marco, I want you to invite Tomiko to live with us."

He nodded. "Yes, I've been thinking of that. We do have a spare bedroom, and—"

"No spare bedroom," Addy said. "She'll live in your room. She'll sleep in your bed."

He smiled wryly. "I think she might have a choice in the matter too."

Addy rolled her eyes. "Please, Poet. The girl is fucking crazy about you. I can see it. And you're madly in love with her. I can see that too. There are blind men in Fiji who've seen it by now, even the ones who've been dead for a century."

Marco grew serious. He patted the cushion beside her, and Addy sat down.

"I don't know if I should," he said.

"Why?" Addy said. "Tomiko is sweet, Poet. She's really sweet. And smart. And beautiful. Hell, if you don't want her, I'm going to dump Steve and woo her myself."

He stared out the window at the sea, but he was gazing at his past. At RASCOM and Fort Djemila. At the battle of Corpus. At the invasion of Abaddon. He thought of his journey through space and facing Malphas in Toronto, of learning a horrible truth.

"She's nineteen," he said softly. "She's so young. Eight years younger than us. And she can't understand. Nobody can. What we went through." He looked into Addy's eyes. "You understand. Ben-Ari and Lailani understand. We might never speak of it, but we understand. Tomiko won't. And I might never be able to speak of it to her."

Addy's eyes dampened. She caressed Marco's cheek.

"Marco, she doesn't need to understand. She needs to make you happy."

He nodded. "She makes me happy," he whispered.

Addy smiled and wiped her eyes. She hugged him. "Go to her. Go to her now. Bring her flowers."

He went to her.

He invited her for dinner again. Then he invited her to spend the night. Then he invited her to spend the rest of her life. And she said yes. And she kissed him and slept in his arms that night, and he was happy.

He still woke up from nightmares most nights. Sometimes, Tomiko told him, he screamed in his sleep. But she was always there to soothe him in the darkness. When the panic struck, Tomiko held him close, stroked his hair, and sang soft lullabies in his ear. And he calmed and slept again.

Most days, Marco still remembered. An insect would fly into the house, and his heart would burst into a gallop, and he would see the scum in the mines. A dish would shatter, and he'd seek shelter, seek his gun, sure the bombs were falling. And during those times too, Tomiko was there to hold him, kiss his cheek, sing to him, and calm him.

But mostly, the memories were softer, more bittersweet. Memories of Caveman in his firetruck pajamas. Of Jackass and her books. Of Elvis crooning. Good memories of fallen friends.

He never told Tomiko about them. He wasn't sure how. He wasn't sure she would ever truly understand what he, what Addy, what the rest of them had gone through. But as the days went by, he realized that it was okay. That Addy had been right. That Tomiko didn't need to understand.

That she made him happy.

And that's what mattered.

Her name was Tomiko, like in his book, and she was meant to be there for him.

Because after all, the world was small.

And after all, the world was good.

And after all, the world was beautiful, and so was she.

One hot night, Marco and Tomiko decided to sleep outside on the beach. They lay on the sand between the seashells, the water just beyond their toes, and gazed up at the stars. She had never been to space. Marco pointed at the constellations, telling her about the stars, about the places he had visited, about the wonders he had seen. About aliens who lived in a watery world, their fins like purple banners. About starwhales who glided through the cosmos, communicating telepathically. About ancient forests that grew in ships of light. About a thousand other marvels.

And then he told her more.

He told her about how during a drill at boot camp, they had peed into bottles and milk cartons, and their sergeant accidentally knocked them over. About how Beast would boast about Russia, but he had actually been from Queens. About how

Caveman would somehow find and pick flowers even in the desert. About the time Elvis would croon old songs in the shower, and once they had all joined him, performing a spirited rendition of "Suspicious Minds." About all those funny tales from his youth. And with every story, Tomiko laughed, wrinkled her nose, and nestled closer to Marco. Finally she slept, a smile still on her lips.

Marco remained awake. He lay under the stars at her side. Then, slowly, he rose to his feet without waking her. He walked to the edge of the water. He pulled the conch from his pack, the soulshell the yurei had given him. A glow still emerged from inside.

"Goodbye, Kemi," he whispered and raised the seashell overhead.

Golden wisps emerged from the shell, coiling upward in the night.

Goodbye, Marco, he thought he could hear her say.

The golden light rose higher, becoming one with the stars.

He hesitated for a moment, then took out the small wooden box Eldest had given him.

When you're ready, open this box, she had said. *This is my parting gift to you.*

Inside, he found a crystal the size and shape of a willow leaf. He recognized it. A crystal from the Tree of Memory aboard the soulship. When he turned it in his hands, the crystal facets showed his memories. The ones he had described to Tomiko. And memories of Kemi—smiling at him, dancing in the forest of the Nandakis, and waving from a field of stars. He had said goodbye to her, but he knew that she wasn't gone. He knew that Kemi, that Caveman and Beast and Elvis, that Anisha, that his father, that all those he had lost would forever enrich his life, would forever live in memory.

He placed the crystal in his pack. He returned to Tomiko and lay beside her.

She woke and looked at him. She touched his cheek.

"You're crying," she whispered. "Are you all right?"

He nodded and held her close. "I'm all right, Tomiko. I'm happy."

* * * * *

Ben-Ari sat in the small transport shuttle, flying toward the starship orbiting Earth.

The *Lodestar* had been designed to look like an old Earth sailing ship, the kind Magellan and Captain Cook had used when exploring the world. She didn't have masts or sails, of course, but her hull was the right shape, silvery and gleaming. A figurehead thrust out from her prow, shaped as Eos, the Ancient Greek goddess of dawn. The ship was several hundred meters long, and five hundred people worked aboard her.

"She's beautiful," Ben-Ari whispered, gazing through the window of her transport.

The shuttle pilot, a young Taiwanese man in a blue HOPE uniform, nodded and smiled. "She certainly is, ma'am."

Ben-Ari wore the uniform too, the fabric form-fitting yet sturdy, navy blue and trimmed with white. Her insignia shone on her shoulders: three blue circles on each shoulder, denoting her the captain of the ship. HOPE had a different rank hierarchy than the military. Back in the HDF, she had once borne the title of *captain* too—a junior officer. Here, a member of HOPE, the same word meant a whole lot more. In HOPE, a captain was comparable to an HDF colonel.

Like my father, she thought.

The shuttle flew closer, and Ben-Ari watched the sunlight gleam on the starship, watched her polished hull reflect the Pacific ocean below. The shuttle floated by letters engraved on the hull, each letter the size of a man, spelling *The Lodestar.*

At the airlock, a jet bridge stretched and connected with the shuttle. Ben-Ari rose to her feet, ready to step on board.

But she hesitated.

What if I can't do this? I'm only twenty-nine. I've never commanded a ship larger than the Saint Brendan *and the* Marilyn. *How can I command five hundred scientists and explorers, many of them older and wiser than me? I'm a soldier. Just a soldier.*

She inhaled deeply.

General Petty believes in me. I found the Ghost Fleet beyond the Cat's Eye Nebula. I twice liberated Earth from alien invaders. I can do this. She released a shaky breath. *I can do this.*

She walked across the jet bridge. And she stepped into her new home.

A lobby awaited her, the floor carpeted, the walls gleaming. Her officers stood here, all in fresh uniforms. They nodded to her, shook her hand, smiled. Engineers. Pilots. Navigators. Scientists. The people she would lead into the darkness—but also the people she would rely on, she would learn from. The people who would guide her among the stars.

I'll miss you, Kemi, she thought. *I'll miss you, Marco, Addy, Lailani. I'll miss you all so much.* Suddenly she could not stop her eyes from dampening.

"Captain!" said one of her officers, concern in his eyes. "Are you all right, ma'am?"

She nodded and wiped her eyes. "She's a beautiful ship. She's so beautiful."

The officer smiled. "May I show you to the bridge, Captain?"

She nodded. "Please do."

He led her through the ship, down gleaming hallways, past labs and lounges and observatories, and everyone she passed greeted her with a nod and smile. There were no salutes here. There were no guns. There was no grimness or fear. There was curiosity. There was nobility. There was optimism. There was hope.

Ben-Ari stepped onto the bridge, a circular room like a planetarium, showing the stars all around her, even beneath her feet. Several officers worked here at control panels, and they rose to their feet when she entered.

A captain's seat waited in the center of the room. Ben-Ari hesitated for a moment, as if she needed permission to sit. Then she raised her chin, walked across the transparent floor above a field of stars, and took her seat.

It was comfortable. Somebody even brought her a cup of tea. She gazed out at the stars.

"Where to, Captain?" asked her helmsman.

Ben-Ari took a deep breath. She pointed forward. "Straight ahead, Lieutenant."

He cocked his head, a line appearing on his brow. "Captain? Where are we going?"

She smiled softly, gazing out at those stars. "I don't know." She looked at her helmsman. "But it will be amazing."

A smile broke through his frown. "Aye aye, Captain. Straight ahead."

The *Lodestar*'s engines thrummed to life. They sailed out into the darkness, leaving Earth behind, heading toward the unknown.

CHAPTER THIRTY-THREE

From her jagged throne, she gazed.

From her pyramid of gold and rust, she saw.

In her city of shadows and starlight, she waited.

She.

Mistress of time. Of glory. Of worship and sacrifice and woven mortal screams.

Her clawed hands creaked, and her eyes narrowed, waiting. Ever waiting. A million years of patience, of festering fury, of rotting vengeance. A brewing storm.

She.

She who lurked. She who hungered. She who felt such hatred. She who had died a thousand times. She who had given birth to a thousand oozing, screeching, feasting things. She who had run upon dark plains, who had burrowed in tunnels, who had dissected, who had pulled the organs and strands from sticky animals underground, who had learned, who had gazed into the past and toward the endless darkness ahead.

She whom they worshiped.

She who had gone to searing deserts where her slaves had rutted in the sand, apelike and squealing and kneeling before her, raising obelisks for her splendor. She who had suffered epochs of exile. She whom they had carved, a hundred times their height, upon great sandstone and iron.

She. Of glimmering claws. Of white eyes, all-seeing. Of a decaying throne. Of a hunger still fresh. Of a lust that burned with eternal flame.

She.

Goddess.

A thousand mothers.

She.

Nefitis.

They moved through the dark city toward her. They walked along the boulevard of shattered bones between the towers of her eternity. Under the stars, they advanced. Her warriors, ankh pendants around their necks. Her angels of retribution. And they carried one of *them*.

Nefitis had no nose like the apes, but her thin nostrils flared. She inhaled deeply. She could smell it. Man-flesh.

The starchildren climbed the black stairs toward her throne, carrying the prisoner. They stepped onto the polished dais and knelt before her. Beautiful warriors. Graceful hunters. Slick. Naked. Gray skin glistening in the starlight. Mouths—thin lines, lipless. Nostrils—shut against the stench of the man. Eyes—oval, black, gleaming, peering deep. Children. Her children. Her creations. Her grace. Her immortality.

"Mistress," they hissed, kneeling before her. "Mother."

Nefitis leaned forward in her throne. "You have brought me one, children."

The prisoner trembled. A human. A man. A mere ape. Trembling. So afraid. He gazed up at her throne, and his face paled. Liquid flowed down his leg. Liquid flowed down his cheeks.

"I . . ." The ape's voice shook. "I am Private Justin Doyle. According to the Galactic Convention, I will reveal my name, rank, and serial number, but I cannot—"

Nefitis rose from her throne, and the human swallowed. Naked. Hairy. Primitive. He trembled like a newborn starchild over its first meal of flesh.

She descended. She moved toward him, robes fluttering, hems burnt. The jagged spikes of her crown, nailed into her brow, dripped her holy blood. Her breasts, bare and painted with ancient runes, dripped her milk. Her ribs pressed against her papery skin. Her eyes shone like stars. Her claws gleamed like polished steel. She reached out those claws. She caressed his cheek.

"Kneel," she whispered to this child of man.

He knelt. He shook. "Please," he whispered. "Please. Mercy."

Nefitis placed her claws on his head. So small. Such a small mind.

"Worship," she hissed.

He bowed lower. His face touched the obsidian floor. "Please don't hurt me. I'm just a private. I—"

Her children grabbed him. They pulled him onto a stone altar, its obsidian surface stained with old blood. Snakes emerged from burrows in the stone, wrapped around the man's wrists and ankles, and pinned him down. He screamed. Oh, how he screamed! Such a sweet sound! He lay, strapped onto the altar, basking in her holiness.

Nefitis placed a claw on his belly. She pierced him, hooked a strand of intestine, and pulled it out. She coiled it lazily around her finger.

"Mother!" the man cried. "Mother . . . Mama . . . I'm sorry. I want to go home. Please, please! I know nothing. I—"

"You know her," Nefitis hissed, coiling, pulling out more intestine, wrapping it around her wrist. The pulsing bracelet glimmered and dripped. "You know Ben-Ari."

The human wept. "No. No! I—" He screamed as she plunged a second claw into his belly. "Yes! I know of her. I know her name. I never met her. Please. Mercy . . ."

Nefitis worked slowly, slicing, carving him open in the shape of an ankh, her holy symbol of immortality. Exposed to the air, his organs glistened. Hot. Sweetly scented. Her nostrils flared.

"Tell me of Ben-Ari." She licked her lips.

"Please," the human whispered. "Somebody, please. Wipe my memory. Like General Petty did. Please. Please. I want to forget. To forget . . ." He screwed his eyes shut. "Just a dream, just a dream—"

He screamed as Nefitis ripped off his eyelids.

He screamed as she worked, pulling out organ by organ, arranging them on the altar around him. She kept him alive. Yes, she knew this art. She kept his heart beating, even as it glistened on the cold black stone. She kept his blood flowing. She kept him awake, feeling everything, screaming, begging, seeing all. Stomach. Spleen. Kidneys. Sweet pancreas. All the parts of him, arranged on the altar around his torso, connected with gleaming strands, pulsing.

She rearranged the organs. She frowned, moving heart and offal, lungs and liver, her claws mixing the blood, scrutinizing.

And in the organs, she saw.

She saw time.

She saw past and future. Dreams. Visions. Prophecies.

Some goddesses gazed upon the stars for signs. Others peered into old bones and ancient books, while some studied the flights of birds. Not she. Not Nefitis. Not the mother of misery. Not she with unending lust. She gazed into *life*.

And in this life, broken down into its components, she *saw*.

"I want to forget," the human whispered, weeping. "Please. I want to forget. I want to forget. I—"

When she cut out his tongue, he could speak no more. But how he screamed!

She shoved the organs back into his body, and she stitched him shut with a metal thread. She carried him toward a towering boulder by her throne, and she nailed his limbs into the stone. She let the vultures descend, let them feed upon him, pecking, savoring the morsels. With her ancient power, she kept his flesh alive. Kept him screaming until nothing remained.

Nothing but that metal thread, coiled on the floor. Her sweet pets flew off, bellies full, dripping blood like red rain.

Nefitis returned to her throne.

She gazed upon her city, and she gazed upon time.

She gazed down at her children.

"Mistress." They knelt. "What is your prophecy?"

Nefitis raised her claws. She licked the blood, savoring, reflecting.

"In the organs, I saw," she hissed. "I saw her. I saw them. I saw their world. The time is near, my children. The enemy is weak. Soon our mighty hosts will march. Soon Earth will be ours, and all will worship me." Her fury flared, white, searing, intoxicating. "Soon Ben-Ari will scream."

"Earth!" her children cried, hands raised, and fell to their knees. "The promised land!"

"It is ours, my children," Nefitis said. "Our birthright. Our destiny. I will lead you there."

She gazed upon her visions, etched in blood and shattered souls.

She gazed upon a distant world.

She gazed upon those she would kill, those she would taste.

Upon her throne, in her city of shadows and glory, she smiled.

The story continues in . . .

Earth Reborn (*Earthrise* Book 7)

DanielArenson.com/EarthReborn

NOVELS BY DANIEL ARENSON

Earthrise:

Earth Alone

Earth Lost

Earth Rising

Earth Fire

Earth Shadows

Earth Valor

Earth Reborn

Earth Honor

Earth Eternal

Alien Hunters:

Alien Hunters

Alien Sky

Alien Shadows

The Moth Saga:

Moth

Empires of Moth

Secrets of Moth

Daughter of Moth

Shadows of Moth

Legacy of Moth

***Dawn of Dragons*:**

Requiem's Song

Requiem's Hope

Requiem's Prayer

***Song of Dragons*:**

Blood of Requiem

Tears of Requiem

Light of Requiem

***Dragonlore*:**

A Dawn of Dragonfire

A Day of Dragon Blood

A Night of Dragon Wings

***The Dragon War*:**

A Legacy of Light

A Birthright of Blood

A Memory of Fire

Requiem for Dragons:

Dragons Lost

Dragons Reborn

Dragons Rising

Flame of Requiem:

Forged in Dragonfire

Crown of Dragonfire

Pillars of Dragonfire

Misfit Heroes:

Eye of the Wizard

Wand of the Witch

Kingdoms of Sand:

Kings of Ruin

Crowns of Rust

Thrones of Ash

Temples of Dust

Halls of Shadow

Echoes of Light

Standalones:

Firefly Island

The Gods of Dream

Flaming Dove

KEEP IN TOUCH

www.DanielArenson.com
Daniel@DanielArenson.com
Facebook.com/DanielArenson
Twitter.com/DanielArenson

30068046R00239

Made in the USA
San Bernardino, CA
21 March 2019